TEMPTED BY HER ROYAL BEST FRIEND

JULIETTE HYLAND

THE PRINCESS WHO STOLE HIS HEART

JULIE DANVERS

MILLS & BOON

First published in Great Britain 2023
by Mills & Boon, an imprint of HarperCollins*Publishers* Ltd,
1 London Bridge Street, London, SE1 9GF

www.harpercollins.co.uk

HarperCollins*Publishers* Macken House, 39/40 Mayor Street Upper, Dublin 1, D01 C9W8, Ireland

Tempted by Her Royal Best Friend © 2023 Juliette Hyland

The Princess Who Stole His Heart © 2023 Alexis Silas

ISBN: 978-0-263-30607-1

05/23

Juliette Hyland began creating heroes and heroines in high school. She lives in Ohio, USA, with her Prince Charming, who has patiently listened to many rants regarding characters failing to follow their outline. When not working on fun and flirty happily-ever-afters, Juliette can be found spending time with her beautiful daughters, giant dogs or sewing uneven stitches with her sewing machine.

Julie Danvers grew up in a rural community surrounded by farmland. Although her town was small, it offered plenty of scope for imagination, as well as an excellent library. Books allowed Julie to have many adventures from her own home, and her love affair with reading has never ended. She loves to write about heroes and heroines who are adventurous, passionate about a cause, and looking for the best in themselves and others. Julie's website is juliedanvers.wordpress.com.

TEMPTED BY HER ROYAL BEST FRIEND

JULIETTE HYLAND

MILLS & BOON

For all the people who've made tough choices
for the sake of their own wellbeing.

You are seen.

PROLOGUE

THE NEXT SHIFT was arriving at London Pediatric Hospital, and Dr. Syver Bernhardt strained his neck, looking for the mess of dark curls.

"You ready, Dr. Bernhardt?"

Syver didn't even attempt to hide his smile as he turned to find nurse Hazel Simpson behind him. "You got me."

"'Bout time!" She clapped her hands and tapped his arm with hers. "I think the current score is Hazel three, Syver five hundred!"

"You've won over three times." It had to be at least ten. Though she was right, this was one thing he took first place in!

"And you've won more than five hundred."

It was a silly game. One he didn't even remember the origins of. Somehow, he'd snuck up on her when they were on opposite shifts to say good morning...or was it good evening? It didn't matter. The game of being first to greet the other had stuck, and he was the reigning champion.

"You'll catch up one day!" He followed her into the staff room, grabbing his backpack as she placed hers in a locker.

"I doubt it. But I don't need to catch up."

This really was the perfect way to begin or end a shift. Hazel was his best friend, roommate and colleague. He saw her constantly and yet never tired of their inside jokes.

Her nose twitched, and he knew she was about to press a point. "You didn't answer my question, though. You ready to be an attending?"

"Yes...and no." He slung his backpack over his shoulder,

wishing he sounded surer of himself. He was excited, ready to finish his residency. Prepared to take on medicine as a full pediatrician. No more student physician, intern or residency. He'd completed today's shift, so technically, he was an attending physician.

It seemed like he'd been in med school, internship and residency for half his life. Which wasn't that far off!

This was his dream. The one he'd set for himself when his old life vanished. The goal that let him reach for something that wasn't home. Or the family he'd been cast out of.

For the first time in his life, he'd truly felt like himself. The real Syver, the one no one wanted to know at home, had flourished here.

He'd trained to be a pediatrician, thought of little else besides that goal. Now the day was arriving. He was reaching his end point.

Now he was Dr. Bernhardt, attending pediatrician. And part of him wondered if he was really ready. If he'd learned enough. If he'd be good enough.

"I felt the same way when I finished nursing school. Ready, *and not*, excited, and a tad terrified. All normal reactions. You're ready, Syver. And we are celebrating as soon as I get home!"

Hazel ran her hand along his shoulder, the connection brief…and friendly. That is what they were, friends and roommates. She'd moved into his flat two years ago, after her roommate's marriage. What was supposed to be a temporary arrangement had flourished into a friendship he'd never expected.

"Movies, popcorn and takeaway!" A Saturday tradition, at least when they were both free.

Hazel tilted her head, her bright eyes meeting his. "If you want to actually go out, we can. Someplace fancy, even. You've certainly earned it." Then she followed him out of the staff lounge and grabbed a tablet chart off the charger.

"And mess with tradition! No way." He'd spent his childhood going to fancy parties, elite restaurants, stuffed into suits and told to stay quiet.

He'd spent years playing a role he never quite fit. There was something special about spending time with a dear friend. Relaxing in confines of your home with no expectations.

And that time was always better when Hazel was by his side.

Besides, she was working the night shift. Even after a few hours of sleep, Hazel would prefer to slip into comfy pants and crash on the couch. And that was where he wanted to be, too. An epic celebration was epic just because they were having fun together. The location didn't matter.

"All right, if you're sure. I need to do patient transfers, but I put a lemon cookie on the counter for you."

"Best roommate ever!" Syver raised a hand as he headed for the door. "Good job sneaking up on me today, but come Monday…"

"Yeah…yeah!" Hazel waved and then turned toward the nursing station.

Syver whistled as he walked up the stairs to their flat. The Tube wasn't very crowded, and he'd hit the station at just the right time. He was officially Dr. Bernhardt and the life he'd carved out for himself was truly taking root.

"Your Highness."

He wasn't sure how the security service had entered his apartment, but Syver didn't care.

He was finally just Syver. Not Your Royal Highness, not Prince. Just Syver. It had taken years to settle into that. Years to accept that the royal family of Fönn preferred him forgotten.

"That isn't a title I answer to." *Not anymore.*

He'd been officially, but secretly, banished as soon as he turned eighteen. The King would never admit his queen had cheated. People suspected, there'd even been a few "news" articles, all quickly hushed up, but it was not discussed. Though the King never hid his distaste for his "second" son. They only thing he'd ever done to please the King was leave.

That was a wound buried so deep in his soul, Syver didn't think it would ever stop weeping.

Dropping his backpack, he stepped into the living room, stunned to see three guards in Fönn regalia standing in formation. "What are you doing here? I've not broken any of the King's rules."

He'd maintained a low profile; no one knew his origins. He'd studied at university, invested the payment the kingdom had given him and kept to himself. There was no reason for the guard to be in his home.

A look passed between the well-trained guards. The world teetered as the air in the room shifted. "What is going on?"

"The King requests you return home."

He couldn't stop the laugh, though there was no humor in the chuckle. "You're going to have to do better than that. After all, it's the King who sent me away."

And told me I was never to set foot back in the kingdom.

That second part wasn't exactly public knowledge, but it didn't surprise him that the security personnel didn't react. Either they were very skilled at their jobs, a distinct possibility, or it wasn't news to them. Maybe both.

"King Eirvin passed this morning."

The security officers parted, then bowed as Syver's brother stepped up. "It's *me* who requires you at home."

His brother's presence stole the wind from Syver's planned responses. The King was dead. The man everyone in Fönn assumed was Syver's father. The man who'd told him he was no longer part of the family was gone.

There were emotions he should feel. Anger, sadness…relief. But nothing came. The news settled like a lead balloon in the room as he tried to process the information. Tried to react.

"You're the last person I expected to see here. Shouldn't you be getting ready for a coronation?" The words lacked the deference he'd been trained to give his brother, but Erik didn't flinch.

"I doubted you'd come if I sent just the guard. Personal touch and all."

Personal touch. The words sounded liked they tasted bad. There was little hint of personal in this.

He came. For me.

No one had come for Syver…ever.

"The Dowager Queen hasn't stopped crying. She also wishes for your return."

Dowager Queen? Why didn't Erik ever call her mum? Titles, propriety, it all came first…and Syver always fell short.

Mum. His heart swelled, then crashed with worry. Was she all right? Probably not. Though he doubted she'd ever show it. But she wanted him home.

Words he'd never expected to hear made his heart soar. His family wanted him.

As if summoned by Erik's words, his mobile rang. "Mum…" She was calling. Calling him.

Syver took a deep breath as he looked around the flat. He'd called this place home for almost ten years. He'd mourned home, hated his banishment for the first year. Now the idea of leaving hurt, too.

"I need you, Syver, Erik needs you, Fönn…well, Fönn needs you, too." Pauses punctuated her words, and he could hear the tears in her voice. King Eirvin had cheated on the Queen regularly, but she'd loved him through it all. The one time she'd fallen for another…well, that had resulted in Syver. King Eirvin had not been as forgiving as his queen.

But if they needed him, wanted him, Syver would come.

"I'll be on my way shortly. I need to finish up a few things here—"

Hazel…

They were celebrating and the idea of leaving her. His throat closed. Maybe she'd like a change of location? The idea of not seeing her again, of not living with her…

"Sorry, Your Highness." The guard's tense words broke through his pained musings. "Our orders are to depart as soon as you have a bag packed."

Your Highness. It took him a moment to realize they were speaking to him, not his brother.

"My presence in England is unknown. And must remain that way. The funeral is tomorrow and then my coronation. You are the heir to the throne." Erik's words were firm, already king-like.

Heir to the throne, a throne he had no right to, and didn't want.

"Fönn needs doctors and a united royal family. You're part of Fönn's future."

Part of Fönn's future.

He'd see the frozen shores, attend the Summer Nights Festival, be part of the family he'd been thrown out of. It was a dream he'd given up when he'd landed in London, one he'd convinced himself he no longer wanted.

He closed his eyes and said a soft goodbye to the life he had here.

"Mum, I need to say goodbye…"

"There isn't time, Syver. You must come now. It is not fair, but it is the role of a prince. Fönn needs you." Her words were soft, but he heard the bite of the Queen behind them. Duty first. He might not have King Eirvin's blood flowing through him, but he'd been raised as a prince.

Forever duty. There were sacrifices to be made, but home and family—he couldn't say no.

His throat closed as he felt the royal mask slip back on. He'd sworn when he'd left Fönn that he'd not step foot back on its shores.

But that didn't mean he didn't yearn for it.

"I'll see you soon." A promise he could finally keep. He heard his mother sigh before she whispered a goodbye.

He slid the phone back into his pocket and walked into the kitchen. The sight of the cookie pulled another lump into his throat. He'd not told his best friend who he was. It wasn't supposed to matter, didn't matter when he was here.

In London he was Dr. Syver Bernhardt. It was a role he loved, the one he'd found solace in when his world was so empty.

But it hadn't been empty after he'd met Hazel. He was her

silly best friend. A woman who saw him as he saw himself...
perhaps the only person in the world who knew the private
man.

He'd not wanted to lose that. Not wanted to see the shift if
she learned he was royalty. *Even cast-out royalty.*

That selfish decision now meant she was going to come
home to an empty flat and a truth he wouldn't be here to share
personally.

It was time to go home, but he'd find a way to get back to
Hazel. Someway.

For now, she was safe and secure. That was what mattered.
He owned the London flat, and she could stay as long as she
wanted.

Forever.

The word slid into his mind, but he pushed it out. He needed
to focus on his family for the moment, but he also needed her
to know she was part of it, too.

Pulling a note from the drawer, he stared at the blank lines.
How did one write *goodbye, I'm sorry* and *give me a few
months to figure things out* in one short missive?

"We need to get moving, Syver." Erik's words were sharp
as Syver heard security tossing things into boxes in his room.

In the end, he scratched out a few words he knew weren't
enough. He'd make it up to her as soon as he resettled in Fönn.

CHAPTER ONE

Five years later

THE NORDIC ISLAND KINGDOM of Fönn was barely visible through the chilly fog, but Hazel Simpson could just make out the outline of the shore. At least she thought it was the shore.

Pulling into the heavy coat, she stared at her new home. The travel nursing contract let her work in Fönn for the next twelve months, though the nursing contractor let her know the kingdom was very interested in those taking contracts staying on.

Would they be if they knew my history?

She closed her eyes, pushing the unwelcome thought away. It wasn't her history. Not really.

Not that anyone in London cared. People who'd known her. People who claimed to be her friends had turned their back in her darkest moment. Her mother, who'd finally reconnected with her, had walked away. Calling her a naive idiot who ruined everything.

She'd accepted that the life she'd known, even if it wasn't a fairy tale, was over.

Alec had led her on for three years. Three years of playing the perfect girlfriend at investment events, of hiding her unhappiness, hoping that things would change. Three years of accepting expensive gifts when he missed a date, or anniversary or was a giant jerk. Three years of not asking enough questions. Three years accepting the bare minimum in a relationship. Three years with a con man whose company was nothing more than a Ponzi scheme.

Three years of her life down the drain. And with it, the career she'd built.

She had known nothing about Alec's crimes. The National Crime Agency cleared her. Though the investigator mentioned it shocked him how blind she'd been as he carted the expensive jewelry and electronics from her flat.

Items she hadn't wanted…not that anyone believed her. No. They thought she loved the fancy life Alec provided. When they'd met, he'd been a penniless stockbroker, then he'd hit it big…or at least that was what he'd told her.

And she'd wanted to believe him. Wanted to think that this was the person who wanted to be with her. The person who finally loved her for her.

Naive. She'd been so naive.

Her colleagues didn't agree with the assessment. They didn't think you could live with someone and not know them. *Twice.*

That was the real rub. She'd lived with a man she hadn't truly known twice.

Prince Syver Bernhardt.

Her onetime roommate and best friend. And the heir to the throne of the island nation where her ferry would land in a little over an hour.

Five years ago, she'd protested. She hadn't known. Like the rest of the hospital, the rest of London, it was shocking to find that a prince resided unknown among them.

No one had realized royalty from the tiny nation was sitting beside them. Working with them, acting like one of them. He'd buried that truth so well.

Or maybe she just hadn't dug deep enough. Maybe, like with Alec, the signs had been there, and she'd ignored them. It was so easy to believe a pretty lie.

The note Syver left on the counter with the cookie she'd gotten him was less than half a page. A quick goodbye, a promise she could stay in the flat as long as she needed.

Like she wanted to be there without him.

Yet it was one of the few possessions she'd brought with her. *Why?*

That was a question that had bounced around her brain each time she boxed up her life. And she had no better answer today than she did when she packed up their flat.

His flat.

Syver owned the flat. Something she should have picked up on. He hadn't cared about her rent, hadn't charged her market price. Another clue she'd ignored because she'd craved stability.

Searching for that stability, grasping for it, clinging to mirages of it, had only caused her pain.

"Careful, Elias!" a woman called as a little boy darted past Hazel.

The child laughed as he raced to the railing.

Hazel's stomach jumped to her throat as the boy reached over the railing, his mother stepping to his side. The child was fine, just enjoying the boat ride.

As a pediatric nurse-practitioner, she'd seen more fall injuries and broken bones in children than she could count.

He laughed and his mother stroked her son's head. Such a simple motion, one Hazel had never experienced. Her mother didn't know the definition of affectionate.

Hell, the woman hadn't wanted her. Maybe another would have hidden that dark secret, not Rita Simpson. She'd made sure Hazel knew from the time she was old enough to understand that she was an unwanted drain on her mother's life and purse. Even her name, Hazel, was after the color of her eyes. And only given after the nurse said she had to have a name to exit the hospital.

Leaning against the railing, Hazel kept her eyes from the young family. Focus on the future. On Fönn.

She bit her lip as the image of Syver danced in her memory. He would have believed she didn't know about Alec's schemes. He'd have listened.

But he wasn't there. He'd left her and never looked back.

He's where I'm going.

Fönn. Where Syver was the heir to the throne. The island nation had expected King Erik and his wife to have a child as soon as they wed. Three years later, the island was still waiting.

Most of London had stopped following the tiny island politics after watching Syver stand in the audience of his brother's coronation.

Not Hazel.

She knew he dated aristocratic women who graced magazine covers. Long blond hair, crystal-blue eyes with legs for ages.

Never for very long, just long enough to get local bloggers hoping he might settle down. The women were her polar opposite, in looks and status.

Not that it mattered. They'd only ever been friends.

Best friends.

Or were they? Friends didn't keep such secrets.

Water under the bridge, Hazel. It wasn't like she'd see him. The blogs and articles referred to him as the doctor heir, but never mentioned him working in medicine. Royal life wasn't exactly designed for a full-time job.

Which was a shame. Syver was a gifted pediatrician, one of the best she'd worked with in her nursing career. But what role did medicine have to play when you wore a crown?

A screech echoed over the boat's engines, and Hazel instinctively turned toward the boy she'd seen earlier. But he was safe in his mother's arms.

The cries came again, echoing from the back of the boat. An accident, and as a nurse, she knew her place. So she made her way toward the commotion. It didn't take long for an announcement to echo over the intercom.

"Is there a doctor on board? If so, please come to the back of the boat immediately."

Hazel wasn't a physician, but she knew the cries of an injured child.

She moved as fast as was safe on the wet deck. A small gathering was accumulating around the injured, and she pushed her way through. "I'm a nurse."

The little girl was sitting in her mother's lap, tears racing down her cheeks as she cradled her left arm.

"It hurts!" The wail broke Hazel's heart as she knelt beside the little one.

"I'm Hazel, a nurse." She smiled at the young girl, then looked at her mother. No other medical professionals stepped forward, but fortunately, and unfortunately for the child, it didn't take a doctor to diagnose the issue at hand.

Her wrist was already two times the size it should be, and bruises were popping up. Broken.

How bad? Only an X-ray could determine that, but the child was going to be in pain until they could get her treated.

"I need you," Hazel pointed to a man standing in the circle of gawkers, "to let the captain know we have a broken wrist. I need transport to the children's hospital available when we arrive. And ask how long it will take for us to reach the dock."

She didn't add *please*; this was an order. In emergency situations, directing someone to do something was better than asking.

Hazel pointed to a woman. "I need you to get me a first aid kit." She'd seen two white boxes with red crosses attached to the wall. Inside should be an instant ice pack, gauze and something she could use to stabilize the wrist.

The woman took off and was back before long, her face dejected. "This was all that was in them." The woman held up what looked like dirty gauze and two packs of Band-Aids.

Hazel looked at the poor offering and made a mental note to make sure she mentioned they needed restocking. But that was a problem for another day.

"All right then, find me a board, or anything sturdy I can use to stabilize her wrist. And ask the captain if he has ice somewhere."

The woman took off, and Hazel pushed the hood of her parka back. A little water slipped into her jumper, and Hazel shivered as she looked at the girl. "Can you tell me your name?"

"Ebba." The little girl sniffed, shifted in her mum's lap, then let out another sob.

"I know it's hard, Ebba, but I need you to stay as still as possible. Okay?"

"We have twenty minutes before landfall." The man she'd sent to talk to the captain coughed as he slid to a stop, barely catching himself.

Thank goodness. Hazel didn't need to add to her patient list.

"There will be transportation to take you to hospital. He didn't call for a medic, though."

"That's fine." Hazel nodded. The broken arm was an emergency but didn't require a medic or ambulance transport.

"This is all I could find." The woman held up a long wooden spoon. Her other hand held a baggie of ice. It wasn't much, but it was the best she could do right now.

"Perfect." Hazel took it from her hands and showed it to Ebba. "I am going to stabilize your wrist, Ebba. That means I am going to tie it to this spoon."

"With what?" Tears ran down her cheeks, but she looked confused. Children, even those in pain, were often full of questions. It was one of the things she loved about specializing in pediatrics.

"With this." Hazel undid the ribbon she'd tied her ponytail with this morning. It was soft, and a pretty pink.

As soon as she undid the bow, her hair popped out, wet curls falling everywhere.

Ebba laughed, a small sound, but a good one.

"My hair gets a little curly when it's wet." Hazel winked as she carefully lifted Ebba's wrist.

"A little?" One always heard the truth from the youngest.

Hazel wrapped the wrist then pulled Ebba's sleeve over the makeshift construct and put the ice on. Ebba sucked in a deep breath, then relaxed a little.

Ice would help with the swelling and numb a bit of the pain.

"As soon as we land, we're going to go to hospital for an X-ray."

"You're coming, too?"

"Of course." She hadn't really planned to. There wasn't a

reason to. She didn't start until tomorrow; nothing like leaving it to the last minute to arrive.

This would let her get an idea of the hospital before starting. *And keep me from thinking about walking into a small furnished apartment on an island where the only person I know wears a crown and left me without so much as a real goodbye.*

"A child crossing on the ferry this morning slipped and fell."

"Broken leg or wrist?" He hated that it didn't surprise him. There'd been far more accidents on the ferry lately. The island nation sat just below the Arctic Circle. Which meant even into the summer there was snow over much of the north, and down by the coast an icy drizzle fell.

The ferry dock was old, slippery and becoming more hazardous. He'd raise the issue with his brother later this week. Though he wasn't sure that it would do much good.

King Erik wasn't as focused on the aristocracy and their problems as his father...but he still didn't enjoy hearing Syver's "complaints."

In fact, he didn't enjoy hearing from Syver at all. His mother might raise the issue for him, but he doubted it. She rarely brought his concerns before the King.

If the crown didn't have interest in the issues, then Syver would use one of his other methods. Over the last several years, he'd become adept at maneuvering without the full approval of the crown.

If the captain didn't have the finances for the repairs, Syver would offer a small no interest loan out of the investment fund he'd set up. The one where he regularly turned down high-profile society projects his brother pitched.

His fund was for those without access to other money. The repairs benefited everyone, and the captain maintained the business his family had managed for at least four generations.

In his brother's five-year reign, Erik had reversed some of the damage his father's reign's focus on the aristocracy created. But he'd not gone far enough, in Syver's opinion.

There were beautiful buildings for the royal family, areas

the average citizen never saw. But the price for their citizens had been steep. Resulting in a large-scale emigration.

He wasn't the only one banished from his home. He wanted as many of Fönn's residents to return as possible. And he could not understand why that made him even more of an outsider in his family.

It was easy to see their citizens struggled under aging infrastructure, bad tax codes and numerous other issues. Issues that didn't impact the insulated aristocracy. Issues many of the leading families of the island didn't care about.

Taking care of the country's health infrastructure was Syver's primary goal, which would be easier if his brother didn't constantly remind him that he wasn't really royal. Or keep him from leading the initiative.

But the imposter heir kept trying. With enough work, maybe he could make Erik and his mother accept that just because he didn't have King Eirvin's blood didn't mean he wasn't family.

"The good news is there was a nurse on board. She took command of the situation according to the notes the captain relayed." Meg, a recent travel nurse from Maine, turned Fönn resident when her contract ended, looked up from the tablet chart.

"That is good news." The words felt stilted, but Meg didn't seem to notice as she turned back to work.

Nurse…taking charge.

Hazel.

She started tomorrow and arrived today. Something the other employees didn't realize; something no one knew the Prince was tracking. He'd watched the manifests for his friend, worrying when her arrival date slipped closer without her name appearing on a flight or the ferry records.

Most of the travel staff they hired arrived at least a week early to get settled. But not Hazel.

He didn't know what to make of her late arrival. Her résumé said she could be available in a week's time. That she was looking to leave England. So why had she waited so long to arrive?

When Human Resources sent out the pack of résumés for

new travel contracts two months ago, his mind had swirled at her name.

He'd picked up the phone immediately. The résumé pack was mostly so the doctors and head nurse knew what the pool looked like. Not to give hiring advice. He hadn't cared. He wanted Hazel here.

Now!

He'd mentioned that he'd worked with her at London Pediatric Hospital. That she was a wonderful nurse and would be an asset to the team. He'd left off that they'd been roommates.

Fönn's media had been consumed with King Eirvin's passing and Erik's rise to the throne when he'd arrived. No one had paid much attention to Syver's return. And Hazel had never given an interview about her relationship with him. Something his brother had worried over, but not Syver.

He and Hazel had been genuine friends. Leaving the way he had was still the biggest mistake he'd ever made. He should have put his foot down, stayed until she got home.

At the very least, he should have called immediately after he landed in Fönn. Invited her to join him, even. But the whirlwind of King Eirvin's funeral, comforting his mother, taking part in his brother's coronation and finally the investigation into the state of the country's health affairs had meshed together in a month of meetings, crisis talks and shakeups to ministry positions.

By the time he'd come up for air, thirty days had passed. Her mobile number suddenly didn't work, or she'd blocked him. He'd flown back to London, and found their flat empty.

The pain of standing in that empty set of rooms, of not being able to reach her. He'd thought of going to the hospital, but after living in the city for nearly a decade anonymously, this time, anonymity wasn't an option.

A diplomat arrived at the flat. And then the media. The life he'd had before…with Hazel…a distant memory. He'd flown out hours later, without ever finding her.

But she was coming here now. He could make it up to her.

And maybe pick back up the friendship he'd cherished most in his life.

"Hi. I'm Hazel Simpson. I've got a seven-year-old female, Ebba."

"Broke her wrist on the ferry." Meg's voice carried over the conversation, but Syver felt each of the nerves in his body light at the sound he hadn't heard in so long.

"The captain called ahead. Dr. Bernhardt is ready for her."

"Syver?"

"At the ready. It's good to see you, Hazel." Syver stepped beside Meg, his body vibrating. She was here. Really here.

Her dark hair was curlier than he remembered, with water dripping from it.

Her hazel eyes held his for the briefest moment before dropping to the little one's level. "You are in expert hands, Ebba. It was so nice to meet you."

"You're not staying?"

"Hazel has a lot to do, honey. It was nice of her to come to hospital with us." Ebba's mum kissed the top of her daughter's head.

"But I have her ribbon."

Syver looked over the counter. A wooden spoon and pink ribbon stabilized the little girl's arm. The ribbon that had probably tied Hazel's curls.

"A wooden spoon?" He looked at her. "That is inventive, Hazel."

A look flashed in her eyes...a warning? It passed so quickly.

"Well, the ferry first aid kit was more than a little lacking. Her wrist has had ice on it to reduce swelling. Bruising occurred immediately."

An orderly arrived. "Someone looking for an X-ray?"

Ebba's lip trembled. "Thank you, Hazel."

Hazel looked to the orderly, then to the child. She hesitated only a moment. "I'll see you when you get out, okay?" She smiled as Ebba's mother mouthed a thank you.

The little girl and her mum disappeared around the corner, and he saw Hazel's shoulders sag before straightening and looking at him. He waited for her to say something…anything, but no words fell from her full lips.

"That was nice of you," Meg murmured, breaking the awkward silence, as she looked from Hazel to Syver.

He could see the questions building behind Meg's eyes. It must be clear they knew each other. *She called me Syver.* No one did that. He was Dr. Bernhardt or Prince Syver. Never just Syver.

Not that it mattered. He had no intention of answering questions. Particularly before he talked to Hazel alone.

"Ebba's grandfather passed last week. They were returning home from his funeral. I guess he moved abroad in retirement." Hazel shrugged. "She's exhausted from travel, as is her mum, and sad."

"Big feelings." Syver made a note to give her mother a pamphlet on helping children with grief. People often saw children as little adults, even though their brains weren't fully developed, and emotional regulation was something many adults struggled with.

"Yes. Combine that with a broken wrist—it's a lot." Hazel looked down the hall to where the orderly had taken Ebba and her mum. "Is there a phone I can use? I need to make sure no one delivers my stuff for another hour or two. Not that there is much of it."

Syver's heart ached at the hurt in that last phrase. Once he'd have known exactly why Hazel was hurt, or tired, or happy or anything. But right now, she didn't even hold eye contact with him.

If this reunion was taking place anywhere else, he'd ask—directly. But Meg had already caught a link between them. He wasn't ashamed of his time with Hazel, but she'd not wanted to stay in touch. He'd wanted to honor that.

So, he didn't talk about his time with her. Even his mother only knew that he'd had a roommate he'd treasured. And lost when he answered the call to come home with no notice.

Meg handed over the desk phone, but Syver jumped in. "I'll put in a call. Make sure everything is set up fine."

"Oh." Meg grinned and looked at Hazel. "That's perfect. Working with a doctor/prince has some benefits. His people will handle it perfectly."

His people. Such a weird statement. One that after five years as the heir to the throne still felt uncomfortable. There were several limitations on Syver; things most people never saw. However, getting her stuff picked up and delivered, that was well within his abilities.

Hazel met his gaze then, her eyes finally holding his. His soul jumped. It was a ridiculous phrase; he knew that. Knew it wasn't even possible, but his inner self felt like it was coming home, finally.

He'd left London, lived in Fönn for years, but home. Home still felt elusive.

Because Hazel was missing.

"You don't have to, Syver... Dr. Bernhardt." Her voice was firm, but he saw her fingers twitch.

Looking at her hands, his chest caught. Each of her nail beds was red, picked over and over. He'd watched her pick her thumb when stressed, but for all of them to be so angry.

What happened?

He couldn't ask that here, but he could try to make her comfortable about using his name. "Syver works." He wanted her to use it. His colleagues referred to him as Dr. Bernhardt, and the people called him Prince Syver.

An upgrade from the barely controlled sneer previously attached to *Your Highness* people used when he first returned. A sign of respect, he knew, but he enjoyed hearing Syver. Just Syver...

Spoken in her sweet alto tone.

He swallowed, uncomfortable at the realization of how much he wanted it. And the sensation that the want bordered up against a feeling that differed from the friendly bond they'd had for so long.

"Well..." Meg's voice was bright, a reminder that she was there.

Syver felt heat burn around the collar of his scrubs. "I'll place the call now, Hazel. I'll handle everything, promise."

There was that look again.

"Haz—"

"If you insist." She crossed her arms and looked at the floor.

"I do." He grinned, though it felt off. She was upset and trying to hide it. And he had no insight…deserved none.

"Why don't I give you a quick tour? You know, cut down on the things you need tomorrow for your first day." Meg stepped around the desk, her eyes meeting Syver's.

Yep, the nurse from Maine had questions…ones she'd ask Hazel and then come for him. Hazel could answer as she liked, but Syver would not break.

Their time together was too precious to be used as idle gossip.

"After I can show you to the room where Dr. Bernhardt will put on Ebba's cast."

"Sounds good." Hazel unzipped her coat, the oversize pink jumper she wore swallowing her slight frame. "I'll see you later, Dr. Bernhardt."

The two women headed off, and Syver leaned against the counter. Hazel was here. She was really here.

And she'd called him Dr. Bernhardt. *Intentionally.*

How he hated that barrier. They'd never had one before. There were things he needed to say, things to apologize for. Better to do it fast.

He picked up the phone, arranged for Hazel's things to be unpacked and for a dinner delivery.

Today was a lot. After all, she'd left her home country, arrived in a new one, given aid to a wee one on the ferry, then come face-to-face with the roommate who'd abandoned her. An overwhelming twenty-four hours to be sure.

At least he could take care of her a little.

"Hazel!"

Shivers raced down her spine as Syver's voice hit her back. She'd stayed long enough to see Ebba's pretty pink cast. Hovering in the room and trying to keep her eyes from Syver.

Now her goal of stealing out was failing before she'd set foot in the parking lot.

She was running from Syver, and the torrent of feelings his sight brought her.

After the cast was on, when saying goodbye, Ebba's mother had quietly whispered that everyone got used to Prince Syver just being among them. She'd kindly explained how being in royalty's presence was a little uncomfortable for everyone at first. But not to worry because he wasn't like most royals.

She knew that. After all, Hazel had lived with him. For two years.

Sort of.

Prince Syver was a mystery. A person she knew of from news and blog articles. The man she'd known was simply Syver. Her best friend.

Her best friend who'd abandoned her.

Left her to fend off all the questions. Not seen the shocked looks and heard the exasperated sighs when Hazel swore she hadn't known. That wasn't the worst, though.

No. It was the loneliness, the lack of his presence. The absence of the feelings she got when he was around. That was what she'd missed most.

It was that feeling that she'd chased with Alec. Pretending that with enough time, enough understanding, she could make those feelings happen again. Then her life had fallen apart.

That wasn't Syver's fault, but she'd wondered more than once what would have happened if he'd stayed.

Was that selfish? Maybe. But when she'd needed someone the most, the person she'd wanted to run to was gone.

And yet, I came here.

"Hazel!" The baritone sound of his voice now heated her blood. What was that? Remnants of the long day? Maybe. Whatever it was, it would disappear. It had to.

In less than sixteen hours, she was going to walk back through the hospital doors. She needed to get to her flat. Settle herself.

She truly hadn't expected to ever see him again. Maybe

part of her had hoped, but working with him, she'd never let herself think of that. There were so many things she wanted to say. She wanted to confront him, tell him how his absence had affected every aspect of her life. How hurt she was.

Underneath that frustration was something else, too. The urge to run into his arms. To collapse into her once safe space. But Syver wasn't that—hadn't been that since he left.

It was clear they were going to be working together. Syver had always worked closely with the nurses, seeing them as part of the team. So she'd see him…a lot!

And as Meg's pointed questions about the looks he gave her reminded Hazel of their connection, the easy one they had, hints of it still simmered beneath the years and distance.

If it was that obvious, better to address it before they worked their first shift.

Turning, she bit her lip to keep the smile her brain wanted to form from appearing. She was lonely. It had been a rough year, a rough few years, and her soul wanted to jump into friendship. To recover something she'd thought lost forever.

But she wasn't the naive woman she'd been. Life had thrust so many choices upon her. From her mother's choices to Alec's, she'd let those choices wash over her rather than address conflict head-on.

The woman she'd been was gone. Hazel faced conflict now. Noticed the warning signs and addressed issues. Truth might hurt, but it was better than a fantasy.

Crossing her arms, she waited for him to reach her. Had he always been so tall…so handsome?

Yes.

It was something all her female colleagues, and a few of her male colleagues, had commented on. How did you live with such a beautiful man and not get turned on by him?

Because he'd been her friend. She'd loved him, but it hadn't felt romantic. Sure, her heart had calmed around him, and maybe she'd felt better in his presence than anyone else's, but that was the definition of their friendship.

Best friends. Two peas in a pod, who'd snuggled on the

couch, laughed at silly and not-so-silly jokes. Made dinner and griped about work frustrations. Her other half who understood when she'd had a bad day. The one she'd leaned on.

Hazel had grown up jumping between small flats as her mother moved from one partner to another. Her mum always hoping the next guy was her knight in shining armor and blaming their abandonment on Hazel when things didn't work out. The seminomadic life hadn't allowed for any deep childhood friendships to form. But it had felt like she and Syver had one.

Then he just left me.

"It was kind of you to come with Ebba and stay while I fitted her cast." Syver pushed his hands into his pockets. Was that still a tell for when he was nervous? "Is your ride on its way?"

She looked at the parking lot, her cheeks heating as she realized she had no ride. Rushing from the hospital as soon as they'd discharged Ebba, hoping to avoid this interaction, had gotten her here. And this was why she was supposed to address conflict head-on these days.

First day failure, because no taxi was coming to rescue her. *So step up now, Hazel.*

"I don't have a ride. I guess that is something I should have thought about." She was glad the hood of the parka offered some cover for the heat coating her face. "Suppose I need to go back in and place a call."

"My shift's over. Why don't I take you to your flat?" He held up a hand. "Before you argue, I don't have to—I know. But let me anyway. I think we need to chat."

They did. This wasn't the case of some man disappearing and wondering why. She knew he'd ghosted her. He was a royal, and she was about as far from blue blood as possible. Still, there were things to say. Better to hash it out before they started working together.

She nodded, not quite trusting her voice.

"I need to change real quick. Don't move, okay?"

"I'm not the one who left with no warning, no ability to call, no forwarding address." The words were out, the years of hurt spilling uncontrolled into the open.

Syver flinched. Her words cut, and she hated that part of her was glad. She'd faced the media, the questions, the hate, alone. While he'd lived in a palace...because his father died. Her throat tightened.

"Hazel... I..."

Accepting confrontation when necessary was one thing, cruelty, another. She held up a hand. "Sorry. That was uncalled for." His family needed him; his country needed him. Hazel Simpson could not compare to those responsibilities.

"Hazel—"

"It's fine, Syver." She nodded to the hospital. "I'm tired and grouchy. Go get changed before I hire a taxi." It was an empty threat. She had no plans to leave, even if she could magic transportation to the parking lot.

He looked back at the hospital, then stepped close to her. Less than an arm's length separated them, and part of her brain screamed for her to move closer. Her heart remembered how safe she'd felt in his arms.

A safety she'd craved but hadn't felt since he left.

Her brain remembered other things, though. Recalled the sleepless nights, the tear-soaked pillows. So, her feet stayed planted.

"I'm not leaving you, ever again."

He raised his hand. For a moment she thought he'd cup her cheek, but then he pulled back.

"I promise, Hazel."

"Big promise." Hazel winked, trying to defuse some of the tension. They'd shared an easy banter once, a push and pull that looked almost scripted but came so naturally.

This wasn't five years ago, though. "And easy promise, when we're in your country." This was his place, where he was a prince. And she was just Hazel. Something that hadn't ever been enough.

"My country or not, it's true." Then he turned on his heel, nearly jogging through the hospital doors.

He returned in record time. So maybe he hadn't completely trusted her to stay put.

But it was the backpack on his shoulder that caught her eye. Navy blue, with patches…the bag she'd gotten him for his birthday.

The bag she'd found in a secondhand store. Vintage patches covering it. She'd purchased it immediately. Then unknowingly given it to a prince. "You still have that?"

Syver patted the strap. "Of course. Best gift I've ever gotten."

"I doubt that." Hazel murmured as she followed him to a car parked in a slot for Dr. Bernhardt. Designated parking… a nice perk.

She slid into the leather seats, surprised when he started the car, but didn't pull out of the parking spot.

"Hazel." His voice was soft, the same voice she'd heard in so many dreams since he'd left. "I need you to know something."

She turned, her brain bouncing between excitement that she was finally with her friend again, uncertainty that she was finally with her friend again, anger and a fourth emotion pooling in her body that for a second felt like desire.

"I enjoyed every single minute of our friendship. It was the best time of my life." Drumming against the steering wheel, he looked at the car's ceiling, then back at her. "I never expected to come home to find Security in the flat…"

His voice died away, but there was a look in his eyes. Uncertainty or longing, or something else entirely? She wasn't sure.

He took a deep breath, reaching for her hand, but pulling back before he actually connected.

She ached to close the connection. But too much time and distance hovered in those few inches.

"But?" She looked away as she asked the question. Her life seemed like a never-ending series of *but*s.

I'd take you with me, but… insert random man Mum was dating *…doesn't like children. So Nan will look after you for a while.*

I'd take you on vacation, but it's just the boys.

I believe you didn't know about Alec's crimes, but the rest of the staff have doubts. You can't be effective if no one trusts you.

"But…" he waited, and she finally turned to look at him. "I should have told you who I was. It was selfish. I didn't think of myself as a prince. King Eirvin…well, let's just say he didn't miss me while I was gone."

Do all royals refer to their parents by their titles? It felt off. A hint of anger…and acceptance.

Unfortunately, a parent not missing you, she understood. She hated that he'd experienced it, too.

"I just want you to know that if I could do it over, I'd change several things in my life, but never the time I spent with you as my friend."

Friend. Why did that word leave a hole in her chest? They'd been friends. It was the right description—so why did she wish he'd embellished it?

All of his words spoke of the past. A friendship that had served him for the time. And now…and now they were colleagues. Just colleagues.

"Thank you, Syver."

He took a deep breath, looked at her, then turned his head and pulled out of the parking lot. Silence settled around them. It wasn't nearly as comfortable as the silences they'd enjoyed as roommates. Quiet times when they were lost in their own thoughts.

But it didn't bother her either. Silence from Alec had been a sign of trouble. A warning that his day had gone off and he might take that frustration out on her.

He'd never hit her, but as her counselor pointed out, abuse came in many forms. He'd honed his blade by leveraging her childhood trauma against her. If her mother didn't want her, why would anyone else? He'd helped her get her job. Without him, she was nothing.

They were just words, but they'd cut millions of slices into her soul.

Syver parked the car in front of a row of flats, pointing at the one on the end. "Palace staff delivered your bags a few hours ago. I asked them to stock the pantries and takeaway is in the fridge, too. Enough for you to have leftovers."

Enough to invite you in.

But she would not do that. She needed to process today. Decompress and settle in. Still. It was the nicest thing anyone had done for her in…well, the nicest thing done for her since Syver left.

"Thank you. Again." Hazel sighed as she crossed off some of the many items on her mental to-do list. "Do you help each of the traveling nurses?"

She'd meant the question to sound lighter than it had come out. However, like all words, once delivered, there was no way to recall them.

"No. But I've been excited since I rushed your résumé to the HR department."

Rushed my résumé…

The hiring official hadn't mentioned that. If he'd recommended her, a prince, could they have chosen a different candidate? Was she here because of Syver?

There's always someone better. Her mother's voice echoed in her brain.

No, Hazel wasn't letting that toxic thought take residence. She was more than qualified, more than a decade in pediatrics and five years as an advanced nurse-practitioner, often called an ANP.

"I'm happy you're here." Syver's face was so open, carefree. Like when they'd lived together.

In the images she saw on blogs and in gossip rags, he was controlled, regal. She reached her hand across the console and squeezed his.

The connection lasted less than a second, but she already wanted a hug. Wanted to invite him upstairs and reconnect. Lay her problems at his feet and rest for a while.

But he was Prince Syver now, and she was still Hazel Simpson. A lifetime of difference hung between the last five years, and she wasn't sure how to cross it. Or if she should.

So she offered a smile instead. "I'm happy I'm here, too." Then she slid out of the car, not trusting herself to stay any longer.

CHAPTER TWO

"QUESTIONS?" CLARA, Fönn Children's Hospital human resource manager, leaned across her desk.

She had one. Not about this morning's orientation or job expectations, but one that had hammered through her brain all night. Not asking meant continued worries. And her brain, once latched on to a thought, rarely released it.

However, asking brought its own issues. *Fear is something you learned to move past. Take control of your situation and hold on to yourself.*

As her counselor had reminded her, humans often thought the worst when the actual result was nowhere close to it.

"One. And it's off topic." Hazel's stomach clenched, but it was best to know if they'd hired her because Syver pushed for it. If she'd landed in a new place just to be chased by the same issues as before.

If once more, her proximity to a man with power had made a difference. The physician at the private clinic had wanted the opportunity to invest in Alec's business. Not her expertise.

Or not *only* her expertise.

"Dr. Bernhardt was kind enough to drive me home last night—"

"You call him Dr. Bernhardt?"

The knot in her stomach tightened as Clara raised a brow, confusion clear on her face. Had she expected her to use his royal title or to call him Syver—because of their connection? "Why wouldn't I?"

She'd rarely spoken of their time together. He was her colleague. Her colleagues in London knew she'd lived with a prince. But after the news ruckus died off, people largely forgot her connection to the royal family of Fönn.

She'd never given an interview, something she was proud of. There were times when she could've used the money. Though she doubted the tabloids really wanted it. Their story wasn't exactly exciting. There were no salacious details to reveal. Just friendly reminders of the man she'd known.

Clara's eyebrows pulled together, and the tips of her lips turned down just barely. "It's just—he indicated when he prioritized your hiring that he knew you personally. He was gone for a while."

Clara's eyes caught hers. The same look Hazel had seen in Meg's eyes yesterday. A curiosity…probably wondering how a nurse from Nowhere, England knew the heir to Fönn's throne by name.

She would not react. The knife turning in her soul would not get the upper hand. Even if Hazel wanted to slink away.

First day and she was here because of Syver.

Should I have seen this sign? Should I have questioned?

How would she have even done that?

And it wasn't the first time, either. That stung. Once more she hadn't really earned her place.

It was her mother's favorite line.

People give you things, Hazel. You never earn anything.

Her mother believed Hazel should be glad she'd kept her when her father left. Glad for the necessities she'd provided. Things Hazel hadn't earned…couldn't earn, no matter her grades or attempts to please.

When her grades came back with excellent marks, her mother insisted Hazel's success was only because of the pressure she'd put on her. *Pressure. Trauma*…apparently those words were interchangeable.

And then Alec used his connections to recommend her to the private clinic she'd worked at.

It didn't matter how hard she worked. There'd always

been someone who'd questioned if she deserved what she'd achieved. And now a prince had prioritized her résumé.

If she displeased him, would the hospital drop her contract?

"So Syver… Dr. Bernhardt…is the reason you hired me?" The words tasted like ash as she forced them out. Better to know than guess was only true if it wasn't the worst-case scenario.

"You were a top candidate but." She shrugged. "I mean, knowing people is how the world works, right? So Prince Syver's recommendation didn't hurt. Was that your question?" Clara looked genuinely confused. Like it was silly to even worry about.

But if you'd had someone take your position because of your ex…

She'd signed a contract. She was in Fönn for a year. Syver's recommendation or not. "I told you it was off topic."

Hazel knew her smile was forced, but there was no good way to segue out of the topic she'd raised.

"You're a qualified ANP, and Fönn is still recovering from years of mass exodus. We're all pleased you accepted the position." Clara's beeper went off, and she looked at it. "I need to run, unless you need something else?"

"No, thank you. I'll find Meg for the next round of orientation." What was done was done. Clara was right. She was a qualified ANP, and people used connections all the time to land positions. That the only connection she had was a criminal con man made her different from most.

I've got Syver.

Her body warmed as his face danced in her mind. And not as just a friend. What was that? Even though it frustrated her knowing his recommendation had, at the very least, been a selling point for her hiring, all her mind wanted to consider was how handsome he'd been carrying the backpack she'd given him.

She'd thought more about him almost reaching for her hand than about replaying his words about the job. Her mind questioning what would have happened if she'd closed the distance.

Nothing. Nothing would have happened.

"Good day, Hazel. I think that puts me at five hundred and one."

Her body ached at the greeting. There were a few times over the years where she thought she'd heard him. It always put her in a sour mood when she reminded herself that the game was over.

She'd missed the game. But they were strangers now. Playing it felt off. "Good morning, Dr. Bernhardt." She didn't acknowledge the count. Didn't make a joke, even though she wanted to.

Colleagues. They were just colleagues.

"You okay?" He wore blue scrubs with a cartoon bird stenciled on the pocket. It screamed *pediatrics*, and the scrubs were tailored to fit his body perfectly.

Of course they are. He is a prince.

At her hospital, a few of the doctors had purchased and tailored their own scrubs. Hazel had always just gotten hers from the bin the hospital provided. Something she planned to do here, too.

But she could appreciate the fineness that was Syver.

Seriously! How did she pull those thoughts from her brain? After all, she'd just learned of his recommendation.

A recommendation most people want, Hazel!

Most people would be pleased. So why was she so determined to be put off by it?

Alec's action had imploded her career. But Syver was as different from her con man ex as possible. He was her friend. Or at least he had been.

And none of those mental ramblings explained why her thoughts kept rotating back to Syver's good looks.

"I'm fine. Dr. Bernhardt."

"Again. I prefer Syver." He winked and held his hand out, gesturing to a hallway. "Any interest in lunch?"

Yes.

"I'm supposed to find Meg. Go over a few things and then, if they need me, help with patients." Hazel pulled at the skin around her fingernails. A nervous habit that she'd never fully broken. One that had worsened after Alec's arrest. "Not hungry anyway."

Her stomach rumbled, and Syver raised an eyebrow as he dug his hands into his pockets. At least she wasn't the only one uncomfortable with the shift that time and distance had done to their relationship. "I don't like to use the term *liar*," Syver teased.

"But it's true." She smiled, unconsciously, then wiped it from her face. It would be so easy to flip back into the friendly scripts they'd used. To play the hello game, to pick back up the inside jokes that had made her days so happy.

To lean on him. Leaning on him was why his disappearance was so rough. Leaning on Alec was why she was here to begin with. Hazel couldn't let herself lean on anyone. Not again.

He pursed his lips and looked toward the stairwell that led to the lower floor. "I've got a bit of a break. So, I'm grabbing a sandwich."

He turned and started down the stairs. She knew he wouldn't ask again. Wasn't pushing. Just letting the offer stand. And that made her want to follow even more.

Still, she hesitated. Then her stomach rumbled again. She had half a shift left, and medical staff learned to take breaks when the opportunities presented themselves.

It was only when she was standing in line behind him that she wondered what people would think of the two of them eating together. Staff ate together regularly, but she was new, he was the Prince.

And he recommended my résumé.

Things she should've considered before following him.

Sliding across the table from him, she wondered how fast she could gobble the hummus-and-tomato sandwich without seeming rude.

"I'm not pushing, Hazel, but your fingernails look worse than I've ever seen." Syver glanced at her hands, then picked up his sandwich. "Are you all right?"

The urge to lay everything out. To tell him why she was

here. To joke that her fingers had looked nearly normal before Alec's arrest. But then she'd have to admit that her boyfriend had been arrested.

And that she'd lived with a man who'd treated her poorly and she'd accepted it. That still stung.

It was a hard lesson, but she'd sworn she wasn't going to accept less again. That no one would question her place in the world again. If someone couldn't accept her as she was, then they didn't get her at all.

She'd applied to be an international travel nurse and planned to start anew.

Then I came to the one other place in the world that I knew someone—how daring.

"It's been a long a year, or a long few years, I guess. I came to Fönn to start over." Her hand slid across the table toward his. His fingers flexed just before she pulled back.

She wanted to cross her arms, keep herself rooted in place so she wouldn't give in to the desire to reach for him. To touch him. That was the past and she needed to focus on the future.

On taking care of herself.

"I need to prove to myself I can do things on my own." She ran her finger over the broken skin of her thumb, the urge to rub it for a few seconds, or longer, hitting hard. But she refocused on her sandwich.

"I appreciate you forwarding my résumé." There, the words were out. She'd acknowledged the connection and his potential role. Address things head-on. That was the best route. The route she'd sworn she'd take now, no matter the consequences.

"I didn't forward your résumé." Syver took a big bite of his lunch and shrugged. "At least, not directly. I saw your résumé on the top of the packet and told Clara we needed to see if you'd come, but your résumé was always one of, if not the, top candidate for the position. I just put in a good word."

A good word…from a prince. Surely, he knew how much his words mattered?

"You're a prince."

"Eh…" He took another bite of his sandwich.

Could he really not see the difference it made? "Still, that was nice of you. I didn't expect it and—" The desire to say what had happened, confide in him, lean back into the safety, welled in her chest. It would be so easy.

Easy routes were the fastest to heartbreak. Her watch buzzed, and she finished the last bit of her lunch. She needed to leave.

"That's my sign to find Meg."

Syver nodded, though she thought he wanted to say more. But he let her go.

Syver saw Hazel walk into the room and knew a frown was forming on his lips. A childhood spent being told to keep his face devoid of any emotion other than polite excitement, a fake emotion, made him hyperaware of the position of his face. Another thing he'd let drift away while in London.

Something he hadn't wanted to return when Erik asked him back. Yet the happy family, the acceptance he'd hoped for... hadn't appeared. It was sad that the ability to hide his thoughts had reappeared almost as soon as he landed.

A necessity for survival in the unfeeling palace.

Hazel's words at lunch ricocheted through his mind. Even if he hadn't put a word in for her, he couldn't imagine Clara not offering her a contract.

People use inside connections all the time.

That thought irked him. It was true and one of the many things he had fought against since his brother ascended the throne. The issue he and the King argued about most often. The aristocracy thrived on inside connections. It was how their world worked.

And the system was decidedly unfair for anyone not privy to the behind-closed-doors conversations.

But Hazel was the opposite of aristocracy. She'd gotten into a preparatory school because of good grades and used scholarships to cover the high cost.

Other than that, he knew little about her background. When her roommate situation had shifted suddenly because of an elopement, she'd said she couldn't rely on family. They'd grown up in different classes, but Syver understood that. He'd offered his place as a short-term retreat, only to love having a roommate.

Well, he'd love having Hazel as a roommate.

In the two years they'd lived together, they'd spent holidays together—working—so others could spend time with family. Despite the distance, his mother always sent birthday and holiday gifts. Small items, items that let him cling to the idea that at least one person in Fönn still thought of him.

The only gifts Hazel received were from him.

If Clara hadn't wanted to hire Hazel…well, if Clara hadn't thought she was an excellent candidate, Syver would have gone to bat for her.

Syver needed her here. Seeing her name had healed a deep wound. He'd have fought for her. Period.

But he hadn't had to, because Hazel's résumé spoke for itself.

"Fourteen-year-old girl exhibiting stomach cramps and fainting in Room Three." Hazel handed him the tablet chart. Her eyes shifted, and he could see words stuck there.

A concern, an uncertainty. Because she was new…or was it something else? "What is it?"

"I'm not offering a diagnosis—"

"I trust my nurses, but you're an ANP so you diagnose patients, too." They'd each worked with physicians who didn't trust other attending physicians or nurses. Those doctors had taught him exactly who he didn't want to be.

"I understand. I also don't want to add thoughts to your mind before you form your own opinion." Hazel shifted, then crossed her arms. "GI issues and fainting can indicate multiple diagnoses."

That was a good reason not to say something. Even if someone watched for it, unconscious bias affected all humans.

"But listen to her mother and watch the way she looks when her daughter talks about her symptoms."

Syver raised an eyebrow then nodded.

"I could be reading into things—"

"I doubt it." Syver looked over the tablet chart. The four-teen-year-old, Ida, complained about stomach cramps and had fainted during her gymnastic meet. "Let's go."

Stepping into the room, he offered Ida a smile. "Ida, I'm—"

"Prince Syver." She smiled as she looked up. Ida was hugging her knees and covered in a blanket.

"She was cold." Hazel answered his unspoken question. So their ability to read each other perfectly in work situations hadn't faded. That was going to come in handy.

Unfortunately, it didn't appear intact outside the hospital. They were stilted. Words clogged his throat, things that needed to be said, but he couldn't push out.

Still, she was here.

"My stomach is better now after the cracker Hazel gave me. It was just a long meet." She sighed and shifted, the blanket slipping off her shoulders.

Her collarbone stood out in the bright lights. He looked to Hazel and saw her attention focused on the same point.

Ida ran a hand over her arm. "Your arm hurt?"

"Oh." She pulled the blanket over her arm. "My skin's dry. It happens."

Anorexia nervosa. The diagnosis he knew Hazel feared. Disordered eating was a complicated diagnosis; it would be easier to treat a GI issue. Dry skin, the thin arms and being cold, he ticked them off mentally. All symptoms related to the body not getting enough nutrition.

There was no quick fix for body dysmorphia.

"Cracker?" Hazel started to cross her arms, and he watched her adjust her stance. Confrontation wouldn't work, but he understood the urge. It was easy to argue that you just needed to eat more. But Ida wouldn't respond to that. "I gave you two packets, eight crackers in each…did you eat more than one?"

Ida's eyes shifted to her mum, who held up the packets. "She handed them to me after the first one. I told you, you should have more." Her eyes shifted to Hazel, pain radiating through her features.

So Mum knew what the issue was too, and either had confided in Hazel or saw a partner in getting her daughter help.

Syver used the tablet chart to alert the nutritionist that they needed a consult. It was possible Ida had a GI bug, but if she did, it was a secondary diagnosis. The cramps were probably hunger pains and the fainting due to a lack of nutrients.

"You need to eat more than a few crackers, Ida. This is just to help with your hunger pains." He kept his tone light as he made another note for the nutritionist.

"I have a big competition next weekend." Ida's bottom lip wavered. "I'm already bigger than all the other girls. I can't even add half a pound."

She needed to add at least fifteen, ideally twenty-five. There was no way Ida was the largest gymnast, which was not a terrible thing. But with body dysmorphia it was likely Ida saw herself that way. And explaining that she wasn't wouldn't work.

That didn't keep her mother from trying. "You aren't. And even if you were, it wouldn't matter." Her mother's voice quivered. "And you need food for fuel, honey."

"I *need* to get extra rotations." Ida lifted her chin. "And to do that, I need to be as small as possible. Coach says so. If I want to compete at the next level, I have to sacrifice."

"Coach…" Her mother closed her mouth and hugged herself. "I want you healthy, Ida."

There was little Syver could do here other than refer Ida to Inpatient Services. Which he planned to do. But with disordered eating, the patient needed to see the problem.

That was one of the first steps on the long road to health. And having an adult in her life pushing for her to reach a next level—to lose weight—was not helpful. He wasn't sure what he could do about a coach encouraging disordered eating, but he'd figure that out after this consultation.

"Is next week the last meet?" Syver thought inpatient treatment needed to start immediately, but if next week was the last meet, holding off a few days might make it more likely that Ida would enter the program willingly. The odds of success went up drastically in those cases.

"There is no last meet." Her mother frowned and pushed a tear off her cheek. "We've been at the gym nearly every day since she turned seven."

"I have a gift—Coach says so." Ida curled tighter into the blanket. "A gift. I just have to sacrifice a little more."

"Ida." Hazel stepped forward, then sat on the side of the bed with her. "Does your hair fall out when you brush it?" Her voice was soft, but there was a tone of authority in it. Syver took a step back and looked to Ida's mum. If Hazel made a connection here, it would help them immensely.

"Everyone's does…" She brushed a tear off her cheek. "But yes."

"That's because the nutrients you get from food keep your scalp healthy and make your hair grow. And your skin itches?"

"No lotion Mum finds works. I've tried… I don't know, it feels like hundreds of kinds." Her voice was soft, tears coating each word.

"That's because the lack of nutrients is drying out your skin. It's also why you are so cold. As you lose muscle mass, your body can't regulate your temperature." Hazel took a deep breath, looked at Ida's mum and then continued, "And you're hungry all the time, right?"

Ida sucked in a breath, "If I were stronger, I wouldn't be."

Ida's mum put a hand over her mouth, and Syver saw tears trickle behind them, but she didn't make a noise. This was going to be a long road with many hills and valleys.

"No. You are so strong." Hazel held out her hand and Ida put her hand in hers. The bones of Ida's wrist so prevalent, Syver was shocked she wasn't breaking bones.

That was coming, though, if she didn't get help.

"Coach…" Ida bit back whatever she planned to say. "I'm tired, too." She leaned her head on her knees but didn't pull away from Hazel.

"Of course you are. Your body is a wonderful machine, but it needs nutrients. You are perfect, just the way you are. You don't owe anyone but yourself your best, sweetie."

"I don't want to give up, but… I think I need help, too. I'm torn, Mama. What do I do?" Ida started sobbing then and Hazel slid off the bed, shifting places with her mum who wrapped her arms around her daughter, sobs echoing between them.

Syver waited a few minutes, let the emotions of the room calm a bit, then started, "I've requested our nutritionist for a consult, and I will make a recommendation for inpatient treatment for disordered eating. As an emergency doctor, I can only do the referral, but if you have questions, call the desk here, ask for me. If I don't know, I will find someone who does."

Ida's mum mouthed *thank you* as he and Hazel walked out of the room. All of this information would be on the discharge paperwork, because he doubted her mother would remember, but that was okay.

Closing the door, Syver turned to Hazel. "That was impressive."

"A tiny baby step on the very long road that Ida is going to walk. Probably for the rest of her life." Hazel clenched her fists. "And her coach…"

"I'll have a look at that." Ida's statement worried him. Young adults were impressionable, but no sport was worth creating lifelong health problems.

Hazel let out a breath, her shoulders relaxing as she looked at him. "Working with a prince has perks, I guess."

"Occasionally." His family didn't give him much responsibility. The King rarely listened to him. The people liked him and that gave him some sway. Still, his suggestions were just that. Suggestions one could ignore.

"But you were the actual hero in there. Sitting with her, walking her through her symptoms, brilliant. Letting her acknowledge each one."

"A trick I saw a nutritionist use at the last clinic I worked at in London. Not my idea." Her eyes darted away from him, and she rocked back on her heels.

Hazel was getting ready to bolt. The uneasiness was already settling around them.

"It wasn't a trick, Hazel. It was skill, and the reason you are here." Before she could interrupt, he continued, "You told

Ida she was perfect just the way she was. That she didn't owe anyone but herself her best."

He stepped closer and almost regretted it as the pull he'd noticed between them since she'd showed up yanked at him. Syver wasn't sure exactly what that was. But he pushed the feeling away as he held her bright eyes. This moment was about Hazel, not his own wants. Whatever those were.

"You can see it in others, so perfectly…why not yourself?" He smiled and stepped back.

Why does stepping away feel like I'm wading through sand?

It should be easy. They'd worked together for years as friends. Joked and had deep conversations on the bad days, but he hadn't felt drawn to her like this.

Had he?

Maybe he was just excited to have his friend back…

"Thank you, Dr. Bernhardt." She patted his arms, friction bolting through his body. Her eyes followed her hands and she yanked them back. Clearly, she hadn't meant to touch him. Hazel opened her mouth, then shifted and started down the hall.

In another lifetime he'd have made a clever joke, walked with her. Joked with her. Now he watched her go, wishing they weren't at work, wishing he could follow her.

CHAPTER THREE

"THANK YOU SO MUCH for agreeing to switch shifts!" Meg was nearly bouncing as she handed the tablet chart over. "Summer Nights is one of my favorite holidays, and I'm not even from Fönn."

And it didn't hurt that her boyfriend had indicated that he might propose this evening. Hazel didn't mention that, though. Meg was already nervous that she'd misread the signs.

The historian she was seeing was full of interesting tidbits and Meg was nearly certain he'd been bread-crumbing hints all week. But now that the night had arrived, the nerves set in.

She understood. How many signs had she misread over her lifetime? That was a list she had no desire to make.

"I hope you have fun."

"Oh, I will. Part of me feels bad that you'll miss the festival's opening. It's your first Summer Nights. At least it should be sl—" Meg clammed up, not wanting to jinx the staff by saying the night should be slow.

Hazel appreciated the concern, but holidays spent in the hospital were something she was very used to. Others had families to spend this time with.

Alone was how Hazel had grown up. Alone was how she'd spent so much time. And not wanting to be alone anymore was how she'd nearly gotten trapped with Alec. That wasn't a pretty realization, but one didn't address internal issues without acknowledging how trauma affected them.

"Don't worry about me." She winked. "The doctor and I will do fine." If the night really was slow, then she'd work through the stack of paperwork that always seemed to pile up, no matter how the staff endeavored to keep it under control.

"Dr. Bernhardt and you will be fine." Meg held up a hand and walked out.

"Syver?" His name slipped out. She still wasn't used to calling him Dr. Bernhardt, no matter how much she tried to remind herself.

"You called?"

Hazel spun and couldn't stop her smile as he leaned against the nurses' station. She wiped it off quickly. Since her first day, they'd worked a few shifts together.

Professionally—professionally they worked better than ever. Syver was now a full physician and so sure of himself. And she was an ANP. In the years they'd worked together, she was still getting her footing as a nurse, and he'd left right after finishing his residency. There'd still been a hint of professional uncertainty when they worked together last time.

The uncertainty was still there, but they were used to it. One didn't practice medicine without worrying that they were making the wrong choice or second-guessing tough choices.

At least good medical professionals didn't. Once you accepted that feeling, it made you a better professional.

Life had thrown them back together, and their ability to pick up on the needs of the patient and relay them to each other with minimal words, or sometimes even a look, was back.

Personally, though. Personally things felt stilted…and heated. It was such a weird combination.

She might be able to overlook it, if there wasn't an undercurrent in her blood every time she saw him.

Desire?

She woke with thoughts of him. Fell asleep thinking of him. Things that hadn't been there before, or maybe they had? History blurred with feelings she wasn't sure were actually there.

They'd been friends. No undercurrents of need or heat or whatever…except she wasn't so sure of that now.

He leaned toward her, and her body ached to close the distance. Something she'd done years ago without even thinking.

They'd touched, friendly…light caresses. Things she'd missed so much when he was gone.

But now…now there were so many layers involved. Once, she might have thought he wanted to renew their friendship. Maybe he did. But she'd misread so many things. So, she kept her distance.

"Why aren't you at the festival?" She wasn't from Fönn, and in London they'd worked all the holidays together, but here he had family. And royal responsibilities. The royal family opened the festival. She knew that; she read up on the festival—on him. Though now that she'd blurted it out, she realized he was never mentioned as attending the opening night. The King and Queen featured prominently on the flyers, but the flyer listed the Dowager Queen, too.

The articles mentioned he always attended the closing night, but she'd assumed he was there other days too.

After all, Syver was the heir to the throne.

"Looking to get rid of me, Hazel?"

She knew the words were a joke, but there was something in his look. Sadness? Uncertainty.

Not really. Though it would be easier to be paired with anyone else tonight. But she couldn't say that.

"Of course not." She reached for his arm again but pulled back. Yep, that was too much of a reaction.

She couldn't pretend it upset her that he was here. She enjoyed working with the other physicians in the small pediatric hospital, but working with Syver was her favorite.

Still, reaching for him, touching him *and* the heat in her cheeks were too much for a work friendship.

We did it before.

"I just figured as Prince Syver you'd be at the festival. Your family opens the festival, after all. A fancy opening ceremony, from what I read."

His eyebrows shifted on the word *family*, a deep crease appearing between his eyebrows for a second before vanishing. "Technically, the King opens the festival tonight. The Queen and Dowager Queen attend too, but my presence isn't necessary." There was a heaviness to the words. An acceptance coated with…coated with something, but she wasn't sure what.

"The last night is my favorite." He was still smiling, but she could hear the heaviness.

"Syver—"

"If you're free, come."

Free to come? Did he want her to, or was it just a slip? Ugh. Just ask!

"Do you want me to come?" It was only after the question was out that she realized he said she should come if she was free, not come with me.

Syver was probably just being nice. How did someone talk about attending a festival without asking the roommate you'd lived with for two years to come along? At least how did a person do it without seeming rude? She held her breath. Waiting for the no. Or the *I'll be sure to wave, if I see you* comment.

She ran a finger over her thumb, the urge to pick at the skin pulling at her, but she was getting better. Her week in Fönn had already calmed her nerves considerably. Not having colleagues cut you out of conversations or finding yourself walking in on gossip that went silent when you rounded the corner would lift anyone's spirit.

Now the only time she was nervous was when she was alone with Syver. Those were different nerves, though. Whether she wanted to admit it, she had a little crush on her former best friend.

Except he wasn't just Syver now. Hazel was crushing on the Prince of Fönn. The heir to the throne.

He'd always been handsome, but now…now she noticed more. Thought of him more. Ached to touch him, and not in the friendly way they'd always shared. The little touches, hugs, things she'd done without thinking before.

Fantasy was all right, as long as she remembered Syver would marry one of the country's aristocratic women. That was the custom. The expectation for the heir to the throne. Something she knew because she'd kept up with him.

"I'll pick you up." Syver smiled, and the air around them popped.

Was that a good idea? Maybe not. Perhaps spending time with him outside the hospital would squash the feelings running too free in her soul.

"So what is the first night of the festival like here?" She asked, trying to force her brain away from the idea of hugging Syver and raising her head and kissing…

He cleared his throat; at least she wasn't the only one uncomfortable here.

"Well, there is a lantern ceremony. The King lights the first one, then the rest of the festivalgoers follow suit. The entire sky looks like floating stars. As a kid I stood on the platform with my mother, brother and the King and just stared into the sky."

She'd meant what was the unit like tonight. The halls of the emergency department were quiet. It was a little unsettling. She and Syver were here, along with a handful of other nurses. And two floater doctors, one from the cardiac unit and one from neurology, were on call on their floors in case Syver needed aid.

It was something she'd not experienced in London. The emergency department had had a constant stream of small patients. Even the clinic she'd worked at after Alec's recommendation was busy from the moment it was open until at least an hour after the last patient walked out. She wasn't used to having any downtime, but life on Fönn was slower.

It was easier to breathe here. Like the weight she'd worn since birth was finally gone.

Like she was home. *Home.* Hazel didn't really have that. And a flat with rented furniture did not a home make. Still, Fönn was a good landing place after the chaos of Alec's arrest.

"Why do you always call your father the King?" The question landed like lead. Syver stood, and she saw the shift in his stance. It happened anytime someone brought his father up.

She'd noticed it before, but in the quiet hallways it was suddenly on bright display.

Her hand twitched as she reached for him, then she put her hands in her pockets. They were alone, mostly, but this was still work. And there was still a barrier between them. The chasm of distance.

She could see the heaviness in his soul. His own weight—one she was sure wasn't there when they'd lived together.

Before he could dash away, a car pulled up. It slowed, and a teenager got out, then it drove off.

The teen walked in, his arm wrapped in a towel…soaked with blood.

"What happened?" Syver was moving around the call desk as Hazel followed suit.

"I fell on my way to the festival." The teen took a deep breath and slowly pulled the towel from his arm, displaying dozens of thorns. "Into my dad's prickly wild rosebush."

Unfortunately, the towel had likely pushed several of the thorns farther into the teen's skin and the grimace on his face hurt Hazel's heart. It wasn't a life-threatening emergency, but seeing a child, and teens were still children, in pain was the worst part of this job.

"Is your dad on his way in?" She'd seen a few parents drop their older kids right at the door, then find a parking spot before rushing back to their side.

"Um—" The teen looked to the door, then to his feet. "He probably went to the festival. Technically, he's my stepdad. Though I don't remember a time…" He blew out a breath and shook his head. "I'm seventeen, so I can handle this."

The grimace reappeared, but he straightened his shoulders. He was trying to maintain his control, something a child shouldn't have to do, particularly when they were in pain.

Age didn't matter when you were hurt. She'd known from her earliest days that her mother didn't want her. Yet on her darkest days, Hazel had still wished for the comfort a mother might give.

She suspected the pain of knowing his stepfather wasn't

coming back hurt as much as the dozens of tiny cuts on his arm. Hazel and Syver could patch those wounds…the others were not so easily healed.

"Of course you can." Syver nodded, but she could see the fury in his eyes. Yes, the young man could handle this, but he shouldn't have to. "Follow me."

The young man stepped beside Syver as they headed for the first room.

"I'm going to get some warm water," Hazel called. "I had a friend who fell in a rosebush. Long story, but it will help with the removal."

She dashed away and was back in a few minutes, carefully carting the water bath with Epsom salt. "It takes about ten minutes, then the removal won't hurt as much."

The teen put his arm in the water and immediately relaxed.

"Does it feel good?" Syver was pulling sterile tweezers from the room's storage supplies and materials for stitches.

"Yeah. Weird."

Hazel nodded, "It is. I lived next door to Annie when we were both around five. Her gran had a bunch of rosebushes in the center of her backyard. Beautiful. Late one night, we were playing tag and forgot where they were. Annie was tangled in the bushes for…well, it seemed like an eternity.

"After her gran got her out, she dropped her into an Epsom bath, then spent the night pulling thorns out." She looked at her watch, almost ten minutes gone. Fortunately for Annie, she'd fallen into a regular rosebush. Which, while painful, it didn't have the same number of thorns as the wild kind.

"We are lucky Hazel had such an experience, though her friend wasn't as lucky." Syver glanced at her, and she could see pain in his eyes, then it vanished.

She tried to read the issue, something they did so well in these situations, but nothing came to her. Whatever the problem, she didn't think it had to do with Carr's physical injury.

"That's ten minutes, Dr. Bernhardt. How do you want to rest his arm for the procedure?" There were thorns in Carr's hand, his elbow, everywhere. There was no position that wouldn't cause him at least a little pain.

"I wish my mum was here." Carr leaned his head back and blew out a breath.

Hazel looked to Syver. Asking to call her wasn't a great idea if she'd passed, but if she was available via phone, Hazel didn't mind asking.

"She's traveling. On a plane over the Atlantic, right now." Syver blew out a breath and looked at Carr's hand.

So that option was out. All right, she and Syver would do what they could to help the teen, but he'd always remember his stepfather's actions.

That damage could last a lifetime.

"Think you can hold up your arm long enough for me to get the thorns out of your hand, then you can rest on your hand while I work my way up the rest of your arm?"

"I can do that." Carr held up his hand. "Let's do this."

"That's the last one." Syver stitched up the last of Carr's wounds. The boy had held strong through the nearly hundred thorns he'd pulled from his skin and the thirty stitches in twenty cuts that wouldn't close on their own. His arm was a patchwork of cuts, but he'd done perfectly.

Carr's eyes were closed, his uninjured arm thrown over his eyes. The procedure had taken close to three hours. Luckily, Dr. Olsen had handled the other three cases that had wandered through the door. All minor injuries from the festival and quickly dispatched.

The teen was exhausted and sad.

Syver understood. He only knew his biological father was his mother's lover. He didn't know the man's name, only that she'd refused his offer to run away together. Probably because it would have meant leaving Erik.

The real royal. Syver was raised in the palace as a prince. King Eirvin had instructed everyone that they were to act as though Syver belonged.

He was part of the royal household, but acutely aware that

he wasn't the same as Erik. He'd never felt loved by the King, and his mother only showed him affection when King Eirvin wasn't around. No matter what he accomplished, what he achieved, it wasn't enough.

He wasn't enough.

It wasn't until he was a teen that he'd understood why he was different, and that nothing he could do would change that.

"Your mobile is ringing. Caller ID says Mum." Hazel held up the phone. "Do you want me to talk to her or are you ready?"

Carr moved slowly, exhaustion coating his expression. "Can you tell her what's happening, then pass me the phone? I just… I don't want to."

"Of course." Hazel offered a comforting smile and sat on the edge of the bed as she answered.

"Hello, this is Hazel at the Fönn Children's Hospital. Carr is fine."

Syver heard the breath Carr's mum let out. It was the perfect way to answer the phone. Put the woman at ease—it was a skill Hazel had exuded in London and one he'd seen repeatedly in the last week.

She was excellent at her job, but it was deeper than that. She was meant to be a nurse. Meant to help people, to make them feel at ease. It was a trick one could learn, but you'd never be great at it, if it wasn't natural.

Hazel went over the basics of the injury and treatment. And Syver could tell from the answers that she'd talked to her husband first. And that the woman was furious her son was alone at the emergency department.

That was good. It meant Carr had a support system at home.

Something Syver didn't have. His mother loved him. But duty to the crown came before everything else. She'd wavered once, and had Syver, but since then she was the personification of duty.

His brother treated his wife, Queen Signe, better than King Eirvin had treated his queen. But it was still a marriage of convenience. A union meant to secure the royal line.

If Syver married, theirs was the type of marriage expected of him. A marriage of convenience where the bride knew the expectation was duty, not love.

His mother had attempted to set him up with a few "appropriate" candidates. *If* a marriage was ever granted for him, it would be one like Erik and Signe's. Syver had given in to so many family expectations. Done so much for them.

But he'd refused that one. Better to remain single than fall into a union like his parents.

"Your mum wants to talk to you." Hazel handed the phone over. "Dr. Bernhardt and I are done. Do you want privacy, or would you like me to stay?"

"Stay, please." Carr picked up the phone, as Syver nodded to Hazel and stepped from the room.

He needed a few minutes to collect himself. Children hurting was the hardest part of this job. He could fix the cuts the rosebush dealt, but the injury his stepfather inflicted…

It was so close to thousands of wounds King Eirvan had laid on him. Wounds that scabbed but never fully healed.

Syver leaned against the wall, closing his eyes.

"I need to find my stepson. Now."

The voice was angry, and Syver opened his eyes.

Let me guess. Your wife called.

It was the first line that came to his mind. The first line of the dress down he wanted to give. But that wasn't professional, and his son still had to live with him. At least until his mum got home. Patient safety had to come first.

"Carr had over a hundred thorns in his hand and arm. He needed thirty stitches. Not all in the same place, instead they had to be placed in the larger cuts with two or three stitches. Your *son* did fantastic."

The man's cheeks were red, and Syver could see the motions of trying to figure out how he was supposed to respond. "If he'd been listening to me, he wouldn't have fallen in the bushes to begin with."

That might be true. It might not be. It didn't matter. Carr had needed him here, and he wasn't.

"My nurse explained to his mum what happened and the treatment."

His eyes shifted to the left, and he clenched his fists before releasing them. "The first night of the festival is huge for my business."

"Yet you left early?" Syver raised a brow. The lantern lighting wouldn't happen until two hours after sunset. Which in summer meant almost midnight.

So he'd been able to step away now.

"My wife wanted me to check on Carr." He stuffed his hands in his pockets. "I wanted to talk to him before she called, but I guess…" He blew out a breath and some of the tightness in his body language relaxed, too.

He'd wanted to save face with his wife. But what of his son?

"Is Carr safe to go home with you?" It was an important question, one Syver needed answered correctly, and in a manner he believed.

"Yes." His stepfather kicked at the floor. "I won't pretend that tonight makes me look good." He ran a hand over his face. "But he's fine with me. I just never clicked with Carr like I did with his brothers."

"Because his brothers are biologically yours?"

The man pressed his lips together. And Syver didn't need confirmation. He'd lived this life; nothing he said would make much difference. It was sad, but this was a deep-seated issue the man in front of him needed to fix, if he was capable of it.

"Carr is a good kid. And you are missing out by not knowing him and loving him." Syver stuffed his hands in his pockets. "Room Three."

He stepped into the staff lounge, walked to the fridge and grabbed a bottle of water. He drank the whole thing down; his brain iced, but it was more comfortable than the thoughts racing through his head.

"Why does it matter whose blood runs through someone's veins?"

"It doesn't." Hazel's words were soft as she stepped to his side. "DNA doesn't make a family."

He'd not meant for anyone to hear the words. But he wasn't upset Hazel was here.

She went on, "Or at least DNA shouldn't. It also shouldn't matter that you get a girl when you want a boy. That was why my biological father left. Or rather, it's the reason my mum gave."

Her hand rested on his arm. It was comfort she was offering, comfort that should flow through him. But the touch felt like fire. Need, desire, the urge to pull her into his arms raced through him.

What is wrong with me?

They were at work. Carr's relationship with his stepfather mirrored his issues with King Eirvin. He'd spent the better part of the evening pulling thorns from a kid's arm. The last thing Syver should be thinking about was how Hazel touched.

Or how much he wanted to touch her.

"You okay?" Her words were coated with concern.

"Of course." He cleared the emotions from his throat, "It just hurts when a parent doesn't see their child as they should. And it's too common." That was the truth. Part of it.

He'd never spoken to anyone about his biological father. Technically, he wasn't allowed to. To hurt the crown meant hurting Fönn. And the royal family never hurt Fönn. At least not through scandal.

His father had banned the man's name from his mother's lips…something she'd followed even after his death. It was like they thought by not addressing it, Syver would be more of a true royal.

Yet, he was still the imposter heir, never quite good enough.

"Syver—"

"I'm fine, Hazel, and I don't want to discuss it any further."

She pulled her arm away, and he wanted to yank the words back. She'd offered him comfort. Despite the uncertainty still lying between them, she was coming to his aid, and he'd snapped at her.

He was a royal. An aristocrat, born with the silver spoon in his mouth. People figured he didn't have problems. Or if he did, they were easy enough to solve for a man in his position.

And most things could be. But not this.

"Hazel…"

"It's fine, Syver." She turned but paused at the door, then looked over her shoulder. "But if you ever want to discuss why *this* upset you so much, I'm still a pretty good listener."

A lifetime of holding on to this secret, the thing he was supposed to tell no one. The reason they'd forced him from Fönn.

He'd gotten a medical degree, but the palace could banish him again if he stepped out of line. And the children of Fönn deserved an advocate. One who wouldn't leave for better opportunities.

But knowing he was always a degree away from being cast out…how did he explain the lifetime of anger, hurt and frustration that left? He knew Hazel would understand, but letting that truth out, voicing the worries, made them real.

Strolling up to Hazel's door, Syver pulled on the collar of his jumper. It was a cool evening, but heat crept up his neck.

He'd expected her to call it off so many times this week. He'd waited for it, waiting to break from it. But she hadn't.

They were going to the final night of the Summer Festival. As…friends? The descriptor felt off. This wasn't a date. Even if part of him wished it was. A tiny part, one he kept trying to ignore.

He was just glad his friend was back. The feelings rushing through him were an over-the-top reaction to seeing Hazel after so long. In a few more weeks, it would settle back down.

Is that what I want?

A lifetime of wondering what if?

Syver didn't want to travel that mental loop. Tonight was meant to be fun. A way to get back the friendship that he'd missed for so long. Tonight was simply two friends reconnecting.

Maybe this would clear the tension pulling through them.

They still worked well together, better than he did with the rest of the staff, even after years away. But they were a bit off.

Even more since his outburst following Carr's procedure. He couldn't retract the harsh words, but he could show her the festival.

The first night of the festival was the biggest, and the crowds lightened as the week progressed. Tonight was the least attended event. But the last night of Summer Nights was one of his favorite things. He'd heard people calling the dimming of the lights sad.

That watching each section of the park go dark made them wish it wasn't over for the year.

For Syver, it was like a rebirth. Standing in the festival darkness with just the few who stayed all night, it was magical. Like starting anew.

And attending it with Hazel was a dream he'd never conjured come true.

She opened the door before he could raise his hand to knock. Her curly brown hair was pulled into a high ponytail, the curls spilling over her cheeks. Her lips were light pink, and so full. He caught himself staring at them and forced himself to look into her eyes instead.

If he'd hoped meeting her gaze would ease the clench in his chest, the butterflies in his stomach or the urge to lean toward her, he'd been sadly mistaken. The green hue called to him, his own special siren song.

"Ready?" His voice sounded hoarse as he stared at the woman he'd never been able to forget.

Hazel stepped out of the flat, her body brushing his for an instant, and Syver couldn't contain the sigh.

"Yes, I'm ready."

Yes. Yes.

He mentally screamed the word on repeat. He wanted to spend the last night of the festival with Hazel. Wanted to walk with her in the quiet, dimming streets. Wanted to see how she'd react to the night so few saw as a celebration.

"It surprised Meg you were going tonight." Hazel stepped

next to him on the sidewalk. Her flat was less than a mile from the festival grounds and they'd agreed to walk. "I guess she didn't realize you always go on the last night. I joked that King Erik opens and Prince Syver closes."

Not technically.

He did always attend the closing, but he never pointed it out. "Who told you I always go to the closing?" Erik was part of the opening ceremonies. He lit the first candle. Syver attended the final night as a civilian. Or as much of a civilian as possible.

Many of the stalls closed once they'd sold out of their wares. It was quiet. Music ended an hour before the final light dimmed. It was almost meditative.

"Oh, I read it online on a…" Hazel's voice trailed off and then she let out a nervous laugh. "I…uh…" She ran a hand along her chin and then looked at him, her cheeks shading pink. Such a beautiful color. He wanted to run his finger over her cheek. He swallowed the thought.

Focus!

"Did you keep up with me on the tabloid blogs?" They focused on the royal family, and occasionally ran pieces on him. Usually when his brother fed a piece of gossip to push an uncomfortable story off him.

Syver wasn't sure what to make of the news that Hazel had kept track of him—sort of. In his mind, he'd figured she'd left their flat in London and rarely thought of him. If she'd followed him, what did that mean?

Syver wrapped an arm around her shoulder and leaned his head against hers. It was an automatic reaction. One he'd done hundreds of times when they'd lived together.

But his body had never jolted, his nerves never fired, reminding him exactly which parts of his body connected with her. Maybe he should pull away, but that was the last thing he wanted, and Hazel sighed, a contented noise that raced right to his heart.

When he lifted his head, she rested hers against his shoulder as they kept moving. That cemented his choice. He'd hold her until she pulled back.

"Maybe." Another uncomfortable laugh followed. "I hated losing touch, and you weren't hard to find."

"If you hated losing touch, why did you block my mobile number?" The words were out before he could think them through. He'd tried…not fast enough, he admitted that, but listening to the dead air when he called, watching the text say undeliverable had broken his heart.

He didn't want to make her feel bad. He was the one who left; she got to react however she needed.

Hazel sighed as she stepped out of his arms. "I didn't."

"Hazel, I tried calling. I texted, I flew back to London, and you'd abandoned our flat. It hurt, but I also know leaving the way I did…"

"You came back?" Hazel stopped. Her mouth falling open as she shook her head. "For me?"

"For you." He pulled her to him then. Not the subtle around-the-shoulder hug they'd had. A full body, holding her as close to him as possible, hug.

His heart nearly exploding when she wrapped her arms around his waist. A piece of him snapped into place. The world felt like it tilted back to where it was supposed to be. Hazel with him. It just made sense—it always had.

When she stepped back, she took his hand, squeezing it. "You really came back for me?" She pursed her lips after repeating her words.

"I did. About a month after. Everything was so crazy when King Eirvin died, and then Erik ascended and the coronation. It was…a lot. And that is an understatement."

"It was." She let out a sigh. "No one believed me when I said I didn't know."

"Oh…" He'd not considered that. He should have. After all, everyone had known they were close. A few of his colleagues even assumed they were dating. He wasn't supposed to mention his title, hadn't figured anyone would ever say it in his presence again. But he still should have told her.

"What happened?" His chest was tight as he waited for her

answer. He'd left her, focused on his family's wants. On their needs. Happy to be included, finally.

The reality that he wasn't really wanted had taken weeks to set in.

"Press. Questions I couldn't or wouldn't answer. I even had a few agents reach out with suggestions for a tell-all book. One had already named it—*My Years with the Prince*."

Hazel laughed, the alto tones radiating through the night. "That was a tad much, as I told them."

"You could have made a lot of money on that story."

"Maybe." Hazel swung his hand and pulled him toward the festival, but she didn't let go. "But there wasn't a price I could put on our friendship. As far as blocking you, I had to get a new phone because someone gave my number to a tabloid. So…that's it."

"That's it." Syver pulled them to a stop again. He'd wasted so much time, and he wasn't wasting any more.

"At this rate, we'll miss the festival." Hazel smiled as she squeezed his hand. "Your favorite night only comes once a year."

"I don't care." And he meant it. Nothing mattered in this moment more than making sure she knew how deeply her words, her continued friendship, even when he hadn't known it, touched him. "Hazel…"

"Why did you come back?"

The question floored him. How could she not know? "Like I said, for you." He swallowed as the enormity of those words settled around them.

"For me?" Her face shifted in the late evening sun. This time of year, the sun didn't set until well after ten, and he was so glad he could see her features clearly.

She was stunned…shocked, and the revelation broke his heart. "Of course. I had this grand plan that you'd come to Fönn. That I'd convince you to leave London behind and join me at the pediatric hospital. We had a mass emigration issue under King Eirvin. Our medical professionals…well, we're still rebuilding."

It was his primary focus—but it wasn't the reason he'd come for her.

He shook his head. "No. That's not right?" He didn't want any misunderstanding.

"No, you didn't come for me to help Fönn?" He heard the tint of concern in her voice.

Syver would not let that stand. "I came because I wanted you with me." He'd thought he'd wanted his friend here. That was part of it, but he'd had other friends, other colleagues, who'd have helped Fönn. He'd not reached out to a single one.

It was Hazel he needed. And he was starting to suspect the feelings he'd associated with friendship were so much deeper even then.

"Oh." Her mouth formed a delicate O as she stared at him. "I'd have come."

The world disappeared as she held his gaze. For so long, he'd assumed she'd been angry. Rightfully so. Assumed she'd run and blocked him. And he'd lost years.

Years…

"Hazel." He lifted his free hand, let his thumb run along her chin. The cord he felt linking them clanged as her breath hitched. Whatever this was, was like nothing he'd felt before. "Hazel."

"You already said my name." She laughed and leaned her cheek against his hand.

"Prince Syver!" The call broke the spell between them.

She pulled back, but he squeezed the hand she still held. If she wanted him to let go, he would, but his heart soared when she squeezed back.

"Are you heading to the festival?" The young lad called as his mother tried to push him along, her eyes clearly understanding that he'd interrupted an important moment.

"Sorry!" She held up her hand, pushing her son, who couldn't be over seven.

"Why are you sorry, Mama?" He waved at Prince Syver. "We're going to the festival, but not for very long because I have to go to bed."

Hazel covered her mouth, but it didn't hide the sound of her giggle. "Yes, we are heading for the festival." Her words were bright, and she pulled at his hand, so they started walking toward the festival, too.

"We'll see you there," Syver called, grinning as the little boy skipped beside his mother.

The interaction was cute and would make anyone smile. But it was the woman still holding his hand that made his body sing.

CHAPTER FOUR

THE LAST LIGHTS of the festival dimmed, and night seemed to sigh in inky darkness. Meg had attended each night of the festival last year, and said she found something sad about the last night. The lights going out across the field, the closed shops. She'd lamented that there was nothing to signify the end besides the lights.

No closing ceremony. No celebration. Just darkness.

Hazel hadn't known what to expect. It wasn't a traditional festival environment. But she saw nothing sad about the dimming lights. It was an acknowledgment that this cycle of time was over and another was on the horizon.

Her eyes found the man beside her. Another shift. One she wanted.

He'd come for her five years ago. He'd wanted her here. With him.

The piece of her heart that had broken when she'd stood alone in their flat healed tonight.

She couldn't have stayed at the flat. People got past the doorman for three weeks straight. He'd always feign surprise or anger, but she knew the reporters were sliding him a few hundred dollars for access.

Hazel did not rate the same level of security as the wealthy residents and a prince. The once friendly looks of her neighbors had turned into nosey questions, followed by icy glares when they realized she wouldn't offer any gossip.

Leaving was the right answer, but she could have left a note.

Something to let him know where she was. Maybe she would have, but she'd figured he'd ghosted her like so many others.

A miscommunication that they'd both been too hurt to reach out after. Humans really could make a muck of things.

Tonight, under the setting lights, the last of the heaviness between them lightened. Now there was no way to ignore the tension, the desire and the need left unbridled in its absence.

He'd nearly kissed her. That was where the moment was headed when the child interrupted them.

It would be easy to pretend she didn't know where this evening was heading. Once upon a time Hazel would have. But she wasn't conflicted. Hazel knew what she wanted.

His touch. The feel of his lips on hers. Syver.

Prince.

The title hung in her mind. Hazel had accomplished much in her life. On her own. But there was no hidden aristocratic link in her bloodline. She'd be seen as lesser—always.

Yet, she didn't want to walk away. After five years without him, she couldn't do that.

"Do you ever tire of being a prince?" She hadn't meant to ask the question. She'd wanted to walk with him, spend the rest of the night with him. Kiss him.

But that title. The one that had hung over them since the day he disappeared. It raised questions. Ones that needed answering.

"Yes. It's something I had no control over, something that still creates." He paused, wrapping an arm around her waist.

"Creates?"

"Tension." His lips brushed the top of her head. But it was a passing caress, one that didn't quite feel like a kiss. "But tonight, I'm just Syver."

Just Syver.

That was nice. Even if she wasn't sure it was possible. However, it was nice to pretend that they'd stepped back in time. That here and now it was just Hazel and Syver.

"So, just Syver, what now?" It was an open-ended question.

He could answer for tonight, could answer for the almost kiss they'd nearly shared, for the friction building between them.

Or in a flippant way, one they could laugh off tomorrow.

"Well, we have a few options." He leaned his head against hers and the feeling she'd had all those years ago of safety and security rammed back into place.

Were we just too busy to realize our bond was more? Or naive? Or scared of ruining the brilliant friendship?

Perhaps it was a combination of all three. And time and distance had stolen their ability to ignore it.

"We can stay here for a while. The park is open until one, and neither of us has work tomorrow. We can walk through the gardens. At night, the rich floral scents reach toward the stars."

That sounded lovely, but her soul craved more.

He moved his head against hers and for a moment she thought he'd kiss the top of it. When that didn't happen, she feared he meant to let her go. Instinctively, she tightened her grip on his waist, then relaxed. If he let her go, he let her go.

She could handle it. She'd put the need away, even if she didn't want to.

Lifting her hand from his waist, he spun her into his arms. Her eyes were adjusting to the darkness. The last bits of space between them closing as her body shifted against him.

Her heartbeat echoed in her ears as she lifted her chin.

Kiss me.

The words were on the tip of her tongue, but she couldn't quite force them out. Instead, she heard a single word slip out, "Or?"

"Or..." he bent his head, his breath warm against her ear as he whispered "...I kiss you."

"Kiss me." She wrapped her arms around his neck, pulling him to her. This might be a mistake, but she didn't care. She needed him.

Her lips met his in the darkness. The scent of summer flowers wrapping around them. If Hazel thought this moment would dampen the desire she'd felt building since she'd first seen him, the reality was so much hotter.

She arched against him, oblivious to everything but her body's desperate urge. Her soul cried out, ages of longing seeming to rush forth.

His lips were soft, but his hands on her back were firm. Holding her in place, cradling her as he tasted her. A small slice of heaven she never wanted to leave.

"Hazel." Her name, whispered in Syver's deep tone, sent tingles floating from the tip of her head to the tips of her toes. If one could see happiness vibrate, she'd light up the entire festival site.

"Syver." She leaned her head against his shoulder. Everything shifted tonight. If she was honest, things had nearly shifted in their friendship before. A look here, a touch that lasted a hair too long. But they'd never crossed the invisible barrier. Never even acknowledged its presence.

Because there was no turning back now.

Once you kissed your best friend, the friendship you'd had, no matter how good, how strong, evaporated. In its place was something new.

Now they needed to figure out what that was. Or they could let it slide away into the night's oblivion.

She waited a minute, but when he said nothing, the nerves that lit when his lips met hers turned on her mind. Why wasn't he talking or kissing her…or something?

"We don't have to talk about it, if you don't want to." She hated those words. But if this was just a onetime thing, an impulsive action to break the fission between them…

"And if I want to talk about it?" Syver dropped a light kiss on her forehead, then another on her cheek. "If I want to talk about it very badly?"

She giggled, then felt ridiculous. She was not a teen or some girl lovesick for the first time. "Here or at your place— or mine?"

"Yours might be easier."

"Of course." She pursed her lips, hoping the darkness covered the wave of uncomfortableness beating against her mind. She wasn't exactly sure where Syver lived. That was something none of the blogs she'd followed ever mentioned—for good reasons.

Whether it was the palace grounds or someplace else, it certainly wasn't a one-bedroom furnished apartment. A place that would highlight how much social distance there was between them.

She'd made the place as homey as possible, but it still looked temporary. Certainly not like a place where'd you'd find royalty.

"What are you thinking? I can practically hear the mental jumps echoing in the night."

"How?" Issuing the challenge was easier than admitting she was worried her flat was lackluster.

Although I loved it when I got here.

It was twice the size of her London rental, and didn't come with a grumpy old landlord who lived upstairs and monitored her comings and goings. Not that there'd been much to monitor.

Syver pulled her hand from around his neck and ran a finger gently over her thumb, just below where the nail bed met the nail. "You were rubbing this. I suspect you wanted to pick it."

It honestly hadn't crossed her mind, but the habit was so ingrained she often only noticed the issue after she started bleeding.

"Having lived with me for two years gives you an unfair advantage." Her bottom lip popped up, and she reeled it back in. She was *not* pouting in this moment.

"It does." Syver chuckled. "And I enjoy the advantage. Hazel, there is no pressure here."

"I know. But it's silly."

"All the more reason to tell me." His lips pressed against her neck. If he was trying to distract her, it was working.

"My flat isn't exactly a palace, and it's not exactly fit for royalty."

She pushed against his chest, enjoying the playful grunt that echoed before he wrapped his arm around her waist.

"Hazel…" He squeezed her side. "I'm just Syver.

Except you aren't.

Rather than voice that truth, she laid her head against his. "Well, then let's head for my place, just Syver."

Rationally, he knew he wasn't just Syver. He was the heir to the throne of Fönn. The full son of King Eirvin, beloved son and brother...at least as far as the public was concerned.

Though if everything continued well with Queen Signe's pregnancy, he wouldn't be the heir for much longer. He didn't mind that loss. But when Erik had his heir, would Syver have any place in the family? When the illusion wasn't needed, would he become even more of an outsider?

Was that even possible?

The constant worries were easier to set aside with Hazel in his arms. With her he could almost forget the royal family's baggage. He was simply a man infatuated with the woman beside him. His best friend.

He'd spent five years missing a part of himself. Had he realized it was Hazel he needed?

No.

Maybe he should have. Those two years with her were the best of his life. At least until they'd kissed tonight.

Even if he had realized it, he wouldn't have searched her out. That knowledge sucked. He'd thought she was gone when he found their flat empty.

Their flat.

That was how he'd always thought of it. The week after Hazel moved in, it was theirs. And he'd left with a brief note. Left her unprotected.

And rather than monetize her fifteen minutes of fame, she'd changed her number and moved out of their flat. To protect him.

He wasn't sure what would happen next now that they'd kissed, but no matter what it was, he was protecting Hazel.

Always.

"Home sweet home," Hazel sighed as she pulled her keys from the small bag she'd carried tonight.

He could hear the tension in her tone, and her shoulders were tight. Over a flat?

Maybe he should have taken her back to the palace. But the head of security was a terror. Now that the Queen was almost through her second trimester, he'd tightened policies further.

Erik and Signe have suffered three miscarriages. Few knew of their upcoming bundle of joy. And the country wouldn't know until she was past twenty-four weeks.

That meant Arne, the head of security, wasn't letting anyone pass, even Syver's guests, without at least a minimal check.

Arne was dismissive of Syver, like most of the staff. Everyone knew Erik didn't give Syver much responsibility, so he was overlooked. The man wouldn't go out of his way for Syver.

It was selfish, but he didn't want any delay. He wanted to talk to Hazel. Wanted to kiss her again. Spend time with her.

"Darling," he kissed the back of her neck, "if you want to go to the palace…"

"No." She opened the door and pulled him into her home.

He was not prepared for the rush of emotions as he stepped into Hazel's flat. There were house plants tucked into the small bookcase. And a vining plant hanging over a shelf on the opposite wall, a soft-looking blue blanket on the back of the couch and a romance novel on the small table by it.

It was like stepping back in time. Coming home.

"I see you found the garden center." He'd joked that their flat in London was half greenhouse. And he'd loved watching her care for plants. He'd even gotten her one of the vine-type ones…though he couldn't remember the type now.

She looked at the plants, then shook her head. "No. You'll have to show me where it is!"

The squeal was music to his heart. The woman loved plants, and he'd enjoyed seeing her baby them.

"These are the ones that were hardy enough to make the journey and fine with customs. I packed their box carefully, then told them what to expect. I've babied them this week. They are bouncing back from the stress." She was smiling, but her face was quite serious.

Her plants were her babies. She could chat about any green thing. Plant talk with Hazel, he'd called it.

Another thing I missed without knowing it.

"You brought the plants?"

"Only a few. I gave the rest to the staff I knew liked plants. But berry arrowheads and pothos are hardy. Remember, the employee told you there was nothing you could do to kill this one?" She moved toward the trailing vine plant on the wall as his heart exploded.

"You kept the plant I got you?" Kept it, nurtured it and brought it to Fönn. There wasn't a good definition for the emotions seeing the plant sent through his chest. A plant... his gift to her.

"It lost a few vines on the way, but a little trim and he was good as new." Hazel shrugged. "I'd never be able to part with it."

"Hazel..." There were so many things to say. But the emotions tumbling through him caught all the words. He'd gotten the plant as a baby green. The garden center employee had sworn that if she didn't like it, it was easy to care for. That if she went on holiday, he'd be able to manage it.

And now it was here. In Fönn. A piece of their past to start their future.

"I couldn't leave it, Syver." She swallowed and shrugged. "I know it's only a plant, but you got it for me."

"I missed you, Hazel. Every single day." There were many things to say, but he needed her to know this most.

Her lips brushed his, the touch brief, but it ignited a flame in his body.

"Do you think we missed signs of..." Hazel pursed her lips, then leaned her head against his shoulder.

"Of this?" He kissed the top of her head, loving the feel of her in his arms again. They'd sworn they were just friends to everyone. Sworn they were roommates, nothing more.

Maybe they'd even believed it.

But he had dated no one while they lived together...and neither had she. They had reserved their free time for movies, garden center dates, walks in the park and her helping him study for exams.

"Yes." They weren't looking for it, and maybe it wasn't the right time then. But they'd certainly missed the signals.

Or willfully ignored them.

She looked up, and he kissed her cheek, then moved his lips to her jaw until he caught her lips.

Hazel. His world had been busy, but it wasn't until she'd walked back into his life last week that he'd realized how empty it was.

She tasted of honey cakes, pleasure and home. His fingers cradled her neck as he explored her mouth. If there was a more perfect moment, he didn't want to find it.

Pulling back, Hazel looked over her shoulder. "It's nearly one."

They'd said they were going back to her place, but he wasn't sure either of them had realized just how late it was. Wrapped up in each other it was easy to miss.

"Should I go?" There were things to say, conversations to have, but it was late. And he wanted time with her.

"You could stay. We can watch a movie, just be together. I've missed just being together." She bit her lip, "I'm not ready for…for…"

Her cheeks blazed and then she nodded, seemingly to herself. "I'm not ready to go to bed with you, but I also am not ready to end tonight. But if you want to leave—"

"A movie sounds perfect." Syver sighed as the rightness of this moment settled with him. A movie with Hazel. "Where's the television?"

"Oh." She looked around and then ran a hand over her thumb before pointing to the door that had to be her bedroom. "Is that a problem?"

"Nope." Did he want her? *Yes.* Crave her touch? *Absolutely.* But she'd left her home a week ago, gone through so many changes all at once. He'd wait however long it took for her to be ready.

CHAPTER FIVE

HAZEL STIRRED THE cinnamon batter and made sure the griddle was warming. Crepes on her day off was a tradition she'd started when she'd lived with Charlotte. Her roommate, who'd met the love of her life on holiday and married on a whim, then needed Hazel to find new lodgings.

Their love story, which now included the cutest set of twins, was the reason she was fixing cinnamon crepes with an apple butter filling for Syver this morning.

Hazel ran her fingers over her lips. Part of her couldn't believe she'd kissed him last night, and woken fully clothed in his arms this morning.

How had they waited so long to kiss?

She'd fallen asleep before the movie they'd selected finished. Then woken to Syver holding her. He'd taken his jumper off, but stayed by her side all night.

That was not something Alec would have done. Particularly after she'd indicated she had no plans to sleep with him.

She wanted to. Wanted to kiss her way down Syver's body. Wanted to hold him tight and do things her mind had conjured quite freely in her dreams.

But for all the friendship and heat between them, they were still strangers in some ways. There were things to say. Things she hadn't wanted to broach so late and when they were both drunk on the emotional high of first kisses.

This morning, with crepes and coffee, it was time.

"That smells delicious. Cinnamon crepes. I haven't had those since I left London."

"Syver!" He'd been sleeping so soundly, she thought she had a few more minutes to get her thoughts together. She turned and some of the batter dropped off the spoon. "Shoot!" Setting the bowl aside, she reached for a towel, but Syver's hand caught hers.

"Hazel." His hand was warm in hers, but the batter was spreading and her cheeks were hot. Nothing like not getting all your mental insecurities set aside before coffee.

He ignored the batter.

"The floor will be sticky."

"I'll clean it." He slipped a hand under her chin, his blue eyes holding hers. "But are you all right? It's not like you to be so jumpy."

"Nervous. There are," she gestured between them, "things to say."

"There are. But I'm so glad I'm here." He grinned then dropped his mouth to hers. Her heartbeat echoed in her ears as her body flushed with need and excitement. This was what her soul craved.

She pulled back, mostly because the smell of the first burned crepe circled them. "Always burn the first one, right?" She moved to grab the pastry off the griddle and turned to find Syver scooping up the dropped batter in the towel.

He stepped to the sink, dropped the towel in, then wet another and cleaned the mess.

Mist covered her eyes. It was such a simple task. It shouldn't make her heart race or her eyes water. But Alec never did anything for her.

And her mother...

Hazel got things done. Because no one was coming to her rescue.

And now there was a literal prince cleaning up the floor in her rented flat.

"Hey," Syver slid his arm around her waist. His fingers brushed across her back as he laid his head against hers. "What's wrong?"

"Nothing." She felt the uncomfortable laugh before she

heard it. Nothing was wrong. "I just can't believe a prince cleaned my floor."

"Just Syver here."

This was the other thing they needed to discuss. Because whether he wanted to admit it made him different or not, Syver was the heir to the throne. Her throat tightened, but she needed to make sure she understood the requirements, the expectations, the rules that came with dating him.

Because Hazel didn't want to mess this up.

"I promise that when you are here or we're alone, you will be just Syver. But you are the heir to the throne. You are Prince Syver and I'm just Hazel."

"There's nothing *just* about you, Hazel." She saw an emotion dance across his eyes that she worried for a moment was anger. It was fleeting, and she didn't think it was directed at her, but she leaned back.

A force of habit from watching Alec and adjusting to his moods for so long.

"What was that?" Syver tilted his head.

"What?"

"You moved away from me. I was frustrated because..." He threw his hands up, took a breath then nodded, like he was mentally arguing with himself. "I came home because my family wanted me to. But my relationship with them...is still strained."

"I'm sorry." She hated that for him. Family was supposed to be your safe place, but for so many it wasn't.

"Family is a frustration point for me, but that has nothing to do with you. So again...why did you lean back?"

She could see the questions in his eyes. Hazel turned, focusing on the crepe, trying to ignore the mist coating her eyes.

"Why did you come to Fönn?"

"Honestly?"

He slipped beside her and leaned against the counter. "I think honesty is best."

"Fönn was the first offer I got. And I needed to leave. I was in a relationship...it wasn't good." That was such an understatement. "He wasn't physically abusive, but I got good at reading the signs that would set him off. And I can read you so well because we lived together." She chuckled, trying to lighten the mood. Alec was her past. But the hints of it were still with her, whether she wanted them to be or not.

"Hazel." He closed his eyes then put his arm around her waist. When he opened his eyes, he sighed, "I hate that you went through that."

"Me, too." She wouldn't offer the statement that it had made her stronger. In some ways maybe it had. But the truth was that it was a period of her life she didn't like looking at. If she could undo it, she would.

She dropped the crepes onto plates. "How about we move to the table? So coming home wasn't what you expected?"

"No." Syver cut into the crepe. "I love my family. I work hard for the royal family, but it never feels like enough. Which is why I like being just Syver." He winked.

Hazel wanted him to be just Syver, but that wasn't the life he'd been born into. And they couldn't simply ignore it.

"We can be just Syver and Hazel here, or even at work, but you are a prince...and with us..." She picked up the mug of coffee she'd poured early wishing there was more heat coming through ceramic. A way to push away the fear. "I'm about as far from aristocratic as possible. *When* we tell people, they will have opinions." She'd experienced that, seen the looks, heard the questions. The media this time would be more direct.

It changed things.

"When? You want to hide me?" Syver pushed his chair back. His tone was light, like he was trying to make a joke, but it felt flat.

That tore through her. She wanted to scream from the top of Fönn's mountains that she was dating Syver. But what if this was a temporary thing? A fling that burned out.

It didn't feel like that...but she'd misread signs before. If this burned brightly only for days...well, it would break her heart and she didn't want others to see that.

Not again.

"What if this is just a fling?" That had come out wrong. Her brain refused to behave this morning. The last thing she wanted was to cheapen what she suspected was between them.

"It's not." Syver's tone was soft, but authoritative.

There's the Prince.

The person so certain of their position in life that they could make declarations.

A foreign idea to Hazel. Her position had never been certain, even when she thought it was. Dating a prince, falling for one. It changed everything.

"What is your worry, sweetheart? Tell me. I can handle it."

The urge to rub her thumb pulled at her. She didn't want to hurt him, but she'd lost so much before. She took a deep breath and leaped. "There were so many questions when you left. They'll be questions again."

"Ones we get to answer together."

Together.

She wouldn't stand alone this time. He'd be by her side.

That didn't mean the questions wouldn't be direct or things they didn't want to answer. "Is it too much to ask for a few weeks of quiet before the show gets underway?"

"No, it isn't. We can wait until you're ready for anything." Syver made sure she was looking at him. "Provided you understand, I'm not hiding you. The second you want the King to know or Meg, or the universe, you tell me. And I will shout it to the heavens."

She opened her mouth, but no words came out. How did you respond to that? No one had ever wanted to shout to the next block, let alone to the universe, that they were with her. Syver's certainty, his unwavering tone, shot electricity through her.

"I missed having breakfast with you." She reached for his hand across the table.

"I missed everything about you."

"Your clothes are here." Hazel smiled as she held up the bag the palace aid had dropped off.

"Thanks," he kissed her cheek, "I'm going to hop in the shower. Pop some popcorn for the next movie. Your choice."

She smiled as he headed down the hallway. They'd spent the day laughing, catching up, talking and bingeing the movies they'd missed together. It was silly and the perfect way to spend a day.

She hummed as she started the popcorn maker.

"Is there anything that smells as good as popcorn?" Syver asked.

Hazel turned, "That was a fast shower." The words were barely out of her mouth before it started watering as she stared at the gorgeous man at the entrance to her kitchen.

After his shower, a little water dripped from his head and the tight white undershirt he wore hugged all the right places. He stepped to her, dropped a kiss on her cheek, but it wasn't enough. Popcorn and movies were distant memories as Hazel wrapped her arms around him and claimed his mouth. Syver's tongue met hers and the electricity his body ignited exploded. Her hips rubbed against his as she molded to him.

"Syver?"

His lips trailed along her chin as his fingers rubbed her lower back. "Yes?"

"You want to watch another movie?" She looked at the popcorn. If he wanted more time, that was fine, but she wanted him. All of him, now.

"I want what you want." His mouth met hers and their tongues danced, meeting each other's rhythms as though they'd done this thousands of times. "If that's a movie, fine…if not."

His fingers slipped under her shirt and ran along her belly.

"You have a way with words, Syver."

"Wait until you see what else I can do with my mouth."

Syver picked her up, and Hazel let out a small gasp. This felt a little fairytale-ish. And she loved it!

Hazel felt perfect in his arms as Syver headed back toward her bed. He wanted to shout to the world that this woman was his.

Syver wasn't sure how his mother and brother would take it. But that was a problem for another day.

"Syver," Hazel breathed his name, and his heart nearly melted.

"You are so beautiful." He nipped her ear before laying her on the bed. "So incredibly beautiful."

Her cheeks darkened, and he ached to know if the rest of her body turned to rose when she received a compliment.

After lifting her shirt to just below her breasts, he pressed his lips to her belly, loving the small hitch she gave when he lowered his attention to just below her waist. The urge to strip her quickly warred deep inside.

But Syver refused to rush this moment with Hazel. He planned to worship her body with his mouth, with his tongue, with his hands. With his whole being.

Her hands skimmed across his head, catching bits of his hair as she moaned his name. His manhood was already aching for release. "Hazel," he sighed her name as he finished lifting her shirt over her head, then watched, mesmerized as she unhooked her bra. "You're so beautiful."

"You already said that." She bit her lip, and he watched the skin on her chest shift to a rose hue as she reached for him.

"It bears repeating." He raised his hand, running a finger along her breasts, circling one nipple, watching it tighten on his touch.

After dipping his head, he let his mouth follow the same path. Suckling her, enjoying the feel of her in his mouth as his fingers slipped her comfy pants down.

She wore no undergarments beneath them.

Dear God, his body was quaking with a yearning he'd never felt so acutely.

His hand ran over her bare bottom and even if he'd wanted to, he couldn't stop his exhale. "I imagined stripping your knickers down all day, but this. This is so much better, Hazel."

"I never wear them with my cotton pants." She let out a small giggle as her hand reached under his shirt. Each touch lighting a flame on his skin.

"That is information I will file away for future reference." He lifted his arms, letting Hazel remove his shirt.

Before her, he'd have never said that stripping clothing off piece by piece was foreplay. Sure, it was exciting, but the ache he got watching a naked Hazel lift his shirt, unbutton his pants and slip them over his hips was something he'd never experienced.

Her soft hands ran along his length and his groan echoed in the room. His body shuddered; he wanted to bury himself in her, hold her as he drove into her. But he was determined she'd remember their first time as more than his frantic need for her.

Lifting her hand, he then kissed the fingers that had stroked him. "I want you, Hazel, desperately."

"The feeling is very mutual, Syver."

She was a siren, with curly hair, hazel eyes and a voice that drove him to the edge. But he was not too far gone yet. "Lay back."

Hazel raised an eyebrow, and for a moment he thought she'd balk at the request. Instead, she leaned herself against her pillows.

He followed her, captured her mouth, enjoying the taste of her against his tongue before he slid his way down her body.

Arousal chased him as he drank her in. After lowering his mouth to her mound, he flicked his tongue against her pleasure bud, loving the sound of his name floating in the room. Her hips arched, offering herself fully to him.

Yes.

Syver gripped her backside, keeping her in the perfect place for his mouth to worship her. Her hands wrapped through his hair, and he heard her breath accelerate.

He wanted, needed, to push her over oblivion's edge. Hazel, his Hazel.

"Syver!" Her pant was music to his ears as her body softened following her orgasm.

He kissed the inside of each of her thighs as he kissed his way back up her body.

She shifted and pulled open the top drawer of her bedside

table. He followed her hand, before grabbing the condom and then ripping it open as quickly as possible. Syver needed her now.

He sheathed himself, then joined their bodies.

"Syver!" Hazel wrapped her legs around him. Her body matching each of his strokes.

Time slowed, then stopped, as they gave in to their desires. He dropped kisses on her cheek, then her jaw before joining their lips.

Her fingers traced down his back as she met each of his thrusts. They claimed each other. It was magical and so normal. Her body tightened again, and he kissed her as he finally gave in to his own climax.

He was right where he was supposed to be. It was a feeling he only truly got with Hazel.

CHAPTER SIX

HAZEL LOOKED AT SYVER, then forced her gaze back to the tablet chart in front of her. It was a slow day. Which normally she'd be grateful for. After all, one didn't really want the children's emergency department overrun with chaos.

But with a little activity, she might be able to keep her eyes from wandering to him. They'd spent the last few days cocooned in her apartment. Reminiscing, exploring each other's body and relaxing.

He'd even had groceries delivered so they didn't have to leave. There were more than a few perks to wearing the crown.

She wasn't prepared to tell anyone that she was dating the Prince just yet. Wasn't ready to explain or face the questions she knew were coming. The pictures, the looks.

She'd had most of them thrown at her when he'd left. She could answer them this time. Say aloud that she was dating Syver. That the man she was with made song lyrics make sense. He made her chest heavy with joy instead of worry, made her feel like herself. All better than great things!

Maybe it was selfish, but she wanted some time to revel in those feelings without the world dissecting it.

And she wanted to be sure. Maybe that wasn't fair, but after Alec…she just needed more than one blissful weekend.

"So did you have a good weekend?" Meg stepped beside Hazel, her eyes looking toward the office doctors used during slow moments. The door where Syver had disappeared only a few minutes before.

There was a hint of curiosity in her tone. The American

nurse was friendly, bubbly…heck, she could step onto a set and play the role of friendly nurse without having to try at all. She was also incredibly observant.

Luckily, it was also easy to distract her.

"Tell me about your engagement party." The event wasn't for another few months, but Meg was already planning…with folders and binders outlining everything.

Hazel wanted a wedding, one day. But Meg's level of planning was epic. If this was the organization for the engagement party, Hazel wasn't sure what it'd look like when it was time to plan the actual nuptials.

"Oh! I found the perfect bakery to make the cupcakes. They can do the design Lev wants. A historical re-creation of Fönn's pastries. Historians."

Hazel laughed. Lev was a university historian specializing in Fönn's history. Meg said she'd learned a lot from him, but it wasn't the cake's decor that mattered, not really.

"I'm sure they'll be beautiful. But what will they taste like?"

Meg clapped and closed her eyes like she was remembering the flavors. "Lemon raspberry cake with the lightest frosting. I ate three of them, and my fiancé, I love saying that…" She practically swooned as she repeated the word. "My *fiancé!*"

"It is a fun word." Her mother had gotten engaged three times. It had never worked out.

That hadn't stopped Hazel from dreaming of her own. Imagining the man who'd stand by the altar and choose her.

"Anyway, my fiancé ate four. Luckily, they were tiny tasting ones, but there was no doubt which we'd choose." She grinned and launched into a list of items she'd checked off her ever-growing to-do list over the last few days.

Hazel smiled and nodded at the right times, keeping her eyes focused away from the door where Syver was working.

"So, now that I have explained everything about my party," Meg hit Hazel's hip with hers, "you can tell me all about your days off." She winked and laughed. "Why won't you talk about your weekend? I can keep a secret."

"I spent the weekend cocooned in my apartment. It was

lovely, but not nearly as exciting as engagement planning." They'd never left, though lying in Syver's arms was more exciting than party planning in Hazel's opinion.

Syver stepped out of the office, and Hazel's eyes lifted automatically before dropping back to Meg.

Meg sighed and looked at the patient area where Syver had disappeared. She met Hazel's gaze, took a breath, then looked over her shoulder again and sighed.

"Something to say?" Hazel probably shouldn't issue the challenge, but it was clear Meg wanted to say something.

"He's different since you arrived." She smiled. "Well, honestly, he's been different since your résumé landed."

Hazel was proud that she didn't make a face. She'd proven herself over the last week. Even if Syver hadn't put in a good word for her, she was the best choice for this position.

But it was the first part of the statement that perked her curiosity. "How is Dr. Bernhardt different?"

Maybe she shouldn't ask, but…well, curiosity was a natural human trait.

"He's happy."

Hazel couldn't stop the spread of her smile. Happy. Five little letters in one word that made her heart sing.

"He wasn't unhappy before, but he was apart. Almost going through the motions. Like he was missing something. And I think he was missing…you."

Hazel's mouth opened, but she couldn't force any words out.

"What are you two discussing?" Syver's words broke the spell holding Hazel.

She'd spent all morning tracking his movements, but Meg's words had transfixed her.

"Engagement planning!" Meg offered. "I found the perfect cake. Now I need to find the best flowers."

"Good luck." Syver smiled, but a bit of the light dimmed behind his eyes.

"What do you think?" Meg leaned on the desk, her face bright. "After all, you're from Fönn. The party is in autumn, any recommendations?"

Syver looked at the chart he was carrying, "I've no idea what might be right for an engagement party or wedding, Meg. Even if I planned to wed, the palace would make all the choices."

Her breath caught, and she saw Meg's head swivel to her. Syver didn't look up, though.

Even if I planned to wed.

Those words shocked her, but it was the other part that hammered home who she was dating. No choices? A royal wedding was a big deal, but it was still the bride and groom's day.

"You aren't ever planning on marrying?" Meg looked at her again, but Hazel didn't react.

Family doesn't have to mean marriage and a baby carriage. She knew that. Believed it. But marriage was a union between two people. Two, not a royal court. If he wasn't free to make choices on his wedding day, what else was he not free to do?

This was not the place for that discussion. But the lines etched into the corners of his eyes worried her.

"Astrid, in Room Three, needs transferred to a room upstairs. The virus has dehydrated her and exhausted her system. A bag of fluids and observation for at least twenty-four hours are necessary. Her parents have done a great job monitoring her fluid intake, but she can't keep anything down. In a few days, the toddler will keep them on their toes again, but for now she needs admitted."

"I'll start the transfer." Meg pushed a button on her tablet and the orders started printing on the desk. She grabbed them and wandered off.

"So, what kind of cake is she getting?" Syver leaned forward, coffee, cinnamon and mint mixing in her nose as he grinned. Many people found it weird that medical professionals could shift so fast, but one had to learn to compartmentalize in this line of work, or you went mad.

"Lemon raspberry." She wanted to know about his previous statement. About his lack of control in his own life. And why he'd said it so confidently…in her presence.

That hurt more than she wanted to admit. What if the palace didn't approve of her? Would the King and Queen step in? And if they did, would Syver listen?

What were the signs she needed to watch for? Would she recognize them?

"Hazel—" His eyes softened, and he leaned as close as was professionally acceptable.

Before he could say anything else, a shout echoed in the bay. Hazel hated the sweep of relief passing through her. They'd spent a weekend together, agreed they weren't seeing anyone else, but that was a far cry from wanting to discuss wedding bells.

The finality of his tone unnerved her, but she'd focus on that later.

"Prince Syver, my daughter needs aid." A blonde beauty was helping her daughter walk in. The teen girl was holding up her foot, tears streaking down her face.

"Mia—" Syver answered.

"Dr. Bernhardt, Astrid is seizing," Meg called and Syver turned, racing toward the room.

She shouldn't have wished for more to do. Hazel met the mother's gaze. At least this emergency wasn't life-threatening. "Are you Mia?"

"No, I mean I am, but you can call me Lady Penve."

If this was a movie, Hazel was sure she'd be able to see Lady Penve's breath as her icy tone lashed out. "My daughter needs help. Why is Prince Syver rushing off?"

Hazel blinked. Meg's call had been distinct. Astrid was seizing. A rare complication for a virus, but one that needed to be taken seriously. Lady Penve's daughter had injured her foot.

Hazel wasn't sure how the injury occurred, but her foot wasn't bleeding profusely. She was in pain, but walking into the emergency room under her own powers. Therefore, she was a lower priority than a seizure.

A much lower priority. Something that shouldn't be hard to understand.

"Another patient has a medical situation." Hazel kept her tone even. Maybe Lady Penve didn't understand the implications of Meg's call. Even though Hazel wasn't sure how she could miss it.

"I heard. However, Hilda needs him." She crossed her arms and tapped her toe on the ground, a motion that was far too close to a cartoon villain.

Hazel had become a nurse at twenty-two and completed her ANP at twenty-eight. At thirty-two, she'd seen all sorts of patients and parents. Worry brought out the best in some, and the worst in many others.

"I'm here to help. So, Hilda, what happened?"

"I slipped outside—"

"She was climbing a tree when she's been told not to. And at your age. You should be past this!"

Hazel pursed her lips, biting back the urge to tell Lady Penve that Hilda was old enough to tell her the issue. The girl was a teenager, at least fifteen, maybe older. "Did you fall out of the tree and hurt your ankle?"

"No." Hilda's voice shook as she looked at her mother, then lifted her foot. A large stick was stuck in the center of her foot. "I landed wrong when I jumped down."

"And she was not wearing shoes."

"I see that." Hazel kept her tone light as she moved to grab a wheelchair. She hated to agree with Lady Penve when she was being so disrespectful, but if Hilda had worn shoes, this injury wouldn't have occurred.

Of course, as a child who'd loved to roam barefoot, Hazel also understood the desire to climb trees shoeless. It was a rite of passage. And teens were still children. In fact, in her experience, they were prone to rash decisions almost as often as toddlers.

"Let's get you into a room." Their triage nurse usually saw patients first, but Hazel could handle the stick removal. And she was loath to subject another staff member to the vitriol Lady Penve seemed intent on dispensing.

"When will Prince Syver be available?"

"Not sure." Hazel kept her words even. "The good news is, this is something I can treat."

"No. We'll wait for Prince Syver." Lady Penve crossed her arms.

"Mama…"

"We will wait." She gave her daughter a look Hazel knew Hilda had seen many times before.

It broke her heart and was a reminder that emotional trauma was not relegated to any class. Children learned parental behaviors…and how to survive them.

"I assure you, Lady Penve, that I am a qualified advanced nurse-practitioner. I am fully capable of numbing your daughter, pulling the stick out and assessing further needs."

Puncture wounds were delicate treatments. Depending how far the stick went into Hilda's foot, she might need the wound packed. And she needed antibiotics. The stick had a plethora of germs.

"The longer the stick is there, the greater the risk of infection."

"Something she should have considered before climbing the tree. You made the mistake and now you'll wait for Prince Syver."

Red danced across Hazel's vision. Being careful was a good reminder, but accidents happened. And delayed treatment was *not* an acceptable punishment. "How old are you?"

"Excuse me?" Lady Penve raised an eyebrow.

Hazel didn't acknowledge the interruption. In Fönn, children sixteen and older had rights in determining their medical care. Hilda was climbing trees, but she was clearly a teen.

"I turned sixteen last week."

"Sixteen and climbing trees."

The cutting remark didn't bother Hazel. It was the age she needed. "Hilda, I do not know when Dr. Bernhardt will be available. He is caring for a two-year-old with a virus who had a seizure after he asked for her to be admitted to the hospital. Your foot is not a priority for him. Do you understand?"

"I do." Her eyes slid to her mother, then back to Hazel. "Can you remove it?"

"I can."

"I said..." Lady Penve put both hands on her hips, straightening her shoulders. If she was hoping to intimidate Hazel, it wouldn't work. "*We* are waiting for Dr. Bernhardt."

"Your daughter has requested I remove the stick. As an ANP, I am more than qualified. At sixteen, she can choose her medical decisions. You can stay and remain quiet. Or you can leave."

"I will do neither!"

"There is a third option, and that is Security forcefully taking you from the room. Your choice." Hazel walked to the sink and washed her hands before donning gloves.

Lady Penve stormed from the room, and Hilda let out an audible breath. "She's probably going to talk to management." *And this isn't the first time.*

She didn't need to say the last words for Hazel to hear them. That wasn't her concern, though.

Directing her attention to Hilda, Hazel looked at the injury. The stick looked to have gone straight into her foot. The surrounding area was red, but the puncture wound was contained. The stick in her foot hurt, but the sixteen-year-old now had another big choice to make. "Let's worry about the problem sticking out of your foot right now."

Hilda looked down at her foot, glared at the stick, then looked to Hazel. "How?"

"I can numb your foot with lidocaine."

"That is going to burn." Hilda pursed her lips and wiped a tear from her cheek as she interrupted. "My friend had an accident on his yacht last summer. He needed over thirty stitches and swore the lidocaine hurt worse than anything."

"Some people describe it as a powerful bee sting, others like lightning. I don't know what your sensation will be. The other option is I can take the stick out quickly without numbing it. I've done a similar procedure before. Once it's out, I will pack the wound and put a local numbing cream on it."

"Both are going to hurt." Hilda's voice trembled, but she didn't look away from Hazel.

"Yes." This situation would require a large dose to make

sure she was numb. The odds of a negative reaction went up exponentially with the amount needed for the procedure.

It was Hilda's choice. Hazel would do whatever her patient wished.

Gripping the table, Hilda nodded. "Pull it out."

Hazel didn't wait.

"Prince Syver!"

Syver wiped his face clear of emotion as he turned to greet Mia, Lady Penve. Astrid was stable, but whenever a patient was struggling, it was difficult for Syver. The plan to transfer her to a regular room had shifted to transfer to the intensive care unit. Three words he hated telling parents.

It was best, and temporary. That didn't change the emotions the unit shift brought.

He needed a few minutes to decompress, but that was apparently not happening. "Mia—"

She didn't wait for his greeting. "I need you to do something about your nurse."

Of course, she had a complaint. Mia was difficult, and that was the nicest descriptor he could give. The woman exuded the attitude King Eirvin's focus on the aristocracy had fostered. She and a group of her friends had floated the idea of a private hospital so their children didn't have to wait.

It was technically part of Erik's Health Initiative. An initiative Syver had offered to aid multiple times. One his mother had lobbied for his participation in. Only for them to be turned down repeatedly. At least his brother hadn't followed through with the private hospital expenditure.

It was bad enough when the aristocracy felt the country owed them special treatment. But wanting a hospital staffed with the best doctors when the rest of the country needed quality medical care—was horrid.

Syver had urged Erik to kill the idea as soon as he ascended the throne. He'd delayed the request rather than remove it. And Erik made sure the aristocracy knew the delay was Syver's recommendation.

If there was bad press to take, or a policy Erik didn't think his sycophants would like, it fell on the imposter heir. That recommendation had earned him a few enemies, but Syver didn't care.

"*I* don't have any nurses, Mia." He pinched the bridge of his nose, knowing the stress indicator would have no impact on Mia's tirade.

Ensuring his voice was level, Syver started an explanation he only planned to deliver once. "Our human resources department hires the finest staff—I have no control over it."

That was mostly true, but he knew people listened when he talked. Because his voice held more weight than it should, he was cautious about how he used it.

"I want Nurse Hazel Simpson fired."

"Not happening." He folded his arms as he leaned against the counter. He didn't know what had occurred with Mia and her daughter, but he knew Hazel would never do something not in the best interest of her patient.

Mia opened her mouth, and Syver held up his hand. "What happened to Hilda?"

"She had a stick in her foot, climbing a tree. I swear she's intent on making a spectacle of herself." Mia crossed her arms and took a deep breath. She'd been trained from an early age that one did not lose their cool in public.

She was failing now, which was only making her angrier. He knew she was trying to rein the emotions in, trying to gain control so she could exude the cool calmness expected of her.

It was unfair that Mia had internalized that toxic belief and unfair that her daughter was growing up in the same environment. But life at its core was unfair and the thing one controlled least was the status of their birth.

"Hazel didn't remove the stick?" Syver felt the yawn at the back of his throat and looked down, trying to catch it.

"I did." Hazel was smiling as she joined their little band, but it didn't reach her eyes. It was the "customer service" grin medical professionals learned to wear with difficult patients or family members. "Your daughter is asking after you."

Mia looked at Hazel, judgement radiating from her upturned nose. "I wanted Prince Syver to remove the stick."

"And your daughter requested I not wait for Dr. Bernhardt as he treated a higher priority case."

"Higher priority." Mia's left eye twitched. "My daughter is a member of the aristocracy."

"Yes, you indicated that, Lady Penve, but once you cross the emergency department threshold, patient priority becomes who needs care the most, not a class distinction." Hazel's eyes held unsaid words.

"I packed Hilda's foot. The puncture wound is just under half an inch. I prescribed antibiotics and showed her how to clean it. Do you want to see the wound before I start the discharge papers?"

"No." Syver shook his head and saw Mia's hands vibrate before she stepped between them.

"You will look at my daughter before this nurse discharges her. I do not trust her. Besides, Hilda deserves to have someone like you look at her."

Hazel blinked but didn't respond. All medical professionals had patients or parents of patients challenge them. Sometimes it was the right move. But this was pure classism.

"I can contact your brother if needed."

That was an argument she could have used with the former King—successfully. King Erik didn't deal with medical issues; that didn't mean he wouldn't hear the complaint. Didn't mean he wouldn't use it against Syver.

The reason he'd called Syver home was to have an adviser on this issue. Syver understood the problem. Erik rarely listened. But when he did, when Syver could make a real difference, it made his return to Fönn worth it.

And eventually he'd earn a full place. He believed that, somehow, Erik would see the wisdom in hearing his counsel. In treating him like a brother. A real brother.

"I want it known that I trust Hazel, and all the nursing and medical staff employed here, Mia. Go ahead with the discharge papers, Hazel."

Hazel started toward the nurses' station, returning a few minutes later with the discharge papers. "I'll take a quick look at Hilda, then should you have questions…"

"My sister has your number. She still talks about you."

Syver caught Hazel's shoulders shift, but he didn't look her way. He'd dated Mia's youngest sister months ago. And *dated* was a very loose term for the two dates they'd gone on before he'd told her he didn't see a relationship developing.

"You need to call the hospital or Hilda's pediatrician, if you have questions."

Mia released a sound that was not an agreement as she followed him to see Hilda. The woman was demanding, but she wasn't the first demanding countess he'd dealt with.

And she won't be the last…

Syver had never monitored the clock on a shift. The hospital and his patients were always his primary focus. In fact, his mentor had instructed him to remember that burnout was possible for anyone, and time away from the hospital was a good thing.

Today, though…today he watched the hands tick toward six.

"If you glare at that clock any harder, it might slow just to spite you." Hazel moved beside him, her presence bringing a wave of calm.

He let out the breath he knew he'd been holding. His shoulders loosened and a bit of the day's drama drifted away.

"Ride home with me?" The words escaped, and he wouldn't recall them even if he could.

He wanted to spend time with Hazel, wanted her beside him.

"Syver…" She'd taken public transportation this morning, not wanting to add to gossip if anyone saw them arriving together.

He had a change of clothes at her house and was planning to head directly there, but he didn't want to spend the extra few minutes away from her.

"I know what you are going to say. Know the thought process behind it, I even understand. But we've both had a rough day. Let me drive you home." He kept the words even so that if someone heard, she could claim he was just being a good friend.

Friend.

He'd associated that word with Hazel from the first day they'd met. Now though…after spending the weekend in her arms. After waking beside her, holding her…it was such a small part of what he wanted to call her.

What he wanted was to shout to the world about her. Let them know about the woman who'd chosen him.

"Let Prince Syver take you home. The bus will add at least another thirty minutes to your commute. And after Lady Penve…" Meg's voice rose an octave as she crossed her arms and pressed her lips closed.

The woman had railed, even as Hilda had walked out of the hospital. Meg had spent most of the day with Astrid and her parents—ensuring the toddler was stable before the transfer.

Meg had had a few choice words for Mia…all muttered under her breath but loud enough for Syver and Hazel to hear.

"If you're sure you don't mind?"

"Oh, he doesn't mind." Meg waved goodbye and started out the door.

"I think she is trying to matchmake with the two of us." Hazel laughed before whispering… "Or she's already guessed it isn't necessary."

"She's quite the romantic. I suspect even more so now that there is a ring on her hand." Syver ached to put his arm around Hazel's shoulder. To hold her hand as they walked to his car, to touch the woman he cared about after their long days. But he also wanted to honor her request to maintain the secrecy for a bit longer.

"Marriage brings out romance for most."

He couldn't stop the cynical chuckle as he slid into the

driver's seat of his car. "Maybe, but it also brings out jealousy, anger, spite and many other emotions, too."

"You don't mean that."

He turned, stunned by the shock in her voice. "I do." Erik and his bride seemed happy enough. Their arranged marriage was doing better than Syver's mother's union.

But it was not the stuff of fairy tales.

Signe and Erik rarely spent their free time together. And she often wore the look of sadness he'd seen on his mother's face. Theirs was a royal union, not a love match.

"In my experience, marriage doesn't create the romance Meg is looking for." The memory of his mother standing outside his father's door. Tears streaming down her face.

He'd been too young to know exactly what their argument was, but he'd known his mother was hurt. Known that the cheerful face they put on for the kingdom was a lie.

"So your parents' marriage wasn't happy? Is that why family is difficult for you?" Hazel's hand lay across his knee and he put his hand over hers.

Technically, my parents weren't married.

The words hung on his tongue. Aching for a release he'd never given. The number of people who knew the truth now were just his brother and mother. The list of those who suspected but never mentioned it was considerably longer.

The one person who'd mentioned it often, though only when in the royal family's presence, was gone from the mortal realm.

"It's part of it. Royal marriages are for power, security and class. Not love."

"I see." Hazel's voice was quiet as she focused on the road.

"Luckily," he brightened, "I've no intention of having a royal marriage." He squeezed her hand.

He wasn't sure the palace would even approve a marriage for him. A prince did not just wed in Fönn. There were agreements and controls.

Nothing like the fairy tales.

A marriage to Hazel was likely a nonstarter. The thought burned his heart. It shouldn't matter, and it never had before she'd shown up in his country.

But the thought of her never wearing his ring, even if they were together for years, cut. Far deeper than he'd expected.

Silence hung between them. Silence was a part of life. So many people felt the need to fill the quiet moments, but Hazel never had. It comforted him...usually.

Today the quiet mimicked a wall. A wall he hadn't suspected was there.

"It's been a long day." The sigh behind Hazel's words cut against his soul.

"We should take a detour." The idea bloomed, and he was already turning the car. He knew the perfect pick-me-up.

"Detour?" Hazel looked at him; he didn't glance away from the road, but his body relaxed as her hand squeezed his.

Mia's attitude, Astrid decompensating unexpectedly...

Those two things alone were a recipe for a tense day. So why was it the discussion of marriage making the car so quiet?

Asking was the right answer...but once the question was out. You couldn't unlearn things you heard. And he wasn't ready to bridge that gap.

They'd been together for a weekend. The idea of a life without Hazel, his throat clenched before the thought even formed. He'd lived that life, and he had no intention of going back to it.

"Where's the detour?" Hazel's tone was bright.

Was she pulling away from the unexpectedly tense subject...or pulling away from him?

"The garden center." He squeezed her hand. "Your place has three plants. You can't convince me you aren't aching to add more."

She laughed, the tone off just a little. Dating your best friend let you bypass the learning curve on many things. It also meant that he knew she was pushing away feelings. Hiding hurt.

"More plants are the answer to every harsh day." She closed her eyes as she leaned her head back.

Plants were the answer today, but what happened when they weren't?

CHAPTER SEVEN

DRIFTING AROUND HER FLAT, Hazel looked at the two floating shelves Syver had helped her hang. Plants poured off each of them. In silly pots that he'd insisted on purchasing for her.

It should have been a sweet treat. A reminder that he knew her better than others. Cared about getting her something that mattered to her. But a cloud hung over the vines.

A week later and she still kept rethinking his statement on marriage. That the palace would make all the decisions. Rather than fight that, he'd just decided not to marry.

Without considering what his future partner might want.

She rolled her finger along the edge of her thumbnail, then pulled back. They'd been seeing each other for a short period. Not enough to even consider marriage.

But the idea that he'd just let the palace decide his fate. It worried her more than a lifetime of just loving each other. So much of her life had been decided for her.

Her mother's constant moves. The job with the clinic Alec had arranged. All her belongings raided by the authorities. She wasn't prepared to live a life dictated by others.

And Syver shouldn't want that either. If he accepted it, what did it mean for them?

Her throat was stuffy as she looked at the plants, worried that she was missing something important. Something that could drive everything.

Fönn's monarchy had more power than most modern monarchies. Though they had a host of advisers, the King's word was still final. An archaic rule she thought needed revised.

However, it was unlikely Syver would ever sit on the throne. And he could renounce his title, gain his complete freedom.

Freedom by renouncing who he'd been from birth.

It was an easy thought, a much harder action to take. With consequences that couldn't be undone.

Pressing her palm into her chest, she looked at the greenery, trying to see it as something other than a distraction from the tension following their marriage discussion.

Alec had used gifts that way. Bought her something when she asked questions about his work or fought over some new fancy purchase she didn't think they could afford. Redirected her thoughts with a pretty bauble. Whenever conversations started about getting engaged, or their future, or any slight argument, she could count on finding a gift on the counter.

Always something expensive. Something she didn't want.

Everyone had told her how lucky she was…of course, they'd also abandoned her after Alec's imprisonment. Gossiped over the fancy electronics and jewelry seized as evidence.

Plants weren't the same. Alec had never gotten her a plant, even though that thoughtful gift would have meant far more than any fancy electronic or jewelry she had no place to wear.

So why did the vines and silly pots give her the same uncomfortable feeling?

"Hazel." Syver swept into the flat, and grinned.

And most of her uncertainty floated away.

She was the one holding back in the relationship. She was the one who'd asked him not to discuss their relationship. Not to announce it to anyone.

Projecting her own insecurities would only hurt their future. Still, what if she was missing something?

"I come bearing gifts!"

Gifts…

And the hint of uneasiness tripped through her as she stepped out of the small kitchen. "I don't need a gift, Syver."

"Well, the Queen will be sad to hear that." He held up a pink-and-blue box with the fanciest ribbon she'd ever seen tied on the top.

"Queen?" Hazel looked at the box, trying to figure out what the Queen of Fönn would send her. "Why would she send something to me?"

Hazel eyed the box. Syver hadn't had to tell his family about their relationship. He wasn't technically living at her place, but he had a few changes of clothes here, a toothbrush and shampoo.

He'd told her more than once that he liked her flat better than the palace. Something she didn't believe the first time, but he'd seemed so sincere and happy when he was here.

It was only a matter of time before the staff at the hospital learned what Meg was nearly certain of. She and Syver were together.

"Gift might not be the best word. It's more invitation." Syver grinned as he set it on the table. He was nearly bouncing.

"You know what this is?"

"I do." He raised his hands and for a moment she thought he'd clap, but he spun the box so the bow was facing her.

"There is a function Queen Signe would like you to attend. She requested you."

His happiness was infectious. Hazel smiled as she looked at the pretty package. An invitation…from the Queen. That excited Syver.

"You want us to attend?"

"I very much do."

"A function with the royal family. If we attend, then I'm officially your…" Her mouth froze. She wanted to say girlfriend. It felt like that, but they'd never actually labeled this.

"My girlfriend. Yes. If you attend, our connection will be official. Meg will feel quite justified. But if you're not ready, I can pass along your apologies."

His face fell a little on the words. He'd do it, but he didn't want to. He was excited for her to attend.

That settled the last of her nerves. "What function are we attending?"

"Open it and you'll see." Syver bounced and tapped the box again. The happiness he wore lifted away most of the worry she had about stepping out of line or doing something that embarrassed him.

A gift from the Queen. That was a plot twist Hazel from six months ago would not have believed. "I take it your brother and sister-in-law approve at least a little of you spending time with me?"

In any other relationship she wouldn't have worried over it, but particularly after Lady Penve's reaction last week, she'd been more aware of the status others would know she didn't have.

"They seem happy enough." His voice was soft, and he didn't look at her.

Hazel tilted her head. "Why does that surprise you?"

"We already know each other's little tells, don't we?" Syver's lips brushed hers.

He was trying to distract her. And kisses were the way to do it, but she would not let this go. "We do. And you're avoiding the question." Hazel crossed her arms, creating a bit of a barrier from the advances she craved.

"Most people would focus on the fancy invitation from the palace."

"You're more important than an invitation or anything else from the palace." A look passed over his face and she hated the surprise she saw there. "Syver." Running a hand over his chest, she lifted on her toes and pressed a kiss to his lips.

His arms wrapped around her waist and, like it had every other time they'd kissed, the world slowed. His lips, soft and warm, wrapped her in a protective bubble. Nothing could hurt them in this moment.

"Why does an invitation for your girlfriend surprise you?" What wasn't he saying? There was something he never said. Something he was hiding.

I'm hiding something, too.

She hadn't found a way to tell him about Alec. He knew the relationship was bad...but not how bad.

Holding her, he put his head on hers. "We were not close growing up. Erik was the heir and I..."

The hesitation surprised her. He'd been the spare. It was a word anyone who followed royal families around the globe knew. A hurtful descriptor that was still part of the everyday lexicon.

"The extra special additional bouncy boy?" She strengthened her grip on him. He was the furthest thing from the spare in her mind.

Syver chuckled. "That is a better phrasing than *spare*."

"Agreed!"

"Anyway, his training, the roles he took on, looked different from mine. He asked me to come home, but I haven't received the roles I expected. My mother and I are closer than when I was in London, but I'm left out more than included. My recommendations…" his voice trailed off.

"You're still uncertain of your place here?" That surprised her. He'd returned to Fönn over five years ago. At the request of the King.

"I am." Syver pulled back but grabbed her hand and tapped the box. "Perhaps that isn't fair. I guess I just thought I'd be more involved."

More involved.

Two words that sank against her heart. Because it wasn't involvement she thought he craved, it was acceptance.

"But this is a big deal. A big thing." He pointed to the invitation. "Open it."

Turning her attention to the box, Hazel looked at the intricate design. It seemed like something out of a movie. "I really can't imagine what the Queen would invite me to."

It was a piece of art—how was she supposed to open this? She couldn't see any seams under the bow, any areas to start the unwrapping.

It was a weird thing to be self-conscious of. But Hazel hadn't received gifts from her mother growing up. Alec had never wrapped the things he gave to soothe over arguments.

The Christmas gifts Syver had placed under their small tree were nicely wrapped, but not fancy like this.

Untying the bow, she let out a small gasp as the box fell

open and paper butterflies "flew" for a moment, then landed on the table.

"The Queen certainly knows how to design an invitation!" Hazel lifted the small card inside, then did a little dance.

"A gender reveal!" The Queen was pregnant. Hazel had an invitation to the baby shower for the heir to Fönn's throne.

"Yes." Syver took a deep breath, a bit of the excitement falling from him.

"This is a happy moment, right?" Nothing about Syver indicated he wanted the throne. But to be unseated…an identity you didn't want was still one you had. The only one he'd ever known.

"Signe has struggled to maintain pregnancies. The palace has not publicized that. Everything is going well this time, but until the little prince or princess is here, I think there will be a fog of worry and concern."

Hazel understood. One in eight known pregnancies ended in miscarriages, and if one counted the number that occurred before a pregnant person realized it, that number was likely far higher. Infertility was a struggle some were very open with and others chose not to discuss. And whichever choice a pregnant person made was the right one for them.

"The gender reveal is happening before they tell the kingdom. I think they plan to announce it the next day."

"And you're okay with the announcement?"

His eyebrows knit together as he looked at her. "Why wouldn't I be?"

"Because it will make you third in line to the throne instead of heir? That might bother some people." She waited a moment, but when he said nothing, she added, "But not you."

"Not me." He dropped a kiss on her lips. "Heir to the throne isn't a title I ever expected." He shrugged as he glanced at the invitation.

She was certain there was more to it, more words trapped in his soul, ones she wished he felt secure enough to let out.

"This will be your first royal engagement, though." He pressed his lips to her forehead.

First...

Royal marriage might be off the table, but the future wasn't. That was lovely and terrifying. What happened if she messed up?

"Are there protocols I need to follow?" His arms tightened. *Was he being protective...or worried...or both?*

"Yes. But there is plenty of time to discuss those. Not what I want to do tonight."

"So what do you want?" Hazel kissed him, meaning it to be a quick peck like his kiss. Instead, his arms pulled her even closer, his mouth opened and everything but her need disappeared from the world.

"You." The word was a growl. In this room there was no prince, no aristocrat. Their tongues danced together, and he lifted her onto the counter. She wrapped her legs around him. Hugging him tightly as his mouth devoured hers.

"I know we were supposed to go to dinner." Syver muttered as he trailed a kiss along her jaw.

"We still can." It was a joke. If he tried to take her anywhere but bed, she'd throw a fit.

His fingers gripped her backside through her pants, and she couldn't stop the whimper of need on her breath.

"Really?" He nipped at her ear.

His manhood pressed against her and she knew a tease when she heard it. Shifting her hips just slightly, she relished the groan pouring from his mouth. "You want me as bad as I want you."

His touch woke the siren in her. Her body sang for him, craved him, and right now, she had a very specific song in mind. She slipped off the counter, her fingers skimmed his hard length as her tongue danced with his.

Syver groaned, and it was music to her needy self. Her fingers undid the buttons of his pants as his hands ran over her breasts. Her nipples tightened, but she knew if he stripped her, she'd lose control.

And this moment, this moment, was about making Syver lose his.

After pushing his pants to the ground, Hazel traced her finger across his tip then slipped to her knees, loving the control she had over this moment.

Syver's hands wrapped through her curls as she kissed her way down his length, cupping him, then working her way back up with her tongue.

Her own need was smoldering as she took him fully, using her mouth to drive him toward the edge.

"Hazel..." His hips rocked, and she looked up, enjoying the pleasure enlivening his features. "Sweetheart..." His fingers stroked her chin, the urgency in his tone as he tipped fully over orgasm's cliff.

Only when she'd taken all of him did she finally rise from her knees.

"Hazel," his bright eyes stormed with desire as he started unbuttoning her shirt, his fingers tracing the inches of skin he'd uncovered. "My turn."

Such promise in two short words.

"Do I look okay?" Hazel smoothed out the light pink dress he knew she'd purchased for this party.

He hated the look of panic that she'd hidden quickly. Today was a big deal. One she couldn't fully understand.

Syver hadn't expected an invitation to this event for himself. Erik rarely invited him to gatherings, but to get an invitation for himself and Hazel. He wondered if his mother had begged her oldest to include them. Either way, it was a significant step.

Maybe Erik was finally ready to fully welcome him *and* Hazel. An acceptance he'd craved all his life, to get it with Hazel. There was no better gift.

"You're gorgeous." She'd left her curls loose, painted her full lips red, and he ached to kiss them. But if he started, he'd likely sweep her away to his room and spend the night ensuring she wore nothing but the lipstick.

And he wanted her at this party. The intimate gathering of a few trusted aristocrats, Signe's family and Security, was the perfect place to introduce Hazel. Ease her into the royal world.

His role in the family wasn't as high-profile as people assumed. The palace used his position at the hospital to argue that he was too busy for some royal obligations. A convenient excuse that kept him away from all but the few events where his absence would be noted.

When the Prince or Princess was born, he'd be able to step back even more. *Able, expected...*

Technically, it was the second of those things. But by couching it as able, it gave Syver the feeling of a little more control.

"I curtsy to the King and then the Queen, correct?"

"Yes." Pressing his lips to her forehead, he sent a silent prayer to the universe that this didn't scare her away.

He needed Hazel. And he wanted to make the family happy. Maybe even happy enough that they'd consider granting them the right to marry.

Doing it without his family's approval... Syver couldn't imagine that. It would be a slight directly against the King. And going against his brother would lose him the little ability he had to support the health initiative. To combat the horrid ideas presented by people who'd never served in a medical setting.

Lady Penve and her like-minded cohorts would swoop in as soon as he held no power. Separating care for their children, leaving the others with what? Who would advocate for all the children of Fönn?

So Syver needed to play by the royal rules.

"And if I mess up?" Her voice wobbled just a little.

"If you mess up, I'll let you know. We all mess up at first." It was true, but Syver also planned to keep an eye out for the head of the protocol office.

If she started for Hazel, he'd run interference. Marge had controlled the office with an iron fist since before King Eirvin's reign. Or at least it felt that way. She relished correcting small slights and had recommended more than one palace ban for slights she considered large.

Erik had reined her in—but she still pushed the boundaries.

Arne, the head of Security, approached and dipped his head. "Your Royal Highness... Ms. Simpson."

"You can call me Hazel."

Arne shook his head. "No, I can't."

Hazel looked at Syver, and he held up a hand. It wasn't worth arguing over. Arne was focused on the royal family, but not Syver. Not really.

The imposter heir got the basics. Nothing more.

"I did not run a full security profile on Ms. Simpson. Given that it was my understanding she wasn't visiting the palace. The invitation..."

Arne didn't complete the sentence, but Syver heard the words. Hazel's inclusion was a surprise, a last-minute gift from the palace.

"Security profile?" Hazel stiffened beside him.

"It's standard, sweetheart."

"It is, and typically completed before anyone has access to the royal family."

Hazel chuckled and looked at Syver. "Well, I had access to the royal family for years in London. Lived with them even."

"Prince Syver was not considered part of the household then. His security was not a priority for King Eirvin."

"Excuse me?" Hazel moved, but he caught her, holding her tightly to him.

Now it was Syver stiffening. Arne was simply relaying the truth. King Eirvin hadn't cared; getting upset didn't change anything.

Hazel wrapped her arm around his waist. "You all right?"

No. But now wasn't the time or place. "Fine." He didn't look at her, knowing she'd see the hurt Arne's words caused. She was already angry on his behalf.

If she knew the words felt like daggers ripping through him, he doubted they'd make it through the garden party. And he wanted this day to go well.

Needed it, too.

Syver's feelings rarely mattered. So he did as he always did, pushed the feelings away.

That was a skill all the royals excelled at.

Arne looked to Hazel. He could see the security officer making judgments. Which was his job but Hazel wasn't a security risk.

"If anything happens to the royal family—"

"Prince Syver is part of the royal family."

"Hazel."

"Syver?" Her eyes blazed as she looked at him. His own champion.

The words caught in his throat. No one championed him. He was the black sheep, the imposter heir. The only role he'd ever known. She was ready to fight the head of security...for him.

A role even his mother rarely took up.

"It's all right." His voice was soft. This was the role he played. His position in the family—one earned through no fault of his own.

"It's not." She lifted her hand, cupping his cheek. She turned to Arne. "But I will not put *any* member of the royal family in danger."

"Syver!" He wasn't sure whether the arrival of his mother into this maelstrom was a calming force or an agitating one. The Dowager Queen could be difficult to read, even for her son.

"You must be Hazel Simpson. The young woman who's captured so much of my son's attention."

His mother smiled at him. "She is gorgeous."

She is. Inside and out.

Hazel dipped into a curtsy. She wobbled slightly, but for a first attempt it wasn't bad.

"Come with me, dear girl." She pulled Hazel to her feet. "We have much to discuss."

Syver followed, but his mother held up her hand. "Syver," she laid her free hand on his arm, squeezing it lightly. "Erik wishes to speak to you. I'll escort Hazel into the garden."

Hazel's eyes widened as she looked back at him. His mother pulled her along, though pull was too strong of a word for the Dowager Queen's actions. But the effect was the same. "Tell me about Syver in London. He rarely talks about his time there." His mother winked, clearly happy to have found Hazel.

"I'll see you shortly," Syver called, wondering how much of their story Hazel would spill and glad that his mother had sought her out.

Hazel wasn't sure what she'd expected for the gender reveal party. It was like those she'd attended for friends in London. The decorations were all pink or blue. Cupcakes swirled with pink-and-blue icing.

But it was clear where the preference lay…and what was expected.

People were putting little blue strips into a bowl, voting for a prince. The bowl for the Princess was empty until Hazel dropped a vote in.

Syver's mother had told her that no princess had been born in the royal line for four generations. When she'd quipped that perhaps it was time then, the Dowager Queen had looked horrified. If hoping for a girl was such an issue, why have the gender reveal at all? Hazel had known enough to keep that thought to herself.

Not that she'd had many people to talk to. Syver's mother had grilled her for stories about her son. They'd laughed and seemed to be having a grand time. Until they entered the garden. Then it was like a shield had fallen in front of the woman.

The Dowager Queen, doing her duty.

She'd stayed by Hazel for a little while, then been pulled away. Queen Signe had nodded to her when Hazel said she was glowing, and the rest of the invited guests had found other places to be as soon as she wandered their way.

The snub wasn't subtle.

It's not supposed to be.

She was being put in her place. Spoiler alert, Hazel knew her place and her exclusion here didn't bother her. But would it bother Syver?

He was different inside the palace. The shift between Prince

Syver and just Syver, as he liked to call himself, was on display. She wasn't sure what to make of it.

Her family wasn't loving, hadn't cared for her, so she knew what toxic relations looked like. She just hadn't expected to find them here. They'd called him home. Flown him home so quickly, reintegrated him into their home for the public eye.

Behind closed doors, though.

"You doing all right?" Syver's voice was calm as he slid his arm around her waist.

She opened her mouth, planning to say yes. To just get through this, but the word wouldn't form. "No one wants me here."

"That isn't true. I do." He grinned, but his eyes shifted, surveying the crowd.

Surveying the enemy.

And he didn't lie and say she was just reading too much into it.

"Why was I invited?" That was what she couldn't understand. They'd addressed the invitation to her. Syver had thought his brother was happy for him. Yet, it was clear that everyone wished she'd stayed home.

"I'm not sure, sweetheart. I think my mother wanted to meet you. But out here, she's doing her duty. Like always." The line between his eyes deepened and a heaviness clung to him.

He'd been so excited for her to receive an invitation. All that joy evaporated as the reality of the day set in.

"Let's just get through the party. We're a team." He squeezed her.

"A team." Repeating the words made her feel a little better. "What did your brother want?"

"To let me know that another petition was put before him regarding a private hospital."

"Private is just another word for exclusive. I worked in one once—we turned away far too many patients. At least, in my opinion." Bitterness floated through her. She'd watched people keep her out because she'd been born to a single mum who lived just above the poverty line.

Those same people had pretended to accept her after Alec's "business" took off. Then relished his downfall, and by association, hers. It was bad enough when people wanted to keep professional and personal relations separate from those they considered less than them.

But medical services.

That was a special brand of evil.

"Did you explain to the King why that wasn't appropriate?"

"I did. And he's listening to me." There was a hint of surprise at the end of his sentence.

"Good." Hazel leaned her head against his shoulder, wishing this day was over. If she never stepped into the palace again, it wouldn't bother her.

"We're cutting the cake in five minutes. If you've not voted for prince or princess, now is the time." The staffer's call echoed across the crowd.

The palace baker had created the cake. If it was pink on the inside, then a princess was on the way, and if it was blue, then most of this party was going to be excited.

"Did you vote?"

"For a princess. You?"

"I'm not allowed to. They are doing a drawing out of the winning bowl. Royal family isn't allowed to take part. Might look bad if we won our own gift."

"Your mother voted."

"Did you see her actually drop her name in the bowl?"

Hazel started to say yes, then replayed the interaction. "I don't recall."

"It's a standard royal trick. Distract and then people think you participated without you actually doing it."

"Cake time." The staffer called and the attendees all moved as one toward the stand.

The excitement she'd witnessed at other parties was nowhere to be found. There was no squealing, no clapping, no last-minute calls for a boy or girl. It was a production, but it lacked any heart.

The King and Queen stepped to the cake and lifted the knife.

"Are they hoping for a prince or princess?" She knew the crowd wanted a prince, but surely in the twenty-first century, the royal couple would be happy with either.

"A boy. If it's a girl, well, then if the Queen has another baby and it's a boy, that will supersede his sister. So the hope is always for a boy first. My brother really wanted to do this, the first royal gender reveal. Even though everyone said it was silly since no princess has been born—"

"In four generations. At least I understand why your mother was so horrified when I said it was time for a princess."

"You didn't!" Syver let out a chuckle, then quickly controlled it. "Mother probably privately enjoyed it. Not that she would show it here."

"I didn't realize it was a misstep. My boyfriend didn't let me in on the secret."

"My apologies."

Hazel looked at the couple. They sliced the cake and she saw Queen Signe's face dip.

It's a girl. And she isn't happy.

Hazel's heart ached. If the queen's husband had pushed this reveal, a fun tradition where the ultrasound technician put the gender in an envelope to give to a baker or family member, so the expectant parents could be surprised at their party.

People recommended not doing a gender reveal if you might be upset by the outcome. But if you'd had boys for four generations and expected a prince…

The Queen's bottom lip quivered for just a moment before she controlled the action.

"Princess!" King Erik announced.

Hazel clapped, the sound clear in the quiet. She saw a few heads turn her way, but she wouldn't act like this was a sad moment. A princess was coming. Signe was pregnant and healthy. The baby was healthy. This was a joyous moment.

She looked at Syver, and he clapped with her.

"Congrats, Signe and Erik! A little niece for me to spoil."

The rest of the crowd started clapping then.

Queen Signe's eyes found hers, and there was a softness in them that had been absent before. She nodded to Hazel.

At least this wasn't a complete failure.

CHAPTER EIGHT

"DR. BERNHARDT'S PHONE."

Syver heard Hazel's words as he opened his eyes. Light was streaming through her window. Rubbing his face, he sat up. Yesterday's garden party had exhausted him, but not hearing his phone was something that never happened.

He wasn't on call, but that didn't mean other physicians didn't ring. Consults and emergencies rarely cared about the schedule.

Work was the reason he was back in Fönn. The way he gave back to the country. The way he'd proved himself.

He slid to the side of the bed and yawned, not quite ready to start the day.

"No, I've not seen it. How would I even do that? No, he doesn't know."

The shift in her tone activated Syver's body. Something had upset Hazel.

Yesterday had been a lot. Erik had told him that he was looking forward to how Hazel did. For a moment, he'd thought the walls were falling around the royal family...for him.

Instead, it had seemed like an intentional snub. At least his mother had liked Hazel, and the Queen had softened toward her, too. Signe had sought Hazel out after the announcement that she was carrying a princess. The heir to the throne was going to be a girl for the first time in a hundred years.

And only Hazel had clapped. Even he'd stood there stunned. The expectation was a boy. A prince. Erik looked stunned as well. The Queen looked defeated. Until she'd caught Hazel's look, seen the happiness and joy in Hazel's celebration. Every bit real—not faked for the Queen's enjoyment.

The first person she'd talked to after the announcement was Hazel. Who'd reacted with warmth and excitement as Signe discussed names and nursery decorations.

The aristocrats could ice them out, but if the Queen accepted her, eventually maybe the King would, too. Then everyone else would fall in line, even if they didn't want to.

Walking into the kitchen, he held out his hand. Hazel dropped the mobile into it immediately. The color was gone from her face, and she was wiping tears off her cheek.

"Why is my girlfriend in tears?" He opened his arms, but Hazel walked into her bedroom, her head hanging and her shoulders screaming defeat.

Someone was going to pay.

"There was a leak from the garden party. *Someone* tipped the press to the Queen's pregnancy and the fact that it is a girl."

And Arne automatically assumed the someone was Hazel. Of course, the head of Security was reaching out here first. "And you think Hazel had something to do with it?"

"Given her previous association with a con man who is serving over ten years for fraud—"

"What?" The word fell out before he had time to think. The royal family could use the slip against her and him. He'd vouched for Hazel. Sworn there was nothing to find.

"Something she kept from the heir to the throne, too."

She had, but he could hardly hold that against her. He'd kept his literal identity from her when they'd lived together for years. Even now, he'd not let her in on the state secret regarding his birth.

He trusted her implicitly. Hazel wasn't the leak.

She would never announce something so important for someone else. "She didn't tip the press. I doubt she even knows how."

That wasn't something anyone discussed, but most "unplanned" photos or news releases regarding the royal family or aristocracy were planned leaks. Public relations in the digital world was an art form, but one noncelebrities rarely knew how to navigate.

"Hazel Simpson is banned from the palace." Arne's voice was tight. "As the head of Security, I will also recommend to the King that your association with her be discontinued."

Syver hung up without responding.

He didn't think Erik would order him away from Hazel. But there were other ways to pressure him. His stomach turned on the thought. Erik could make Syver's life difficult. Could withhold money from the projects he sponsored.

He could send me away again.

The tiny voice in the back of his head sent fear ringing through him. It had felt nice to get away from Fönn when King Eirvin was in charge. But he'd missed his family, even if they weren't the picture-perfect example of love.

He didn't want to lose them. Not again. But he couldn't lose Hazel either.

"I didn't call anyone."

"I know."

She sank into the bed on those words, her shoulders collapsing as a sob left her chest. "You believe me."

"I do." Syver sat beside her and pulled her to him. Running his hand along her arm, he kissed the top of her head. He didn't want to push, but he needed to know about the con man issue.

"But I need to know about—"

"Alec was my boyfriend. I met him not long after you left. I was lonely, and he said all the right things."

Her shoulders shook, but Hazel didn't stop. "He was starting a business. In medical research, a lot of technical IT jargon. Or at least that was what he said. Maybe it was even the truth at the beginning. That was his defense at trial. But the reality is I don't know."

Syver said nothing. He didn't quite understand what she was saying.

"We lived together for two years. I told you it was bad, but I thought, well, I thought it would get better, or I hoped it would.

And the business, it wasn't real. All fraudulent investments, robbing Peter to pay Paul."

She blew out a breath. "He helped me get a job at one of the private clinics 'funding' his tech. Nursing manager at a high-end pediatric clinic, all private patients. I liked it. No, I loved it."

She ran a finger over her thumb, and he grabbed her hand before she could pull at the skin. She was hurting, but she didn't need to hurt.

"I was good at it. Managing care, ensuring the patients got what they needed, and I could bring in pro bono patients, too. I felt fulfilled in my career."

Her being good at something was the least surprising thing he'd heard. "Of course you were good at it. You're an excellent nurse."

"Alec's tech, the stuff he claimed would revolutionize patient care…a figment of his imagination and greed. Everything came crashing down a little over a year ago. The police raided our flat. All the fancy things he'd purchased were confiscated to recoup damages."

"Hazel…"

"The worst was no one believed I didn't know. Everyone thought he was so charming before the arrest. Thought the presents and the attention were perfection, never mind that my dreams were materializing. A settled life, a place that was really ours, not a rented flat, a family. A person who didn't belittle me. All of it kept slipping further and further away."

She laughed, but there was no humor in it. "He was perfect…until the raid. Suddenly, they'd all suspected something. Seen a glint in his eye or heard the way he talked about something and just *known* something was off."

"And they believed you knew." He squeezed her tightly; if there was a way for him to wipe away the pain, or take it on, he would. He cared for her, was falling fast for her.

Hell, who was he trying to kid? He loved her. Maybe he had for years, or it had just happened fast. Either way, the truth was there. He loved Hazel Simpson. And this was the absolutely worst time to mention it.

"How does one live with a prince and a con man without knowing? Either you're incredibly naive or a liar." Her tone shifted, and he knew she was mimicking the words she'd clearly heard more than once.

"Hazel."

"And I was naive." She stood, wrapping her arms around herself. "That is something I hate to admit to myself, but it's so clear. I lived with a prince for two years and never suspected."

"Hey—"

She kept pacing, ignoring his interjection. "I dated a con man for years. Lived with him for two. I accepted his gifts, thanked him for helping me get a job. It frustrated me that he stopped talking about our future. But I never guessed. I missed all the signs. I didn't know or suspect…"

"Why would you?" He wasn't even sure she was hearing him.

"And I was naive to think it was possible I could just restart, leave Alec and the past behind. It always finds you. No one remembers the good stuff…but the bad. That will haunt you forever, even if you did nothing wrong."

"You are not naive." Syver stepped in front of her. She bumped into his chest, and he wrapped his arms around her. Holding her in place, taking in the sobs and just letting her be as she needed to be…with him. "You are kind, trusting—"

"All things that he used to take advantage of me."

The bitterness in those words. That way of thinking was damaging. And it wasn't true.

"Someone taking advantage of you says more about them than it does you, Hazel." Running his hands over her back, he held her while she sobbed and waited for her to gain some control.

"Kindness, empathy, trusting others makes you an excellent nurse and a good person. Qualities that I wish I had at the same levels as you."

"You are kind." She sniffed.

"If you could be in my brain right now, you wouldn't think so." Alec was out of his reach.

She pulled out of his arms, sniffed again and wiped her nose with the back of her hand. "I must look a real fright."

"You're gorgeous."

Hazel raised her brow. "Come on, Syver. I have puffy eyes...my nose is runny from tears..."

"You are gorgeous," he repeated, and reached for her hand. "Puffy eyes and runny nose included. You are gorgeous, period."

"At least you know all my secrets now. No more skeletons hiding in my closet."

The words hit him, and he let out a breath. She'd told him everything. All the sins that weren't hers but still weighed against her soul. And he still had a giant one.

"I'm not King Eirvin's son." The words were out. The state secret he technically couldn't tell anyone. The imposter heir and the truth behind why he'd been sent away.

And even after his recall...they didn't treat him as an equal. People assumed it was because he was at the hospital so often. Assumed those duties kept him too busy to be at the opening ceremony of Summer Nights, or state visits, or any other number of things that would normally be expected of a proper heir to the throne.

"Hazel..."

"I know."

Two little words. Two little words and a smile. His ears buzzed, his brain rattled, and now it was his turn to fall into the bed.

Hazel wasn't sure what reaction Syver had expected to his announcement, but it obviously wasn't her admitting that she knew. The truth wasn't as surprising as she was sure he thought it was.

He didn't have the traditional *E* name. All the girls' names Signe had discussed with her were *E*, and when Hazel commented on it, she'd said it was the tradition for royals.

That all members of the family had an *E* name. The tradition went back for more than a hundred years. She'd said it with such grace, such certainty. Like she'd forgotten that Hazel was dating a royal...who did not have an *E* name.

Her reaction when Hazel pointed it out, the color tinting Signe's cheeks as she made an excuse that made no sense, raised several questions. Ones Hazel didn't know the Queen well enough to ask.

Then there was Arne's statement that Syver wasn't considered part of the royal family when she lived with him in London. That he was there at all, blending in, acting like he wasn't a royal. None of that added up to a son King Eirvin was proud to have carry his name.

His birth, the scandal it must have caused, none of it mattered to her, but it clearly did to him.

"You're still Prince Syver." His mother had had an affair, but he was still a royal. Some might whisper about his bloodline, but those whispers shouldn't matter.

Shouldn't.

Who was she to talk? Hazel had fled London to avoid whispers. And nearly collapsed in a heap on her kitchen floor when she'd heard Arne's accusations. Whispers did damage.

"Am I?"

"Do you want to be?"

Syver opened his mouth, closed it, then opened it again. But still no words came out.

"You weren't Prince Syver in London. And you mention that inside these walls you're just Syver. You seem to crave it. Do you even want to be a prince?" She doubted anyone had ever asked his preference. By the circumstances of his birth, he was royal...and not, at the same time.

But what did Syver want?

"I want my family to want me. All of me—without reservation." The words were so soft that she knew he didn't mean to speak them. And they broke her heart.

Because she didn't know if that was possible. It had taken her a lifetime and a solid therapist to understand that her mother wasn't capable of accepting her. Alec had used her, his love as fictitious as the company he'd used to scam people.

Syver couldn't control what others thought of him. Only how he reacted to their actions.

Sliding into his lap, she put her hands on either side of his face. "All you can be is your best self."

"That's never been enough."

Leaning her head against his, she held him as the sad words washed over them. He should be enough. The man was kind, intelligent, well-spoken. And none of it should matter, because as the Queen's son, the King's brother, they should love him just for that.

His pain ricocheted through Hazel's soul. His hurt, and her inability to pull it from him. If she possessed one wish, she'd use it to make him feel how he made her feel.

Whole.

Since the moment she'd seen him, her heart seemed to beat with his, her eyes looked for him. They'd been friends in London, but if he'd stayed…if he'd stayed, this would have happened.

Maybe even the night he left. All the signs were there for everyone but them to see. He was her person. The man who made her feel all the things she'd read in the romance novels she devoured.

"I love you." Maybe this wasn't the right time but waiting for some perfect moment wasn't her style. "I love you, Syver. You are enough."

Her body was lighter; speaking truth did that. She loved him. His lips skimmed hers, as his hands firm against her back pulled her even closer.

"I love you, too."

She laughed. It wasn't funny, but her body released the sound. "Syver, it feels like we have always known this. We're hopeless."

"I know. But there is no one else in the world I'd rather be hopeless with."

"How romantic!" She pushed on his shoulder before dipping her lips to his again. Movies, books, the world made a big deal out of these moments.

Videos went viral on social media with people telling others they loved them. This was such a small moment, and she wouldn't change a thing.

He held her as they kissed, enjoying each other. There was passion, but it was subdued by the morning's heavy topics.

She wrapped her legs around his waist, then leaned her head against his shoulder. Holding him as tightly as possible. "I love you."

His fingers caressed her back. "You already said that. Though I can't imagine I'll ever tire of hearing the words." His lips grazed her temple.

"Now what?" She hated to interrupt this moment, but life moved forward. If the King or Queen believed she'd leaked information, it would make life difficult for Syver.

He wanted a relationship with his family, but she wasn't willing to give him up either.

"We go to the palace."

Her blood chilled, and she knew he felt her stiffen. Maybe it was the right choice, but it was hard to catch her breath. "I'm not allowed on the grounds."

It was the second thing the head of Security said at her this morning. And he'd been very serious.

"I was told the same."

If he was nervous, his tone didn't suggest it. Was that a princely cover…or something he'd learned because he was unwanted? A way to blend in even when the world felt like it was ripping apart?

"So…"

Maybe there was some secret entrance. Some way past that only royalty knew. Arne wouldn't appreciate Syver showing her any secret entrances.

"We call his bluff."

She knew her mouth was open and her eyes must be fully bugged out. "Bluff? Syver—"

"Yep. And I think the quicker we leave, the better."

She pulled her hand across her face as she moved off his lap. "What does one wear to this type of meeting?" She was only half joking.

"Something nice."

"The nicest thing I had was the garden party dress." She wasn't planning on playing girlfriend to the Prince when she took the job on Fönn. Her closet was mostly comfy clothes, items she could change into quickly when she got off shift.

"Palace wear" wasn't filling her closet.

"Choose whatever makes you most comfortable, sweetheart. It will be okay, promise."

Promise.

She knew he meant that word, but there was a look in his eyes. Concern…worry…fear. He wasn't sure it was going to be okay.

All right, whatever happened, they were going together. Syver and Hazel, and that was all that mattered.

Syver knew his grip on Hazel's hand was tight, but there was no way he was loosening it as they walked through the palace's family entrance.

The security person raised his head, frowned and picked up his radio. An interaction he'd had thousands of times, one that barely elicited the wave of a hand or more than a *Hello, Your Royal Highness*, was now interrupted. And he was dragging Hazel here.

He wasn't sure it was the right choice, but he also didn't know what other path to take.

"You're free to enter, Prince Syver, but Ms. Simpson—"

"Is coming with me." Syver nodded, and he kept moving. "Tell Arne that I disobeyed you. It's the truth."

No need for the young captain to get in trouble with his boss, but this was nonnegotiable, and he was making that clear now.

"Syver…"

"It's fine, sweetheart." *Man, I hope that's true.* He picked up his pace, glad Hazel followed his lead.

At least today was Sunday. The day King Erik allowed himself some rest. Until noon, King Erik and Queen Signe were in their private chambers. Up three flights of stairs, immediately to the left. He could beat Security, but it would be tight.

The King's chambers appeared, and he could hear the commotion coming down the main hall. Syver didn't bother knocking. Hopefully, Erik would forgive the intrusion.

"What—" Erik's jaw tightened as he met Syver's gaze. "She is not allowed on the grounds."

"Why? Because some article appeared, please, anyone could do that."

"Who else would have told such personal news?"

Hazel flinched, her shoulder shifting into his body.

His brother couldn't be this naive. "Many people might have shared the impending news."

"I had everyone in attendance fully vetted, except." Erik's eyes slid to Hazel.

I vetted everyone but the one you brought, Syver.

Erik didn't say it, but he didn't have to. Putting so much faith in vetting, in believing that members of the aristocracy would protect the information because of their association to the crown. It was the height of wishful thinking.

Syver would never harm his family. He'd kept secrets from the time he'd learned to talk. And he'd never fall for someone who wouldn't do the same.

The woman he loved was beyond reproach in this issue.

"Your Royal Highness," Hazel said as she pulled away from Syver just as raps started on the door.

Erik held up a hand, and Hazel stopped talking. He stepped to the door and told Security they were to wait in the hallway. It wasn't much of a win, but at least he hadn't let them through the door.

Turning back to Syver and Hazel, Erik raised his hand again. "You were saying, Ms. Simpson."

She took a deep breath, clasped her hands, then met the King's gaze. "That I didn't leak the information. You don't know me, but I swear I wouldn't share such personal information. I wouldn't even know how."

"A lot of fancy words. A quick text to a friend or a line dropped into a website tip site. It's easy."

Erik wasn't wrong. It was remarkably simple to alert people when one wanted to.

"If I wanted to out the royal family, why didn't I sell my story about Syver? Living with the Prince for two years while he acted like a regular person in London is the bigger story."

Erik's jaw twitched again, and Syver reached for Hazel's hand, but she kept going. "I am not saying your impending joy isn't big news."

"It is the heir to the crown, the true…"

He caught himself as his eyes flicked to Syver. Would the dismissal ever not sting? He didn't care about being the heir to the throne, but Erik's happiness of ensuring he was out of the line of succession, in a way that didn't mean confirming palace rumors, smarted.

"You are having a child. That the baby will wear a crown one day is not massive news." Hazel held up her own hand as Erik opened his mouth.

Silencing the King.

Syver was proud and also horrified.

"I could have had a book deal, could have done daytime talk shows. I had my chance when the crown was paying no attention and the story would have gained me something. Then it would have run on the world stage for weeks, maybe months, if I was the type of person to embellish."

She looked at Syver, her face so open. Turning, she raised her chin. "Whatever you think of me, I gain nothing from this leak."

"She's right." Signe's voice was soft, barely carrying across the room.

"Signe." Hazel didn't hesitate. She moved to the Queen's side. "How are you feeling?"

Not well.

That was obvious from the Queen's pallor.

"Faint. I can still feel the baby move, though, and I'm not bleeding."

"All right." Hazel put her arm around Signe's waist. "We are going to the couch. Can you make it that far?"

"Signe…" Erik was at his queen's side, sliding his arm on the other side of his bride.

Their marriage wasn't a love match, but Erik cared for his wife. Signe had never stood outside these chambers begging for entrance where she should be welcomed without question.

"I gave everyone different names." She let out a heavy breath as Hazel and Erik lowered her to the couch. "The names mean it's…"

"We'll worry about that after." Hazel's words were tight.

"Afraid my wife will name you?"

Hazel didn't bother to answer the King's accusation. "Her pulse is racing, Syver."

Hurrying to the in-suite phone, Syver picked up the receiver, pushed one button and didn't wait for the palace operator to respond. "I need medic transport for the Queen from the King's chambers. Alert her ob-gyn to meet us at the hospital."

Hazel ran her hand over Signe's forehead. "She doesn't feel feverish, but she is sweating. Signe, what have you eaten this morning?"

"Nothing. I had so much at the party, I felt a little sick last night. The baby didn't seem to appreciate the fancy treats, I guess." She let out a small laugh, the sound bordering on hysterical.

Like all physicians, he'd done a rotation through obstetrics, but his knowledge was a decade old. He'd paid attention, but his rotation through pediatrics had come first, and he'd felt at home in the specialty from the first moment. So the other rotations had gotten his attention, but not his love.

"Medic here."

The door opened and two paramedics and most of Security raced in.

"I told you—"

"Not the time, Arne. Ban me from the palace after we secure the Queen." Syver kept his tone cool, as the head of Security openly glared at him. That was unusual—and he recovered quickly, wiping the expression from his face.

"Her pulse is more than a hundred beats per minute. I couldn't take her temperature, but she doesn't feel feverish. However, I noted perspiration on her brow, and she has not eaten since around…"

Hazel looked at the Queen.

"Around six last night." Signe's eyes met Hazel's, and she reached out her hand. "Thank you, Hazel."

Hazel smiled, but Syver could see the concern in her eyes. Like him, she had limited expertise in obstetrics. She knew Signe had struggled with infertility, even if she didn't know her full patient history.

They were limited in the care they could provide. And, at least for him, the ability to only provide basic care, and no reassurances, was difficult.

"Do not leave the palace grounds until I give you leave." Erik's words were stern and clearly for the security team.

Hazel waited until the King and Queen were gone before hitting Syver's hip. "Guess I'm now banned from *leaving* the grounds." Her words were bright, but he could see the frustration and concern on her face.

"Why don't I show you my wing while we wait?"

"Your wing! How fancy."

"Somehow, I thought you were joking." Hazel couldn't help her mouth falling open as Syver showed her the different rooms in his wing of the palace. "A wing, and I thought our flat in London was the height of grandeur. It was a proper step down."

"I thought of it as a step up." Syver kissed her fingers as he led her to his suites. "Most of the rooms here are empty. I have an office, which I never use, my bedroom suites and a library. Otherwise, the guest rooms are available for palace functions and such."

"It's almost like you have your own not so little flat back here." It had taken nearly twenty minutes to walk from the

King's suites to Syver's rooms. And it was clear from the decor changes and lack of ornamentation that only Syver used this wing.

"I think King Eirvin preferred me as far away as possible."

"You lived down here as a child?" That horrified her. It was one thing for an adult, always in the public eye, to choose to step out of it in the privacy of their own place. But for a child to be banished in their own home.

"Syver." She reached for his hand, hating how similar their upbringings had been. Her mother hadn't had the option of sending her twenty minutes up the road to live. But if she had, she'd have exercised it at first chance.

"I got free run of the place down here, and mother visited every evening. Read me books and such."

Righteous anger stormed through her belly as those words echoed in the empty hallway.

Visited.

One did not visit their child in the spare wing of a palace.

"Ever thought of leaving? Getting your own flat in the city, nearer the hospital?"

"Hazel, are you asking me to move in with you?" The grin on his lips suggested he was joking, but there was a look in his eyes. One that called out to her.

She hadn't been suggesting that. Not really. They'd been dating for less than a month. One didn't move in that quickly... except he was already basically living at her place.

And they'd lived together once. Platonically.

"I mean, you can do better than my place, Syver. I have a rented bed, for heaven's sake."

"But the mattress is comfy." He pulled her into his arms, dropped his lips to hers, then let his hand trail along her lower back. "I'm not trying to put you on the spot, Hazel."

"I know, but you didn't answer my question. Have you thought of getting your own flat? Someplace that isn't a half-mile walk from the rest of your family."

They were the wrong words. His lips fell into a frown and his hands on her waist loosened. "Syver..."

Maybe she shouldn't push, but he deserved more. And she wanted to give him that. Show him.

"No. No, since I got back from London, I've not considered leaving. My family…" He pursed his lips and she could see him trying to find words.

Words she knew would either be a lie or a hard truth.

And she wanted him to know she understood. "My mum never wanted me, and I am not saying that your family is the same, but moving out might help. Some distance…"

"If I left completely, I would lose the little access I have to Erik. Mother tries, but there are aristocrats who are intent on having control over all things. You heard Mia—if she could convince him to create a private hospital or private wing of our hospital, she would."

"And you think Erik would do that?" Hazel understood the concern, but was it realistic?

"You saw him today. He can't believe that the vetted aristocrats at the party could have leaked, when it's clear they did. He was raised with them, sees them as friends."

"And you don't?"

"I was raised with them. No one discusses the rumors of my birth, but…"

But he'd never been part of the inner circle. Not welcome, even though his title should have granted him access. It was what made him the man she loved.

However, her heart ached at the reality he'd experienced. And it hurt for the acceptance he was seeking. Acceptance she didn't think his family could fully give.

"I think you should move in with me." She hadn't really thought through the words, but if he was officially at her place, maybe he could see that he deserved more than the crumbs his family offered.

He deserved the world.

"Hazel…"

"I'm serious, Syver. Maybe it's a wild idea, but we've lived together before. We're excellent at it. My flat is smaller than our London place, but…" She grinned as she reached her arms around his neck, "We only need the one bed this time."

"Hazel."

"Don't think about it. Just jump with me. We can pack while we're hostages! Syver, you're already there all the time. This is just pulling your clothes and the few personal items you might like. I don't have room for the library, but for our next flat…"

"Our next flat." Syver's thumb ran across her jaw, and he brushed his lips against hers. "I like the sound of this, Hazel, of being with you."

"I love you, roomie. Now point me toward your suitcase!" She was serious. As soon as King Erik released them, they were out…period!

CHAPTER NINE

"THE KITCHEN SMELLS WONDERFUL."

Hazel grinned as she lifted the crepe from the griddle. Their first Saturday as live-in boyfriend and girlfriend and she was resurrecting their old tradition.

And not getting sidetracked by the bedroom. At least not for a little while.

Syver wrapped his arms around her waist and pressed a kiss against the back of her neck. "I used to love waking up and smelling the cinnamon on Saturday mornings. I looked forward to it all week."

Lifting her head, she kissed his cheek. "I loved it, too. The first crepe I had was in the university cafeteria."

"Really?" Syver pulled back and moved to the coffeepot. "Your mum never made one?"

The mention of her mother sent the same stab through her heart as it always did. She'd cut the woman off after Alec's arrest. Not that her mother had noticed for almost a year, when she called asking for a loan, telling Hazel in crude terms that she must have hidden something away when she was sleeping with the con man. She didn't believe her when she said no, and Hazel had finally snapped. She had informed her then that she had no interest in a relationship.

Which was only partly true. She wanted a relationship. One that was loving and meant for her and her alone. But her mother wasn't willing to offer that. That didn't mean that she didn't wish the phone might ring one day with an apology, a genuine apology, and an offer to start over.

However, Hazel was wise enough now to realize that was unlikely. Maybe even impossible.

"Mum was not exactly a cook-a-morning-breakfast type of mum." Or a cook-or-care-for-you-at-all mother. She'd kept a roof over Hazel's head, but that was about it.

He'd asked after her family several times this week. She knew it was because he was missing his. She couldn't fix that for him.

His mother had called each night. A quick call, never lasting long but at least it let him know he wasn't forgotten completely. His brother had not reached out at all. He deserved more than a quick call. They should miss him. Want to know why he was gone. Beg for him to come back.

But she also knew that just because family should do something didn't mean they actually would.

"You always talk about her in the past tense."

Hazel flipped the sides of the crepe, then put it on the plate she'd laid out. "Here you go." She spun the batter, then dropped it on the griddle.

"Sorry, Hazel. I guess I just have family on the mind right now."

Letting out a deep breath, she looked over her shoulder. Syver's neck was slumped. His eyes were tightly closed. She understood; she really did.

This was a process, and it was one she could help him with. Support him each step of the way. But she couldn't walk the path for him. Only he could do that.

If he wanted to. If he didn't, then he was in for a lifetime of pain.

"I cut my mother off. I haven't spoken to her in a year."

"You just cut her out of your life? She's family." He pursed his lips as he looked at the crepe.

Family.

A word that brought some people comfort. All it had ever brought Hazel was pain.

"Sharing DNA does not make a family." He was in the same spot. Surely he saw that?

"I spent my life trying to be the perfect daughter, trying to earn my place in her life, then trying to earn my place in Alec's. I'm not doing that anymore. I like who I am. I don't need to earn my place. Maybe I still falter with that sometimes, but I know my worth."

And you should know yours, too.

Those words were trapped in her head. She couldn't force them out. He was always going to be the imposter heir. That wasn't fair. But he couldn't change it. It didn't make him unworthy, though.

"Do you think your mother could do anything to earn your trust?"

"No." One syllable, two letters, and a world of pain behind them. She could hope, but realism was best here. If her mother ever decided she loved her, for her, Hazel would weep with joy. That was almost as unlikely as the moon shifting places with the sun.

She knew that…now.

Putting her crepe on her plate, Hazel turned, her knees nearly buckling as his horror ran through her.

"She isn't good for me, Syver."

"I just can't imagine giving up."

"I couldn't imagine it either. Until it happened. The break was sudden. I mean, a long time coming. So long. But then one day, it was just severed. I can't explain that. In the moment, it was pain, and freedom, spun together in a horrid mixture that will be with me forever."

Syver ran a hand over his brow, then held up his crepe. "It's crepe morning. Happy times, together."

He moved to the table and she followed.

"So, I was thinking, maybe we put up a few more shelves. I know you're aching for more plants."

It was a unique way to change the subject. An offer for more plants, a treat after an uncomfortable conversation. Hazel took a sip of her coffee, then reached her hand across the table. "I'd love a few more shelves, but…"

"But—" Syver raised a brow. "Never thought I'd hear you say *but* when a plant was involved."

"Syver, I don't need a gift after each hard talk. You can ask me any question you want about my mum. I know moving out…"

"I'm not cutting my family off."

What if they cut you off? Could he live with that? Would he choose her, if they made him choose?

"And I am not saying you have to. What was right for me doesn't have to be right for you."

"I know."

Do you?

The words were on the tip of her tongue, but she couldn't bring herself to say them. This morning had been heavy enough. "As much as I want a few more plants, I wonder if it might be better to look for a new place. Somewhere a little bigger."

Syver blinked. Clearly, that was not something he'd considered. Her place was nice, but with his stuff from the palace, it was overstuffed. They didn't need a giant location, but something a little bigger, where they weren't always bumping into each other.

Though she didn't really mind bumping into him.

"Just something to think about."

"Yep. But in the meantime, plant store today?"

"Sure." Hazel raised her coffee mug, hoping it hid the downturn of her lips. She wanted him happy, but if his family never came around, could he be happy with just her?

Was Hazel a big enough gain compared to the loss of the royal family?

His phone buzzed, but Syver knew it wasn't his family. The constant rings and buzzes were from colleagues and friends, all asking the same question. Had he seen the poll?

All equally disappointed when the answer came back no, that he'd been on shift. That he'd look at the links they sent when he got home.

Home. A smile twitched across his face. Hazel's place, their place, was small, but it was home. Though she'd brought up looking for a new place a few times.

He wanted to say yes. Needed to, but part of him kept hoping his brother might reach out. Hoping his mother's short calls might turn into a visit.

The palace was only one of the residences the royal family owned. He hoped that after the initial sting of his departure evaporated, they'd ask if he'd like one of the flats or country homes.

Some indicator they wanted him close.

He'd thought of reaching out, even drafted a text then worried that the method was too little. He'd written a letter…one that was still sitting on the counter in an unaddressed envelope.

It felt more personal than an email. He could call. His mother asked each night if he was sure of the path he was taking.

And each night he lied. Said he was. But it wasn't true. Not really. He'd second-guessed himself repeatedly. However, in Hazel's presence, most of the worries slipped away.

She was his person. He knew that deep down. The one he'd looked for without knowing it. She was the strongest person he knew.

Strong enough to cut her mother off. That made a person strong. Strong. He kept repeating the word, forcing himself to choose it over the other that rattled in his brain.

Heartless.

He hated thinking that. Hated that he couldn't stop the words from appearing. Hazel was the furthest thing from heartless.

Yet, he knew she wanted him to do the same. She wouldn't say it, not yet anyway. That didn't mean he didn't see the look in her eye.

But how did one cut off one's family? How did one walk away from them? He'd done everything asked of him. Maybe he was still an outsider, but it wasn't as bad as it had been under King Eirvin.

If Hazel could see the difference...see how much better life was with his brother and mother. Maybe it wasn't perfect. But what family was?

Pulling into the small parking facility for their apartment, he smiled, pushing away the uncertainties. He was steps away from the woman he loved. He needed a shower, and he'd do his best to get her to shower with him.

"Tell me you have looked at the poll." Hazel laughed as he stepped through the door. "My phone has been ringing off the hook. And I keep having to tell people, I don't know."

"I haven't. I've gotten texts and voice mails all day, but I do not know what poll it is and why people think I should see it."

"The paper did a poll on who the favorite royal was." She looked at him with such an expectation.

He wasn't sure what reaction she was waiting for.

"Oh." Syver laughed. "Yeah, they do that every couple of years. An online thing. Not super scientific but fun for the kingdom. The King and Queen are always the favorite."

He couldn't remember a time when that wasn't true. It made sense; Erik and Signe were the ones people associated with the crown. Of course, they'd be the top answer.

Hazel's eyes widened. "Syver, you're the most popular."

He squinted, trying to see if she was pulling his leg, then he smiled. Always nice to win something. "How fun. Surprising, but fun."

Was this really what people had called him over? A poll run on a website for clicks? Either way, it didn't matter. Nothing to worry over or get too excited about.

Next year, or whenever they ran it again, it would be Erik, or maybe the new Princess.

"It's not close, Syver." Hazel's words were soft, but he could hear the concern in them.

Why would that bother her?

"Really?" He shrugged as he kissed the top of her head. "Want to shower with me?"

"Syver?"

"Hazel?" He ran his fingers along her collarbone, just the

way she liked. It had been a long day. He needed a shower, but he wanted her with him.

"You are the most popular. You don't think the palace will notice? Your brother?"

His mood took a hit, and he stepped back. "If he does, I'm sure it will be a minor discussion point. They talk about the polls every so often. However, no one makes a big deal of them."

"How many of those 'not a big deal' polls did *you* win?"

He didn't like the bite in her tone. This wasn't a big deal. He doubted Erik did more than grumble over it. "None." Syver's phone buzzed again. He pulled it out of his pocket. "It's just a silly poll."

If it made his brother notice him…made him reach out… No, he would not travel that thought pattern. This was just another day. And what he wanted was the woman before him.

"If you say so." Hazel's grin was forced as she reached for his hands. "I guess your friends, colleagues and girlfriend are just excited for you."

"That is nice." He meant it, too. It was sweet that people thought the poll mattered. Lovely to know his friends were happy for him. But it didn't mean anything had or would change.

After running his finger along her chest, he let his thumb hover over her nipple. "So…join me in the shower?"

Her gaze caught his, and she hesitated, then let her hand dip to his pants line. "Absolutely."

CHAPTER TEN

"A LETTER ARRIVED from the palace. Do you want to read it before we head to the hospital or wait?"

Her words were lead weights as she held up the envelope with the King's Seal. He wanted to rip the seal off and devour the message, throw it unread in the trash and burn it all at the same time.

The first missive to arrive in weeks. And one that was not expected.

A week after he'd moved out, Erik had sent his apologies for his accusations against Hazel. Sort of. The few words delivered by a security guard who explained that Signe had been testing her youngest sister.

A test she'd failed by revealing to the press the names she'd strategically given to her sister. Apparently, there were a handful of wrong names dancing around the aristocratic circles.

If anyone knew the real name, he thought it was Hazel. Signe had been so happy after Hazel clapped. The Queen had gravitated to Hazel following the announcement.

Since he'd moved out, Hazel had had two meetings with Signe, though Hazel referred to them only as get-togethers. Informal meetings discussing the upcoming baby and checking on Signe after the food-poisoning scare that had kept them trapped in the palace for almost six hours.

If she knew the Princess's name, Hazel was keeping it to herself until the baby was born. Even he didn't know the names Signe told her. She refused to break the Queen's trust.

It meant Hazel had earned a close confidant in the royal

family...while he had lost them all. His mother still called, but she was distant, mentioning his brother and how it looked for Syver to be living in such a small place. The conversations were short.

Even his attempt to reach out to Erik about the health initiative had been rebuffed with a simple *The King is busy*.

He'd heard nothing since.

He wanted Hazel and his family.

Is that too much to ask?

It felt like his time in London—except now hundreds of miles didn't separate them. It was harder to pretend the actions didn't cut.

"Syver?" Hazel's hand was warm against his cheek. "You can do whatever you want with it. Or you can think about it while we are at the hospital. There are no wrong answers here."

Except there were. Maybe she didn't realize that. There was a wrong answer. In fact, there were several wrong answers. Answers that would make him an internal pariah. Or even more of one.

In the world he'd grown up in, he knew there was one right answer, a few half-right answers that would get ridiculed or result in small punishments, and a host of wrong answers.

"Read it for me."

Hazel pressed her lips to his. A quick kiss, a reminder that he wasn't alone.

"Brother—"

"He started it *brother*?" Erik always addressed him as Prince Syver. A formal address of titles. A reminder of who was in charge.

"He did." Hazel handed him the letter.

He barely resisted the urge to rip it from her hands. A frown passed over her features before she moved to where their bags were by the door, ready for their shift.

"He's inviting me to a family dinner. Just family..." His words drifted away.

"Family." She sighed as she slid her pack over her shoulder. "I suspect that doesn't include me."

It didn't. "I'll send along our apologies." The words were hard to say, but they were the right ones.

"No," Hazel shook her head, "you should go."

"I'm sure it's an oversight." It wasn't, and he hated the lie. Technically, they weren't married or engaged, so the family wouldn't consider her. That didn't mean he didn't consider her family.

She was, and he'd make sure they understood that at dinner. This was a onetime situation. He and Hazel came as a pair from here on out.

Hazel looked at her phone, then held it up. "We're pushing our time, Syver. We need to get moving. You haven't seen your brother or mother in weeks. Besides short phone conversations with your mother you haven't heard from them since we packed your things."

She frowned at the corner where many of his items were still in boxes.

"We need to find a new flat." Syver gestured to the boxes. The flat wasn't large enough to store his things long-term and live comfortably.

"We do." Hazel had brought it up several times. She'd even looked for a few places, nothing fancy, but a two-bedroom flat, a place that gave them a little more space.

He'd dragged his feet. Hoping for news from the palace. Hoping they'd offer them something. An olive branch…one she hadn't wanted to wait on. Now the palace was reaching out and not including her. It was time to act.

His family could doubt this relationship if they wanted. He would not let Hazel do the same. "This weekend. We will look for places this weekend."

"I'm holding you to that, Syver. Now…" She tapped her wrist.

No watch was there, but he understood the universal sign. He laid the letter gently on the table. Dinner with his family. He was having dinner with his family.

* * *

"I swear this is the third time we've been in the emergency room for something like this in the last four months."

"Sorry, Mum." The teenager looked at his mother. Tear streaks ran through the dirt on the boy's cheeks. "I really thought I had the trick down this time."

Her eyes rested on her son, and despite her frustration, Hazel could see the love radiating through the look. And the worry. "I want to support this. I do…but Niko…it's so dangerous."

"It's not, Mum. Not really." Words only a teen who still believed they were part superhuman and nothing bad would ever happen to them could utter.

"You've broken both your wrists, had more stitches than I care to remember, and now a broken ankle."

"We don't know it's broken." Niko huffed, crossed his arms, then cringed as the movement jostled his clearly broken ankle.

"It is." Syver commented as he strolled through the door. "In two separate places, I'm afraid."

He flipped the tablet around and showed Niko and his mother where the breaks were. Though it didn't take a doctor or an X-ray technician to see the lines between the bones that shouldn't be there.

"Maybe now you will reconsider this extreme biking sport." Niko's mother barely caught the sob as she looked from the tablet to her son.

"Mum. I love it." Niko's lip wobbled, and he pushed away another tear, whether from pain or worry over the sport he loved, Hazel didn't know.

The teen closed his eyes for a second, shifted, though he was careful how he moved. When he opened his eyes, no one could miss the resolution in his features. "How long will I be in a cast, Prince Syver?"

"I don't know." Syver pulled up the swivel chair, sat and looked at the ankle. "This is a complicated break." His gaze shifted between Niko and his mother. "It requires more than just a cast."

"More how?" His mother stepped to the edge of her son's bed. "Is he going to be okay?"

"Yes, but today all I can do is splint it. You'll need to follow up with an orthopedic surgeon. I'll make the referral as soon as I splint it. They should be able to see him at the ER consult tomorrow morning or afternoon."

"Surgeon?"

Hazel grabbed the splint from the cabinet, handed it to Syver and went to stand by Niko's head. When Syver fastened the splint, it was going to hurt. He had to get the bones in the right place and secure it. Once the procedure was done, Niko would feel some relief, but there was no way to dull the initial pain of moving the bones. So Hazel would hold his arms, keep him as still as possible, so it went as fast as humanly possible.

"I'm supposed to compete in two months, Prince Syver. That's why I was trying the new trick. The tail whip is complicated, but I can do it. And if I complete it, I will definitely kick Johan off the gold medal stand."

"There are things more important than medals." Niko's mother's whisper was meant to be heard. "You are very talented, but—" She gestured to his broken bone. "This is so much to ask of yourself."

"Why can't you just support me?"

"Niko!"

"Why don't we get the splint on, Hazel?" His interjection didn't surprise her. Medical staff was often seen as background to life. Nursing school had prepped her for the injuries and diseases, but she'd not expected to be a witness to so much family drama.

"Niko, I am going to hold your arms while Dr. Bernhardt places the splint. To keep you as still as possible."

Syver nodded to her. "Niko, this is going to hurt."

"It already hurts."

Niko's mother looked to Hazel, and she could tell the woman wanted to roll her eyes. Teens were full of bravado, but their brains weren't fully formed yet, so long-term consequences were often difficult for them to imagine.

"I know." Syver's voice was patient. The exact right level of understanding and doctor authority. "But when I splint this, it's going to slide the bones back into place, and the splint will hold them there until you can get in to the orthopedic surgeon. Some describe it as fire lighting up your body. There is no way to numb it, so we go as fast as possible."

"If you need to scream, just let it out." Hazel had found that giving patients permission to let loose helped sometimes. She gripped his arms and looked at Syver.

"Ready?"

Niko's face shifted from Syver to his mother before nodding.

Syver splinted his ankle, and the scream made Hazel's ears ring. It took less than two minutes, but Hazel knew Niko would remember those two minutes for the rest of his life.

If this injury didn't make him want to stop his sport, and Hazel saw no indications that it did, then nothing would.

"We're done."

Niko let out a sob as Hazel released her grip on his arms. "I'm still going to complete the tail whip."

"Just make sure you wear a helmet."

Niko's mother's eyes widened. She opened her mouth, then shut it tight.

Syver continued, "The discharge nurse will be in with the papers shortly. And follow up with Dr. Mathias as soon as you can." Then he gestured for Hazel to follow him.

"I think his mother was hoping you'd convince him to give up the sport." Hazel kept her words low as the door closed behind them.

Syver looked at the closed door; there were thoughts running through his mind, but he didn't voice them.

"It is dangerous." She wasn't sure what the right answer was, if she was honest. She'd patched up more sports injuries through her career than just about anything else. But if a hobby made you happy, brought joy into your world, who was to argue it was wrong?

"It'd be nice if family supported the ones they were supposed to love."

A knife slid into her soul. That was commentary on his family, not Niko's. And she understood. If her mother loved her…wanted her, how different would her life be?

But would he be okay if they didn't? If he never got the support he deserved? Once more she worried that she wasn't enough. Her chest was tight; if he had to choose, would he choose her? And if he didn't, what would she do?

"Syver…"

"That sounded wrong."

Because you're speaking of you, not your patient.

"I just mean, this is clearly something that is important to Niko. That should be enough."

"And if he was an adult, I'd agree."

I want your family to support you. Want them to support us. However, I want to be first in your life. Is that too much to ask?

"But he is a child. She is trying to protect him. *That* is her role as his mother."

A role our mothers should have taken more seriously.

Hazel took a deep breath, then quietly added, "This isn't the same situation as yours."

His eyes flashed as he took a step back. "I didn't say it was."

"Syver." They were like two pieces of a whole. She knew his tells. Knew how much he wanted to be part of his family, truly part of it. Falling for her might not make that easier.

Actually, she knew for a fact it would make it more difficult. If he married, the expectation was that he'd marry a princess, or lady or heiress.

Though she figured his brother would prefer if he fell out of the public completely. And his mother seemed to let what his brother wanted go. It wasn't fair, but Syver couldn't seem to see it.

They'd called him back to Fönn because they'd needed his expertise. And the timing of today's missive coupled with the poll showing him as the most loved royal…it was suspect at best.

Deep down, Hazel thought he understood that. But accepting it...that was something different.

Loving her meant slipping further away from the royal expectations. She was not a princess or lady or anything more than a nurse. But she liked who she was. She didn't want him to have to choose, but...

In an ideal world, family loved you, flaws and all. But Syver's "flaws" weren't his.

The thing a person got the least choice over in their entire lives was the status of their birth. One did not choose their parents. Heaven knew, Hazel wouldn't have chosen her mother.

But a person got to choose as an adult who they associated with. And she feared a day was coming when Syver would have to choose, too.

What if he doesn't choose me?

Syver pulled at the collar of his shirt as he stepped into the formal dining room's entrance. Blood pounded in his ears, his heart wanted to jump out of his chest and he wished for at least the hundredth time since setting foot on the palace grounds that he had thought of a way to bring Hazel.

That would have meant standing up to his family. Choosing sides in the explosion that he'd known since he was a teenager was always hovering under the palace floors. A hum of friction that no one acknowledged but had the power to rip everything away from him.

And he wasn't ready for that.

"Your Highness." A man he recognized as part of the security team, but didn't know, offered a curt bow. "I'm Viggo. Arne's replacement."

Only a lifetime of ensuring he didn't react to bad news kept him from responding with an energetic *What?*

Arne had been with the royal family since before he was born. The man was almost an institution within the grounds. Whatever shakeup had happened in his absence must have been epic.

"Congratulations." He offered a palace smile, then stepped

into the dining room. King Erik and his mother sat in their traditional places, and Queen Signe was next to his brother.

Signe sent him a soft smile, but he could see the uncertainty in her eyes. So this was an ambush. One they'd instructed him not to bring Hazel to. And like a fool, he'd listened.

"It's good to see you." His brother nodded and smiled.

Some of Syver's tension released as he met his brother's smile. Erik rarely smiled, a habit he'd picked up from his father. Smiles were treats, rewards, things he'd never earned from King Eirvin.

"It surprised me to get the invitation." May as well acknowledge the elephant in the room. Family dinner was not something the royal family traditionally did.

His brother looked at him, clearly trying to decide Syver's mood. "You left so suddenly I thought a little breathing space might be good for everyone."

"I left after you had your former head of security block my girlfriend from the palace over a lie that your queen could have easily cleared, if you'd been willing to ask."

Erik's head literally bounced back.

He hated the small joy blossoming in his belly. He'd never spoken back to King Eirvin; he'd simply agreed to move abroad. He'd even enjoyed getting away.

Meeting Hazel made all of that worth it.

With Erik, he challenged issues that impacted the hospital, children's health and a few priority projects, but as a rule, he was careful with his words and actions. He never pushed too hard. He wasn't really sure what had come over him tonight, but he was leaning into it.

"Boys." His mother offered him a smile. "You're brothers… remember. Family."

Erik didn't acknowledge their mother's statement, but it sent a small wave of comfort through him.

"Arne was so sure."

"He's always been aloof with me. For reasons I've never understood, but I suspect whatever the bias was…" Syver shrugged; whatever it was, Arne was gone.

"I loved his brother." His mother's voice was so soft, Syver wasn't sure she meant to speak.

"Your father." Her eyes shone with tears that didn't fall. "King Eirvin had him resettled abroad and he passed not long after the King. I am not sure Arne ever forgave me—but he decided to retire and your brother accepted it.

His mother's words stole the wind from Syver's lungs. The mystery of his parentage dropped so casually into the conversation.

"What was his name?" His father, at least genetically, was gone. No hope of knowing him...of finding out if he was wanted.

The room tilted and if there was air, his lungs couldn't find it.

"We aren't here to discuss the past."

"Erik—it's my father."

"A man you never knew."

Syver looked to his mother, saw her brush a tear off her cheek, then take a deep breath.

"The past is gone, Syver. Sit down." She nodded, the mask of the Queen sliding fully into place.

Duty first.

He wanted to argue, but his brain was buzzing as he fell into a chair. What was he supposed to do with information no one wanted to discuss?

"Ms. Simpson."

"Hazel." His mind might race a million miles a minute, but he would not let them other her. He knew the tricks. It was one thing to employ them against him, another to use them on Hazel.

"What are your intentions?"

"Intentions?" Repeating the phrase didn't unmuddle his mind, but it bought him time.

"Yes." Erik shook his head. "As a reminder, marriages of Fönn's royals must be approved by the crown."

Marriage.

He wanted to marry her. Wanted his ring on her finger, but

he'd never believed the crown would approve a union. If there was hope…he'd do nearly anything for it.

Signe turned to look at him. There was hope in her eyes. For Hazel, for herself, for him? He wasn't sure, but it calmed his nerves.

Focus on the future. On Hazel and the family he still had.

"I love her. It's as simple and complicated as that. My future is with her. We are looking for a new flat this weekend. Hers is—"

"Too small for a prince." His mother's voice was firm. It was the same refrain she'd repeated each time she talked to him on the phone.

"Her flat is small, but that isn't the reason we are looking for something new." It was part of it, but he would not add to his mother's dismissal tone. The flat was nice, but it had rented furniture. It wasn't hers or his and she wanted something that was.

Something he should have agreed to the first time she'd asked. Though the way his brother was looking at him, the hope that he might be right, that the crown might offer them a place, seemed possible. That would solve so many things.

Wouldn't it?

"I agree. It looks," Erik tilted his head, clearly weighing his words, "off for a member of the royal family to be living in such a situation. The good news is that I have a solution."

"A solution?" Syver looked from Signe to his mother, but neither met his gaze. The King was in charge, duty first. "Meaning?"

"Meaning I had Protocol find a location that is suitable for you and Ms.—Hazel. It is downtown, a penthouse—you can use furniture from the storehouse, move your bed."

Syver blinked. It was what he'd wanted. But to hear his brother offer it. His voice was hoarse as he bent his head toward the head of the table. "Thank you."

"There will be some functions that we might want to host at your place. With," Erik paused again, "with Hazel."

"Of course." Syver nodded. His heart was close to exploding. His mother smiled, and for the first time in his memory, he felt like a member of the royal family. A full member.

He'd worried this was a meeting to convince him to give up Hazel, something he wasn't willing to do. Instead, he was getting the best of both worlds.

His family was bringing him and Hazel into the fold. If only she was here to hear it, too.

"The penthouse is ready to move into—simply let the staff know what to take out of storage. Once your place is set up, we plan to have a photography spread done, showing the modern royal family."

Pushing for modernization, away from a focus on the aristocracy and their wants, was a goal he'd nearly dropped. Now he and Hazel could do that…together.

"For the next family dinner, I'll bring Hazel."

"I'd love that." His mother reached for his hand as Erik looked away.

Erik motioned for dinner to be served, but he looked unhappy. Like this wasn't what he really wanted. A tinge of worry pierced the back of his mind, but he pushed it away. After a lifetime of trying to belong to his family, really belong, it was happening. And Hazel would be by his side, with his family's blessing.

CHAPTER ELEVEN

"WHAT DO YOU THINK?"

Hazel knew he wanted her to be excited, but as she looked out the penthouse window, her mouth refused to utter any words. A warning bell rang in her soul. She'd ignored them before…and lost everything with Alec. She didn't want to listen to them now, but her body was screaming that she didn't want to live here.

"This place is enormous." Syver exuded over-the-top energy that she couldn't replicate for him.

That was true. It was larger than any flat she'd lived in. "Is the size important to you?"

Syver's face fell as he shook his head. "Not really."

He'd learned about his father and seemed to push away the hurt that reveal caused. She'd tried to discuss it, tried to see if he wanted to broach the subject with his mother. But Syver repeated what he said Erik had said, it was the past.

It was…but an important part. And she worried the approval of his brother was overshadowing everything else.

Syver wanted to believe this was approval. Wanted this to show there was a thawing in the relationship. That the future was bright.

Maybe it was the start of something. Maybe she was just being too sensitive, but she didn't like Syver's mention that there were expectations that the royal family would use this space for photo opportunities.

She'd asked if the royal apartments were used in such a manner. Syver had said, of course, not. Such a quick response with none of the follow-on thought of why their place would have that expectation.

No worry over why this place would be the foundation for the "modern" royal family. No thought his reputation with the people had something to do with it. That it wasn't really Syver they wanted, but the ability to leech off his goodwill.

Syver was popular. Maybe not with his family, but with the people of Fönn. She saw it every day in the hospital. When they walked around the gardens or visited the garden center. He was one of them, truly.

King Erik could not make the same claim. In fact, she'd heard more than one rumble it might be better if Fönn's monarchy had less control. That in this day and age, having a powerful king made little sense.

Something Hazel privately agreed with.

Syver held far more power than his brother...but she didn't think he realized it. *Or he doesn't want to.*

"You're picking at your thumb."

Hazel pushed her hands into her pockets. Her nail beds were healthier than they'd been in years, but there was an undercurrent of worry she couldn't quite force herself to ignore.

The same feeling she got the last time she saw her mother and when she broke up with Alec. A feeling that she was about to be cast out. She'd thrown walls around her heart when she'd felt the end coming with Alec. She hadn't expected the raid, but it was her naivete that had broken her, not her love for the con man. Her childhood had created nearly impenetrable barriers with her mother...once she'd finally announced her boundaries and stuck to them.

She had no protections with Syver.

Because I don't need them.

She wanted to believe that inner voice. Wanted to believe that this penthouse was a gift with no strings attached. That if they turned this down, life could be happy.

That there wouldn't always be the need to worry about what the palace thought.

"What if I want to keep looking?" She pursed her lips as Syver's mouth opened then closed with no words coming out.

"We found a few other places." The cottage she'd found, the one she loved, was perfect for them. It gave them privacy, a little more room. Their own place.

Something truly theirs.

"None were as nice as this, though, right?"

His challenge surprised her. Crossing her arms, she shrugged. "I guess that depends. As nice as this is aesthetically, no, but the other ones don't come with strings attached. Which I think makes them nicer."

"That isn't fair." Now it was Syver burying his hands in his pockets.

Maybe it wasn't, but it didn't make it less true. "Syver, we don't have to choose this place. Can we at least look at some others? Maybe you'll fall in love with one of them."

He bit his bottom lip and looked around the penthouse. "I'm not sure Erik will understand if we pick another place. I don't…"

She waited for him to finish the sentence, but when he didn't, she guessed at the end. "You don't want to make him angry."

"I've never been asked to do anything other than help re-build the medical infrastructure. And even my participation in that is limited to the crumbs he gives me."

"And you've done a fantastic job, even with the crumbs, as you say."

What would happen if he just stepped out as Syver, no title to his name? People without titles worked on important causes all the time. He could make even more of a difference. He could.

"The children's hospital will one day be one of the best in the world. I do not doubt that." His work in the medical field was an impressive accomplishment, one he'd earned on his own!

"For once, I feel like it's possible for me to be part of the family. I got invited to dinner, and he's offering this and hosting events here."

"What happens if you upset him? Or I do?"

Syver reached for her hands, and she let him take them, needing the connection. They were so close to a fight, one she didn't want to have, but feared might be inevitable.

"We aren't going to upset him."

That didn't answer her question.

"What if we do? What is the punishment? Is it banishment?" She laughed, but the sound died in her throat as she looked at him.

"Syver…"

"A prince needs permission to marry."

"Only if he wants a royal wedding." She remembered the words, too. And she wanted to marry him, wanted him by her side forever. But she didn't need or want a royal wedding.

But getting married without permission would cut him off forever. Her heart clenched. So they'd lived together forever, if necessary. She'd made peace with that already. She loved him. A marriage certificate didn't change that.

"We've been together for less than two months. We can worry after marriage agreements and permissions in a year or so."

"Hazel—"

"Syver." She couldn't stop the interruption. This flat was beautiful. Made for the camera, even, but she couldn't agree to it. At least not right away. "Can we just look at a few other places? Please." If they took this option, they'd live in grandeur. But the consequences…they might not survive them.

"Hazel showed me the cabin you were looking at yesterday. If you don't snap it up, Laura and I might swoop in." Dr. Lindgren, the pediatric cardiologist, grinned as he passed Syver some paperwork to sign.

Syver made a noncommittal noise. He knew exactly which place Dr. Lindgren was talking about. A small place, at least compared to the penthouse his brother was offering. The cabin overlooked the sea. It had a greenhouse, and three bedrooms that were warmed by the sun. It was all wood and felt like walking into a faery cottage.

It fit Hazel perfectly. She loved it, but it wasn't the penthouse. Choosing it would be seen as a direct statement against Erik. Maybe that wasn't fair. It was their home, but Syver had played this game his entire life. He understood the rules.

Choosing the cottage would cut his ties to the royal family. The only family he had left.

Maybe forever. He wasn't ready for that.

Moving out was the correct choice. Hazel was right about that. The penthouse was a gift; sure there were strings attached to it. That was life in the royal family, and it wasn't like his family was the only one that attached strings to things.

It was human nature.

"Hazel loves it."

Dr. Lindgren laughed. "Can I give you some free advice from a man that's been married for almost three decades?"

He didn't wait for Syver's approval. "If it makes the woman you love happy, it's the right choice. I would be happy in a hole in the ground if that was what Laura chose."

"Even if it meant angering your family." He hadn't meant for those words to escape his soul.

Dr. Lindgren looked at him, really looked at him, and Syver had a difficult time not shuffling his feet as the older man's eyes took him in.

"Family is important."

Exactly.

Before Syver could agree, Dr. Lindgren added, "But family is what you make it. It doesn't always include those that society says it should. Love is worth risking it all."

It was a nice thought, but life was more complicated than that. His mother hadn't chosen romantic love. His father, a man gone before Syver even knew he'd existed, loved his mother. And she'd chosen duty. The royal family. That was a form of love, too.

Dr. Lindgren looked at his wrist, took in the time and

raised a hand. "Laura's expecting me for dinner. Good night, Dr. Bernhardt."

"Night." He turned and saw Hazel walking up the hallway.

Her quick steps and the deep worry line on her forehead set off warning bells in his brain. He loved her, but he could see the fires of concern in her mind, too. The little tells that often took months, or even years, for partners to recognize, were visible to each of them even though they'd been together less than two months.

"We've got a sixteen-year-old in Room Three. Lars is presenting with anemia and has a history of acute lymphoblastic leukemia. He's been in remission nine years."

Syver blew out a breath. Acute lymphoblastic leukemia, commonly called ALL, was considered the most survivable childhood cancer. It had a five-year survival rate of over ninety percent.

But cancer, no matter the survival rate, was always terrifying.

"Who is his oncologist?"

"Said the doctor emigrated seven years ago. He'd been in remission for three years then, his mother should have gotten another, but..."

Hazel shrugged and looked at the floor. It was a story they heard all too often, should have followed up, meant to follow up, then life got in the way. It seemed fine until it didn't.

"He's scared."

"I bet." Syver took a deep breath. There was little they could do in the emergency room. The point of the place was stabilization and moving on, and the terror seeping through the teen's veins, only hearing the words *cancer-free* could clear that.

Words Syver could not utter.

"All right, let me check him and we'll see if he needs to stay for observation or if I can discharge him to see Dr. Holm."

"Meg already texted her. I guess they worked at the same place in Maine. When Dr. Holm returned home, she convinced Meg to come, too."

Syver nodded as he took in the information in Lars's chart.

He was tired, had some aches in his bones and was anemic. All symptoms he presented with when he had cancer the first time.

However, those symptoms didn't mean his cancer had returned. The aches and tiredness were symptoms of anemia. A diagnosis with a range of causes.

"Before you go in…" Hazel hesitated, looked to the room then back at Syver, "There is some family drama. Not sure what kind, but the mum's been on the phone. Some heated words and tears were exchanged."

It wasn't an uncommon theme. Emergencies brought out a range of emotions, even in families that weren't experiencing any other crisis moments. And more families than people wanted to admit were in the middle of a crisis.

"Thanks for the heads-up." Syver raised his hand. "Shall we?"

Hazel fell into step beside him and, even with the ripple of tension between them, Syver's spirit raised. He and Hazel together. This was his happy place.

"Good evening, Lars. I'm—"

"Prince Syver." Lars smiled, though it wasn't bright. "I've always wanted to meet you. Though not this way."

Syver reached out a hand, and Lars shook it. "I'd rather our greeting was in another location, too. Where is your mum?"

"Fighting with my aunt…like usual." Lars's cheeks colored, and he looked at the floor. "They own a bakery, inherited after my nan passed a few years ago. They are always arguing about the direction of the place."

Syver looked at the door, then cleared his throat. Fighting with your sister while your son was in hospital was not a choice he'd make, but his focus was on Lars.

"I'll see if I can track her down." Hazel headed back through the door.

"What's the palace like?" Lars's feet kicked the air as Syver pulled his stethoscope from his pocket.

Lonely was the most accurate description, but not what people wanted to hear. "Busy. There is always something going on." Which was also true.

"But we aren't here to talk about the palace." Syver kept his voice light, but Lars still grimaced.

"Nope. We're here to talk cancer." He laughed, but it quickly turned into a sob.

"We're here because of your anemia, which can happen without a reemergence of your cancer." It was possible his cancer was back, more possible than Syver wanted to admit, given his medical history. But it could be something else causing it, too.

"Tell me your symptoms."

Holding up his fingers, Lars started ticking off, "One, I'm tired. Two, I'm pale. Three, my stomach hurts after I eat."

"Wait, your stomach hurts?"

"Yeah. It started a few weeks ago—before that I figured the tiredness was because I was studying for exams. I want to be a doctor, which means I need high marks for university. I remember the stomach pains from last time. I'd eat something and I couldn't keep it down. I lost so much weight."

"But you were on chemo?"

"Right." Lars sighed. "Not looking forward to that again."

Lars didn't understand what Syver was saying, but that was all right. If he was right, the cause for the anemia, while serious, likely wasn't a cancer recurrence.

"Do you eat tuna or salmon?" He knew he was on the right track by the grimace passing over Lars's features.

"Not anymore. An hour or so after I eat them—"

"Your stomach burns."

"Yeah." Lars blinked and leaned back in the observation chair. "How did you know?"

"Medical school." Syver winked and then requested a gastric consult for Lars. "If I'm right, you still need to see Dr. Holm, our oncologist, to get back on your annual checkup schedule, but you also need to see our gastroenterologist. The anemia could be because of a peptic ulcer."

"Found your mum." Hazel's cheeks were red, and she was having a bit of trouble catching her breath. "She'll be in shortly."

Had she chased the woman down?

"Good." Syver turned his attention back to Lars. "I'm going to chat with your mother until you see the gastroenterologist. She'll need to adjust your diet. No fatty foods, and you need to make a list of any foods that trigger the pain. The anemia is likely because the ulcer is bleeding."

"It's weird to be happy about that." Lars covered his mouth with his hand and his shoulders shook. "I've been prepping… and…"

"And worrying. That is completely normal." Hazel stepped to the side of the observation chair and patted Lars's shoulder.

Syver made eye contact with her, and she nodded. She'd stay with Lars while he talked to the mother.

Stepping into the hall, he nearly bumped into a tiny dark-haired woman who was furiously typing away on her phone.

"Excuse me," Syver started, but she waved a hand at him. He waited a moment, then cleared his throat. "Are you Lars's mother?"

"Yes. I just need to send one more text to my sister. The woman is insisting on instituting some new pastry with the supply chain the way it is right now. But she is the oldest and thinks she knows best. Like the place would even be the spot it is without my marketing skills—on top of baking most mornings, too."

"I'm sure that is frustrating, but Lars."

"Has been through this before, Doctor."

The cold statement made him want to slap the phone out of the woman's hand. He was pretty sure her son had a peptic ulcer, something less serious than cancer, but still serious. And she was fighting over text!

"I don't think his cancer is back."

"So an overreaction."

"Put the phone down and listen to me." He saw one nurse turn his head, but Syver didn't look away from Lars's mother.

Looking up from the phone, she opened her mouth, likely to yell at him, then realized who he was. Sometimes being a royal doctor had its perks.

"Prince Syver."

"At the hospital, I prefer Dr. Bernhardt, but yes."

"Lars will be so happy to meet you. He wants to be a doctor."

"He mentioned that." Syver took a breath, trying to grant his patient's mother some grace. He didn't know what the argument with the sister was over and honestly didn't care. His focus, and hers, for the moment at least, needed to be Lars.

"The good news is that I think the anemia is the result of an ulcer. I am going to send you home with some recipes that will help balance his stomach acids until the gastroenterologist can fit him into her schedule."

Syver took a breath but didn't want to wait for her to say something or look back at her phone. "I will set up a consult with Dr. Holm, our oncologist, as well. Lars needs to be keeping up with his regular checkups."

"Thank you for the information."

Hazel slid from the room. "Lars was hoping you'd wait with him while Dr. Bernhardt fills out the discharge papers."

Her cell dinged, and it took all his patience not to roll his eyes as she looked at the text.

"Never go into business with the family. It always gets messy." She tapped a quick reply, then pushed through the door.

"I gave Lars my email address." Hazel whispered as they stepped away from the door. "I told him I'd forward questions about medical school and the process to you."

"You could have given him mine, Hazel."

"Syver, you are a prince. I am not dropping your email into a teenager's hands, or anyone else's, for that matter. And if his mother got it. That family business sounds like a nightmare."

"All family businesses have their difficulties." Syver tapped out a few things on the tablet that forwarded his consult requests and initiated the discharge papers with directions for a bland diet.

"Sometimes the best thing to do is drop the family." Hazel let out a sigh and leaned against the wall.

"You don't mean that."

The green in her eyes flashed under the fluorescents. "I do. You are not required to keep toxic people in your life. Cutting my mum off was best for my mental health—I don't regret having no contact with her. I waited too long to see the signs, but they were there and I acted. It was the right move."

The look he'd seen in her eyes was back. The challenge, the acceptance, the statement that if she'd done it so could he.

"Hazel." Meg raised a hand as she walked over. "We've got a set of twins in triage with coins up their noses. Help me with the extraction?"

"And that's my cue." Hazel hit his hip and wandered off.

Syver watched her, his blood cold. He knew her mother hadn't wanted her. Knew their relationship wasn't ideal, but the idea of cutting off family, of going without contact. What if she asked him to do that with his family?

She wanted to…he was nearly certain.

He was overreacting. He was tired; the first night on night shift always took adjustments.

She'd recommended he move out of the palace. But she was the one hesitating on the penthouse. Hesitating on his family.

The royal family was far from perfect. He understood that. But cutting his family off wasn't an option. It simply wasn't.

And Hazel isn't asking me to.

Not yet.

CHAPTER TWELVE

"ERIK CALLED."

Hazel didn't put a smile on her face as she looked up from the oven. "Asking after the penthouse again?"

Why was the King so insistent on them taking that offer?

Syver wanted to believe that by him stepping away from the palace, his brother was finally seeing his worth. Hazel's view differed.

She thought the royal family knew his worth. That was the problem. The people liked Syver. He worked among them, treated their children, offered smiles and everyday greetings.

That wasn't possible for the King and Queen, at least to the extent that it was for Syver. They wanted to use his connections. Give the royal family a facelift. Which would be fine if they wanted the changes to be more than surface level.

If Syver was the face of modernization, fine. But if he was simply a bright Band-Aid to hide the rot...

She'd been that Band-Aid once. She hadn't realized it with Alec, even though the signs were obvious once she stepped away. The signs she'd ignored. The pretty girlfriend who worked in healthcare...he couldn't be scamming the health facilities.

Hazel had no interest in playing that game again. Even though she worried she was ignoring signs again.

She wanted Syver to have a genuine family. One that loved him for him, not for what he could bring them. She could be that. She was that.

"Are you going to tell me what he wanted?" The hesitation

bothered her. Their relationship was great, except for the tension regarding the royal family. Tension she wasn't sure how to alleviate. Tension that was pushing its way into all aspects of their lives lately.

You are dating a prince.

"He says he has a surprise for us. At the penthouse."

"I still like the cottage better." She shook her head, trying to clear the complaint out. This was an ongoing discussion, but not the point of this conversation.

She took a moment, then asked her question, doing her best to hide the agitation. "What is the surprise?"

"If he'd told me that, it wouldn't be much of a surprise."

Well, that was true.

His arms wrapped around her; his lips pressed against her neck. "He invited both of us."

Leaning against him, Hazel pulled his warmth to her. This was her safe space. Wrapped in his arms, it felt like they could tackle anything...but his family.

She wanted to be as excited as he was. Wanted to see the positives, but Syver was grasping at bread crumbs. They were a couple. Why shouldn't she just be included? That was the expectation, not a prize to be won.

She bit back the words, but they tore through her soul.

"When are we supposed to go?" She brushed her lips against his. If only the connection they had wasn't hiding behind their individual wants...and fears, now.

It had seemed so easy. So natural for them to slip from friends to lovers. They'd been like one. Now, though, they were drifting. They both knew it, but how did they fix it?

And should I?

Her soul shook at that thought. Syver was her person; she didn't doubt that. But she wasn't sure it was enough. She'd been so burned by Alec. She wouldn't do that again.

"Now...well, as soon as we get dressed."

Hazel looked at her overalls and bit back the retort that her comfy overalls were nice enough for the cottage. This was important to him. "I might need to *invest* in a few more nice clothes."

She meant the words to sound funny, but Hazel knew the exasperation was obvious, too. She didn't have the budget, or inclination, to spend money on "royally appropriate" clothes.

"I can always help if you need it."

"I don't." The words came out too fast, and she hated the flinch passing over Syver's face. "I just mean, I..."

Syver stepped in front of her. "I love you."

A sob caught in the back of her throat. It was exactly what she needed to hear. "I love you, too." They'd get through this tension, figure out their place in the royal family together. "We're a team, right?"

"Of course." Syver kissed the top of her head. "And if you want to wear the overalls, do it. I love anything on you, though I love you in nothing more!"

She unhooked the straps of her overalls. "We could always say it took us a while to get dressed."

"You are too tempting!" His lips trailed down her throat and for a moment, the world, its problems and all their expectations slipped away.

Syver's cell dinged for the fourth time as they approached the parking garage for the penthouse. "Are you sure you don't want me to check that?" He'd rebuffed her previous attempts, probably because it was the King, or the protocol office or something.

She'd considered texting Signe, asking if there was an issue she should know about. She and the Queen were getting on well, but she didn't want to pull Signe into any drama. The woman was making the best of the life she had, and was seven months pregnant. She didn't need any additional worries.

"I'm sure Erik just wants to know where we are."

"Maybe the delay wasn't the best idea."

Syver reached for her fingers, pulled them to his lips, then pressed a kiss to her palm. "I wouldn't change that delay for a second. Though I don't feel like explaining it to my brother either."

"Signe is pregnant—I suspect he'd understand."

"Erik only understands the crown." Syver's words were so soft, she wasn't sure he'd meant to speak them. "We're here, now. So he'll see us shortly."

Syver leaned over, kissed her cheek, then sighed. "I appreciate you agreeing to this. I promise, we are not committing to the penthouse, at least not today."

She'd scheduled another showing for the cottage. A place she figured was only still on the market because it was her and Syver looking. The Realtor had called in a favor to put it on hold while they discussed it, and the seller had agreed. Something they couldn't continue to do. It wasn't fair.

Syver slid a key card into the elevator, and the option for the penthouse lit up. Security was nice, but they worked with the public every day. And the residents of Fönn had given them space in their private lives.

Hazel didn't want to live in a gated community or in a high-rise where she had to have a special key card to gain access. She wanted to live some place that was theirs. A place no one could yank away.

A place where they didn't have to perform. A place where she wouldn't worry about expectations, if she was meeting them, or look for signs of something going wrong. No place the palace offered could ever give her that.

The doors of the elevator opened, and camera flashes immediately started.

"What!"

"Syver!" King Erik's voice sounded over the clicks.

Syver dipped his head toward hers, an act that she was sure would look lovely when the photographers were going over the snaps later. "Smile—act like we knew."

His breath was warm against her ear as he slid his arm around her waist.

Hazel's bottom lip was shaking. She wanted to scream, wanted to hit the buttons on the elevator and return to the garage. Go back to her little flat, get into her overalls or comfy yoga pants and pretend they'd told Erik they needed more details, or they weren't showing up.

Instead, her feet followed Syver as he moved toward the King. Someone had furnished the place. There were even a few pictures of them together at the baby shower.

God, it looked like they already lived here.

"We're here to announce, publicly, Prince Syver's relationship with Ms. Hazel Simpson. The palace is thrilled these two are happy and moving into this penthouse. Prince Syver's work at the hospital has kept him from participating in many royal engagements."

Syver stiffened as the lie fell from his brother's lips. He took part in everything asked of him. The royal family just hadn't asked much of him.

"However," Erik raised his arm, gesturing in a rehearsed way, that looked off. Like he was preparing to toast Syver. Had he rehearsed this speech with a champagne glass that he was now missing? "On my mother's suggestion, I plan to make him the face of my health and family initiatives."

They'd kept the imposter heir away, but now that he was more popular than his brother, now that the people of Fönn showed Syver preference, he was important.

It wouldn't last.

"And of course, we plan to have Ms. Simpson by his side." Erik met her gaze, daring her to argue.

The words clawed at her throat, ached to escape as she stared at the man who was using his brother, a man who only wanted to be part of his family.

Then he looked at his brother. "I suspect we'll be having a royal wedding soon."

A royal wedding. The thing Syver had never expected to get. Erik had given the man she loved everything he thought he wanted.

But it wasn't a genuine offer.

More camera flashes went off as questions spilled from the lips of all the gathered journalists.

"Syver." She wasn't sure he could hear her quiet plea, but she wanted away from here. The crown had trapped them.

The hint about the royal wedding was as good as a proposal. And none of it was for them.

Her eyes met his, and her heart sank. Syver's face was brilliant. He was getting what he wanted, finally. The imposter Prince made real by the brother who'd used him but never made him family.

And he could yank it all away if Syver didn't perform. If she didn't perform. "Syver, we have to talk now." The words were quiet, but she saw the female journalist to her side raise a brow.

"Syver." She grabbed his hand. "Please."

"I think my love is a little overstimulated. If you'll give us one moment."

Erik's face fell for an instant before the King threw a pleasant mask back on. "Ms. Simpson isn't quite used to this. But she will be."

They moved to the master bedroom, and Hazel wasn't shocked to find it empty. "So the palace only decorated the public areas for this ambush."

"I know it feels like an ambush, but sweetheart, Erik is offering me," Syver shook his head, "offering us a place, an actual place, in the royal family."

"Is he?" Hazel crossed her arms as she moved to look out the window. "Because weeks ago, he held us hostage in the palace because he thought I spread information about the Queen. Ignored us completely when you moved out. Then that stupid poll came out showing that you are the most popular royal, Syver…"

He had to see this, he had to, for what it was. A ploy to make sure the King controlled the narrative. He was giving Syver what he wanted, but it wasn't real, if it wasn't honest.

"He can take this away as soon as his image is rehabbed, or if you do something wrong, or if I do. We don't need this."

"I need my family."

What am I?

Pain echoed across her thumb as blood trickled into her

palm. She'd pulled at the skin, not realizing how tender she'd made the flesh.

"They need you. But you don't need them. You don't." He was owed more than an ambush, more than a sliver of acceptance.

"I'm never going to cut my family off, Hazel. Yes, we have our differences, but they are my family. I know you did it, but I can't. I won't give up on them."

Words hurt. She'd always known that, but she'd never thought they could break her. "Is that what you think I did? You think I gave up on my mother?"

"If she reached out tonight, would you take her call?"

"No." It was the truth. If her mother reached out now, it would be because of Syver. Not for her.

His jaw clenched as her truth landed between them. "Sometimes you have to look past the failures of others. Meet them where they are. Not everyone can be perfect. I choose to look past their faults, to accept them for who they are. Even if they aren't what I want them to be."

She'd made each of those excuses once, too. Tried so hard to believe that she'd find a way to be enough for her mum. Maybe marrying a prince would do it. But if the only reason her mother wanted her was because of who she was dating or married to…well, Hazel was enough without that.

"I choose me. Maybe that is selfish, but I tried my entire life to be what she wanted, whatever that was. An outstanding student, a nurse, a woman living with a wealthy man. Nothing was good enough."

She held up her hand. She needed to get these words out before her heart finished shattering. "If she wanted me, *for me*, she could have me now. If she reached out, and I believed she wanted me. Just me. It would heal a torn part of my heart that will never feel full without her."

"And you think Erik doesn't want me for me?"

Hazel could see the hurt. And the determination. This was what he wanted. Pain ripped through her soul.

She'd seen all the signs this time. Knew he wanted his family most, and she'd overlooked them. Hoping that his family might give him what he wanted. But it was Syver doing the bending…and it always would be.

She took a deep breath, took in his face, reached for his hands, knowing it was the last time she'd hold them. She wanted a Pause button, a Rewind machine that let her go back to this afternoon. Relish his touch.

If she'd known it was his last, she'd have memorized every soft kiss, every brush of his tongue, every touch. "What I know is that I love you, for you." She put her hand on his chest, knowing the tears were streaming down her cheeks.

"But I also know that isn't enough. You want…" She gestured to the closed door and the illusion of acceptance that was behind it. "You want his attention, acceptance. I can't fill that hole for you.

"I won't have my home or my job threatened because I don't follow a script. He just basically announced our engagement—you haven't asked me—we haven't talked about it. Not seriously. Syver…"

"I mean, I love you. He's just putting the royal stamp of approval on us."

And that was the issue. The heart of all the tension. He needed the stamp, and it was the last thing she wanted.

Her eyes slid to the door, then back to him. "I can't walk this path with you, but I hope it is everything you want it to be."

"Hazel."

Lifting on her tiptoes, she pressed her lips to his, then pulled away.

"Good luck, Prince Syver."

She was gone. And yet everyone had continued on. Acting like nothing was wrong. That this was just another royal engagement, another random party or announcement made by the palace.

It was like the reporters hadn't seen Hazel step out of the unfurnished bedroom, tears streaming down her face, head held high. Hadn't asked her questions she refused to answer as she left. Even to the most untrained eye, it was obvious they'd fought.

Fought.

That word indicated there was a chance. A way to patch things up. He'd chosen his family. Made it clear he wouldn't lose them. Made it clear he *couldn't* lose them.

So he'd lost her.

The world had shifted forever.

Yet, the night moved on.

Unlike Syver, Erik's tongue wasn't tied. He'd changed the topic, made an excuse for Hazel, like he knew her. Transitioned the night to the palace's priorities. Because he was the King, the audience he'd used for the "surprise" followed his lead.

Which was good, since there was no way to vocalize all Syver's thoughts. No descriptors to place on the magnitude of hurts, nothing but mental anguish at the breaking of his soul.

Reporters weren't owed that coverage.

"I think that went well."

Syver couldn't stop the hurt chuckle from breaking through. "Well? Well! You ambushed my girlfriend and I."

"Ambush is such a petty word. You and Hazel were not moving fast enough. You moved out of the palace almost a month ago. I offered you this place two weeks ago."

Just after the poll came out.

Hazel's voice echoed in his mind. And the voice wasn't wrong. The timing was suspect.

"It was a nice offer. I appreciated the palace thinking of me." *Remembering me, choosing something for me.*

Erik rolled his eyes to the ceiling before wandering to the kitchen and grabbing water from the fridge. "Living in a little place, it looks bad. Mother agrees."

He knew their mother agreed, but that didn't make it true. "It is not that small." It was a nice flat. They just needed something bigger, something that was theirs.

Ours.

His heart broke as he looked around the penthouse. It was

nice, better than nice. It was elegant, with lots of lights for plants…plants Hazel would never bring here.

"The point is, the palace needed action."

"Action?"

Erik ignored the interruption. "We'll plan a wedding in, say, December? Holiday themes are always brilliant."

"Wedding?" Syver shook his head. "How can you possibly think the woman who walked out of here in tears will meet me at the altar under your order?"

Only the fury building in his chest allowed those heart-breaking words to escape. Hazel would not meet him at the altar. Erik had seen to that.

He'd made his choice. His family. He'd serve as the head of Erik's health and family initiatives. Two things incredibly close to his heart, but there'd be no wedding.

Is it worth it?

Why was his brain offering that question now? He'd made his choice. The palace was finally seeking a place for him. Bringing him into the royal family, truly.

"A hissy fit." Erik shrugged. "Signe's had them before, too."

Hissy fit. It was a good thing Hazel wasn't here to hear the words. She'd launch into him. And Syver almost wished he'd get to see it.

"I have things I need to do tonight, Erik." Like gather his things from Hazel's, try to move forward with the life he'd chosen. Make peace with his choice. "But before I leave, I want to run a few things by you regarding the health initiative."

"Mother suggested you, but you were my choice. It's yours to run."

My choice.

Warmth flooded his system. He was his brother's choice. Words he'd never said, likely never thought. Syver was right; his family could change. Could accept him.

"That's good to hear. We need to focus on recruiting medical professionals. Many professionals that left during King Eirvin's reign—"

"Father did his best."

Erik's interruption didn't surprise Syver, but he would not react either. King Eirvin hadn't focused on all of his subjects. He'd reserved his kindness, his affection and his favorable decisions on those he liked best. Those with access to stroke his ego, to make him feel big. Something most of Fönn had no opportunity to do.

Whether his brother wanted to admit it or not, the former King's focus on the aristocracy had driven many people to other opportunities. Students seeking to study abroad rarely returned. It was a deficit he wanted rectified.

But that was not an argument he wanted to have this evening.

"If I can convince doctors, nurses, techs to return, maybe other professions will follow, too." That was the easiest initiative.

"Do what you need to do. I don't need to be involved."

"Don't you want to be?"

Erik pulled his phone from his pocket and sighed as he flipped through a few messages.

Syver's stomach rumbled as he watched his brother. The health initiative was near and dear to his heart. He'd lobbied for control, or at least input, since the moment he landed on Fönn. His brother had finally chosen him.

But what if he'd only chosen him to keep him close now that he was pulling away? Syver had expected to be an integral part of the conversation for years, only to be rebuffed. What if he'd never been allowed close because Erik didn't want him around, even for projects he didn't care about?

Those were poisonous thoughts…

Only if they aren't true.

He needed to focus. Tonight was a lot. Too much, but right now, he needed to focus on what he had, not what he'd lost.

"As far as the family initiative…" His tongue felt like it was plastered to the roof of his mouth. What did he know of family? He'd lived apart from his, metaphorically, if not physically, for most of his life.

Children needed secure environments. Needed to know their needs, physical and emotional, were met. If they weren't…

If they weren't…well, many people ended up in a cycle of chasing admiration. Doing their best to make their families happy without ever gaining success. The trauma produced often lasted a lifetime.

If she wanted me, for me, she could have me now.

Hazel's words echoed in his mind. She'd been born in conditions so opposite from his. Her life growing up had produced trauma, knowing she was unwanted.

Unwanted…

Being born with a literal silver spoon in your mouth didn't protect you from that. Class didn't matter if your family didn't want you.

"Did you offer this flat because the poll showed I was more popular than you?" It wasn't the conversation they were meant to have, but the words refused to stay buried.

"What does that have to do with the family initiative?"

That wasn't a refusal. Redirection was a skill they learned just out of the cradle at the palace. Get asked something uncomfortable, redirect. Usually the person won't even notice.

"Nothing, and everything, if you think on it. Our family isn't exactly functional."

His brother laughed. Laughed.

The sound was so cruel after everything he'd done for the royal family. He'd bent himself into their mold—and now, now his brother, his king, was laughing. "It's not a joke."

"Of course it is. Syver, you aren't even royal. Or at least you shouldn't be. If Mum had had more control—"

How long did this argument have to play out? Erik was just over forty, and Syver would turn thirty-five this year. This family history did not need rehashing. It was buried, in more than one way.

"There is enough blame to lie at both of our parents' feet, but I never asked for this. The thing you control least in this life is who you are born to."

"You're right. You've done nothing. You weren't in charge of anything. You work for a living. *You* left the damn country!"

Sent away…not left. Syver wasn't dragging those semantics into the argument.

"But the country loves you best. Explain that!" Patches of red coated Erik's face and water spilled across the counter as he slammed the bottle down.

The fury on Erik's face tore the mental cushions Syver had always placed around his family. The cushions that let the mean, cruel, insensitive and terrible things bounce off him. Let him take the hits they'd delivered.

The dam broke. The cord severed…just like Hazel said her relationship with her mother was. He'd been willfully blind.

"So all of this," he gestured to the penthouse, to the documents Erik had held up earlier showing he was in charge of the health initiatives, "it's because I was the most popular royal in some stupid poll?"

"Those polls matter, Syver. If the royal family isn't popular…"

Syver waited for Erik to fill in the blank space of his statement, but he just fumed.

The quiet tore through the flat. "This isn't the age of executing unpopular royals. The problem is the crown hasn't acted for the everyday people in years. If ever."

"How dare you!"

Syver shrugged, the chains he'd wrapped around his controlled responses dropping away.

"It would take so little to please people. Focus on the health initiatives, the emigration issues, family, poverty—you could bring so much aid to those areas. Issues the people care about, issues I've championed without the royal family's support.

"That's why I'm liked. Because I care. Not for the gain, just because it is the right choice."

"And that popularity is why we offered you this chance."

We…not I. My mother is choosing duty. Indirectly, not that it matters.

Duty would always come first. Hazel was right. Though

part of him had known that hours ago. Weeks ago…his whole life. He just hadn't wanted to admit it.

"If I don't perform the way you want, what happens to the penthouse?"

It didn't matter; he would never live here. But he needed to know just how blind he'd been.

"Why wouldn't you perform?"

That was a punch in the gut.

Erik didn't even consider it a possibility that he wouldn't fall in line. That he wouldn't jump at this chance.

He'd always done what was asked of him. Even when it hadn't gotten him any affection, any love. He'd stayed in London, he'd stayed out of the way in the palace, kept himself out of the spotlight. And none of it had ever been enough.

Looking at his brother, he saw their similarities. They had their mother's bright blue eyes, her full lips, but Erik bore the broad nose of his father. And his personality was King Eirvin's, too. Whether that was because he was in his father's shadow, because of genetics or a combination of the two, Syver didn't know.

They bore some of the same DNA. But genetic material did not make a family.

"I have no intention of performing. No intention of acting the part anymore." The words were freeing. His body was light as he let go of what he'd wanted for so long.

"Syver!" Another way Erik and his father were similar. But the sharp tone, hovering on disappointment, no longer made his insides curdle. "Walk out that door, and I will strip your title from you. Strip your family. Mum will stand by the royal family."

She would. He knew that, and it didn't change his mind.

Syver looked at his brother and sighed. "You can't strip something I never truly had."

Erik opened his mouth, but no words left, and Syver wasn't waiting any longer.

He was free. Something he should have been years ago. Better late than never.

"Good night, Your Royal Highness."

CHAPTER THIRTEEN

THE WORLD HAD lost its color. Rationally, Hazel knew it wasn't true, but her entire body ached as she stepped through Meg's front door. She'd walked from the penthouse suite, wandered through darkened gardens for hours before finally texting and asking Meg if she'd come get her and let her crash on her sofa.

At some point, Syver was going to come back to their flat, and she was too cowardly to see him tonight.

"You going to tell me what's going on?"

Hazel shook her head. Even if she wanted to, she wasn't sure she could get the words out.

After losing her home, her career, her country following Alec's crimes, she'd sworn she'd never let others decide her destiny. Promised herself she'd look for any indication she was in danger of losing her heart, of having her life turned upside down.

Falling in love with royalty wasn't in her plans. But she'd done it and lost at love again.

Her body was hollow.

She'd made the right choice, hadn't she? Syver wanted to impress his brother, wanted to belong.

Was that so bad?

She was not traveling that path. She'd made excuses before. Hung on and lost everything.

Except it felt like she'd lost more than everything this time. What was a home, a career, even a country compared to her losing her heart?

"Tea?"

Hazel nodded as she fell onto Meg's sofa. The overstuffed blue couch enveloped her as she pulled into herself as much as possible.

"I only have green tea." Meg passed her the mug. "Probably should have mentioned that."

"It's fine, Meg." Green tea might not be her favorite, but at the moment she was looking for warmth. Fönn was chilly at night, but Hazel didn't think she'd ever feel warm again.

"My fiancé is out tonight."

Hazel flinched at the term fiancé. She'd thought she and Syver would meet at the altar. Not with the royal blessing, but just as themselves. One day.

They'd not discussed it, but it felt like that was where it was heading. Hell, even the palace had seen it.

A Christmas wedding.

She didn't want to make the palace happy, but being married to Syver by the end of the year… Her bottom lip trembled, and she lifted the mug to her lips, knowing the tears were going to spill over again.

"Did I ever tell you why I came to Fönn?" Meg crossed her legs and continued before Hazel could offer anything.

"My ex-fiancé left me at the altar. Literally. I was standing in my poofy white dress with wilted roses looking at a door I knew he wouldn't walk through."

Hazel blinked, not sure what to say. Meg was the happiest person she knew. And thrilled to be engaged—even though she'd clearly done it once before to tragedy.

"Yet, you're marrying Lev."

"*Yet*, I'm marrying Lev." She held up her hand, admiring her ring. "I ran from Maine—I mean, I flew, but…well, you know. I had no plans to find love again. In fact, when Lev asked me on a date, I turned him down. Told him I wasn't interested in dating, period. And he told me to let him know when I changed my mind.

"No pressure, no additional asking me out. Nothing. He was just there. And I realized that if I let fear drive my future, I'd never find happiness. Not really."

"Fear can keep you safe." Hazel closed her eyes, hating the words she'd said, but hearing the truth in them, too. She hadn't listened to her gut before…and it had cost her everything. "The royal family…"

"Is a bit much." Meg winked. "But Syver is different. It's why everyone likes him."

"Everyone does." With a few exceptions. His family tolerated him, and she…her feelings were much deeper than admiration.

"He's still processing his family," Meg offered.

Hazel felt her eyes widen at Meg's words. "What…? Why…? Um…" It wasn't her place to talk about Syver's family, or how much he wanted them to love him. A task she didn't think they'd ever be up to.

"One benefit of marrying a historian is you learn all sorts of facts."

If Meg wanted to distract her with history facts now, Hazel wasn't really in the mood. "Meg—"

"His name starts with an *S*. Did you know that on Fönn it was common for bastards to be given *S* names before the turn of the nineteenth century?"

She hadn't. And she hated how much it made sense. She'd been an unwanted child. Named for the color of her eyes. And his family had followed an ancient tradition.

"So the whole country knows?"

"No, but they suspect. Whoever it was, the royal family covered it nearly completely. If they'd given him a traditional name…" She sighed. "He was gone for a while, banished, though it's not discussed. He's almost broken away. Leaving the palace to live with you, dating a commoner, he's leaving and they're grasping, trying to pull him back. But it won't work."

Hazel couldn't stop the laugh. "Don't be so sure."

Meg hadn't seen the need in his eyes tonight. Hadn't seen the desire, the craving. It was a hole she couldn't fill, a tear she couldn't patch. She knew that, because the hole in her soul was still there, too.

"You didn't see him before you came. Whatever happened tonight, it won't matter. He's seen them for who they are. Maybe he isn't willing to admit that yet, but once you see it, you can't unsee it."

"So what, I just wait? I just hope that one day he chooses himself? Chooses us without conditions or the hope that his family will swoop in?" The words tumbled out, and the tears poured over her cheeks.

"I can't tell you. But living in fear that it will never happen..." Meg's mobile rang, and she looked at it and held it up. Syver's number was clear on the screen. "Want me to answer?"

"No."

Hazel held out her hand, and Meg laid the mobile in it. "I'll be in my room."

Pressing the Answer button, Hazel pulled the phone to her ear. "Meg! Do you know where Hazel is? I'm at our place, and she isn't here. We fought and her phone goes right to voice mail. I need to find her, please."

"I turned my mobile off." Her voice was quiet, but she knew he heard her.

"Sweetheart, I know I don't deserve trust right now, but I'm asking. Meet me at the cottage."

"It's nearly midnight, Syver. It's late, and we've had a bad day, and..."

"I know. I know all those things. And you're right, but meet me at the cottage, Hazel."

"How would we even get in? Asking the Realtor..."

"I called in a favor. Say you'll come."

Fear wanted her to say no. Wanted to throw up the walls she'd put around herself so well. But her heart refused to utter the words.

"All right. I'll be there shortly." Hazel blew out a breath as she hung up the phone.

"Road trip?" Meg was smiling as she leaned against the doorway.

"It's late. I can hire a car."

"Absolutely not. Let's go, Princess!" Meg grinned.

Hazel shook her head. "Not a title I'll ever have."

"Good. Titles are dumb, but I'm still calling you Princess!"

Hazel didn't have the strength or will to argue, so she just followed Meg to the car.

The cottage didn't have furniture. He'd bought a few plants on his way here, and hung some tiny lights to give them some ambiance. The heat wasn't on, but it felt like home. Or it would, once Hazel was here.

He'd called in a favor, one of his last acts as Prince Syver. Gotten the keys from the Realtor on the promise that he'd close on the cottage by the next week.

His mother had sent a text. A text…a short missive asking him not to try his brother. It was always him bending. Never them.

He didn't doubt the threat from his brother. The title would vanish, his limited access to his family would evaporate, too.

There weren't words to describe the hurt that caused. However, it didn't change his decision. He had his own life. Something he was proud of.

Now he just needed the woman who held his heart.

A car drove up the gravel path, and Syver blew out a breath. He needed Hazel more than anything. Letting her walk away this evening was a mistake he wouldn't repeat.

Opening the door before she could knock, Syver hated her red eyes and puffy cheeks. He'd hurt the woman he loved, because she saw him for who he could be. He'd spend the rest of his life making sure she never felt that again.

"Hazel." The urge to reach out to her, to pull her close and never let her go crawled through him. But he wouldn't rush this.

"Why are you out here?" She stepped inside, but didn't touch him. "At this time?" Hazel looked around the cottage, her eyes catching the plant holder in the corner and the lights.

"I talked to the Realtor. Promised we'd close on the cottage by next week, and she agreed to give me the keys."

"Benefits to being a prince." Hazel swallowed and clasped her hands. "Sorry, I didn't—"

"You did. And you're not wrong. There are benefits to a title. I figured I may as well use them one more time before it's stripped."

"Stripped." Hazel shook her head. "No. That is not fair."

"I thought you didn't want me beholden to my family?" Maybe it wasn't a fair question, but she'd seemed so certain this afternoon.

Her nose twitched. "I want them to want you for you."

"Well, I don't think that's possible."

Hazel stepped forward but stopped before she reached him. "Syver..."

"You were right. It's not me, not really, that Erik wants. It's an image, a reflection, one that I'm never going to fully meet."

"I'm sorry." Hazel reached for his hand.

Her warmth centered him. "It's me who needs to apologize, sweetheart. You were right, and I threw some horrid words at you earlier. You didn't give up on your mum. You just stopped letting her control you."

"It hurts to do." Hazel squeezed his hand. "It hurts a lot. But it was the right action for me."

It burned. That was the best description he could give. A heat pressed into his heart, a longing for a world he craved, but doubted would ever be in his grasp.

But that didn't mean he couldn't have a loving family. A family that would choose him, just him. "I can't describe the pain. Not yet. But I know that it's nothing compared to the pain of losing you. You're my family, Hazel. Now and always. I will do whatever it takes to convince you of that. However long it takes, but you and the life we build together are the family I choose."

"Wow." Hazel stepped into his arms. "Those are the sweetest words you could ever say to me, Syver."

"Because they're true." After pressing his lips to the top of her head, he sighed. This was his place. Beside this woman, creating his own path in the world, rather than trying to follow someone else's.

"I wish it hadn't taken you leaving, or me pressing my brother. I wish I could have seen what must have been so obvious to you. I know it was only hours ago, but it feels like everything shifted."

"Because it has." Hazel lifted up and kissed his cheek. "I also wish I'd stayed. I wish you hadn't had to press him alone. I let fear that you'd never see what he was doing drive me out. I let my fear, my past, drive my reaction, too. I regretted it as soon as I left. I love you, and I promise, whatever path we create, we do it together."

"Together." There was not a better word in all the world. *Together.*

EPILOGUE

THE BELLS OF the church rang, but it wasn't for Hazel and Syver's union. She was a holiday bride, though Christmas Eve was still a week away. However, there was no royal regalia, no international press corps.

Erik hadn't formally stripped Syver's title, but he no longer used it in any form. The palace gates were sealed to him like they were to all citizens without an appointment. His life looked very much like any other doctor's on staff at the hospital.

And it was perfect.

But it meant instead of standing in the giant church in the middle of the capital city, she was in the hall of their cottage. Dressed in a red wedding dress with a white faux fur coat over the top, ready to meet the man she loved more than all the world in their backyard, with just the friends they saw as their family.

There was no other place she'd rather be.

"Rethinking getting married with snow on the ground?" Meg dabbed a tear from the corner of Hazel's eye. "You'll mess up your makeup."

"No, I'm not upset about the snow. The makeup, well, I was always going to meet him with happy tears on my cheeks." Happiness coated every fiber of her being. She'd never thought it possible to love and be loved so well. And her eyes refused to stop their joyful watering.

"Well, I'll be in tears too, though I blame the hormones." Meg ran her hand over her very pregnant belly.

The music started and Meg handed Hazel her flowers. "Here we go."

Here we go.

Hazel waited for Meg to reach the makeshift altar they'd put in their backyard. Light snow was falling, but her body never felt warmer. She was marrying Syver.

Her best friend.

The "Bridal March" started, and she almost raced to the altar.

After reaching for her hand, Syver kissed her fingers. "I thought brides walked slowly down the aisle."

She didn't try to stop her giggle. "I could blame the cold, but the truth is I didn't want to wait." She knew her smile was brilliant as the officiant offered a small cough.

They turned in unison, without dropping their hold on each other. They were entering the next chapter in their story of forever, the same way they did everything else.

Together.

* * * * *

THE PRINCESS
WHO STOLE
HIS HEART

JULIE DANVERS

MILLS & BOON

To WAB, the best online writing group
a girl could ask for.

CHAPTER ONE

A MILLION DISTRACTIONS vied for Dani's attention in the busy ER. She fought to tune out the chatter of nurses, snippets of conversation from patients and the pounding from the construction work that had gone on all summer and never seemed to end.

Dani let the noise fade into the background as she reviewed the chart in front of her, hastily jotting notes into a pad. It was the last day of her residency in internal medicine, and she was determined to arrive prepared for rounds. She was scheduled to present on a patient, and Dr. Benson, the senior training physician, had a reputation for challenging residents with difficult questions. Dani had seen trainees leave rounds in tears because of his gruff, intimidating manner.

But Dr. Benson hadn't made Dani cry yet, and she was determined that he never would. She had every intention of finishing her residency with her reputation for withstanding Dr. Benson's intense gaze—known as the Benson Glare—intact.

Despite Dani's focus, one sound rose above the general hubbub and penetrated her concentration. A sharp cough, followed by a gasp, as though someone couldn't get enough air. It was the gasp that made her look up sharply and scan the ER.

Boston General Hospital was an extremely old building, which meant construction was constantly taking place somewhere. As Dani looked for the source of the gasping cough, she saw that a construction worker had dropped his hammer and was hunched over, catching his breath. When he noticed Dani watching him, he gave a quick, reassuring nod and wiped his forehead, then retrieved his hammer and returned to work.

Dani hesitated to return to her notes. Something about the man's cough hadn't sounded right to her. But he seemed to be returning to work without any trouble. And none of the other doctors and nurses in the ER seemed to notice anything amiss. She looked back at the chart in front of her.

Only to have it slammed shut by her best friend, Kim, who bounced up to the nurses' station with her usual exuberance.

"Hey!" Dani protested. "I was reading that!"

"Of course you were." Kim's dark eyes sparkled with mischief. "Only you would be studiously brushing up on patients on the last day of residency. Don't you think there are more important things to do?"

Dani pulled at the locks of her chestnut ponytail, as she always did when she felt fretful. "What's more important than preparing for rounds?"

"Hmm…" Kim pretended to think. "How about taking some time to say good-bye to dear old Boston General? Saying thanks to the senior doctors who've mentored us, the nurses who've kept us from screwing up…and, most importantly, planning all the drinks and get-togethers that need to happen before our residency cohort scatters across the country to begin the next phase of their careers?"

For a moment, Dani almost felt tears prick at her eyelids, but she tried to hide them with a forced smile. Kim was too perceptive not to notice.

"Oof, sorry, Dani. I didn't mean to bring that up. I just meant to say…don't work so hard that you forget to say goodbye to everyone."

"It's okay. You don't need to be afraid to mention it—it's no secret that I'm not taking a position anywhere. I've accepted it. I'm just sad that everyone's leaving Boston in a few weeks."

"I still can't believe you don't have a job or a fellowship lined up. You're one of the best residents in our program."

Dani tried to appreciate her friend's compliment, but her feelings were bittersweet. After three years of residency in internal medicine, the rest of her cohort was about to leave Boston. Most would begin fellowships in their chosen specialty areas, while others had found positions in hospitals and private practices around the country. Kim would be in Miami for an oncology fellowship. All of Dani's friends were about to take the next major step forward in their medical careers.

But not Dani Martin. Or rather, not Princess Danielle-Genevieve Matthieu DuMaria, twelfth in line to the throne of Lorovia. Dani's home was a tiny country on the north coast of the Mediterranean Sea, nestled between France, Monaco and Italy. What Lorovia lacked in size, it made up for in wealth, as the third-richest country in the world. The chances of Dani ever ruling were miniscule—she was the youngest daughter of a youngest son—but her royal duties were still significant enough to interfere with her medical career.

Dani had told her friends and supervisors that family obligations prevented her from continuing to practice as a physician, but no one knew just how extensive those obligations were. When she'd announced her intention to enter medical school, a pitched battle had ensued amongst her family members. No one in the royal family had ever had a profession before, and most of her family members were convinced that Dani's royal duties would keep her far too busy to allow her time for a career in medicine. Studying medicine would be tantamount to turning her back on her family and her country.

Dani loved her family, and it hurt when her uncle accused her of abandoning her responsibilities. But becoming a doctor had been Dani's dream since she was fourteen, when a bad fall from a horse had resulted in numerous injuries, including a compound fracture in her leg that required two surgeries. She'd been inspired by the physicians who cared for her and she formed the dream of one day helping others in the same way her own doctors had helped her. During her university years, she decided she wanted to be a cardiologist—after all, the heart powered everything.

Dani's parents supported her dream, even though many of her older family members had reservations. After a week of arguing, the family agreed on a compromise: Dani would be allowed to attend medical school in the United States, where there was less emphasis on European politics and therefore less of a chance that Dani would be recognized as a member of the Lorovian royal family. Her family insisted she keep her status as a princess a strict secret, for security purposes, and that she use the family pseudonym of 'Martin' as her surname. In return, they allowed her to complete her three-year residency in internal medicine immediately after medical school, so that she could have the chance to practice as a full-fledged physician and give back to the medical community. But when Dani finished her residency, she was expected to return home. She would set medicine aside and focus on responsibilities more relevant to her royal status.

Dani hated that her medical career had an expiration date. Quitting after residency meant that she would never be able to pursue a specialty like cardiology, because of the years of extra training that were required. But that was part of the sacrifice of royal birth. If she couldn't have her whole dream, she would have to settle for having part of it.

Her family's status impacted everything from her friendships to her love life. She'd only made a few forays into romance, but she'd had enough experiences to learn that trying to date as a royal was fraught with problems. If she dated someone who knew she was a princess, she could never be certain they liked her for herself and not for her family's power and influence.

Several years ago, at university, she'd come close to giving her heart to someone entirely. Peter. He hadn't known at first that she was a princess. But she'd had to tell him eventually, and when he found out, everything had changed. His family, once extremely wealthy, was facing troubles on public and financial fronts. Peter seemed to view her royal status as the solution to his family's problems. Dani would have supported Peter wholeheartedly, but no matter what she offered, it was never enough. When he went so far as to sell pictures he'd taken of her to a salacious tabloid—pictures he'd promised no one would see but him—Dani knew it was over.

Her heart still stung at his betrayal, even though so much time had passed. After that, she'd made the decision not to reveal her status as a princess unless someone had earned her absolute trust. Only a few of the medical staff at Boston General and Kim knew the truth.

Keeping her princess status a secret for the past several years had been a welcome change. She'd made friends who she knew were true friends, not people who attached themselves to her simply because she was a royal. It was still easier to avoid dating entirely, even though she still couldn't let go of the hope that she might someday meet someone who made her feel special and maybe even fall in love. It was a nice dream, even though it was incredibly unlikely. Even aside from the complications of dating as a royal, Peter's betrayal had hurt her deeply, and she couldn't imagine ever trusting someone with her heart again.

Now, with the time to honor her promise to her family fast approaching, she'd have to stop indulging in dreams. No matter whether she dreamed of falling in love or having a career she loved, the result was the same: as a princess, her life was not her own. In a few weeks, she'd be back to the life of a princess, and her medical career would dissolve into a distant memory.

Dani hated good-byes and preparing for rounds was a welcome distraction. She wanted to make this last presentation her best. After all, it would probably be the last time she ever had a chance to discuss a patient with a group of colleagues.

The sharp cough she'd heard a moment ago echoed across the waiting room again, followed by a longer gasp this time. Dani and Kim both looked up. The construction worker in the corner was half standing, hunched over his bent legs.

"Think he's okay?" asked Dani.

Kim looked uncertain. "None of the nurses seem to be alarmed. And he's still breathing."

The man took another labored draw for breath.

"That's not breathing. That's gasping," Dani said as the man toppled to the ground.

Dani dashed across the waiting room. The man was pale and rapidly losing consciousness. She couldn't feel a pulse.

"He's in cardiac arrest," she told Kim. "Get help."

Kim ran off to call the code.

Instinct took over and Dani acted. She placed her hands on the man's chest, her elbows locked, and began compressions. The alarm she'd felt seconds ago began to melt away as a combination of training and adrenaline took over her body. She ran through proper procedure in her head as she worked, which always helped her to feel more grounded in a crisis. *Push at*

*a depth of two inches. Interlock your fingers. Make sure they
don't touch the ribs. Start with thirty chest compressions.*

Relief flooded through her as an emergency team arrived.
They'd probably only taken seconds to get there, though it had
seemed much longer.

The team consisted of several nurses and a doctor she didn't
recognize. He was younger than most of the other doctors, with
sun-streaked hair and a stubbled beard. Dani wondered if he
might be a new staff member. If so, this was hardly the time
for introductions. He merely nodded at her and said, "You're
doing great. Keep going until we get to the cath lab."

The team lifted the patient onto the gurney. Dani straddled
the man and continued compressions while a nurse delivered
oxygen through a bag ventilator. The gurney sped through the
ER doors and down the hall to the cardiac catheterization lab
as Dani fought to keep her balance and give compressions at
the same time.

Dani's arms were shaking by the time they reached the cath
lab, though the journey couldn't have taken long. She was so
focused on counting compressions that she barely heard the
sandy-haired doctor. He had to shake her arm, gently, to get
her attention.

"You can stop now," he said. "We're getting him hooked
up to an AED."

He held out one hand to help her from the gurney, and for
a quick moment Dani was in his arms as he lifted her bodily
down to the floor. Doctor Whoever-He-Was had some serious
muscles underneath those scrubs.

But she barely had time to consider those muscles or to be
shocked at herself for having such a thought at *such* a moment.
Because by the time her feet hit the floor, he was already saying, "We've got it from here. Can someone take her outside?"

Dani felt herself guided from the room by a nurse. She stood outside the cath lab, the patient lost to view as the emergency team crowded around him.

After three years of residency, Dani had learned to expect the unexpected. But it was still a shock to see how quickly the situation had gone from normal to critical. One minute the construction worker had been hammering away at the floor. The next, he'd been in cardiac arrest. His life had changed in an instant. Assuming, of course, that he was going to live. She'd only have been in the way if she'd stayed in the cath lab, but she wished she'd gotten the handsome mystery doctor's name. It would have given her some way to follow up with the patient.

As if on cue, the cath lab doors swung open and the unknown doctor stepped out. "Good, you're still here," he said. Now that she could see him outside of a scene of complete chaos, Dani grew more certain that he wasn't from anywhere in Boston. His hair wasn't just light, but bleached in places, as though he spent a lot of time in the sun. His arms were tanned as well—and all signs indicated that she'd been right about those muscles.

"That was pretty heroic for your last day of residency, doc."

How did he know she was a resident? Dani had assumed he was a new staff member, unfamiliar with the hospital. "I don't think we've met," she said.

He smiled, and when he did, one eye closed ever so slightly, as though he were winking at her. "I'm Dr. Logan. Cade Logan." He stuck a hand out for her to shake.

Something was making it a little hard for Dani to get her words out, and if she hadn't had adrenaline coursing through her veins a moment ago, she might have suspected that it had a lot to do with Cade Logan's wink and the warmth of his hand as he shook hers. As it was, she felt as though she could barely force the words out of her throat as she replied, "Dani Martin."

"Well, Dr. Martin, I'm pleased to let you know that thanks to your quick thinking, your patient is on the road to recovery. He's very lucky you happened to be nearby when he went into cardiac arrest—and that you recognized what was happening."

"He's going to be all right?"

"We've done a catheterization to stabilize him for now. He's first on the schedule for a triple bypass tomorrow. It could have been much, much worse if his heart problems had continued to go undetected. It probably saved his life that he happened to go into arrest while working on a construction project in an ER. Seconds counted in a case like this. The fact that you took action immediately gave us valuable extra time."

Dani breathed out, relieved.

"You've managed to do two things today that don't happen often—help to save a life and impress me."

"I'm just glad I was in the right place at the right time," she said.

"Come on, give yourself credit where it's due. CPR, performed competently, at just the right time can make the difference between giving a patient a lifesaving operation, or sending him straight to the morgue. You jumped in when needed, and you had the skills to back up your confidence."

She nodded, letting herself appreciate his words as the familiar bittersweet feeling washed over her. She should appreciate that she'd done well today, even though it would be her last chance to jump into action during a medical emergency.

As though he had a knack for guessing the subject she least wanted to talk about, Cade pressed onward. "Boston General seems about to lose one of their best. May I ask which fellowship you're headed off to, now that your residency is over?"

She hesitated. Even with years to get used to the idea that her career had an expiration date, it was still difficult to talk about. "I'm not going on to a fellowship."

The surprise in his eyes was the same surprise she'd seen in the eyes of her supervisors when they learned she had no plans to specialize as a physician.

"Will you be working as a generalist, then?"

"No. I won't be working at all. Today isn't just my last day of residency. It's my last day as a physician, full stop. I have family obligations that will make it far too difficult to continue."

The concern in his eyes seemed genuine. "I'm so sorry. Is everyone in your family all right?"

"It's nothing like that. My family is… Being in my family means being committed to the family…business. It takes up a lot of time."

"It must be a large business. Are you some kind of pharmaceutical heiress?" His voice was half-teasing, but she saw genuine curiosity in his eyes.

"Something like that." She hated to outright lie to anyone, but misleading Cade Logan wouldn't hurt anyone; she'd probably never see him again after today.

"That's a shame," he said. "The world needs good doctors. Frankly, more than it needs pharmaceutical heiresses."

He was joking, but she could also hear the truth in his voice, behind his smile. Perhaps she could hear it because part of her agreed with him. If she could make her own choices, she'd decide to stick with medicine in a heartbeat.

But her family needed her, and her choices weren't her own.

And who was he to judge her situation before he even knew anything about it?

"Unfortunately, my decision's already been made," she said

curtly, hoping that he'd take the hint that she no longer wished to discuss the matter.

"I understand, but…"

"There's no *but*. I need to be there for my family. End of story." She hadn't meant for her words to come out with so much heat, but she was surprised that Cade was pushing her for answers. Usually, people backed off when she explained that family responsibilities kept her from maintaining a medical career. Only Kim had pried further, and that was after she'd become a trusted friend.

He held up a hand. "Okay. Family first. I get it. But answer me this—why put so much work into becoming a doctor, only to have to walk away after such a short time… What was the point if you were only going to quit?"

She didn't owe Cade any explanations—she'd only just met him, after all. But she found she wanted to answer his question as much for herself as for him. In the toughest times during medical school and residency, she'd found herself wondering why she was putting herself through the sleepless nights, the endless stress of worrying over patients, if she didn't plan to commit to medicine for the rest of her life. But the answer she came back to was always the same.

"Because medicine is a miracle," she said. "It's full of miracles—birth, recovery from illness, overcoming impossible odds. It's science, of course…but there's no other field where you get to see something miraculous every day. Even if I only get to see those miracles for a short time in my life, it's better than never getting to experience them at all. No matter what happens in the future, I'll always look at life differently because I was a doctor. Even if I'm not practicing, I'll know what a miracle it is for a human body to exist, especially one that's suffered through illness or injury. Medicine has showed me that people go on living even under the most extraordinary circumstances, and I'll never forget that."

He was looking at her with an odd expression, as though she'd said something completely unexpected. Suddenly she felt foolish for rambling on about miracles. He probably thought she was hopelessly naive. Nevertheless, it was what she believed.

"And is that enough for you?" he asked. "To have just a few years' worth of memories of all these miracles you've witnessed?"

No. Of course not. She loved medicine. Practicing for just a few years would never be enough. But a princess had a duty to make the best out of the situation she was in. She tilted her chin up and looked straight into his eyes. Blue with flecks of green, giving the effect of an aqua hue. His expression was thoughtful, penetrating. Challenging. She'd met with enough of those expressions during her training that this one didn't faze her.

"It'll have to be," she replied.

She waited for him to tell her that she was utterly ridiculous but, instead, he said, "You're very passionate about medicine for someone who's about to leave it."

"I care about a lot of things. Unfortunately, sometimes those things get in the way of one another."

"For example, your family and your career."

She nodded, glad that he understood.

"Do you know why I'm here in Boston?"

"I assumed you were a visiting physician."

"Not exactly. I'm a fellow in my last year of a unique cardiology fellowship program at the Coral Bay Medical Center on St. Camille—it's an island in the Caribbean."

"I've heard of St. Camille." The island had a reputation for aquamarine waters and white sand beaches. And cardiology was the specialty she'd dreamed of pursuing in her wildest moments—but cardiology had never been an option, with its requirement of an additional three years of training beyond residency.

"There's a need for experienced doctors in St. Camille, but recruiting the right people is a challenge. Lots of students attend medical school in the Caribbean and then want to move back to their home countries once they finish their studies. Not many want to do it the other way around. It's difficult to convince top-talent trainees that it's worth it to move to a small island with limited opportunities."

She nodded. "So you're here on a recruiting mission."

"Exactly. I'm looking for qualified residents, but qualifications aren't enough. The program needs residents who have passion for their work. Residents like you, for example."

"Me?" she was stunned. For one wild moment, she tried to imagine her uncles' reactions if she told them she was planning to spend the next several years in the Caribbean. They'd complained often enough that Boston was too far from Lorovia. St. Camille would be out of the question. "I couldn't. I'm sorry, but…it just isn't possible. My family needs me."

"Of course," he said. "I knew it was a long shot. But if you change your mind, give me a call. There would be an interview, of course, and you'd need strong recommendations from your supervisors. But I have a feeling you'd be a shoo-in."

He smiled again and she felt a pang inside. The way those blue eyes of his almost seemed to sparkle when he smiled… It reminded her of the last time she'd seen the light from the sun hit ocean waves.

His eyes reminded her of home, of all places. She wasn't able to visit as often as she wanted to, but she made sure to return at least once a year during the holidays. It had been several months since she'd walked along the Lorovian coastline, but she could see the water shimmer in her memory as clearly as though she'd been there yesterday.

How odd, she thought, that she could be here in Boston, listening to Cade speak of the Caribbean, and be reminded of home.

Those eyes of his didn't seem to miss much. They might sparkle, but they were penetrating, too. Dani had a small, nearly imperceptible scar just above her upper lip—a remnant from a riding accident when she was young. Most people didn't notice it. But she could feel his eyes on her, tracing the shape of her lips, noticing that something wasn't right.

Why was he looking at her lips that way? It was just a scar. It was imperceptible in photos. Most people didn't notice it unless she pointed it out first—which she rarely did, because she was a little self-conscious about it.

In fact, maybe her self-consciousness was the reason she assumed he was looking at her lips at all. Perhaps he was simply trying to find some feature of hers that stood out, the same way she sometimes tried to make note of a mustache or a pair of glasses when she met someone new and thought she might not remember their name later.

Still, she wasn't used to having her lips stared at with such intensity. She groped for something to say that could end the pause in their conversation, which felt as though it was growing by the second. "What's it like? Living on a tiny island in the Caribbean?"

He raised his eyebrows. "Don't tell me I actually have a shot of reeling you in."

"No, no. I'm just curious."

"In my extremely biased opinion—the word 'paradise' doesn't do it justice."

"But you must live far from your family, unless they're from the island. Isn't that difficult?"

She was surprised by the shadow that passed over his face at the word "family."

"The program is very flexible. There are lots of options to travel home for those who want to. And for some of us, the island's remote location is one of its biggest perks."

Biggest perks? How could that be possible? Dani couldn't imagine living on an island without regularly scheduled trips to see her brothers and cousins. "And what about for you?" she couldn't help asking. "Do you consider the distance a 'perk'?"

"This is the first time I've left the island in six years. Let's just say the distance from family is an asset rather than a liability."

"You haven't left in *six years*?" Dani tried to imagine it. She'd spent so much of her life ruled by family obligations, family history, family traditions. Every decision she'd ever made was influenced by how it would affect her family. And even though she often felt confined by tradition, her family meant everything to her. She couldn't imagine what life would be like without them.

Was family not a priority for Cade? "There must be someone you miss. Family members or…someone important."

"I have everything I need on St. Camille. But the program is very supportive of those who want to visit home." His voice was firm, and Dani had the distinct feeling the subject was closed. Her curiosity burned. Cade had seemed so warm, so relaxed just a moment ago. Right up until the subject of family had arisen.

Of course, family could be a touchy subject for many. Dani

of all people could understand that. But to think of Cade going for six years without seeing his family? It was…it was…

It was none of her business. "I didn't mean to pry," she said.

"It's normal to be curious. But…from what you've said about your family obligations, I'm guessing your curiosity isn't strong enough to get you to seriously consider applying."

She gave him a rueful smile. "It sounds like a great program." That was an understatement. It sounded like the perfect program. The kind of adventure she'd jump right into if her life were her own.

But a princess didn't go back on her word. Even if she was presented with one last chance to become the doctor she'd always wanted to be. Even if that chance was presented by someone with light, wavy hair, bleached blond by the sun.

"It's just…with my family situation, it's out of the question."

He shrugged. "Well, I had to try." He shook her hand. "Maybe our paths will cross again sometime."

"I hope so," she said, although she knew he was just saying it to be nice. What were the chances of ever seeing him again when he lived on St. Camille? Especially when he seemed to have little to no interest in leaving the island.

He turned and headed back into the OR, leaving her standing in the hallway.

A princess always did her duty. She'd done the right thing by turning him down. She'd fulfilled her obligations and kept her promise.

So why did she feel as though she'd made a terrible mistake?

One week later, Dani stood outside a bar across the street from Boston General. She and her friends had shared many drinks there over the years, and they'd planned one last gathering before everyone left Boston.

She could already see a few of her friends inside, but she couldn't bring herself to go in. She didn't feel the least bit celebratory. The end of her residency felt like the end of one of the most meaningful periods of her life. She'd only had a few shining years where she'd really felt like herself.

But of course, Dr. Dani Martin wasn't who she really was at all. Tomorrow, she'd have to go back to her real life as Princess Danielle-Genevieve in Lorovia. She already had a plane ticket in her purse.

There were too many emotions at war within her, and this was supposed to be an evening of joy. She didn't want her feelings to cloud her classmates' celebration. She stood outside the door, longing to go in, but dreading the inevitable good-byes.

As she stood, an older man stepped out of a taxi and moved beside her. She reeled in surprise.

"Dr. Benson?"

Despite his gruff manner, Dr. Benson had never intimidated Dani as he had her colleagues. Perhaps it was because she was used to dealing with her older relatives, who could be demanding and overbearing. Working with Dr. Benson had sparked Dani's competitive spirit, and she'd been determined to live up to his exact and demanding standards.

His expression was markedly different from its usual scowl. In fact, he looked positively pleased to see her. "I never miss the good-bye party for a residency cohort," he said. "And I had a feeling that if I dropped by, I might see you. I would have hated to miss the chance to say good-bye to one of our brightest residents."

Dani couldn't help flushing with pleasure. It was a compliment she'd worked years to earn. "Sorry I missed rounds last week."

"No need to apologize. I understand that a more urgent matter arose. And that you performed admirably under pressure. No less than I would expect of you, of course."

"Thank you. That means a lot to me."

"But I didn't come over here just to throw compliments at you. I wanted to talk to you about something even more important. Your future."

As a senior attending physician, Dr. Benson was one of the few people at Boston General who knew the truth of Dani's situation.

"Dr. Benson…my future involves going home to Lorovia tomorrow. I was only allowed to pursue a medical education on the condition that I return home to resume my duties immediately afterward."

He nodded. "I know your situation is complicated. But as I've gotten to know you, I've realized that like all the best physicians, helping people is truly your calling. And there are so many different ways to help. Not everyone needs to be a doctor. Certainly, one could argue that being a princess offers one a wide scope for helping others. But you, Dr. Martin… I believe that *you* may be called to this profession. You have what it takes to be a cardiologist, if you wanted to continue in that direction. Are you sure that abandoning your career now is the best path forward?"

She held out her hands. "Even if I wanted to continue, how could I? All the fellowships are assigned for this year."

"Not all of them. There are spots at small programs with unusual circumstances. For example, yesterday, Dr. Logan and I were discussing the Coral Bay Medical Center's fellowship program in cardiology. And he seemed particularly interested in you."

Cade had asked about her? Even after she'd told him that it would be impossible for her to move to the Caribbean?

"Dr. Logan left for St. Camille yesterday. But he asked me to speak with you one more time, to let you know that it's a door that's open to you if you're interested. There's no guarantee on how long that door will stay open. But it's open for now. He asked me to give you his number, just in case." He handed Dani a business card.

Even as she took the card, she started to protest once more that she couldn't possibly continue her career in medicine, but he stopped her. "Just take a little while to think about it. And while you're thinking, I want you to have this."

He handed her a pastel-covered envelope, about the size of a greeting card. She opened it, to see a card that looked as though it came from a hospital gift shop.

She read the note scrawled inside.

Dear Dr. Martin,
I can't thank you and all the other doctors enough for being there for me. My own father passed from a heart attack when I was young, but thanks to you, I'll be around to see my own boys grow up. This card is small thanks for what you've done, but I hope you keep it and know that I'm forever grateful.
Thank you for saving my life.
Charlie.

"The man you saved last week is named Charles Brownlow, and he has a wife and two children," said Dr. Benson. "I know that your responsibilities at home are quite serious. But opportunities like the Coral Bay program don't come along often. Frankly, neither do clinicians with the gifts and skill to succeed in such a program. There are lots of ways of helping, Dani. I think being a doctor might be yours."

Dammit. Dani had spent three years maintaining her stoicism under the Benson Glare. But now she felt the tears begin to flow. Dr. Benson had finally made her cry.

"Think about it," he said, giving her a quick pat on the shoulder before he entered the bar.

Dani wiped the tears from her eyes and put both the letter and Cade's business card into her purse. As she did, her fingers touched the plane ticket to Lorovia. She pulled Cade's business card and the plane ticket out and stared at them. She felt as though she held two very different futures in her hands.

Thank you for saving my life.

What could be more important than those words?

She'd made a promise to her family. A princess wasn't supposed to go back on her word. She had obligations to meet and a duty to fulfill.

But wasn't a princess's highest obligation to care for her people?

And as a doctor, she had the skills to care for everyone—not just the Lorovian people, but anyone who needed her help.

What was the point of being a member of the royal family if she couldn't help people?

Thank you for saving my life. She'd thought her future was a settled thing, but those six words placed her on the verge of a decision.

Cade had already left for St. Camille yesterday.

The news left an unexpected emptiness in her heart. He was gone.

Gone, but not entirely out of reach. She had his number.

If she let herself think, she'd never go through with it. She couldn't stop to imagine what her family would say or how they'd react. *Don't think, just do.* She felt the same rush of adrenaline that she'd felt in the ER when she'd jumped into action and started CPR. She pulled her phone from her purse and dialed.

She'd expected it to go straight to voice mail, but to her surprise, he picked up. His "hello" came out deep and resonant, despite the crackling connection.

"Dr. Logan? It's Dani Martin. I'd love to speak more with you about the Coral Bay fellowship program."

CHAPTER TWO

DANI PULLED HER extra pillow over her head, but it did little to block out the thunderstorm that raged just outside her dormitory room at the Coral Bay Medical Center. She glared at the clock on her nightstand. The time glared back at her in neon green digits: four in the morning. She'd gone to bed after midnight, but sleep had been elusive.

She'd been at the medical center for two weeks, yet it felt as though she'd experienced a decade's worth of family conflict. Her spur-of-the-moment decision to continue on with her career had not gone over well with her uncles. She'd known, of course, that they would oppose her choice. Her parents had responded wonderfully, and she was still touched by their words of support. But her father was the ruling queen's youngest son, and as such, he still had to defer to the judgement of his older brothers when it came to broader family matters. It was her older uncles who needed to be convinced, and they were stubborn and used to getting their own way.

It was heart-wrenching for Dani to make a decision that caused so much arguing among her family members. But for the first time in her life, she was willing to fight for what she wanted. Faced with the possibility of losing her medical career forever, she'd realized that she couldn't give up such an important part of her life. Not just for herself, but for the people she could help as well.

Which meant she had no choice but to appeal to her grandmother, the queen.

Dani had always been a little intimidated by her grandmother, who was warm and loving but very strict, especially on matters related to public perception of the royal family. For the most part, the queen left the running of family business to other members of the extended family. But sometimes disagreements arose that were impossible to resolve, and in those cases, her grandmother's word was final.

Dani knew there was a risk in taking her case to her grandmother. If the queen didn't see her side of things, then she'd have to give up her medical career forever. And at first, it did seem as though her grandmother was inclined to agree with her uncles. But everything changed when her grandmother caught the name of the Coral Bay Medical Center.

Apparently, the medical center was more well-known than Dani realized. It was a well-kept secret among the wealthy as a place to obtain discreet health care away from the prying eyes of the paparazzi. In fact, her grandmother revealed, Dani's own grandfather had once been a patient there, and her grandmother credited the doctors there with adding years to his life before he passed.

Her grandmother had spoken to the entire family on Dani's behalf. Perhaps, she'd said, they'd all been too narrow in their idea of what a princess's responsibilities were supposed to be. If Dani had the skills and the ability to save lives as a physician, then she also had a duty to practice those skills. It might be a break from tradition for a royal family member to hold a profession, but weren't those traditions supposed to be for the good of the people? Moreover, her grandmother felt that a debt was owed to Coral Bay, one that could never be repaid. If Dani wanted to practice medicine there, she could do so with the full support of her family.

She would have to continue keeping her royal status a strict secret, for security purposes. And she'd have to continue using the surname Martin. In Boston, the dean of her medical school and a few senior physicians had known Dani's true identity in case Dani ever needed extra security measures or a leave of absence for royal events. But living and working on St. Camille would be different from medical school and residency. There would be no one to hold accountable except herself if her secret got out. The chances of the news spreading, even if she only told one or two people, were far too high. She was, therefore, expressly forbidden to tell anyone of her status, no matter how trustworthy she thought they might be.

Dani agreed to continue concealing her identity without hesitation. It seemed like a small price to pay for the chance to pursue the career she loved.

She was thrilled to finally have her family's consent to work at Coral Bay. But once she arrived on St. Camille, nothing else seemed to go right.

The island's internet had been up and down all week, and she'd been out of contact with everyone. There'd only been one text from Kim—Did you get another chance to feel Dr. BeachBum's muscles yet?

Dr. BeachBum was the nickname Kim had adopted for Cade after hearing Dani's story of how they'd met at Boston General. Dani hadn't been able to get a response through. Due to the unseasonable tropical storms, she hadn't been able to see much of the island's famous white sand beaches and crystal waters. The weather also made it impossible to search for any permanent housing. The Coral Bay Medical Center provided spacious dormitory rooms for all its staff, but they were still rather impersonal, and Dani hoped to find a place of her own as soon as possible.

Her desire to settle in was made more urgent by the loss of her luggage. The medical center had a helicopter pad for flying in patients, but the island was too small for its own airport. Dani had flown by private jet to a larger island and made the last leg of her journey to St. Camille by boat. The ship's captain had seized the chance to travel through a break in the storms. Dani had survived the choppy waters; her luggage, unfortunately, had been loaded at the exact moment an extremely large wave arose, and most of the belongings she'd brought with her were now at the bottom of the sea. It had mostly been clothing and nothing she couldn't live without. But it would have been nice to have some of her own things while she adjusted to a new place.

The medical center staff had given her some spare scrubs to wear until the weather abated and she could shop for clothes. But Dani's frame was petite and they were out of smaller sizes, which meant that Dani had to fold the arms and legs of her scrubs back several times. She felt like a child playing dress-up.

Lightning crackled outside her dormitory window and Dani gave up on any hope of sleep. But it wasn't just the storm that was keeping her awake. She'd risked so much to follow a dream, and now she was far from everyone she'd ever known, living in a room that wasn't hers and wearing clothes that didn't fit.

It was enough to make her wonder if the universe was telling her she should have stuck to being a princess.

It's only temporary, she thought. *I just need time to adjust to the island and to the staff at the medical center.*

But time was a luxury she wasn't sure she had. Because if

she had to work with Cade Logan for much longer, she was likely to lose her medical license for assaulting a colleague.

Dani took a deep breath, trying to keep her blood pressure down as Cade came to mind. He was only trying to help. Probably. But if he was also trying to drive her insane, he was doing an excellent job of it.

As the senior fellow in the cardiology program, Cade was responsible for overseeing most of the training that went on at the medical center. Dani understood that Cade took this responsibility seriously. Over the past two weeks, she'd noticed that he was conscientious, attentive and that he listened with genuine concern to his patients. She admired those things about him.

Unfortunately, he was also the biggest micromanager she'd ever worked with.

If she needed to call down to the lab to request a rush on test results, Cade was at her elbow asking why—was there some emergency? And if so, why hadn't she told him? When she was invited to sit in on a surgery, he'd watched her scrub in like a hawk—as though Boston General would have let her go through residency without knowing how to prepare for a surgical procedure. If she got lost in the labyrinth of the hospital's basement and happened to run into him—and she was always running into him; it seemed impossible to turn a corner at the hospital without coming face-to-face with those piercing blue eyes—then he couldn't just help her with directions. He wanted to know where she was going, what she needed and how she'd gotten lost.

And it didn't only affect her. That morning, Dani had been explaining correct procedure for inserting a central line to one of the hospital interns, Matthew. Dani's instinct was to hold back, letting Matthew find his footing on his own and build his confidence. Cade seemed to take a different view—he jumped in almost immediately.

"Keep your hands steady," he'd said to the intern. Dani scowled. As she'd predicted, criticism only served to worsen Matthew's shaking hands. A moment later, Cade jumped in again as Matthew placed a discarded needle tip in the wrong section of the surgical tray.

"Not there. It goes in the top left-hand quadrant of the tray. Keeping your items organized to a standard procedure makes everything run more smoothly." Dani agreed, but thought Cade could have waited until Matthew was finished to provide that feedback. But seconds later, it didn't matter anymore, as Cade took over the procedure and put the central line in himself.

"Better luck next time," he said to Matthew, and then, to Dani, "Make sure you take some time this week to run all the interns through the procedure more thoroughly."

Her blood boiled. Cade turned to leave and she followed him into the hallway.

"Excuse me? Dr. Logan? A quick word?" Her tone was brisk and sharp and he looked up from his chart, confused. His expression was one of total innocence, as though he had no idea why she sounded upset. It was hard to be mad at him when he looked as though he actually cared about what she had to say—but his micromanagement had to stop. She couldn't work like this.

"Is something wrong?"

"Yes, something's wrong! What just happened in there?"

"As far as I can tell, an intern tried to perform a procedure he wasn't ready for, and you seemed hesitant to do it yourself. I took over for the good of the patient."

She gritted her teeth. "First of all, I wasn't *hesitant*. Every intern is nervous the first time they put a central line in. I

wanted Matthew to see that he could trust his training to overcome his nerves. But you jumping in with criticism when he'd
barely even started did nothing to put him at ease. And taking
over the way you did will just make him feel incompetent."

"Hmm. Perhaps we should ask the patient whether he pre-
fers that Matthew feels good about his skills, or that his procedures are performed by qualified physicians."

The suggestion that she hadn't considered the patient's
needs was infuriating. "I would have stepped in if the patient
were the slightest bit at risk. But training interns is important,
too. And now Matthew's going to be jumpy the next time he
tries to put a central line in, which is going to be worse for
future patients."

To her surprise, Cade's expression softened. She'd been
gearing herself up for a heated argument, but Cade seemed
thoughtful. Worry lines appeared on his forehead and she realized that he wasn't about to snap back at her.

"Tell Matthew to hum next time," he said.

"Hum?"

"Yes. Have him and the patient both hum a tune together.
There's research indicating that humming during central line
placement prevents changes in the patient's central venous
pressure, and it'll calm Matthew down, too. It's simple but
effective. Have him try it…*after* he's observed the procedure
a few more times."

It was a good suggestion, she realized. Why couldn't Cade
have simply offered up that idea in the first place instead of
jumping all over Matthew and leaving her feeling so unsettled?

"That's a good strategy," she said. "I wish you'd mentioned
that to Matthew, instead of taking over."

He smiled at her, one eye closing as he did. "Maybe I was
holding back to see if you'd suggest it to him."

And with that, he walked off down the hallway, leaving her even more irritated than she'd been before they'd spoke.

It was Dr. Benson all over again, she realized. Cade was trying to keep her on her toes. She had to stop letting him get inside her head.

Thunder broke outside her window again. Dani decided that since she wasn't sleeping, she might as well do some early morning rounds. It wouldn't hurt to double-check on the patient Matthew had been working with, either. Cade's involvement had made her anxious—that was what always came of micromanagement—and she wanted to make absolutely sure that the case went smoothly.

She slipped out of bed and pulled on her overly large scrubs, determined to set aside the memory of the way Cade's brow had furrowed when she'd questioned him, making his gaze appear even more piercing than usual. She hadn't spent three years withstanding the Benson Glare just to let Cade Logan and his ever-watchful blue eyes drain her confidence. If Cade thought she was going to be fazed by his constant vigilance, he was about to find out that she was made of sterner stuff.

Dani worked her way through the labyrinthine halls of the medical center, nodding at the nurses she encountered through bleary, sleep-deprived eyes. After two weeks, she felt she was beginning to get to know the staff. Aside from Cade, everyone else seemed to be developing trust in her clinical skills.

When she reached her patient's room, she found that Cade was already there.

Why am I not surprised?

He was reviewing the chart at the foot of the patient's bed. Did he not trust her to look after her patients herself? As the senior fellow, Cade should be available for consultation if needed, but there was no need for him to check on each patient personally.

Unless he wasn't checking on each patient, but specifically on *her* patients, because he doubted her competence.

She reminded herself that it was normal for medical teams to take time to work together comfortably. When she'd first started her residency, she and her colleagues had had to learn to stop being competitive with each other so that they could work together, and some of those colleagues had become her closest friends. Maybe this would be the same.

None of her past colleagues, though, had had Cade's twinkling blue eyes or the condescending wink that came along with them. Still, she had to try.

"Ahem." She cleared her throat to alert him to her presence, but a loud thunderclap swallowed her voice. She waited for the noise of the storm to pass, then said loudly, "Excuse me?"

Cade jumped at the sound of her voice. "Surely there's no need to shout, Dr. Martin."

She was glad the lights were still dimmed for the overnight shift; hopefully it made her blush less apparent. "Just wanted to make sure you heard me."

"Well. You certainly accomplished that." He smiled again and, as usual, the quick change in his blue eyes—from steady and focused to bemused—caught her off guard. His eyes were as variable as the ocean; they seemed to pierce her at one moment and mock her the next. It was unsettling—to never know what to expect.

It's no different than the Benson Glare, she reminded herself. *He may be smiling, but he's here because he thinks he needs to check up on your patients. Just stay calm and don't let him see that you're ruffled.*

She returned his smile with a steady gaze, determined to show him that she wasn't in the least bit on the defensive.

"What's got you up so early?" he asked. "Fellowship isn't like residency. You should be taking advantage of having time to get a full night's sleep for the first time in three years."

He wasn't wrong about that. Despite her rocky start at the medical center, one change she'd already felt the full advantage of was the ability to have a regular sleep schedule. Working through sleep deprivation was a normal part of a doctor's training, but the worst of it happened during the residency years. She'd dreaded the weeks when she was scheduled for night shifts and twenty-four hour calls.

"It has been nice to feel well rested for the first time in…" She paused. "Actually, I can't remember the last time I got a full night's sleep. Maybe back in the first week of medical school?"

He laughed. "I felt the same way when I first started fellowship. At first I had so much energy I thought I needed to get my blood work checked, but then I realized that that was just what it felt like to be a normal person going on eight hours of sleep."

It was nice to hear Cade sounding a bit more relaxed. Most of their conversations so far had been discussions about patient care—discussions that left Dani feeling frustrated because Cade so often seemed to give her instructions or information that was already part of her plan. For once, he seemed more interested in connecting with her, rather than correcting her every move.

Still. She didn't need him hovering anxiously over her work or her patients.

"Dr. Logan," she began, wondering how she could explain this to him in a way he could understand.

"Please. You've been here a couple weeks now. You should call me Cade.

"Cade. Can we go out into the hallway for a moment?"

He accompanied her into the hall. "Why do I get the sense that I'm in trouble?" he asked.

"No one's in trouble. We just need to talk about…this." She waved her arms toward the patient.

He raised his eyebrows, his blue eyes becoming even more clear as he did. "And 'this' refers to what, exactly?"

She tried to find the words to be as diplomatic as possible. "It looks to me as though you're checking up on my patient."

"Is there something wrong with that?"

"Not necessarily. But in case you haven't noticed, *I'm* here to check up on my patient. In fact, ever since I arrived, it seems as though every time I'm about to take care of something, or learn something new or finish something on my own, you're right there to make sure that it gets done."

"I'm the senior fellow, Dr. Martin. Making sure that procedures run smoothly is a big part of my responsibilities."

"Yes, but there's a big difference between making sure procedures run smoothly and believing that they won't unless you take care of them. Quite frankly, most of the feedback you've given me has all been related to things you would have seen me do anyway, had you waited just a half second longer."

"Can you give me an example?"

"Cade. We're *standing* in an example. When I see you here checking up on my patient, it makes me worry that you don't trust me to have things under control, or to seek you out when I need to."

Cade looked pained for a moment, and Dani worried she'd gone too far. But then he said, "It's not you I don't trust."

"What do you mean?"

He hesitated, as though trying to find his words. "I was a resident here for three years, and a fellow after that. This island, this medical center, means everything to me. It's my intention to stay here on St. Camille permanently. And this is the first year I've had primary responsibility for the training program. I want everything to run smoothly. But what if I can't? What if I miss something? What if something preventable happens on my watch, because I ignored my instincts?"

Dani absorbed what Cade was saying. She'd seen him as confident, capable and in control. But until this moment, it had never occurred to her that Cade Logan, certified micromanager and control freak, might be *nervous*.

He's not really a control freak. He's just feeling the weight of responsibility, and he's worried about all the things that could go wrong. She could relate to that.

His next words confirmed her thoughts. "I know you're a good physician, Dr. Martin. I read your application, and I've seen you work. I know I should be able to trust you with any patient in the medical center. It's myself I don't trust. What if I'm not ready for this?"

Something about how vulnerable he looked evaporated any lingering frustration she felt. She'd spent the past two weeks wanting to throttle him, but now that he'd finally dropped his air of confidence and admitted his uncertainty, she only wanted to offer reassurance. A shock of blond hair fell over the crease in his forehead, and it was all she could do to resist the urge to push it back and tell him not to worry. Instead, she said, "Well, first of all, you *can* trust your instincts. In fact, you had a good one just now."

His eyes were quizzical. "How so?"

"When you said it was time to be on a first-name basis. Enough of this Dr. Martin business. Call me Dani."

He smiled, and although his eyes had the same sparkle, somehow it was different; less jarring. The warmth of it enveloped her instead of taking her off guard as it had over the past two weeks.

"I can do that," he said.

She thought for a moment. "I appreciate what you said about trusting my skills. But I think what we need to work as a team is to trust *each other*. And that takes time, but we really haven't known each other for very long. So what do you need from me so that you can trust me?"

He mulled this over. "Transparency," he said, after a moment's thought.

Well, you walked right into that one, she told herself. There was nothing wrong with the idea of transparency, unless one was keeping a fairly large secret. Such as being twelfth in line to a throne.

Cade was warming to the idea. "Yes. Transparency. I think the whole team has got to feel more comfortable with transparency, especially in these early days. And I've got to work on letting go of control. I think the more open and honest we can all be with one another, the more comfortable I'll feel letting go."

Dani gave a weak smile. "Honesty is the best policy."

But how well could she follow that policy?

Most of the time, she didn't mind keeping her royal status a secret because she understood the need for discretion and security. But it felt different to hold on to that secret with Cade standing in front of her, openly stating how much he felt the need for honesty and transparency.

It felt different, too, to notice his eyes once again fall along the line of her upper lip, just as they had back in Boston. His eyes rested right where her scar was, tiny and imperceptible to anyone. Almost anyone.

But perhaps not to Cade.

Back in Boston, she'd thought he was simply trying to make note of her features, as anyone might when meeting a new colleague. Except his expression then hadn't exactly felt collegial, just as it didn't now. Something about the way he was looking at her made her lips feel dry. She tried, desperately, to resist the urge to lick them…and failed.

The moment she licked her lips, she saw Cade swallow. There was no mistaking it.

But why on earth should Cade swallow, simply because she'd licked her lips?

You're making far too much of this, she told herself. *People swallow. People lick their lips when they're dry. You're a doctor, you know all about basic bodily functions. Stop acting as though he's looking at you in any particular way.*

But *why* was he looking at her?

Before she could decide how to interpret his intense, piercing expression, the lights went out.

A thunderclap sounded so loudly that Dani jumped. The lights in the hallway went dark and she could barely see Cade's faint outline, let alone his expression.

"The backup generators should come on within the next few seconds," he said. "Don't worry. This happens sometimes during the worst storms."

They stood together in the darkness, waiting.

"Should we be concerned?" Dani asked after a moment.

"Give it just another second," said Cade. Then, when the lights still didn't come back on, he said, "Okay, let's move back toward the wall."

Dani started to move, but as she did, one pant leg of her

overly large scrubs came unfurled and she slipped backward with a yelp. Firm arms enveloped her before she hit the floor.

She froze in his embrace for a moment, too embarrassed to move.

"Careful," he said. "Here, I'll hold you up while you get your footing."

He kept his arms around her, turning her toward him as she slowly stood upright. She'd never been close enough to him to notice before, but she could swear he smelled of cinnamon.

She sighed with relief as the lights came back on—but his arms were still around her.

"Are you all right?" he asked.

Now she knew he could see her blush, no matter how dim the lighting was. He was too close to miss it.

"It's just these scrubs," she said. "They're a little long for me, so they're hard to walk in." After a moment, she added, "You can let go." When he seemed reluctant, she added, "Really. I'm perfectly capable of standing." Her exasperation came flooding back. They'd just had an entire conversation in which Cade had acknowledged that he'd been too controlling, and now he was doubting whether she could even stand on her own two feet.

"Of course," he said, moving away from her. "Can I walk you back to your room? Or to the charting station, if you're planning to stay up?"

She rolled her eyes. "There's no need for you to walk me anywhere. It was only a few minutes ago that you were saying some very nice things about backing off and letting go. Here's a chance for you to do just that."

"And you were agreeing to be transparent. But there's something you haven't told me."

Her heart was in her throat. What did he know?

"Those scrubs they gave you. They don't fit you at all, do they? Have you been walking around in oversize scrubs for two weeks? Why didn't you say anything?"

She hesitated. But he was right about transparency. If she couldn't be honest about her one big secret, she could at least try to be forthright about the smaller things. "The admin staff said it might be a few weeks before any new medical supplies come in, especially with the storm delaying shipments."

He shook his head. "The storms can't be helped. But we can put in a rush order for certain things."

"I don't want to be a bother," she began.

"Nonsense. I'll see that it's done." With that, he headed out the door, leaving Dani alone with her mind swirling.

Now that she'd noticed the scent of cinnamon that seemed to cling to Cade, she noticed its aftereffects as well. Traces of cinnamon lingered in the room, faint but clearly there—now that she knew what to look for.

She thought again of the way his gaze had lingered on her lips. Why the hell had he been looking at her like that?

She hadn't had any time to make sense of his expression before she'd almost gone sprawling to the floor.

She could still feel the pressure of Cade's arms against her body. He'd held her for much longer than he'd needed to.

Because he's a control freak who can't let go of anything until he's completely certain that absolutely nothing will go wrong, she thought.

Or…because he hadn't wanted to let go of her.

But that was utter nonsense. She'd fallen in the darkness and Cade had helped her up, the way any civilized human would help another.

The truth hit her harder than the thunderclaps outside the window. She hadn't wanted Cade to let go of *her*. She'd wanted him to continue that embrace for as long as possible. For him to pull her closer with those strong arms, to hold her against the solid chest and the warm, beating heart she'd felt—just for a moment—when he'd had his arms around her. Steadying her.

The thoughts she was having now were far from steady. And far from anything professional. Her mind raced, despite her attempts to bring herself back to reason. She breathed in the last traces of cinnamon in the air and imagined that Cade *hadn't* let go. What would it feel like, for the top of her head to rest in the hollow beneath his chin? For his stubble to graze her forehead? Her skin felt hot as she thought of quite a few other sensations she'd like to have while Cade held her…kissed her…and perhaps did more than kiss her.

Stop. This was pointless. She and Cade worked together, and she couldn't be effective at work if she was distracted by her attraction to a colleague.

Attraction. That's all it was. It couldn't be anything more. For one thing, she had no solid evidence that Cade felt anything for her. She could be completely misinterpreting the way he'd gazed at her. The fact that he'd swallowed when she licked her lips could mean anything. And even if he did feel an attraction, it would probably evaporate the moment he learned the full truth about her.

For a member of the Lorovian royal family, dating didn't exactly lend itself to romance. When she was quite young, her uncle Xavier had sat her down and explained The Rules: Anyone she officially dated would have to sign a nondisclosure agreement. A certain number of public appearances by herself and her consort were required each year. Her consort had to sign legal documents promising not to engage in any public behavior that reflected negatively on the royal family. And that was just for starters.

The rules and regulations were only part of a problem that had plagued Dani since childhood. Even if she hadn't promised to keep her royal status a secret, revealing the truth still wouldn't solve the problem she'd struggled with for most of her life: that of wondering whether people liked her for herself or for her title. And Peter's betrayal, years ago, had left her wary and mistrustful of love.

Which was why the flicker of attraction she'd felt when she'd slipped straight into Cade's arms had taken her by surprise. But now that she was aware of her attraction, she had no intention of allowing that flicker to grow into a flame. She'd come to the Caribbean to learn, to help and to make the most of her medical career while she could. Acting on an attraction was out of the question—especially an attraction that was so fleeting and circumstantial. She was certain that if she ignored her feelings, they would eventually fade.

Her only worry was that maybe glances *did* mean that he was beginning to feel something for her. But even if it was true that he felt something—even if she wasn't just in the throes of wild, sleep-deprived speculation—then he couldn't possibly feel that much for her. They'd only met a few weeks ago; hardly enough time for any strong feelings to develop. If she did her best to communicate a complete lack of interest, then any potential attraction he might feel for her was sure to die down.

She ignored the small pang in her chest that suggested she might not *want* to communicate a complete lack of interest. She'd been a princess long enough to know that what she wanted didn't matter. It was her duty that mattered.

And doing her duty meant doing her best to make sure she didn't reveal her true feelings. That wouldn't be too hard, she thought. She was used to secrets, and she'd become very good at keeping them.

CHAPTER THREE

THE LONG WALK along the beach to Coral Bay was Cade's favorite part of every morning. Cardiology staff were required to live close to the medical center, and on his way to work, weather permitting, he walked along the beach to get to Coral Bay, pacing himself to arrive just as the sun became level with the palm trees.

The solitude of the morning should have been welcome after the recent storms. But Cade found he couldn't enjoy the quiet as he usually did.

His thoughts kept returning to Dani and the conversation they'd had not twenty-four hours ago. He hoped she wasn't regretting her move to St. Camille. She seemed to be adjusting well to the medical center—as far as he could tell, all the staff loved her—but he wanted her to love being there, too. The island needed as many good doctors as it could get, and from what he could tell, the medical center had been extremely lucky to snag Dani right off her residency.

Is it really just about what the island needs, though? He tried to swat the thought away, but it persisted.

He could tell himself that he wanted Dani to fit in for the good of the island. But his reaction during the momentary power outage suggested otherwise.

No—in fact, it had been just before the power outage that his thoughts had started to betray him, despite all his best efforts.

He'd noticed the tiny divot near the right corner of her upper lip when they'd first met. The mark seemed like a scar, perhaps from some childhood accident. She'd have a perfect Cupid's bow if it weren't for that little indentation in the corner. But her mouth wasn't perfect. It was unique, which was even better.

He tried not to think too much about the shape of Dani's mouth, though. Because if he did, then it was only a short step away to start thinking about whether her lips might be soft, which then led to thinking about her skin…which he had no business thinking about at all. Because those weren't the kind of thoughts one had about a colleague. And he very much wanted Dani to continue at Coral Bay as a colleague.

The problem was, he could no longer deny that he wanted other things as well.

When she'd slipped and fallen against him, he'd been exquisitely aware of how close her body was to his. Her hair had brushed against his chin. She'd been wearing it swept back from her face, with loose curls cascading around her shoulders. For an instant, he'd had an insane urge to gather those curls in his hands and let his fingers luxuriate in them. He knew that it was only a fleeting attraction, a kind of momentary madness. But the intensity of his reaction had startled him.

Intense or not, it was still nothing more than an attraction. His feelings would die down soon enough if he ignored them, and it was necessary that he ignore them. He'd sworn off relationships years ago, for reasons that made perfectly good sense at the time and still held true today. Even if he hadn't, getting involved with a coworker would invite exactly the kinds of complications he preferred to avoid.

There was also no telling how long she'd stay. Island life wasn't for everyone, and if her family situation was as complex as she'd hinted at back in Boston, then he worried she might find it difficult to stay for the three-year duration of her fellowship. He'd seen plenty of doctors arrive in the Caribbean excited to complete their fellowship in a tropical paradise, only to find the distance from home too stressful. If Dani decided to quit, she wouldn't be the first.

She didn't strike him as someone who gave up easily, though. He thought of how her eyes blazed when she'd accused him of being a micromanager. Had he really been that bad? Probably. He knew he had a tendency to seize control when he felt nervous. And there was plenty about Dani that made him nervous. Nothing that had to do with her clinical skills, of course. No, it was more about the wayward tendrils of hair that fell lose about her face and the dark lashes that framed her eyes. He was nervous that he wouldn't be able to stop thinking about her, and he very much needed to.

It was essential that he and Dani be able to get along, as coworkers, because there was a genuine need for her to stay. In addition to providing free care to island residents, Coral Bay Medical Center served a steady stream of wealthy clients who were used to receiving top-notch medical care in luxurious settings. But in order to maintain their reputation, the hospital needed to recruit the most talented staff, and the most talented staff typically wanted to work on the mainland. So no matter how much Cade might notice himself noticing Dani's curly locks or rich brown eyes, he needed to keep such thoughts to himself. If she eventually decided that Coral Bay wasn't for her, it wouldn't be because he'd made things complicated.

Her introduction had already been rocky enough. Until last night, he'd blamed that on the relentless storms. But now, it appeared that he was to blame, too.

He hadn't meant to micromanage Dani's cases. For all his talk of transparency, he'd only given her the partial truth when he'd said he was nervous about overseeing the training program. There was nothing that would have stopped him from hovering over Dani's patient, because that patient was diagnosed with an atrial septal defect. The same diagnosis his brother, Henry, was given, after it was too late to do anything about it.

Henry had passed away at the age of fifteen. If Cade had been a doctor back then, and not merely an eight-year-old boy, maybe he would have noticed that something was wrong. Like the way Henry was always winded after running up the stairs. Or the way Henry sometimes alluded to a tingling in his fingers, as though that happened to everyone. As a cardiologist, Cade could look back and see all the signs of an undiagnosed congenital heart defect.

But no one had noticed the signs in time to help Henry. He'd collapsed after a track meet, and although he was rushed to the hospital, there was nothing anyone could do.

Without Henry to hold the family together, things began to fall apart. Cade's father had never been good at expressing his emotions, and instead of acknowledging his grief, he turned his anger toward the world instead. After their divorce, Cade could tell that his mother was much happier, but he still longed for the family they'd once had.

He escaped his own grief by throwing himself into his schoolwork. He was determined to become a doctor. He might not be able to save Henry, but he could save other families from befalling the same tragedy.

Coming to St. Camille had been an unexpected detour. He had never expected to live in the Caribbean. After graduating medical school, he'd planned to settle down in Boston, where he'd done his training. He'd spent three years with Susan, his medical-school sweetheart, and they planned to marry as soon as he began his internship.

Cade felt as though everything was starting to work out. He had the career he wanted and a life with the woman he loved. A woman who he thought loved him back.

Two days before the wedding, Susan eloped with Cade's best man. Cade did not take it well. He felt as though everyone he'd ever counted on had let him down. His parents, lost in their grief, had failed to rally to support their remaining child. His best friend, his chosen brother, had betrayed him. And Susan, who he thought was the love of his life, had been lying to him for months. He'd been so busy with his training that he hadn't even noticed they were having problems in their relationship.

And as much as he blamed everyone else, he blamed himself, too. For not seeing what was happening with Susan. Not noticing. Not having any control over the situation, nor any way to stop the helplessness and pain. Just as he hadn't had any control with Henry.

When he'd lost Susan, he stopped attending classes and his ranking fell from first in his class to nearly last. He rallied and took up his studies again just in time to graduate, but by then, his grades had taken irreparable damage. He almost didn't get an internship. After months of languishing in heartbreak and letting his grades decline, there was only one internship program that was willing to consider him. The doctors at the Coral Bay Medical Center were impressed by the passion he showed for medicine. They looked at Cade's history, and the strong recommendations from his professors, and decided they were willing to take a chance on him.

Moving to St. Camille had changed his life, in every way for the better. And if it was far from home, well, there wasn't much at home that he was sad to leave behind. He was better off without relationships in his life—they only led to pain and heartbreak. He found friends among the staff at Coral Bay, and he enjoyed the slower pace of island life.

As he neared the hospital, his phone vibrated. He had a text from his mother: Heard you had some bad storms. Everything ok?

She was the only person he missed, but she'd understood his need to move and they talked frequently.

Aside from his mother, he didn't talk with anyone from his past. He'd anticipated a solitary life on the island, but island life was anything but solitary. Because everyone knew everyone else, there were no secrets. No devastating revelations. He'd had more than enough of those in his life. Secrets always came with sudden, unexpected grief.

After so many complications in his early life, he was determined to spare himself the pain and grief that came with permanent or meaningful attachments. He'd sworn off relationships when he'd moved to the island. He'd had a few brief flings over the years, but nothing more. It was best that way. With no attachment, there could be no loss.

He made a mental note to check on the status of the scrubs Dani needed. Normally such tasks wouldn't be within his purview, but he had a feeling that Dani was the kind of person who wouldn't want to make a fuss over trivial things, and he didn't want her needs to be overlooked. She needed clothes that fit, and those oversize, folded cuffs of her pant legs were a slipping hazard.

Also, the sooner they eliminated the danger of her falling into his arms again, the better.

Her body had been so light in his hands. She'd clung to him, even as she'd insisted she didn't need to.

Of course she clung to you, his rational mind berated him. *That's what people do when they've just slipped. They grab on to whoever's there. It doesn't mean anything.*

And yet. Sometimes he thought he saw her glancing at him, her gaze lingering on him just a moment longer than expected. It probably meant nothing. Or it meant that she was annoyed with him, as she had been last night.

Maybe she'd think better of him if he could back off a little bit. Showed her that he did trust her as a physician and knew that she could handle herself without his constant input. And maybe if he stopped thinking about the way tendrils of her hair came forward to frame her face, he could be more relaxed around her, instead of jumping in with advice to distract himself from the way she made him feel.

And if he ignored his attraction for long enough, it would fade and become a nonissue. It was simply a matter of willpower. This was a good plan. Cade loved plans: they eliminated surprises. He took a look at his schedule for the morning and saw that he and Dani were slated to review some infant screenings. Perfect. He headed to the neonatal care unit, determined to put his willpower to the test.

Dani wasn't sure if the infants on the neonatal care unit today were particularly squirmy, or if all babies were like this. Not one of them seemed interested in holding still long enough for her to wrap the small soft sensor correctly around their hands and feet.

She muttered something under her breath that made Cade give that irritating, half-winking smile of his. "What?" she all but snapped at him.

"You just don't hear a lot of curse words in the NICU," he replied. "Not that I'm judging. After all, our patients are a little too young to understand most words, let alone the naughty ones."

"I wish I could get them to understand how to hold still." Dani tried adjusting the sensor again, only to have it fall out of place.

Of course, she *would* have to struggle with the procedure while Cade was watching. Dani appreciated that he seemed to be trying to hold back today, watching her do the procedure rather than taking over. But she also had to ignore the traces of cinnamon that wafted from him and the way his blue eyes contributed to the flip-flops her stomach was performing. Neither of those things was assisting with her concentration.

It also didn't help that Cade's shoulders were shaking with laughter. When she looked up at him and glared, he quickly put his hand over his mouth, trying to suppress a smile.

She hadn't worked much with newborns, and she'd never done a pulse oximetry screening before. It was such a routine part of screening for congenital heart disease that she wanted to be familiar with it.

But her tiny patients weren't interested in cooperating. Any hopes she'd had of impressing Cade had been quickly foiled by babies less than twenty-four hours old.

"Keep trying," Cade said. "You're doing fine."

Dani maneuvered the sensor again and reminded herself that it wasn't Cade's fault that her stomach did gymnastics whenever he smiled.

"Ha! Got it!" The sensor finally stayed in place, and Dani took her reading. She looked at Cade in triumph, but his expression was bemused.

There's something I'm not seeing, she thought. *And he knows and he's just going to enjoy not telling me what it is.*

Her hunch was proven correct moments later as she read the

infant's pulse-ox levels. The numbers she was getting didn't match the baby's presentation at all. A baby with oxygen level readings as low as this little infant's should be in significant distress. But the baby in front of her was a hale and hearty newborn with good weight and what she could swear was a wide smile, even though he was technically too young to smile.

"Well?" Cade asked. "What's the verdict?"

Dani shook her head. "It doesn't make any sense. How could his levels be so low?"

"You tell me. Ninety-five to one hundred percent is normal, so below ninety percent means…what?"

Dani really wished that Cade's eyes didn't fix on her quite so intensely every time he asked a question. She started listing the problems out loud: "It could indicate an infection or lung problems. Maybe we should do an echocardiogram."

"Hold on. Let's try something else before we jump to additional tests." Cade scooped the baby out of his bassinet. "This little guy is way too active. Plus, babies are small, so equipment slips around on their bodies. I'll hold him, and we'll see if you get a more accurate reading."

Dani flushed. Of course. She'd been overthinking things. And she'd been trying to rush to a solution in order to get Cade to stop looking at her with that piercing gaze, but she couldn't tell him that.

To add insult to injury, the baby, which had been so fussy with her, instantly became relaxed in Cade's arms.

"There," he said. "This should make things go much more smoothly."

"He calmed down right way," said Dani, her frustration dissipating in the face of the magic of the baby drifting off to sleep. Babies were so vulnerable, yet so trusting. She couldn't remember the last time she'd seen any creature so completely at peace.

"Well, I've had lots of practice," Cade replied.

Dani realized, not for the first time, that she knew next to nothing about Cade's life outside the medical center. "You mean with pediatric patients? Or with children in general?"

"With patients. Kids are great, as long as I can give them back to their parents at the end of the day. I couldn't imagine having one of my own. Having to be responsible for a tiny, vulnerable human, twenty-four hours a day. I don't know how parents handle it."

Dani looked at the way the baby had curled itself against Cade's chest. "I think a lot of it is just instinctual."

"In that case, my instinct is to do whatever I can to heal children, not to raise them."

Dani felt an unexpected sense of loss as Cade spoke. She'd always thought she'd have children of her own one day, even though she couldn't imagine how that would come to pass. Given the difficulties she'd had with dating, it was hard to believe she could ever trust her heart with anyone again, let alone fall in love.

But in light of all the complications of romance, all the obstacles in the way of having a family, she often felt that having children of her own was another dream she should give up. Maybe it could be fulfilling enough to help children heal, rather than raising children of her own. It wasn't what she'd always wanted...but how often did anything in life turn out just the way she wanted it to?

With the baby finally asleep, Dani was able take her readings. "Here. Why don't I hold him so I can slip a sensor around his foot?" she asked. But when she tried to take the baby, he stirred and became squirmy again.

Cade laughed. "Anyone can see that you don't hold babies very often."

She blushed. "How can you tell?"

"You're trying to hold him like he's made of glass. Babies like to feel contained; it's why they're soothed when they're swaddled. Here. Put your arm like this, and don't be afraid to firm up your grip a little. You're not going to break him."

He settled the baby into Dani's arms. She felt more confident, following his advice, even though she was nervous to hold something—*someone*—so delicate.

"Look," Cade whispered. "He's fallen asleep again."

As he leaned toward her, Dani once again caught the notes of cinnamon that seemed to linger about his body. Between his scent and the heat she could feel from his body as he stood close to her, Dani was about at her limit.

Cade's gaze flitted away from the baby and back to her. Once again, he was looking at her with that particular, penetrating gaze. The one that made her lips feel dry.

That did it. A woman could only handle so much.

She placed the baby back in the bassinet and then stood up straight to give the front of her scrubs a brisk brush-off. "Well. Looks like we've got the readings we needed. Turns out his pulse ox was normal after all. Nothing to worry about here."

Cade was quiet. He was still looking at the baby, but his mind seemed far away.

"Cade?"

He shook himself. "I'm so sorry. My mind was somewhere else."

"Where, exactly?"

"It doesn't matter." He gave her a quick smile, but something felt off about it. In the time she'd known him, every time he smiled, his left eye had closed in an involuntary wink. But both eyes had stayed open this time. He was forcing the smile, Dani realized. It wasn't genuine.

She knew she should let the matter drop. If Cade didn't want to talk about something, then it wasn't her business to pry into it.

But what if he needed to talk, but wasn't sure how to start?

"Do you want to grab a coffee from the commissary?" she asked, purely on impulse. Given her attraction to Cade, she should be trying to spend *less* time with him, not more. But she'd been taken aback by his distant expression, just now. Wherever his mind had gone, it didn't seem very pleasant.

"It's not necessary." His voice took on a brusqueness she was beginning to recognize. It was the tone he used whenever a conversation broached personal subjects.

"Are you sure? Because I really don't mind—"

"I said no," he replied curtly.

There was an awkward silence. He had the grace to look shamefaced. "I'm sorry. That was rude."

She shrugged. If Cade didn't want to talk, that was his choice—there was plenty she didn't want to tell him, either. "Not a big deal."

"I only meant that I was busy. I have a full day."

"Okay," said Dani, slowly. "Well, consider it a standing offer, then."

"I will. Another time." And he practically ran from the room.

Great, thought Dani. *He couldn't have left any faster.*

If Cade were that eager to get away from her, then at least she wouldn't have to worry about hiding her attraction from him. But for some reason, the thought didn't make her feel any better. Not even a little bit.

Cade headed down the hallway outside the neonatal care unit, thoroughly frustrated with himself. All Dani had done was invite him to the commissary for a cup of coffee and he'd been cold and abrupt.

He ran his fingers through his hair, mentally running through how things had taken such a sudden downturn. He'd been looking at the baby, his mind lost in thoughts of how different things could have been for his brother Henry if pulse oximetry screening had been a routine part of care when Henry was born. He'd been so wrapped up in thoughts of the past that it had taken him by surprise when Dani jolted him back to the present.

And with that jolt, the immediacy of the moment had hit him with full force. His thoughts had wandered to an emotional place, and with Dani there next to him…his guard had been down. He'd momentarily strayed from the plan of ignoring his attraction to her. Everything had been going so well during the screenings, when they'd both had tasks to focus on. But the moment he'd become lost in his reverie—no, the moment she'd called him back to the present—everything had fallen apart.

He'd realized that he was standing next to a woman he was extremely attracted to, while thinking about some very personal things. And as she'd said his name, he'd found himself acutely aware of her lips again, as well as the way her dark curls settled around her neck and the way her still-oversize scrubs hung about her petite frame.

He knew that he needed to get away from her. He just hadn't planned to make his exit so abruptly. Or so awkwardly. He couldn't imagine what she thought of him now.

He needed to fix this, he realized. Not this week or later today, but immediately. They needed to be on good terms to work together, and he didn't like the idea of Dani being upset with him. He might not want her to suspect his attraction, but he didn't want her to hate him, either.

He went to the commissary but didn't find her there. He bought two coffees and headed back toward the neonatal care unit, hoping he'd see her somewhere along the way.

He didn't have to search for long before he ran into her, almost spilling one of the coffees as he rounded a corner in his haste to find her again.

"It's okay," she said as he tried to brush her with napkins. "You didn't get any on me."

"Good," he said. "I'm glad I ran into you. I wanted to explain about earlier." He held out one of the coffees to her and was relieved when she took it.

She took a sip and smiled. "You know, the coffee here really isn't that bad."

Her nose crinkled just the tiniest bit as she savored the smell from the cup. She pulled her hair back from where it fell around her shoulders so that it all cascaded down her back instead, revealing the delicate outline of her neck. Cade swallowed and took a sip of his coffee, too, just to get his bearings. This was going to be more difficult than he'd thought.

"You see..." He tried to launch into an explanation, and then immediately realized that he had nothing prepared. What could he tell her? The truth? He'd never told anyone at work about Henry.

She motioned toward an empty exam room nearby. "Why don't we go in there? You look like you could use a little more privacy."

He followed her into the exam room, and she shut the door and turned toward him. "What is it, Cade?"

"I just wanted to say that I was sorry—for brushing you off

so rudely. You were trying to be friendly, and I want us to be friends, too. But the way I acted was…inexcusable."

She set her coffee down, giving him her full attention. "Apology accepted and appreciated. But is that really all there is? Something seems to be on your mind, and if you want to talk about it, I'm right here."

Her hair had slipped back over her right shoulder, curving inward where her neck met the scoop of her shoulder. His fingers itched to gather her loose brown curls in one hand and reveal the swan-like shape of her neck once again.

Focus, he thought.

"I've been a little distracted, lately," he said. "There's all the responsibility with the training program here, as well as you getting started on the right foot, both at the medical center and on the island."

She nodded and her eyes met his; twin brown pools that he could drown in if he let himself look for long enough. "You've already mentioned that."

"Right," he said, his voice coming out gravelly and low. It was a small room, and she was standing very close to him.

"Cade, in the interest of transparency, why don't you just tell me what's going on?"

She reached out, and Cade realized she was picking a thread from the shoulder of his white coat. He caught her hand. "It's fine," he said. "You don't have to do that."

In spite of himself, in spite of his determination to be an absolute gentleman, he held on to her hand for perhaps a second longer than was proper. Just for a second. It couldn't have been long…and yet, it was long enough that he could take in the softness of her skin. His thumb brushed against the inner curve of her wrist, which was just as soft as the back of her hand, and he knew that same softness would extend to her forearm, and her shoulders and the rest of her, too.

Their eyes met and he swallowed. He let go of her hand, but not before he felt that same electric jolt he'd felt earlier in the neonatal unit.

She took a step closer to him so that there was barely any space between them at all. Her chin was tilted upward, almost begging for him to cup it, and then suddenly he *was* cupping it. He placed his hand against her jawline and tilted her face toward him as he bent to kiss her—tasting citrus lip gloss, a trace of coffee and *her*.

It was over in a second. Or at least, it should have been. He broke away from her, furious with himself and wondering how the hell he could possibly apologize enough for this. He opened his mouth, uncertain of what he could possibly say, but before he could say anything, she was kissing him right back.

Her arms went around his neck and pulled his body close to hers. He held her as his mouth delved into hers, searching again for that indefinable taste that came from her alone. He inhaled the sweetness of her; some soft vanilla scent that mixed with the taste of citrus on her lips, leaving him with the impression of sherbet. He touched the soft locks of her hair, lifting her curls and letting them tumble over his fingers. He was acutely aware of her breasts against him. Her whole body was soft and warm and closer to his than it had ever been before— and yet, not close enough. Not anywhere near close enough.

Cade's pager sounded and they broke apart, meeting each other with startled gazes.

He checked his pager. "It's an emergency."

"Then you should go take care of it."

"But—"

"There's no 'but.' We'll figure this out later. Go!"

She was right. Whatever had just happened between the two of them would have to be addressed later on. He was needed in the cath lab.

As scattered as his thoughts were, his mind registered one thing: Dani had kissed *him*. He'd been the idiot who'd gotten swept up in the moment and kissed her, but then she had kissed him back.

Which meant that she felt something for him, too.

But that made things even worse. Because Cade could handle his own fleeting attraction. Or at least, he'd thought he could, right up until that kiss. But he didn't want Dani to get hurt, and if she became attached to him, she might. Cade had spent six years not allowing himself to get attached to anyone—because getting attached meant you had someone to lose.

He could still taste her lip gloss. He savored it, knowing it was a mistake to do so. He needed to stop things with Dani before they even began. Before either one of them got hurt.

CHAPTER FOUR

THE REST OF the day passed in a blur for Dani. She clung to her training and her professionalism; they were the only two things that allowed her to get through a day filled with patients, lectures and chart reviews after Cade had kissed her.

Kissed her! That was putting it diplomatically. She'd been determined to hide her attraction from Cade, and yet at the first tiny sign of encouragement, she'd practically thrown herself at him. She'd accused him of being a micromanager, of needing to control everything, and then she'd gone and demonstrated that she could barely control herself. She couldn't be more embarrassed.

Somehow, for the first time since she'd arrived at Coral Bay, she'd managed to avoid him for an entire day. She wondered if he was caught up in the cath lab or if he was actively trying to avoid her. They'd have to discuss things eventually, but if he was trying to put off their inevitable awkward conversation, she really couldn't blame him. She wasn't looking forward to it, either.

The more she thought about their kiss, the more she dreaded seeing him again. She couldn't imagine what would be worse: learning that Cade had enthusiastically enjoyed it, or that he felt it had been a huge mistake. Her emotions roiled within her, changing every minute. Wild fantasies of a whirlwind romance with Cade fought with the cold, hard realities of her obligations as a princess and her history of heartbreak.

When she was finally done with her shift, she decided to leave the medical center's campus instead of going to the dormitory. Ever since her arrival, she'd been immersed in work. She longed for a chance to explore this island she'd heard so much about, and with the break in weather, she finally had her chance.

Dani only had to take a few steps outside the medical center's doors before she reached the beach. She felt the tension melt from her shoulders as a light, warm breeze surrounded her. She could just barely taste a hint of salt on her lips, and there was a faint floral scent she couldn't quite identify— hibiscus, or perhaps even orchids, which she knew grew wild on the island. The sun wasn't ready to set yet, though the deepening indigo of the sky promised quite a show in an hour or two. Palm trees swayed on the beach over smooth, flat rocks that jutted out from the white sand.

She made her way toward the rocks and sat down, tucking her knees beneath her chin and wrapping her arms around her legs. *This* was the Caribbean she'd been looking forward to. After a tumultuous start, she could finally start to enjoy the paradise that everyone told her she was living in. She just needed to figure out how she'd managed to mess things up so quickly first.

How had she gone from being so determined to keep her attraction to Cade to herself, to kissing him in an unused exam room?

He said he wanted transparency between us. And he'd gotten what he asked for. After that kiss, he couldn't possibly be in any doubt about how she felt.

She, on the other hand, was mired in confusion. She knew

why she'd kissed Cade. She'd done it because she'd lost control. In a split second, she'd made a bad decision, and now she had to learn how to live with it.

But Cade had returned her kiss. In fact, Cade had *initiated* their kiss. Or had he? She was the one who'd stepped close to him just a moment before it happened. Maybe he'd just been leaning forward and she'd drawn the wrong conclusions.

No, that was wishful thinking. This would all be so much easier if Cade *hadn't* welcomed the kiss. But all the evidence suggested their moment together was more than a misunderstanding. She shivered, remembering his fingers buried in her hair; the urgency of his lips against hers. He'd been just as caught up in the moment as she was.

That's all it had been, though: a moment. A second in which they'd both let their guards down and made a mistake. A single moment didn't mean that anything meaningful had happened. A single kiss didn't mean that either of them wanted anything more from one another. It was just one kiss. One really great, exciting, passionate kiss.

She wondered how far things would have gone if his pager hadn't gone off.

It's a good thing you'll never know, she told herself sternly.

But what was she supposed to do now?

More than anything, she wished she could confide in someone. Her phone buzzed in her pocket, and Dani sat up straight. She wrestled her phone from her pocket and rejoiced to see the bars indicating reception in the corner of the screen. For the first time in days, she could use her phone.

She texted Kim immediately: emergency, can you talk now? Miami might be far away, but at least it was in the same time zone as St. Camille.

OMG great to hear from you. What's up? Kim texted back.

Dani hesitated before responding. Maybe she shouldn't put this in writing. But the chances of some tabloid getting ahold of Kim's texts and printing a salacious story were miniscule. And Kim had proven her trustworthiness time and again. Just like Peter, Kim had had chances to sell stories to the tabloids—but Kim had turned them all down. The urge to talk to someone she could trust, someone who knew her better than anyone, overrode any of Dani's worries about security.

I kissed Dr. BeachBum, she texted back.

Her phone rang immediately. Dani swiped to answer the call.

"Tell me every single detail, and don't leave anything out," said Kim.

After Dani finished explaining, Kim said, "Okay. This is all good. This is nothing to stress over. Everything's going to be fine."

"What? How can you say that? Everything will not be fine. I've only been here two weeks and I've already ruined my fellowship."

"Not possible. You can't ruin an entire fellowship with just one kiss." Kim paused. "It was just a kiss, right? You're not leaving out any other salacious details? Because there are absolutely no datable physicians at my oncology fellowship. Everyone here is well into their golden years. So I have to live vicariously through you."

"Kim. Could you please be serious for at least thirty seconds? I need your advice. How am I supposed to talk to him now? How are we supposed to work together?" The thought of even looking at him made her want to cringe with embarrassment.

"You talk to him like a mature adult. You acknowledge that the two of you did indeed have a moment, but now that moment has passed, and you want to keep working together as colleagues regardless of whatever may have happened between you personally."

Kim's voice sounded polished and well rehearsed. Dani had a sudden suspicion. "Kim, why do I get the impression you've had this conversation a few times?"

"Never mind that. We're here to talk about your love life, not mine. And what I want to know is, what do *you* want to happen next?"

Dani paused.

"Dani? Hello?"

"I'm just thinking."

"What's to think about? Do you like him, or not?"

Did she like him? She liked the way he smelled, the way his body moved. She liked the way his lips felt against hers and the waviness of his sun-streaked blond hair. Hair her fingers itched to tousle.

"He's very attractive," she said.

"But not relationship material?"

Dani hesitated. Cade was clearly kind, caring and dedicated to his work. His micromanaging style sometimes made her want to throttle him, but she'd seen enough to learn that even that flaw came from a caring place.

The problem wasn't that she didn't like Cade. The problem was that she could imagine herself liking him quite a lot.

But liking him was out of the question. A fleeting attraction was one thing. Having deeper feelings for someone, getting more attached…that could lead to something more serious over time. And anything serious between her and Cade would be impossible.

"It's not that he isn't relationship material," she told Kim. "It's that I don't think *anyone* would be."

"Because of the princess stuff?"

"Exactly. Even if I could tell him who I really am… I can't put so much obligation on someone else. It's too much to ask. No one would want to be involved in all of that."

"Mmm-hmm. And what about what you want, Princess Danielle-Genevieve?"

Dani sighed. "I'm not sure how much that matters."

"Dani, is being royal really the only issue?"

"What do you mean?"

"Well, I know you had a lot of heartache over what's-his-name. Peter. That guy from college. He caused you a lot of pain. He completely betrayed your trust."

Dani tried to regain her composure. Any mention of Peter always unsettled her. Not because she still had feelings for him, but because even years later, his betrayal still stung. Kim's words were too close to the truth for comfort.

The island's spotty reception was beginning to weaken. "You're breaking up," Dani said, but before she could finish her sentence, the call was disconnected.

What *did* she want now? It was a question that had plagued her for most of her life. Usually, the answer was that what she wanted didn't matter because she had responsibilities.

But that wasn't completely true, she realized. Wasn't she on an island right now, looking at the Caribbean Sea? Wasn't she practicing medicine, just as she'd always wanted?

There were still stipulations. It wasn't permanent, and she had to keep her true identity a secret. But she'd made her dreams come true, at least partway. And partway was better than not at all.

If only it were possible to make things happen partway between herself and Cade. She thought again of Cade's fingers running through her hair. His hands gripping her shoulders.

In that moment, she'd known exactly what she wanted. She shivered, remembering the pressure of his hands and the way his mouth had almost devoured hers. He'd wanted her, too. Or at least, he wanted the person he thought she was.

Cade valued transparency. But if she couldn't tell him who she really was, then she had no business allowing herself to even *think* about entering a romantic relationship with him. It was one thing to keep her identity a secret at work. It wasn't an ideal situation, but she did feel she had the right to keep her personal information private from her colleagues. But if she and Cade were to become more than just colleagues, then keeping her secret would be more than just a lack of transparency. It would be a lie of omission.

The sun was meeting the horizon. The sea was still and serene and offered her absolutely no solutions to her problem.

She couldn't tell Cade the truth any more than she could deny her attraction to him. In the past, when she'd revealed her true identity, it had been under very specific circumstances. Kim was her best friend, someone Dani had known for years before she trusted her enough to tell her the truth. She'd only known Cade for a little while. They might be attracted to one another, but they were light-years away from the kind of relationship where she could trust him with her deepest secrets.

The trouble was that being a princess wasn't *just* her deepest secret. It was also an integral part of who she was. But revealing that part of herself was fraught with danger. What if she did decide that Cade was trustworthy enough to know the truth? She'd been through that before, believing that Peter could be trusted to know her true identity, and she'd been betrayed. The fiasco with Peter was a big part of why her family had made her promise not to reveal her identity to anyone else. Her family had never blamed her for Peter's actions—these things happened in royal families—but they did expect her to do everything she could to prevent it from happening again.

But for once, it wasn't her family's fears that consumed her the most. It was her own fear of having her trust broken once more. She couldn't bear the thought of going through heartbreak again with someone else. And if Cade learned the truth about her and didn't react well... Dani knew she was a resilient person, but something deep within her told her that she wasn't ready to experience the emotional roller coaster of trust, love and heartbreak with Cade. Going through it with anyone would hurt, but going through it with Cade might break her.

She pushed the thought away. She was letting her fears get the best of her. There was no reason to start worrying that Cade would break her heart, because she wasn't going to let things get to that point.

She had to tell him, in no uncertain terms, that this could not continue. There was no future for them. She'd have to find a way to explain it that he would believe without revealing her true identity. And she'd need to be convincing, because after the way she'd practically leaped into Cade's arms that morning, he could rightfully claim that she was sending some pretty mixed messages.

She needed to tell him tonight. He was off work, and they could clear the air before their next shift together. Kim was right—no matter what had happened between the two of them personally, they were still colleagues and they should act accordingly. She'd tell him that perhaps they could be friends, and nothing more.

You don't want to be just friends with him, though, a small, knowing part of her whispered.

No, she didn't. Her body didn't lie to her. She knew she wanted Cade. Knew it from the way her breath caught when he'd leaned toward her and the way her heart raced when he'd kissed her.

Those were also the reasons she knew things couldn't go any further.

Partway is better than not at all, she reminded herself. At least if they were friends, she'd still have him in her life. Maybe a friendship with Cade wouldn't be so bad.

Who was she kidding? It would be torture.

But she couldn't see any alternative. If she couldn't tell him the truth, and therefore couldn't be with him, then cutting things off before they got too serious was the responsible thing to do. And if there was one thing a princess was good at, it was meeting her responsibilities.

Cade loved his cottage on St. Camille. Like most houses on the island, it was painted in bright pastels—in his case: yellow with aquamarine shutters. It was happily situated near a beach, which gave him lots of lawn space and an unparalleled view of the ocean from his front yard.

He'd set up a fire pit and two Adirondack chairs in his front lawn, right where the grass met the sand. At the end of the day, there was nothing he liked more than relaxing by the fire, watching the sun set the sky alight before it met the horizon. But today, the calm oceanfront view wasn't bringing the peace it usually did, and he knew why.

He couldn't stop thinking about the kiss he'd shared with Dani. He'd never been so surprised by his own behavior. His plan to hide his attraction hadn't even made it twenty-four hours.

The worst part was that he didn't even feel guilty about it, although he knew he should. He knew perfectly well that he didn't want a relationship. But in that moment, during that kiss…he'd wanted Dani, and once things had gotten started, he hadn't been able to hold back.

He knew he needed to talk to her. The sooner the better. He'd managed to avoid her for most of the day, but he couldn't put their conversation off forever.

Figures dotted the beach: people enjoying the last rays of sunlight. Children played in the light of the setting sun, and a few fishermen began to turn toward home with the day's haul. In the dim light, he could make out another figure walking along the beach, and as it came closer he realized that it was Dani.

He'd known, of course, that he couldn't avoid her forever, especially on an island this small. He'd just hoped he might have an evening alone to figure out what he could possibly say to her.

"Mind if I have a seat?" she said as she approached.

He waved his arm. "Go right ahead. How did you know where I lived?"

"I'm learning that it's remarkably easy to find out anything about anyone on this island. You mentioned that you lived a little south of town, so I walked down to a little group of houses and found out that *was* town, and then a group of children out walking with their pigs told me—and I quote—that this end of the beach is where 'the lonely doctor' lives. So I just walked another four minutes down the path away from the village and found out the lonely doctor was you."

He'd heard some of the island residents call him that. He didn't love the nickname, but he supposed it was accurate.

"What if it had been someone else?"

She snorted. "I thought the risk of anyone else on St. Camille fitting that description was very low."

Fair enough.

There was no need to ask what she was doing here, at his home. He geared himself up, bracing himself to explain… something. But he couldn't fathom how to begin.

"I came to apologize," Dani said. Her words came in a breathless rush, as though she, too, had been struggling with how to start and finally decided to just blurt things out.

"What on earth for?"

She threw her hands up in exasperation. "The kiss, of course! It was a huge mistake. I should never have initiated it."

He knew he should feel relieved that she felt this way. And yet part of him felt disappointed to hear her call their kiss a huge mistake. And why was she apologizing for something *he'd* started? He'd never skirted responsibility for his actions before, and he wasn't going to start now.

"Dani, you have nothing to apologize for. I'm to blame. I was the one who initiated our…*my*…indiscretion."

"No, you weren't. I stepped close to you."

"But I was the one who kissed you."

"Yes, but then I…continued things."

Why was she arguing with him about this? He was fully prepared to take the blame.

Unless she really was trying to spare him pain. He realized that he'd been so focused on protecting her feelings that he hadn't thought about whether she was trying to protect his.

"Let's just agree that it was a mutual mistake," he said. "But to be clear, just because it was a mistake doesn't mean I have any regrets about it."

And he didn't. It may have been a terrible idea that invited far too many complications into his life, but, of course, mistakes were meant to be learned from and not repeated, so he didn't have to regret the taste of her lips or the feeling of his fingers in her hair.

He did, however, regret anything that might cause her pain, and so he quickly added, "I think we also both agree that it shouldn't happen again."

She leaned back in the chair and let out a sigh of relief. Again, he felt a pang of disappointment. The kiss might have been a mistake, but hopefully it hadn't been *bad*.

"I do want you to know that I'm truly sorry if I caused any offence," he said.

"No! I... It was a great kiss, Cade. It's just that...by kissing you, I feel that I sent a message that wasn't true to who I am. Relationships are...complicated for me. And I'm not looking for one right now."

Her words mirrored his own feelings exactly, and he felt a tiny sense of relief for the first time since that morning. His biggest fear had been that she might feel he was leading her on. Offering something more than he could give. But if Dani truly wasn't looking for a relationship, then maybe she, too, had merely been acting on a fleeting attraction. All of this was, indeed, a mistake. A misunderstanding. They could work through it, he was certain.

"As it happens, neither am I," he said.

"Please don't say that just because you're trying to make me feel better. I'm trying to apologize for throwing myself at you. I can't believe I was so unprofessional."

"I'm serious," he said. "You can ask anyone on the island. They call me the lonely doctor for a reason. I haven't had a relationship since—" he stopped, unwilling to face the emotions that came up when he broached the subject of his abruptly cancelled wedding "—since I decided to move to St. Camille," he amended. "I came here to get away from all that."

He knew he was being vague, so he could hardly be surprised that Dani raised a quizzical eyebrow.

"And by 'all that,' you mean…"

"Relationships. The complications they bring. The heartache, the disappointment."

"What about the other aspects of them? Having someone to rely on, someone to care for who cares for you? What about love?"

The sun had dipped below the horizon, and he couldn't read her expression in the dusky shadows cast by the light from the fire pit.

Love. He couldn't remember the last time he'd heard the word, let alone spoken it aloud. He found that he couldn't even form his mouth around the word now, so he settled for saying, "I found out a long time ago that handing your heart to someone is the easiest way to get it crushed."

Even though he meant every word, he wondered if he was coming across as too cynical. Dani, he thought, was probably someone who believed in things like love and romance. "I suppose that sounds very negative."

"No," she said. "What you're saying doesn't sound negative. It sounds accurate."

In the short time he'd known Dani, she'd struck him as optimistic, hopeful. It was a change to hear her sound so world-weary. Had she been hurt before? Something within his chest roiled at the thought of her being hurt. In his opinion, believing in love was the adult equivalent of believing in Santa Claus, and the sooner one dropped such fantasies, the better. But there was real pain in Dani's voice. If, like him, she'd given up on love, she didn't seem glad of it. She seemed sad.

"I'm guessing relationships haven't been all hearts and roses for you, either," he said gently.

She gave a low chuckle. "Well, maybe the thorny parts of the rose."

"I'm sorry. I didn't realize you were hurting."

"Oh—I wouldn't say hurting. Not anymore. I had a bad relationship—a long time ago—and it taught me some life lessons."

"Such as?"

"That love…love can be a trap. Love creates these expectations, and then when one person doesn't turn out to be who you thought they were, it's absolutely devastating."

"Like there's this whole different side of them that you never knew about all along."

She seemed to shift uncomfortably in her seat. "People are complicated. You can never really know a person all the way. Everyone has…things they need to keep private."

Her voice seemed strained in the darkness, and Cade surmised that this was difficult for her to say. Whoever had hurt her had left a deep wound.

"Secrets can be so destructive," he said. "It's why I can't abide them."

"Oh," she said, her voice small. "Not at all?"

"Well, I agree with you that everyone has a right to keep certain things private. But when it comes to love, secrets only cause pain."

She appeared to be thinking this over. "So for you, if someone were holding back personal information about themselves, something that was really only meant to be known by the closest people in their lives, that would be a deal-breaker?"

"It depends. If I'm one of the closest people in their lives, then yes. I'd want to know that secret eventually. But if it's just a colleague or a casual relationship, then of course I assume there's plenty that people aren't sharing, just as I'm not sharing everything with them. I think the real trouble comes when you start getting close to someone and they're not being honest about what they want or who they are."

Susan had never told him, until the very end, that she wanted completely different things than he did. He'd wanted to stay in Boston; she'd wanted to move close to her family. He'd wanted to travel frequently; she'd wanted to put their money toward a large house. But she'd never spoken about any of this until after she'd betrayed him with his best friend. He'd felt as though he'd never really known her at all.

"Right," she said. "And then you fall in love with the person you think you know, and then they turn out to be someone completely different. And that person you were in love with just evaporates into thin air. They were never real."

"Exactly," he said. "But, for what it's worth, I'm sorry you know how that feels."

She brushed him off. "It was a long time ago. A *very* long time ago." He couldn't tell, in the dim light, if she was blushing, but she sounded a little embarrassed as she said, "I think that may have been part of why I kissed you the way I did."

"What do you mean?"

She was definitely blushing. "It's been a long time since I've had much intimacy with anyone."

Now *his* eyebrows were the ones that raised. "May I ask how long?"

She buried her face in her hands. "I'm too embarrassed to say."

It seemed that they both had something to be embarrassed about. Normally he wouldn't share this kind of information with a colleague. But he and Dani were having an important and necessary heart-to-heart after the events of the morning, and he thought it might make her feel better if he revealed a secret of his own.

"Dani…if it makes you feel any better, it's been four years for me. And then two years before that." Both women had been tourists who were visiting the island for less than forty-eight hours. Both had been very clear about what they wanted and what they didn't.

She took her face out of her hands. "Really?"

"I was telling the truth before. I don't do relationships, and I'm not looking for one."

She mulled this over. "But if it weren't a relationship. If it were just sex and nothing else…"

He shrugged. "Once in a while I have a chance to end the dry spell. But the opportunities are few and far between."

She cocked her head to one side. "Why did you move to St. Camille, Cade?"

"Here's the short version. I had my heart broken, I moved here and now… I do my best not to get my heart broken again."

"Which means not getting close to anyone."

"Exactly. So you see, you're not the only one who has something to apologize for. I kissed you, knowing full well that things wouldn't go anywhere after that. It was unconscionable of me."

"Okay, but if you felt it was such an unconscionable thing to do, then why do it at all?"

He paused. All the reasons he *had* kissed her were hitting him full force as she sat next to him in the dusk. The angle at which her hair fell against her neck, begging him to stroke it, to cup her cheek and tilt her face toward his. Her lips were gently parted. He wondered if they still tasted like citrus, or if she hadn't reapplied her lip balm since that morning.

He mustered every ounce of restraint within his body. "It was just a mistake."

"Cade. Forgetting a patient's name is a mistake. Wearing mismatched socks is a mistake. What was this?"

He couldn't hide it anymore. "It was a momentary lapse in judgement. I let my attraction get the better of me."

Her ears perked up. "Attraction?"

He shook his head. "That was the wrong word."

"Okay, then what's the right word?"

He searched for a moment, then admitted, "Attraction."

So much for his plan to hide his feelings. It was all out there now, under the stars. He hoped he hadn't made Dani feel uncomfortable.

"Six years," she said.

"What?"

"That's how long it's been for me. Six years. Do you realize that between the two of us, that adds up to a decade without physical intimacy?"

"When you put it like that, it does sound like one hell of a dry spell." He was trying to keep his tone light, but the truth was, all this talk of celibacy was doing little to diffuse his attraction. He was acutely aware of Dani's body near his in the darkness. It was more than the warmth of the nearby fire that made his face flush.

She turned her face toward him, and he was surprised at her agonized expression. "Cade, I know this might sound crazy. But I've been doing a lot of reckless things lately—moving here, starting this fellowship. I told you back in Boston that I have a lot of family expectations. But I'm ready to make some choices for myself. And you were brave enough to say it, so I will, too—I'm attracted to you as well. That's why I kissed you this morning. Because I couldn't help myself. And I felt so embarrassed about that, but now, after talking to you, I think… I think that's why you kissed me, too."

He swallowed. "But you aren't looking for anything serious."

"Absolutely not. And neither are you."

"So…where does that leave us?" he asked.

She sighed. "Right where we started. We're colleagues, friends. Anything between us would be incredibly complicated."

She paused, and they sat in silence for a moment. Then she added, "Unless we both decided that it wouldn't be complicated."

"What do you mean?"

"I mean that it's been ten years between the two of us. Ten years of unwanted celibacy. We have an opportunity here to help each other out. All we'd have to do is remove romance, and love, from the equation."

He thought he was beginning to understand, but he wanted to be sure. "How would that work?"

"All it would take is one night together. One night to get this out of our systems and move on."

Part of him couldn't believe she was saying this. The other part of him was screaming at him not to let this opportunity go. But if she really was suggesting what he thought she was suggesting, he needed to be absolutely certain they were on the same page.

"One night. And then in the morning?"

"We go on together as friends and colleagues. That's it. No ongoing relationship, no expectations."

Well, he could understand the appeal of that. But what about her? He couldn't risk hurting her feelings, no matter what she said. "Dani. Are you sure that's what you want?"

"Ten years, Cade. Six for me. Four for you. In one night, we can end something that's been going on for years for both of us, and prevent weeks of awkwardness while we wait for whatever this is between us to die down. If it dies down."

He hesitated. His body ached to finish what they'd started with their kiss that morning. But he'd never, in his wildest dreams, expected Dani to find him on the beach and propose something like this. He believed he could protect his own heart, but what about hers? He couldn't bear to think of Dani being heartbroken and him being the cause of it. How could he know she wouldn't regret it?

She stood up, and suddenly he realized she had taken his hesitation for refusal. "This was silly," she said. "I never should have brought it up. Let's not mention it again. I'll see you at work." She stepped away from him, toward the beach.

"Dani, wait!" He jumped after her and reached for her wrist. She turned to face him, and he saw her eyes were blurred with tears. "You're absolutely sure? No expectations? No additional involvement or commitment to each other? Complete freedom from obligations? That's all you want?"

"Cade, you have no idea. It's all I've ever wanted."

He pulled her to him, and found that the taste of her citrus lip balm was indeed still there, strong and sweet as ever.

CHAPTER FIVE

DANI FELT AS though her body was melting into Cade's. The moment he'd stopped her on the beach, the moment he'd made it clear that he considered her insane proposal to be an actual, real possibility, she'd given up trying to hold back. He'd pulled her to him and met her lips with a kiss that made her drop all the restraint and professionalism she'd been doing her best to maintain since she'd arrived on St. Camille.

No. If she were honest with herself, she'd been hiding from her own feelings since they'd met in Boston.

But there was nowhere to hide now as Cade kissed her on the beach with an urgency that matched her own. The cool of the night air hit the back of her neck as he gathered her curls in his fingers, while the heat of his body sent a warmth spreading through hers.

He leaned his forehead against hers, looking straight into her eyes.

"My house is right over there," he said.

"Then I guess all we have left to do is go inside." She couldn't believe how bold she sounded. All her life, she'd been everything a princess should be: biddable, demure, responsible. But from the moment she met Cade, something had changed. Suddenly she was chasing her own dreams. And apparently, now that she'd gotten a taste of it, she wasn't going to stop.

Her recklessness shocked her. But she wasn't afraid of it. She recalled the pressure of Cade's lips against hers. Maybe it was a mistake. But if the two of them had just one night together, she wasn't going to end it with any regrets.

Cade put his arm around her and walked her through his front door. The beach had been fairly quiet, but the second they were inside, with the guarantee of privacy, she found herself overcome, not just with wanting but with *need*. She barely caught a glimpse of his home before she turned her face to his again. Her arms wrapped around his neck.

He put one arm around her waist and pulled her close while his other hand traced her jaw and tilted her face upward to meet her lips with his. She parted her lips for him and his tongue entered, exploring her mouth with a slow kiss that flared the fire of deeper sensations within her body.

His hands stroked her shoulders, then fell to her breasts. He filled her senses. She was consumed with the smell of cinnamon, sweat and *him*. Her skin felt hot where he stroked her, and the taste of his lips made her insatiable. She already had her arms entwined around him, and as she leaned back against his front door, she was unable to stop herself from entwining her legs around him, too. After years of meeting her responsibilities, years of denying her own needs, she was finally getting something she wanted. She had neither the will nor the inclination to restrain herself. She wrapped her legs around his body, and he slipped his hands beneath her bottom for support. He turned and set her down on what she realized must be his kitchen table, but she was too preoccupied to take in the decor.

She sat on the table with her legs on either side of him. One of his hands was in her hair, while another reached under the skirt of her dress to trace her leg. He moved her skirt aside and pulled her bare thigh closer to his body as his mouth once again sought entry to hers. Her yearning deepened as his hand slid higher up her thigh and found the nook of her hip. A thin layer of lace was all that separated her from his touch, and now his fingers slid beneath that layer, and she shivered as he tantalized her with steady strokes.

She wanted him closer to her, though it seemed he could never be close enough. She pulled off his black T-shirt and took a moment to appreciate that his body was everything that had been promised: taut, muscular and lean. Her hands went to his belt buckle and, after a moment or two, with very little effort, he stood naked before her.

But she didn't have long to look at him, because he moved close again to kiss her neck, working his way down her clavicle, and then to the side of her breast.

His hand went to the back of her neck, where she'd tied the knot of her halter-top dress.

"Do you know what I love about these types of dresses?" he murmured into her skin. "They're like a magician's trick. All you have to do is know how to undo the knot." His hands worked at the knot she'd tied, and all at once, the dress fell around her with the soft *whoosh* of crumpled fabric.

She suddenly felt nervous. She was wearing nothing but her panties. A bra wouldn't have worked with the halter dress. Unconsciously, she lifted her hands to cover her breasts.

He caught her wrists. "Please. Just let me look a moment. Don't hide yourself from me."

She relaxed. Or at least, she relaxed as much as she could under his piercing gaze. His eyes were the cerulean blue of the ocean, and they washed over her now. He reached for her and pressed his lips against her neck. He traced his finger down her shoulder, and then her breast. She felt her nipples rise at his touch.

"I don't think I'm going to make it to the bedroom," he murmured.

"Neither do I." She glanced over to where her purse had been flung onto a chair. "Let me just grab a condom from my purse." She gave silent thanks to Kim for having put the condom there years ago, despite her own protestations that the chances of her ever needing such a thing were extremely slim. Dani hadn't believed she'd ever need it, but she'd never bothered to take it out of her purse, either. She'd jokingly thought of it as her wishful thinking condom.

Well, all of her wishes were coming true now.

"Let's not wait for the bedroom," she said, handing him the foil packet. "Both of us have been waiting long enough."

He gave her that half-winking smile of his and put the condom on. And then laid her down on the floor.

She felt his hands reach to strip her panties off. And then his body was once again melding into hers. He entered her in one smooth, slow motion, and she felt her body adjust to his.

It had been so long. Their motion felt like a dance her body had been awaiting for years. Her hips swung as though to a familiar tune, but somehow, everything felt brand-new.

Her hands clutched his arms as they swayed together, and then fell over the precipice together. She felt his body jerk and heard him say something with his face buried in her hair. It was her name, she realized.

He slipped out of her, exhausted, and lay on his back next to her. He had just enough energy to pull her body against his. She lay with her face pressed against his chest, one arm draped over his chest, and one of her legs draped over one of his.

She couldn't believe what she'd just done. None of it was

typical for her at all. The spontaneous sex. The fact that she'd been so forward, so aggressive, in giving herself to him. The whole idea of a one-night stand with no expectation of a relationship, and with a coworker, no less. It was all so *unlike* her.

And yet, at that moment, she felt more like herself than she had in years.

Cade blinked his eyes against the bright morning sun streaming through his shutters. Last night, after their initial unrestrained episode on the kitchen floor, they had eventually made it to his bedroom. It had been a close call, with numerous opportunities for both of them to distract one another along the way, but they'd made it.

The morning air was cool and he tried to pull his bedsheets closer around him, only to feel a resisting tug.

Dani was still asleep, the majority of his sheets wrapped around her, leaving him only one relatively small corner.

Ah. So she was a blanket thief. Somehow, he wasn't surprised. After last night, he was forced to admit that his initial impression of Dani—that she was quiet and didn't like to be a bother—was mistaken. Last night, she'd shown him that she was the kind of woman who took what she wanted—in all the best possible ways.

Blankets, though, were up for negotiation.

He lifted the sheet and pulled it toward himself, revealing her naked body underneath.

She stirred as the cool air hit her. "Hey. I was using that."

He stretched the sheet so that it covered both of them, and then moved closer to her so he could warm her with the heat of his body. "Better?"

She smiled. "Mmm. Much."

He held her like that for a while, still reveling in the satisfaction of the night before.

It should have been the perfect morning, with the sun streaming into his room and Dani in his bed. But he couldn't relax completely. Guilt nagged at him.

Dani had been very clear last night that she was completely open to a one-night stand between the two of them. Hell, it had been her idea. And in the heat of the moment, he'd been perfectly willing to convince himself that they could enjoy a single night of physical intimacy, and then return to being just coworkers in the morning.

But now that the moment had arrived to put their intentions to the test, he wasn't certain if things would play out exactly as planned.

Now, as he held her, his discomfort grew. He felt the familiar urge to *do* something about it, but he didn't know what. Dani was dozing peacefully; he didn't want to disturb her with questions about their arrangement.

Just take it one step at a time, he thought. Dani was sleeping; there was no need to wake her. And it wouldn't be productive to worry—right now—about what things would be like later today at work. They'd cross each bridge as they came to it.

Breakfast. That's something you can take care of right now. French toast might not solve every problem, but it would give him something to do with his hands and something to focus on besides his worries.

He kissed the top of Dani's head and said, "I'll be in the kitchen. Come in when you're ready."

He made coffee and sliced some good brioche bread. He'd just put the first two slices on the stove when Dani padded into the kitchen, his bathrobe wrapped around her.

"Is that coffee I smell?"

He nodded toward the coffeemaker. "I have cream and sugar in the fridge, and the French toast will be ready in five minutes."

"My hero." She poured coffee into the mug he'd set out for her and lifted it to her nose, savoring the scent.

He handed her a plate of French toast, and they sat at his kitchen table together. She took a few bites and then stopped.

"Something wrong?" he asked. "I can put it on for a few more minutes if it isn't cooked well enough."

"No, it's perfect."

"Then what's wrong?"

She hesitated and then said, "We both got pretty carried away last night."

A jolt of worry shot through him. "I hope there aren't any regrets."

"Not at all," she replied, and his relief was palpable as she gave a small, reminiscent smile over her coffee. "Last night was... Let's just say last night is going to remain a lovely memory."

"And what about the future?"

"Well...this is it, right? We agreed. Just one night."

"Right. I just wanted to make sure we were still on the same page."

She gave him an irked expression. "Cade. Why are you still asking me about this? I told you last night—I didn't want any attachments or expectations. Isn't that what you said you wanted, too?"

"Yes. I just wanted to make sure you don't get hurt."

"Cade. That's sweet of you to care, but please rest assured that I am perfectly capable of protecting my own feelings."

"I just worry that—"

"Oh, my God!" For a moment he was afraid that she was

upset, but he saw she was laughing as she set her coffee cup down. "You're doing it again. You're worrying about my feelings, so you're micromanaging and trying to be in control."

He was about to argue, but then realized that that was, in fact, exactly what he was doing. "Sorry," he said. "Force of habit."

"See? If this were anything more than a one-night stand, I might be upset. But since it's not, I can brush this off as a charming personality quirk that you're working to change. Seriously, Cade. Let me worry about my feelings, and you can worry about yours. That's what friends and colleagues do, right? And that's what we are."

"Of course," he said. "So at work, we'll just…keep things professional."

"Professional. And secret," she said. Suddenly, her face was stricken. "But you hate secrets. I didn't think of that before…"

"This can be our secret," he said quickly. "It's our business. There's no reason to tell anyone else. It's not really about secrecy, but about privacy."

He saw her shoulders drop with relief. "Thank you," she said.

"Of course." It had never occurred to him to breathe a word about their tryst to anyone else, but it never hurt to officially agree on these kinds of things. He was glad that he and Dani seemed to feel the same way.

They were so compatible, he thought. For example, they were both early risers. There were still three hours left before either of them needed to be at work.

He noticed that Dani was also glancing at the clock, and then back at him, as she sipped her coffee.

"You know," he said. "It occurs to me that we have quite a

window of time this morning before we need to go in to work and put on our professional game faces."

She set her coffee cup down and turned to him, her eyes sparkling with mischief. "What exactly are you suggesting?"

"That maybe our night together doesn't need to end until we walk out that door. Which doesn't need to be for another two and a half hours."

"Hmm." She licked some of the syrup from the French toast from her lips. "Whatever could we do to fill the time?"

He moved toward her and slipped off his robe. "I have a feeling I can think of something."

And he did.

Several days later, Cade's face was drawn with concentration as he monitored the patient's vitals. Taking a patient off of a heart-lung machine was always an unpredictable process, but so far, this was one of the smoothest cases he'd ever seen.

He had to give credit to the team in the room. The nurses and the perfusionist at Coral Bay were all top-notch, and it helped immensely to have Dani on the team as well. The more he worked with her, the more he noticed the difference her presence made. Not only did she fit in seamlessly with the rest of the staff, but she also had a way of bringing them together around her. He'd always been proud of the way the team at Coral Bay responded to a crisis, but with Dani there, he noticed a shift in tone. It was as though the team wasn't just reacting, but responding. Rising to a challenge instead of scrambling to deal with an emergency.

The ascending aorta they'd just replaced was no exception. Unexpected difficulties inevitably arose in this type of surgery. The patient had been put into circulatory arrest, his body cooled to less than twenty degrees Celsius. The team had sailed through the procedure with ease, but now they faced the complicated process of weaning the patient off the heart-lung machine. No two patients ever responded the same way; it was always a matter of trial and error to see what worked and what didn't.

As nerve-racking as these procedures could be, Cade relished the opportunity. He felt as though these situations called for what he did best. Preparation. Control. Offering direction and suggestions. He took pride in being someone who knew what to do in a crisis, and he felt his team drew reassurance from that.

The team pushed O-negative blood into the patient, gradually warming his body. As minutes passed, Cade began mentally ticking off the plans for unexpected changes. Things were proceeding so well that it was making him uneasy.

"Medication ready?" he asked one of the nurses.

"Syringe is in the tray if we need it," she reassured him.

"Dr. Martin, defibrillator ready to go?"

"The moment we need it," she replied.

"Good. I know things are going well, but we still need to be ready for anything. A case like this can take a turn for the worse fast if we're not ready with the right intervention at the right time."

The team *was* doing well, though, and so was the patient. Cade hadn't missed the flash of annoyance that crossed Dani's face when he'd asked if she was ready with the defibrillator. And in all fairness, that look of annoyance might have been inappropriate if he'd asked her once…but he'd asked her three times already. He hoped it was only three. The rest of the team was used to his obsession with checking every detail, but Dani was new… She might assume that once again, he was micromanaging the situation.

Perhaps he *was* micromanaging. But how else was he supposed to alleviate his worry that he might have missed something? He knew, deep down, that his patient was in good hands and that his team would do everything they could to the best of their ability. But what if *he* made a mistake? What if he overlooked something, the way Henry's doctors had overlooked the signs of his condition?

You've got this, he thought. He'd double- and triple-checked everything. And the patient's response to treatment so far had been very encouraging. He let his shoulders relax by a fraction of an inch.

At that moment, the heart monitor gave an erratic blip.

"A-fib," he called out. "Dani, get the—"

But Dani already had the defibrillator paddles at the ready. She gave the patient a single shock to the heart.

Everyone in the room held their breath. Dani charged the paddles for another shock—and the heart monitor began a steady, rhythmic beep.

Cade couldn't help the smile that burst over his face as a cheer filled the room. The patient was breathing on his own. His heart was beating on its own. A patient who could have been facing death would now have a new lease on life. It was a feeling that never got old.

He looked across the room and locked eyes with Dani. She, too, was flush with excitement. He could tell she shared that same feeling of awe at how a patient so close to death could suddenly have their whole life in front of them.

He wanted to share that moment, that excitement, with her. But he forced himself to tear his eyes away.

Over the past few days, he'd done the best he could to be cordial and professional when they worked together. He was finding it to be more difficult than he'd expected.

It was only supposed to be one night, he told himself fiercely. *One night to get our attraction out of our systems. And then we move on.*

But the "moving on" part wasn't happening as quickly as he'd wanted it to. Despite his efforts not to think about it, his night with Dani was burned into his brain. He'd thought that once he'd finished what they started with that kiss, he'd be over her. That was hardly the case. Whenever he had a free moment, he found himself thinking about her. The way she smelled, the way her body had felt in his hands, the way her bare skin had melted against his.

So he did his best to make sure he didn't have many free moments. He was back to filling his time up with as many tasks as possible and avoiding Dani whenever he could. Which wasn't often, because they had to work together so closely.

The team filed out of the room, exchanging high fives. He suddenly found himself face-to-face with Dani. And then, just as suddenly, he was alone with her for the first time in days, as the rest of the team spilled into the hallway and dispersed.

Her eyes were still alight with excitement. "Is it always like that?" she asked, breathlessly.

He had to smile at that. No matter how conflicted his feelings toward Dani might be, it was impossible not to feel inspired by her love of medicine.

"It's different every time. That was an unusually smooth procedure—but as you saw, anytime you take a patient off of a heart-lung machine, there are going to be complications. It's like a puzzle, figuring out what the patient needs and how each body responds differently."

"It was a miracle," she breathed.

He remembered that when they'd first met, she'd told him

she loved medicine because it was full of miracles. "I couldn't agree more."

"Can I ask you some questions about the dose of inotropic drugs we used?"

"Sure. I have some medical journal articles in my office you can borrow." The second he made the offer, he realized that they'd have to go to his office to get them. Which would mean a few more moments alone with her.

But he couldn't rescind the offer now. He'd promised that nothing would change between them, and there was no way for him to backtrack without looking awkward.

Her eyes were still glowing with the thrill of success. He swallowed. His office was only a short walk down the hall. It would be a matter of seconds to reach into his filing cabinet and give the articles to her to read on her own.

"So, uh, let's just head over to my office and get them," he said.

They walked to his office in silence. Cade's mind was screaming at him to say something, but his mind was completely blank. All he could think of was how to get out of being alone with Dani as quickly as possible, because the more time he spent with her, the more preoccupied he became with thoughts he needed to leave behind.

One night together. That's all it was. She agreed. You agreed. So leave it in the past where it belongs.

After what seemed like an eternity, they arrived at Cade's office. He handed her the journal articles and then didn't let go. They both stood there, holding on to either end of the paper. Cade knew he was being foolish. He needed to get himself under control before he did something completely stupid.

But it was too late. Dani pulled the articles toward her, but instead of letting go—as any sane person would have—

he maintained his grip on the paper. Which meant that Dani pulled *him* toward her, too. He hadn't meant for that to happen; he just wasn't thinking clearly. And he *definitely* wasn't thinking clearly when he bent his head down, and she pushed herself up on her toes and kissed him.

He knew he should stop. He certainly shouldn't wrap his arms around her waist and pull her close as he did. But the flavor that lingered on her lips tantalized him, and the light vanilla scent of her threatened to block out everything else.

He was in danger of getting lost in that kiss when she broke away from him.

"I'm so sorry," she said. "I can't believe I just did that. After all we talked about—everything we agreed upon. I don't know what's wrong with me."

With her? What about him? Despite all his good intentions, they'd ended up exactly where neither of them wanted to be.

Well, that wasn't entirely true. It wasn't that they didn't *want* to be there, but that they *shouldn't* be there. Because neither of them wanted a relationship, and if they weren't careful, they were going to end up getting attached.

Unless they made sure they didn't get attached.

An idea was beginning to worm its way into his head.

"I shouldn't be leading you on like this," Dani was saying. "There's absolutely no way there can be anything more between us, and here I am sending you mixed messages once again. I promise to keep this under control. It won't happen again. We can be coworkers and nothing more. I swear."

Her words made Cade even more certain of his next step. Dani clearly believed that *she* was leading him on, that *her* difficulties were preventing the two of them from having a relationship. He was starting to learn that that was who Dani was. Unless someone spelled it out for her, she would assume that everything was her fault. And he was determined to prove to her that it wasn't.

"Dani," he said gently, "I don't think that's going to work."

Her eyes widened. "It has to work," she protested. "I just need to try harder. Be more professional."

He took her hand. "That's not quite what I meant. We've both been trying hard to be professional, but it's not working. We keep ending up in situations like this. I think maybe we need to keep trying, but in a slightly different direction than we have been."

"What do you mean, a different direction?"

"I think we need to make a modification to our original plan. Originally, we thought that one night would be enough for both of us to work out our mutual attraction to one another. But I think we need more."

"But we agreed not to have a relationship."

"This wouldn't be a relationship. This would be a purely physical arrangement, with no strings attached. No expectations of anything more."

"So an extension of last night, essentially."

"Exactly."

She mulled this over. "I suppose we would need to have some ground rules, to make sure neither of us gets hurt."

Now she was speaking his language. Cade valued rules, order and control. It kept things safe. Unpredictability might be fun, but it was also dangerous.

"For example," she continued, "What if you get to a point where you do want something more than what I can offer, and you meet someone who wants the same things? And perhaps we should discuss shelf life, too. How long is this going to go on?"

"How about, it goes on as long as we're both having fun?

If it starts becoming stressful, or if it stops being fun, perhaps we should stop. Or at least agree to take a moment to reevaluate where we stand."

"But what about the other part? About you meeting someone else."

"Dani." He looked at her with as much conviction as he could summon. "There is absolutely no chance of me meeting someone else and wanting anything more than this with them."

"You say that now, but—"

"No. I need to explain."

He paused, trying to find the right words. It had been so long since he'd talked about his reasons for avoiding relationships that he wasn't sure where to start. "There's a reason I've lived on an island for six years. I'm not looking for any strong attachments. I was engaged to be married once. Right at the end of medical school. She left me for my best friend, just a few days before the wedding."

Dani winced. "That's awful. But to swear off relationships entirely—all because of that? Wouldn't you someday want a second chance at love? Or if you don't believe in love, then maybe…happiness?"

He hesitated. It had been years since he'd talked about Henry with anyone. Years since he'd had to explain exactly why getting close to anyone meant reactivating all the old worries about loss and heartbreak.

But he was spared from trying to find a way to talk about Henry when Dani put her hand on his arm. "You know what? You don't have to explain. I shouldn't even have asked. Those kinds of questions are meant for relationships. And we're discussing something very different."

He was relieved that she was willing to let the matter drop.

Although, just to be on the safe side, he asked, "And what about you? What if you meet someone?"

"I can absolutely guarantee that's not going to happen." At the look of consternation on his face, she said, "Okay. How about this? We both agree that we're entering into this arrangement for as long as it's completely fun and stress-free for both of us. If, at any time, either of us wants to end the arrangement, whether it's because we've met someone, or we just don't want to continue—for *any reason at all*—then we agree that it's over."

"Fair enough."

"And we should continue keeping it a secret from our co-workers as well."

"We can try. But it's very difficult to keep a secret on St. Camille."

"All the same, I'd like to try keeping it private for as long as we can."

"Fine." He smiled. "If it's that important to you, then we can keep it to ourselves."

"Thanks. I appreciate it."

"So…see you at my place tonight?"

She gave him a wink as she went out the door. "Count on it."

CHAPTER SIX

DANI SAT FACING the ocean, luxuriating in one of the biggest perks of working as a doctor in the Caribbean: the warmth of sand against the soles of her bare feet. The medical center's cardiac wing boasted a courtyard that led straight out to the beach, and Dani loved taking her midmorning coffee there and relaxing by the water. She usually had a short break before she began her afternoon rounds, which gave her just enough time to decompress from her morning cases.

She'd never been able to relax like this back in Boston, but at Coral Bay, breaks were actively encouraged—and Dani was starting to enjoy them. Today, she'd removed her shoes and worked her feet into the dry, sun-warmed sand, reveling in the sensation of each grain slipping between her toes. The courtyard's palm trees swayed gently above her. The aroma from her coffee wafted toward her nostrils, and she felt the lingering stress from work melt away as her feet absorbed the heat of the sand and the azure expanse of the ocean that stretched before her.

Even though Dani's fellowship kept her busy, she'd never felt so relaxed in her life. Part of that was simply because life in the Caribbean was beginning to have a positive effect on her. The slower pace of island life, the beauty that surrounded her and the sense of community that came with living in such close proximity to her colleagues and patients were all affecting her in positive ways.

But the biggest change that impacted her was the arrangement between her and Cade. Six weeks had passed since they'd begun their experiment in being together without being emotionally involved. They'd spent more time in one another's bedrooms, had clandestine meetings at work and exchanged meaningful glances when they were certain no one else was looking.

As far as she could tell, no one at work suspected a thing between the two of them. For once, she was able to enjoy a connection with someone else that was about what she wanted, rather than expectations or obligations. And Cade continued to surprise her every day. He was an excellent cook, and he proved to be very helpful in her ongoing search for living quarters because he knew so much about the island and its residents. For someone who claimed that he preferred to be alone, he certainly knew plenty of people. He was always introducing her to groups of island children and shopkeepers in town.

She felt a whirring in one pocket of her white coat and saw that Kim was inviting her for a video chat.

Dani hesitated. Internet connection on the island was so spotty that she hadn't spoken to Kim for weeks. Not since they'd discussed having a calm, professional conversation with Cade about how the two of them weren't going to kiss again. And now things had gone in a very different direction. What if Kim was disappointed in her?

But Kim had never judged her before. Dani decided that if the subject of Cade came up, she'd tell her friend all about it. Kim had never revealed any of her secrets. Not telling her would be unfair and an insult to her friend's loyalty.

Who knows, she thought. *Maybe it won't even come up. I*

shouldn't assume she's been thinking about it. Kim's probably got other things on her mind than my love life.

"So, how's it going with Dr. BeachBum?" Kim asked, the moment Dani swiped to accept the call.

"How did you know anything was going on?" Dani blurted, surprised by her friend's directness.

"Ah, so there *is* something. I didn't know. I only suspected. Spill it, bestie. What's going on between you and the sun-bleached beach boy?"

Dani couldn't suppress the smile that crept over her face.

"I knew it! There's more, isn't there? Tell me everything. What have you done, Dani? And don't forget—I know you better than anyone, so I'll know if you're holding back."

"Cade and I—"

"Oh, so it's *Cade* now, is it? Not Dr. BeachBum anymore. You two must be getting cozy."

"Yes and no. We've decided that while physically, things are going *very* well, neither of us is interested in a relationship right now. So we've agreed that it's just sex. No additional commitments."

She was surprised to see Kim make a face.

"Dani, are you sure that's going to work out for you?"

"Why shouldn't it? You used to do this kind of thing all the time during residency."

"Okay, first of all, ouch, but fair. You and I are very different people, though. I know you, Dani. You're a softhearted romantic. You like things that are heartfelt, you like tradition, you like feeling attached."

Dani shifted uncomfortably in her chair. Everything Kim said was true, but it wasn't the whole truth. She might like all of those things, but that wasn't what she needed from Cade right now.

"Maybe I'm trying to discover a different side of myself," she said.

"Are you sure that's what it is? Because I know Peter hurt you pretty badly."

"This isn't about Peter. And that was a long time ago." The entire reason things with Cade were going so well was because the situation was completely different from the way it had been with Peter. Without the emotional attachment, the expectations of a relationship and the royal obligations, she didn't have to worry about being devastated when things inevitably ended.

"Then what is it about?"

"It's about…having something that's just for me, just for right now. It's not for the public, and it has nothing to do with my royal obligations. As long as Cade and I keep things casual, and as long as no one else finds out, then everything we do can stay between the two of us. I've never been able to have a relationship before where it doesn't feel as though the entire state department is involved."

Kim paused. "I just don't want to see you get hurt."

"There's no chance of that. We've both been very clear about our ground rules."

"If you say so. Just…know that I'm here for you if you need anything, okay?"

Before Dani could reply, her emergency pager went off. Dani checked it and said, "Kim, I've got to go. There's a patient coming in on the helipad." She brushed the sand from her feet as she hung up, then jammed her socks and shoes back on before heading for the elevator to the roof of the medical center at a fast clip.

Dani was among the first to arrive on the helicopter landing pad. The unconscious patient was being unloaded onto a gurney, and a nurse had started bag ventilation. "Give me the vitals," Dani shouted above the thunder of the helicopter blades as they wheeled the patient toward the end of the landing pad.

"Twenty-seven-year-old female, recent surgery to repair a complex fracture to the right femur," the nurse shouted back. "Pulse rate and blood pressure low and falling, respiratory decreasing."

So everything bad, essentially. "You said recent surgery?" She said as they went on to the elevator.

"Patient was in a skiing accident last week and suffered a serious break to the right femur, requiring surgical intervention. Surgery was successful, but she's been slow to heal. Blood pressure has been variable."

"Any history of heart problems?"

"None known to us or to her previous hospital. She was meant to be transferred here because her family wanted a second opinion—the last hospital wanted to continue monitoring her low blood pressure, but her family wanted answers. She was stable during the trip here, but took a sharp decline just before the helicopter landed."

The nurse was keeping up the bag ventilation as she spoke. Dani couldn't see the patient's face very well, but she glimpsed a head of striking blond hair with a few purple streaks. Something about that hair sent off a faint alarm in Dani's distant memory, but she wasn't sure exactly what it reminded her of. She turned her attention back to the clipboard the nurse had handed her. The patient had recently suffered a complex broken leg. Either something had gone wrong with the patient's recovery, or some new problem had arisen. In either case, Dani felt out of her depth. With no immediately clear diagnosis, this was a case for a team, not for one doctor working alone.

She was relieved when the elevator doors opened on the cardiac wing and Cade stood there, ready to help. For once, she was more than ready to hand a case over to his expertise. They reviewed the case as they brought the patient to the OR and had her stabilized. They were joined by the head of the cardiology unit, Dr. Briscoe, as well as several interns.

As Dani ventilated the patient, her mind was racing. The patient might be stabilized, but this was a case with numerous questions. What could a broken leg have to do with a dangerously low heart rate? Undiagnosed bradycardia? This was a young patient, but perhaps that meant an undiagnosed congenital condition.

"We have a narrow window of time here," Cade announced to the team. "Opinions? Recommendations?"

"Could be an undiagnosed congenital condition," one of the interns suggested.

"Maybe," Cade replied. "What about the broken leg?"

The room was quiet. "Maybe that's just an extraneous factor," said another intern. "Or maybe the trauma to the leg created conditions for an undiagnosed heart condition to manifest."

"It's a valid theory," said Dr. Briscoe.

"No," said Dani. Everyone turned to hear. "The broken leg isn't extraneous. It's a key factor."

"What makes you so sure?" Dr. Briscoe asked.

"It's possible that trauma to the leg affected the patient's condition. But it's also possible that there's continued bleeding at the surgical site—that while repairing the leg, her previous surgical team nicked a femoral artery or vein, which would account for continued, unexplained bleeding."

Dr. Briscoe frowned. "Testing that theory would mean re-opening the site for an exploratory surgery. If you're wrong, this could risk exposing the patient to unnecessary complications and a much longer recovery."

"It does put the patient at risk," Dani agreed. "But the risk of not reopening the site is greater."

"Agreed," said Cade. "I think Dani's reasoning is sound."

Dr. Briscoe gave Cade a long look. "It's your call," he said.

"Then let's see if Dr. Martin is right," Cade replied.

Eight hours of surgery later, Dani was back in the courtyard, exhausted. Cade sat next to her, breathing hard. There was no solitude this time—instead, every member of the surgical team had come along, sharing both the exhaustion and the enjoyment of a job well done.

Dani had been right. They'd reopened the site of the complex fracture to the patient's leg, only to find that somehow, the femoral artery had been completely severed. Dani surmised that the artery may have been nicked during the patient's first surgery, leading to a slow bleed, but over time, additional movement had put more stress on the artery, ultimately leading to a rupture during the patient's helicopter ride. She'd been in danger of bleeding out before the team had gotten her stabilized.

Dani was basking in the admiration of her colleagues.

"I'm extremely impressed you were able to form a diagnostic impression so quickly, Dr. Martin," Dr. Briscoe said. "I'm sure Miss Berlini and her family will be relieved to know that we've gotten to the bottom of her troubles with recovery and have been able to finally put her on the mend."

Dani's stomach dropped. "Did you say Berlini?"

"Yes—the family is quite prominent, I understand."

Those purple streaks in the hair. In the heat of working on the patient, Dani hadn't paid much attention to the patient's identity, and she'd been even harder to recognize because she'd been on a ventilator.

Dr. Briscoe was right about one thing. The Berlini family was indeed prominent. Angelica Berlini was the daughter of one of the wealthiest families in Europe, and she was also one of the biggest gossips Dani had ever met. They'd never exactly been friends, but they were more than acquaintances, having gone to the same school and most of the same social events over the years.

"Excuse me," she said. She needed to be sure. She went back to the patient's room. A nurse was recording vitals.

Now that Dani could get a good look at the patient, she confirmed that yes, certainly, this was Angelica Berlini. And the moment she woke up, she was bound to expose Dani's secret.

"How's she doing?" she asked the nurse.

"Extremely well," the nurse said with a smile. "Excellent work, Doctor. Everyone's very impressed. Now that she's on the road to recovery, she could be off the ventilator soon. Probably ready for discharge by the end of the week."

"Wonderful," Dani said, and she meant it. She was glad Angelica was going to be all right. But Angelica's arrival meant that the time for secrets between her and Cade was at an end.

She'd done her best to keep her promise to her family. But this was beyond her control. Angelica was Cade's patient as well as Dani's, and there was no way Cade wasn't going to talk to her as she recovered. And if Angelica saw Dani and Cade at the same time, she would recognize Dani instantly.

Even if there was some way she could contrive to speak to Angelica first and beg her to keep the secret from Cade, Dani found the idea distasteful. It was one thing for her to keep her royal status private. But asking someone else to actively help her cover up her identity felt too much like deception. Cade himself had said there was a difference between secrecy and privacy. Simply not mentioning her princess status to Cade felt like keeping her personal information private...even though it was a fairly important bit of personal information. But keeping that secret was the only thing that had allowed her to have a semblance of a normal life during her medical career.

But if she asked Angelica to outright lie about it... It didn't seem fair to Angelica or to Cade. And what if Angelica promised to keep silent, but then let something slip by accident? No. It was time to tell Cade. Sooner rather than later.

She braced her shoulder and left the room, determined to find Cade and explain that she needed to have a private conversation with him. But she immediately ran into Cade and Dr. Briscoe in the hallway.

"Ah! Here's our star fellow," Dr. Briscoe beamed. "Just the person I was looking for. Dr. Martin, I'm so impressed with the diagnostic and surgical prowess you've just displayed that I want to reward you. I'm sending you away from Coral Bay."

She blinked in surprise.

"Just for a few days," he added quickly. "I'd like you to go to Horseshoe Cay at the end of the week on a recruitment mission. It's an island about half an hour away by seaplane. It's quite a bit larger than St. Camille, with three top-notch medical schools that are coming together to have a recruitment event. It'll be hospitals from all over the Caribbean giving presentations, trying to convince the brightest and best graduates to continue their training here instead of heading to the mainland."

"And you want me to go? I've only been here a few weeks."

"That's why I'd like it to be you especially. You're in the process of adjusting to island life right now. One of the biggest reasons doctors are hesitant to build their careers in the

Caribbean is because of the adjustment to island life. Most of the doctors here at Coral Bay have been here for so long that those adjustments are only a distant memory—but they'll be fresh in your mind, of course. And the case we've just worked on would be an excellent one to present to new graduates. It's just the kind of exciting case that attracts top talent, and I'd like you and Dr. Logan to be able to talk about it firsthand."

By Cade's surprised expression, Dani could tell that this was news to him. "You want both of us to go?"

"It's up to the two of you, of course. This is a request, not an order. But it's something I hope will do both of you good. Dr. Logan, you've booked more time in the OR and cath lab than anyone else on the surgical team over the past few weeks."

"Well, I was needed," Cade murmured, but Dani noted the fine lines around Cade's eyes. Had he been overworking himself? She knew Cade well enough by now to know that he was the kind of person who would put in as many extra hours as needed, whether he was exhausted or not.

Dr. Briscoe huffed. "You're needed at your best, which means you need to slow down and let yourself take a break once in a while so you can be refreshed for your team and your patients. Now, there's a little room in the medical center's budget to spring for something a little more luxurious than usual. We're going to put both of you up in the Horseshoe Harbor Grand Hotel. Er, separate rooms, of course. The recruitment event is only for the weekend, but if the two of you would like to take a few extra days to relax, we can arrange for that. Let me know what you decide."

He headed back down the hall, leaving Dani and Cade together.

"Did Dr. Briscoe just send us on vacation together?" said Dani.

"I think so," Cade replied. "I've done a few of these recruitment events, and it's always a wonderful time. It's fun to explore the other islands, and Horseshoe Cay is quite beautiful. The hotel itself is something to see." He turned toward Dani, concerned. "But if it feels like too much, we don't have to do it. Or we can just go to the recruitment event and then leave, without staying for the extra days. You know, if spending that much time together feels too much like it's against the spirit of our arrangement."

Dani hesitated. She'd been worried he might be thinking the same thing.

"Of course, a little time off the island might be ideal," he continued. "We'd be away from anyone we know from St. Camille, so we wouldn't have to be as vigilant about keeping things private. It's a chance to have a little fun."

Fun. Wasn't that what Kim was always telling her she needed more of in her life? And what better chance to have fun than during a getaway with Cade, at what sounded like a fairly posh hotel?

"I can't wait," she said.

"Great. I'll tell Dr. Briscoe we're all in for the long weekend."

Dani was so excited by the idea of the weekend getaway that she didn't recall why she'd gone looking for Cade in the first place until after he left. She'd been prepared to tell him her secret until she'd gotten distracted by Dr. Briscoe.

Now, she realized there was a good chance that Angelica would be discharged from the medical center, and quite likely off St. Camille, by the time she and Cade returned. She didn't have to break her promise to her family. She didn't have to reveal anything.

Except…even after Angelica left, something like this could

happen again. One of the reasons her family had allowed her to accept the fellowship was because Coral Bay had such a prestigious reputation among elite circles as a place for private recovery and excellent care. If Angelica Berlini could get medical care here, then so could any number of people who might know Dani's family. Her secret was safe, but only for now.

Once again, certainty hit her with blunt force. She had to tell Cade the truth.

But why? They'd agreed to keep things purely physical. No romantic entanglements, no attachments, no obligations, they'd said.

So why did she feel obligated to tell Cade a secret she'd promised her family she'd keep?

Because you care about him. You care about how he feels. You care if he feels that you lied to him.

Fine. Perhaps that was true. She cared about Cade—as a person. But that didn't mean she had feelings for him. She respected him. She didn't want him to be hurt. And she knew Cade would be hurt if he felt she'd lied to him. If she actively tried to cover up her royal status, she *would* be lying to him, no matter how she tried to rationalize it.

She couldn't tell him yet, though. She thought about what Dr. Briscoe had said about Cade being overworked. Now that someone had mentioned it, Dani couldn't forget the tired lines around Cade's eyes. She knew he needed some time away. And that settled the issue in her mind. She wasn't going to do anything that would prevent Cade from having a relaxing break, including revealing something that could result in additional stress for both of them.

After they got back, though, she'd have to tell him. And she'd have to find some way to explain to her family that telling very few trusted people about her princess status was necessary, even unavoidable.

For a no-pressure, no-strings-attached situation, her affair with Cade was causing a surprising amount of stress. She knew she could find a way to deal with it. First, though, she was going to make sure Cade enjoyed their trip to Horseshoe Cay to the fullest.

Cade was glad to find that Dani was just as excited to leave St. Camille for a brief getaway as he was.

For one thing, he was excited to show Dani Horseshoe Cay. Even though St. Camille was, in his extremely biased opinion, the best island in the Caribbean, Horseshoe Cay had plenty to offer. The fine dining options were excellent, and he knew there would be a festival going on while they were there. And though their relationship was purely physical, he was excited at the idea of being able to spend more time with her. St. Camille was so small that the gossip flew at light speed, and any time he and Dani spent together outside his own home, they risked becoming fodder for rumors. On Horseshoe Cay, they'd be able to enjoy themselves away from any prying eyes.

In fact, he was already enjoying the benefits of taking their affair off-island. They were in the back of a small seaplane to make the short journey from St. Camille to Horseshoe Cay. Since they were the only two people on the plane, besides the pilot, he was able to hold her hand—something he hadn't been able to do in public for the past several weeks. He was glad that she gave his hand a returning squeeze. These short flights always made him nervous—it felt as though there was almost nothing between him and empty sky.

"I hate small planes, too," she said, noticing his apprehensive expression. "You can always feel the turbulence so much more."

Fortunately, it wasn't long before they were back on solid ground.

The medical center had very generously reserved two rooms for them. They were ornate, with four-poster beds and claw-foot bathtubs.

"It seems a shame that we're only using one of them," said Dani, sitting down on the king-size bed in his room.

"You're certainly welcome to stay in your own room," Cade replied. "I'm sure you're eager for some space after living in the medical center's dormitory for so many weeks."

"Space is nice," Dani said. "But this room comes with certain…amenities…that make up for having to share it."

"Oh?" he cocked an eyebrow at her. "What kind of amenities might those be?"

"Well. Take that bathtub over there. It's huge. Just think, if either of us had to use that bathtub alone, we'd practically get lost at sea."

"I see. So you're saying that it's much safer for *two* people to use that bathtub at once?"

"Only one way to find out," she replied.

Much later, after they'd spent quite a bit of time enjoying the bathtub, Cade suggested they go out and explore the town surrounding the harbor. Dusk had fallen by then, but Cade could hear music coming from the street.

"There's a fancy French restaurant about a block away from here," he said. "Or there's the festival going on this weekend—we've missed the parade, but the opening party will go on all night. There'll be street food and dancing. Which would you prefer?"

"Definitely the festival! Especially if there's food. I'm starving."

"Great. We can get stamp and go."

"Stamp and what?"

"You'll see. Let's go."

As they headed to the main part of town, the sound of calypso, drums and banjos filled the air. The town square was surrounded by food stalls and trucks, and in the center, people were dancing.

Stamp and go turned out to be a salty battered fish cake with sweet dipping sauce. Cade bought a large order from a food cart for them to share.

He smiled at seeing Dani licking her fingers with relish.

"This is wonderful," she said, her eyes closed with pleasure. "But why do they call it stamp and go?"

"It was the way British officers used to give orders on their ships," he said. "If they wanted something done in a hurry, they'd say 'stamp and go!'"

"That's not it," said the vendor of the food cart who'd overheard. "It's because it's so good that people used to stamp their feet while waiting in line for it."

Cade motioned toward the vendor. "Trust the expert," he said.

"Well, wherever it gets its name from, it's delicious."

They walked among the festival, admiring the various wares for sale. Dani kept turning an eye toward the dancing, and Cade had a feeling she'd want to join in as soon as they were done with their meal.

As they perused the various stalls, a man with a camera approached Dani.

"Excuse me," he said, "but I'm covering the festival for a travel article in *The Sunday Times*. Do you mind if I take your picture?"

Cade was ready to jump at the chance, but to his surprise, Dani seemed hesitant—even startled. She went so far as to take a few steps back, positioning herself behind him. "No thank you," she said.

"Are you sure? I'd love to get a shot of—"

"She said no," Cade replied firmly. He put his arm around Dani and maneuvered her away from the stalls. "What was that all about?" he said, once they'd put some distance between themselves and the photographer.

"I just…really hate having my picture taken," she said.

"Really? Why?"

For the first time since he'd met her, she seemed at a loss for words. "I just do," she said. "I can't explain it. I'm just not comfortable with it."

"Enough said. If you don't like it, that's reason enough for me." Privately, though, he was a little confused. The request had seemed innocent enough, and it might have been fun to find their photo in the paper, or online, later. He knew that some people disliked seeing themselves in photographs, but he was surprised that a woman as gorgeous as Dani would feel self-conscious about how she appeared on camera. The two of them had never taken a photo together. He hadn't given it much thought until this moment, but now that the subject had come up, he realized that he'd never seen her take a selfie, or suggest that they pose for a picture at any of the areas of natural beauty he'd shown her on St. Camille. Was she concerned that a photo could make others suspicious of their secret arrangement? Or was she simply camera-shy?

He wasn't able to ruminate on Dani's reluctance much

longer, though, because a moment later, she pulled him into the dancing.

Cade had been to many festivals, but he hadn't been dancing in years. Dani was wearing a green dress with small white dots, and her skirt flared from her waist as she spun. She seemed to find the beat right away, falling into step with the dancers around her.

The last time he'd danced had been just before his wedding date. He'd taken classes to prepare for dancing at the reception, and then, of course, that hadn't happened. He'd given up dancing as part of his old life—and even if he hadn't, who on earth would he have danced with over the past several years?

His first instinct was to stay on the fringes of things. He was hesitant—uncertain of what to do with his hands and where to put his feet. But then Dani grabbed his hand. She pulled him close, right there in the middle of the street. The other dancers whirled around them.

She pressed her hips against his and they swayed together. He could *feel* the drumbeats vibrating from the cobblestones of the street through the soles of his feet. But then he felt something else. It was the rhythm of him and Dani, a rhythm they'd perfected over the past few weeks, but one that promised there was still more to be discovered. He fell into that rhythm, trusted it, and suddenly, his body knew what to do.

He'd never danced with such confidence, but he was confident now. He followed the music and the natural motion of their bodies, and his heart thrilled when he heard Dani laugh with excitement.

Neither one of them wanted to stop moving. But for one moment, he did pause, bending his head toward hers. A hundred dancers surrounded them, twirling, clapping, laughing. But as his lips met hers, he felt as though they were the only two people in the world.

CHAPTER SEVEN

DANI FELT LIKE a different person when she and Cade returned to St. Camille. She was surprised to find that she even looked forward to returning to her cramped dormitory quarters. The medical center was beginning to feel like home to her.

During medical school, she'd enjoyed her time in Boston, but it was never more than a city she was passing through. She always knew she'd have to return home to Lorovia someday. She'd made friends, she'd grown as a physician, but she'd never really felt at home.

But St. Camille was different. She could see the palm trees swaying from the window of the plane, and she felt like they were waving hello. Her fellowship was only meant to be for three years, but she could see herself staying in a place like this forever. Making a life here.

But that was foolish. Thanks to her grandmother, her family was supporting her choice to work at Coral Bay, but would they continue to support her if she wanted to stay forever? Even if they did, what was here for her? As much as she was enjoying her time with Cade, her affair with him would only ever be an affair.

Even though she couldn't imagine how it would be possible, she did want more, someday. She'd always imagined herself having children. And as unlikely as it was, given her complicated situation, she'd dreamed of falling in love. But for right now, she was finding her situation with Cade to be enough. The fact that Cade *didn't* want those things took off a great deal of pressure. She could enjoy the moment.

Sometimes a little too much.

On their first day back at work, Dani had to acknowledge that both she and Cade were failing miserably at their attempts to avoid having physical contact with one another at work. If anything, their foray off-island only seemed to have inflamed their desire for one another. Dani had come to Cade's office to ask him a simple question about a recent surgery. The next thing she knew, she'd once again caught that cinnamon scent that wafted from his skin. A moment later, his hands were running through her hair, his body pressing close against her. His hands traced her side, caressing her breast—and there was no knowing how far things might have gone, had there not been a knock at his office door.

They broke apart, both startled. Cade smoothed his hair and Dani hastily checked her blouse buttons and straightened her clothes. They seated themselves on either side of Cade's desk, and Cade called, "Come in."

Dr. Davidson came in. "I'm glad to find you both here. I have an update on that case from the other week."

Dani tried not to panic. She and Cade had just returned from their trip. There hadn't been time to explain anything to him.

"I'm sure Miss Berlini's family was glad to have her home safe and sound," she said.

"Actually, she's still here."

Her stomach turned to ice. "What? I thought she'd be discharged by now."

"She was supposed to go home yesterday. But she insisted on staying an extra day. She wanted to thank you both for saving her life. I thought you'd want to have the pleasure of speaking with her. Her recovery's gone very well. You should both feel proud."

"We'll make sure to see her this afternoon," Cade said. "Just have the admin staff put it on our schedules."

"Yes, of course," said Dani faintly.

"Will do." Dr. Davidson gave another smile as he left the room. Had it been a knowing smile, Dani wondered? Or was Dr. Davidson just being friendly?

It didn't matter. She had to tell Cade.

But before she could, he said, "You know what? I think you should go to meet the patient by yourself."

Her mouth was dry. "You…you don't want to talk with her?"

"I don't want to steal your thunder. The way you handled the case was outstanding, Dani. You should get all the credit. I'd only steal your glory."

He was handing her exactly what she wanted on a silver platter. She was in inner agony over what to do. Here was the chance to keep her secret and her promise to her family. On the other hand, he was bound to find out eventually—and wouldn't it be better if she told him sooner rather than later?

On the *other* other hand, telling him could change everything between them. And she wasn't ready for that.

"I don't know, Cade," she stalled, racked with indecision.

"Well, I do. Honestly, you'd be doing me a favor. I have an absolutely packed schedule thanks to that bit of time off we took. You'd really be helping me out."

She decided. If Cade didn't meet Angelica now, that would give her time to gather her courage and plan things out. She could tell him the right way.

"Well, if it'll help you out," she said.

"Thanks. I really appreciate it."

* * *

Dani sat at Angelica's bedside. "You're looking well, Ange. I'm so glad your surgery was a success."

"Me, too. The other doctors told me it was touch and go for a while. The worst skiing accident I've ever been in. I almost *died*," Angelica said with relish. Dani suppressed a small smile. Angelica was going to have quite a story to tell when she got home. She just needed to make sure Angelica was cautious about the parts of the story that she shared.

"I still can't decide what's crazier—my near-death experience or the fact that *you* were the person responsible for saving my life," Angelica continued.

"Ange, that's something I want to talk to you about," Dani said. "I've become a doctor. I work here at Coral Bay as a cardiology fellow."

"My goodness. A princess working as a doctor, of all things! How remarkably eccentric of you. But you always did have that unconventional streak."

"It is a little unusual for a member of my family to hold a job."

"Is something wrong? Has your family lost all their money?" Angelica's eyes were alight with the hope of fresh gossip.

"No, it's nothing like that. Being a doctor is just something I feel I'm meant to do."

Angelica's eyebrows furrowed. "I suppose everyone has their little quirks."

"But I need a favor from you, Ange."

"Anything. After all, you did save my life."

"My family is keeping my position here very quiet. We're not broadcasting it to anyone, or telling anyone outside the family about it. You're the *only one who knows*." Dani tried to put as much emphasis as she could on those last words, knowing they would appeal to Angelica's sense of the dramatic.

"A secret! How delicious. And I suppose you want me to keep it for you?"

"If you would. Please. It would just make things so much less complicated not to have to worry about photographers popping up unexpectedly."

"Well, I suppose I do owe you. All right, Dani. You don't need to worry about me. I won't tell anyone you're here."

"Thank you," said Dani, relieved.

Dani spent a few more minutes catching up with Angelica, who enjoyed having Dani listen as she spoke of galas, red carpet premiers and parties. The more Dani listened, the more relieved she felt that she was in St. Camille, living the life she wanted, instead of being paraded around at events.

Later that day, when Angelica was finally ready to leave, she did so amidst much fanfare, giving tearful good-byes to the staff who'd taken care of her. At one point, just before leaving, she took Dani by the arm and said, "By the way, some of the doctors here are *extremely* handsome." She sent a meaningful glance in Cade's direction. "If all of them look like that, I can understand the appeal of working at a place like this." But as far as Dani knew, that was the only interaction Angelica had with Cade. So her secret was still safe. For now.

Over the next several days, Dani tried to find the right moment to tell Cade exactly who she was. But somehow, the right time never seemed to arise.

She couldn't help it. Not only had it been a long time since she'd had a relationship, it had been a long time since she'd had any *fun* in a relationship. It was nice for the two of them to be able to focus on each other. And Cade did seem incredibly focused on her. She could make no complaints about his attentiveness.

When they were apart, she wrestled with whether she was deceiving him. When they were together, all of her worries melted away. They were having so many delightful moments together, and it seemed a shame to spoil any of them with cold realities.

Cade had suggested he and Dani have a picnic on one of his favorite secluded beaches on the island. It was a little difficult to access because of rocky outcroppings, but the advantage of that was that hardly anyone ever used it, so they'd have the whole beach to themselves. Dani could see why this particular strip of beach was a well-kept secret: the sand was blindingly white, the water a perfect turquoise, and wind erosion had carved beautiful rock formations along the coast that kept the beach hidden from prying eyes.

They weren't quite alone, though. At the far end of the beach, a small boy was fishing.

"Looks like we'll have company for a bit," said Cade. "But no matter. The little fellow will probably head home once he's caught enough."

Cade spread a blanket for them. He'd brought along a picnic basket, which Dani was grateful for. They'd spent the morning enjoying the market in town, and she was hungry and tired after a long morning of shopping.

But before they could dig into their apples, cheese and white wine, a sharp cry echoed from down the beach.

Cade was off and running before Dani could even see what was happening, but she followed in the direction of the child's cry. As she drew closer, she saw what the trouble had been. The boy, who was probably no more than seven, had been fishing with a hook and a strong piece of wire. His line had become tangled, and in his frustration, he'd gotten it wound around his wrist. Now the wire was giving him some nasty cuts, though they didn't seem deep—Dani had a feeling the boy's cries were more from fear than actual pain.

Cade had his arm around him and was gently untangling the wire.

"Come now. Stay calm," he said, in a low voice. "We'll get everything sorted out in just a moment. Best thing you can do is stay still."

He unwound the wire and looked back to Dani. "Just a few cuts and scrapes here and there. He'll be up and running in no time." Indeed, the boy's tears had already dried, and he was looking at Cade with wide eyes.

Cade showed the boy how to coil his wire so it wouldn't tangle, which was no small feat for seven-year-old hands. Dani was struck by how patient Cade was, making sure the child could make the coil on his own and then demonstrating the best way to cast and recast the line into the water. Anyone who saw Cade like this, she thought, would be shocked to learn that he didn't want children. He had a natural instinct for talking to the boy at his level, and he waited patiently for the boy to master one step before moving on to the next.

Cade looked up at her. "This is Anton," he said. "He says it's his first time fishing, and his brothers told him he probably wouldn't catch anything."

"Well, then we'll just have to prove Anton's brothers wrong," said Dani. "I think he's been very brave, so far."

"I think so, too," said Cade. He gave the fishing line a practiced cast, then reeled it back in and handed it to Anton. "All right, kiddo. Try it again. Just like I showed you. It might take a few more tries, but I have a feeling that if you keep trying, you might be able to make your brothers eat their words. And your fish."

The little boy threw the line out, holding the coil just as Cade had shown him. Dani held her breath. She had never seen anyone fish before. The ocean was so vast that it was hard to imagine Anton's tiny hook catching anything. But the boy's face was so hopeful, so determined. And then, all of a sudden— "A fish!" he screamed.

"All right, slow and steady, let's reel it in," said Cade.

Dani was absolutely enthralled, watching the boy reel in a small fish and put it into a nearby net with Cade's help. Little Anton caught two more fish before he trotted happily away from the beach, hauling his catch home.

"That ought to keep those brothers of his quiet," said Cade, his voice satisfied. They returned to their blanket and their picnic basket.

"You're great with kids," Dani said. "Can you really not ever imagine having any of your own?"

The smile dropped from his face. She'd obviously touched a sore spot, but she couldn't help feeling curious.

"I suppose I haven't told you why I became a cardiologist."

"We've never discussed it, no."

"It was because of my brother. Henry."

"I didn't know you had a brother."

"I used to. He passed away from an undiagnosed heart condition when he was only fifteen. I was eight at the time."

"Oh, Cade, I'm so sorry. I didn't know."

"Hardly anyone does. I've moved far away from the people who know this story."

"Can I ask how it happened?"

"Henry was a track-and-field star. But the running was too much for his heart, and his condition wasn't diagnosed until after he collapsed at a track meet. After he died, my parents started having problems. We all had different ways of dealing with it—my dad by leaving, my mom by checking out emotionally. And I dealt with it by going to medical school. I thought maybe I could make Henry's death mean something. Maybe I could prevent other kids from dying unexpectedly, the way he did."

"That's a lot of pressure to put on yourself."

"I can see that now. But at the time, it made a lot of sense to me. And I don't think I ever really let go of the idea—that it was my responsibility to fix everything. I believe some people may have experienced it as micromanagement." He smiled at her, and she smiled back.

"I think that's why I was in such a rush to get married right out of medical school," he continued. "I thought that if I couldn't fix my own family, at least I could create a family of my own. Start over. Start fresh. But then Susan left me for my best man—my best *friend*, a person who was essentially a brother to me. I'd cobbled together a family of choice out of friends and people I trusted. Losing those people made me realize that I couldn't handle loss, period. So I decided that relationships weren't for me." He shrugged. "You can't get hurt if you don't let anyone get close."

"What a hard thing to go through. I'm so sorry."

"Things have gotten better over the years. And I realized that I wasn't cut out for things like families or relationships. I decided that I didn't want children, because what if I passed on the heart defect that Henry had? Even if I didn't, children get into accidents, or they can catch illnesses. Anything could go wrong. The same with relationships. The more you get attached to someone, the more it hurts when you lose them. And

I am never going to experience the loss of a loved one again if I can help it."

He meant it, she realized. And she couldn't blame him. After those kinds of experiences, who would want to get attached to other people? And why would Cade ever want to have a child, knowing the potential pain he could be facing if something went wrong? There were, of course, all of the positive sides to having a family, but she couldn't bring that up now, knowing the grief he'd experienced.

The strength of his belief that he would never want a family began to make her feel sad, and she knew why. Despite all of her intentions, she was beginning to feel attached to him. Even though they'd promised each other, over and over again, that that wouldn't happen.

She already knew the answer, but she asked him anyway. "Cade… Do you ever see your feelings on any of this changing someday?"

"I doubt it."

"Yes. So do I."

He looked taken aback. "But you're still okay with what we have, right?"

"Yes, of course." She gave him a faint smile.

"So there's no reason to change anything?"

"No," she said faintly. "I suppose there isn't."

Hours later, they loaded their picnic things into the back of Cade's car as the sun touched the horizon and created a golden path on the waves that stretched all the way to the beach.

It had been a perfect day, Cade thought. Somehow, his time with Dani always left him feeling more like himself. Like when they'd visited Horseshoe Cay and he'd felt so awkward when he first tried to dance. Something about Dani's presence let him relax and be himself. He'd felt it when he'd spoken about Henry earlier. He hadn't talked about his brother in years, and yet with Dani, it felt natural to do so.

Even though their relationship was just a fling, she brought out a deeper, truer side of him. It wasn't like the fleeting relationships he'd had in the past. They had fun, but they talked about meaningful things, and he could tell he was better for it. He'd expected talking about Henry to feel painful, but instead it felt as though a weight of grief had been…not lifted, exactly, but eased.

He noticed that Dani had been very quiet for the rest of the afternoon. He hadn't thought much of it because up until now, the silence between them had felt peaceful, agreeable, but as it stretched on, he began to wonder if there was more to her silence than he first realized.

Suddenly he worried he might have put too much pressure on their relationship by telling her about Henry. This was just supposed to be a fling, after all. He'd brought up something emotionally heavy and, in doing so, had stepped out of bounds of their arrangement. She'd just confirmed that she didn't want to change anything about their agreement— that she was fine with what they had. But now he'd gone and brought up a very private piece of his own past, and he realized it could seem to Dani as though he'd made things too complicated, too personal.

"Is everything okay?" he asked as they folded the blanket together. "You seem a little distracted."

"Hmm? Oh, yes, everything's fine," she said, her gaze drifting away from him. Then she abruptly dropped her end of the blanket and turned to face the water.

He balled up the blanket and shoved it into the trunk. "What is it? Dani, if things got a little heavy for a moment, I'm sorry. I didn't mean to…"

She shook her head. Were those tears forming in the corners of her eyes? "No, it's not that at all. Please don't think that. I'm glad you told me about what happened to your brother, truly. It means a lot to me that you would share something so important with me. But Cade…it's made me realize that there's something I do have to share with you."

He reached out for her hand. "Hey. No, you don't. Everyone has a past. But this thing between us is about what's happening right now. Anything you might feel you have to tell me about the past isn't going to change how I feel about you today, or make me think differently about the person I know you are."

She met his gaze. Those *were* tears in her eyes, threatening to spill over. "That's the problem, Cade. I'm afraid that telling you this will change how you feel about me. I'm afraid it will change everything."

"Then why say anything?" He couldn't imagine what she could possibly disclose that would have an impact on how he felt about her. "We have fun together. Why should anything need to change?"

"Because despite our efforts to keep things uncomplicated, we're getting closer. I feel it, Cade. And I think you do, too."

Dammit. This was what came of unburdening himself, of sharing some of his most personal memories with someone. He had no one but himself to blame. By bringing up Henry, he'd opened the door to emotion, which they'd strictly agreed to keep out of their relationship.

And yet, he'd brought up Henry because he'd felt safe to do so. Some part of him had yearned to talk about his brother, and Dani, more than any other woman he'd met, made him feel safe when talking about his past.

Which meant that she was different from the women he'd known in the past. Which therefore meant that she was right: he was starting to care for her.

And from what she was saying, she was beginning to care for him, as well.

There were feelings between them now, no matter how hard he might try to insist there weren't.

"You're right." His words came out quietly, almost inaudible over the lapping of the waves.

"That's why I have to tell you this now. If I go on pretending, then both of us are going to get hurt."

"Pretending what?"

"To be a normal person."

His brows furrowed as he wondered where she was going.

"Cade, there's no easy or practical way to say this. I'm a princess."

He shook his head, at a total loss. "I don't know what you mean."

"I'm twelfth in line to the throne of Lorovia. My grandmother is the queen."

Lorovia? He'd heard of that country. His mind went back to high school geography classes. Lorovia was supposed to be a tiny country with a massive amount of wealth. Focusing on the details was helping him to control his rising disbelief that Dani could have kept such a large secret from him from the moment they'd met.

Perhaps that was unfair. In Boston, they hadn't known if they'd ever see each other again. But then she'd come to work at Coral Bay, and she hadn't told him. They'd been colleagues, and she hadn't told him. They'd become friends—they'd been intimate together—and she hadn't told him.

"Cade? Say something, please."

He was trying to, but his mind couldn't keep up with events. Everything seemed to be changing around him, even though he and Dani were standing completely still.

He couldn't stop thinking about what this information about her might mean, let alone all the opportunities she'd had to reveal it to him. He'd thought he'd known who she was. This wasn't like revealing a mistake from the past, or having some sort of painful family secret. Dani had deliberately kept a fundamental fact about who she was from him.

"How could you lie me?" he blurted out. "Why didn't you say anything sooner?"

Dani looked extremely uncomfortable. "I never lied," she said, her voice miserable. "I just…didn't bring it up."

Her words were so similar to what Susan had said when he'd discovered she'd betrayed him with his best friend. Susan had never lied directly to his face, but she'd omitted so many truths that it amounted to the same thing.

Thinking about Susan brought back all the old pain—and the old anger—fresh, as though it had happened yesterday instead of years ago. "So everything that's happened between you and me—it was all, what, just some kind of prank? Or some way to amuse yourself?" His voice came out tight and brittle.

"No! Absolutely not." She was horrified. "I had to keep it a secret for security reasons, Cade. It was never about keeping a secret from you, specifically. It's a secret I've had to keep for years from everyone but the most trusted people in my life. I know this must come as such a shock, but please try to understand. This was never supposed to hurt you. I never wanted to lie."

He wanted to believe her. Wanted to believe that she would never willingly hurt him. Moments ago, he'd been so certain that he knew exactly who Dani was, even though he was well aware that they both had much in their pasts that the other didn't know. He'd thought he didn't need to know any of the details. But that was when he'd thought he knew Dani.

"Cade, please don't stay quiet like this," she said, breaking into his thoughts. "I'll tell you anything you want to know. I'm not supposed to—my family won't like that I've broken protocol and told you about my royal status. But you're important to me. Please believe me when I say that I never wanted to hurt you, and that I'm telling you this now because I trust you."

She was saying that she trusted *him*? Right after revealing that she'd kept a huge secret from him? Doubt from the past kept setting off alarm bells in his mind.

"Is Dani Martin even your real name?"

She blushed. "No. My full title is Her Royal Highness Princess Danielle-Genevieve Matthieu DuMaria."

"Matthieu?"

"It's a family name."

He nodded slowly. "Okay. So your name isn't what I thought it was, you don't come from where I thought you did and you're not who I thought you were."

"I tried to explain, back in Boston, that my family situation was complicated. I couldn't tell you anything more then. I barely knew you, and my decision to practice medicine has always been a source of tension in my family. They've only allowed me to come here because the Coral Bay Medical Center helped my grandfather years ago. I'm not close in the line of succession, but I still have royal duties and a responsibility to uphold my family's image."

He thought of her refusal to be photographed on Horseshoe Cay. Had she been thinking about her family's image then?

All he could think about was how it had been yet another opportunity for her to tell him the truth…and she hadn't.

The rational part of his brain could understand that there might be some logic to what Dani was saying. He knew that once he got used to the idea of her being royalty, he might be able to understand, on an intellectual level, that everything she was saying about needing to keep her secret very close made sense. But for right now, her words stirred the hurt of past betrayal. He couldn't shake off his shock at the news of her identity and that she had been capable of hiding it from him so well.

"Is…is there anything else you want to know about it?" she asked, her face streaked with tears. "I can explain more about the security measures or my family's expectations."

He shook his head. "The only thing I want to know is where it leaves us."

She took a deep breath. "It can leave us right where we are, if you want it to. With exactly what we agreed on. No emotional involvement, no attachment. It's the only kind of relationship I *can* have, Cade, because the obligations of a royal consort are so extensive that I can't casually date anyone otherwise. Trying to date when you're a princess is like… Imagine immediately having to decide whether you're going to marry someone on the first date and then asking for that kind of commitment."

As angry as he was, he tried to think about things from her perspective. "So there are a lot of rules regarding who you're with?"

"Not so much rules, as expectations. Anyone I was *officially* dating would have to sign an NDA, which tends to suck the romance and spontaneity right out of things. There are agreements to do public appearances and holiday events—

and those are contractual obligations because otherwise the tabloids start making a fuss about every little thing in their search for a scandal, just because someone didn't make it to a holiday parade or a state dinner. And then there's the whole issue of living under a microscope—the press analyzing everything you do. So everything has to be kept secret, unless it's really serious."

"And we weren't serious." That had been the whole point, but he still felt a pang in his chest as he said it.

"We weren't supposed to be," she replied. "I thought the fact that this was just an affair would protect us. All of those expectations are a lot to put on someone. And the one time, years ago, that I was able to get someone to agree to all of them, it was a huge disaster. The only reason they agreed to put up with all of it was to get close to me, so they could make money by selling pictures to tabloids. I never know what's real, Cade. As a princess, I never know who's using me or who likes me for who I am. But with you I could just be myself."

His anger softened, just a little. Hadn't that been what he liked about being with Dani? Around her, it was easy to be himself.

"Please believe me when I say that I was trying to spare you," she continued. "And since our relationship was *just* a fling, there was no need for you to have to sign anything official or participate in anything formal. But if the press got wind of it, or if I made any public appearances with you, we'd have to decide very quickly if we wanted to keep seeing each other. Otherwise, if the press thought we were in a relationship, but we had no formal agreement in place, the paparazzi could create a scandal out of thin air. I've seen it happen before."

"It sounds like you're saying that if someone else found out, we'd have to end things."

"We'd have to…make a choice. We could end our fling and let any rumors in the press die out. If there's no fire, there's no smoke. Or we could continue, but we'd have to present you to my family and formally commit to being in a relationship. Which is full of obligations I don't want to put on you." For the first time since she'd made her revelation, she looked at him with a glimmer of hope in her eyes. "Does this mean you…*don't* want to end things?"

What he wanted was a time machine that would let him go back to the point before Dani had revealed her princess status. But no, he realized, even that wouldn't fix things. He hadn't known the truth, and he couldn't be in a relationship with someone who wasn't truthful.

But she was being truthful now. She was telling him everything, even though it clearly cost her great effort to do so. Didn't that count for something?

She was waiting for his answer.

"No," he said, finally. "I don't want to end things. But maybe we should slow things down for now."

"I understand," she said, her voice tinged with sadness. "Take all the time you need."

The disappointment in her eyes pained him, but he couldn't bring himself to respond in any other way. He didn't want to end things with Dani. But he didn't want to relive the pain of Susan's betrayal, either. And no matter what Dani's intentions had been in keeping such a huge part of her life a secret from him—no matter how justified she might be—he was still in the position of hearing someone he cared about explain that they'd kept important information from him. Years later, the pain was still fresh, and he wasn't ready to face it.

But he wasn't ready to let go of Dani, either.

Something had to change, though. Dani's revelation that

she was a princess was shocking enough, but the pain came from the fact that she'd been hiding such a huge part of herself from him for so long. The only way he could think for them to get through this was to take a few steps back. From what Dani was saying, it sounded as though a serious relationship between the two of them would be far more complicated than he'd ever realized, and he worked hard to avoid complications under ordinary circumstances. He needed time to wrap his head around everything and to know that he wouldn't risk getting hurt if further revelations came out. He hoped there wasn't more, but he needed to be prepared for the possibility.

"There's one more thing before we move forward," he said as they finished packing up his car. "Are there any other big secrets I should know about?"

"Just the one. I swear."

CHAPTER EIGHT

DANI TUGGED HER sweater tightly over her scrubs as she took the lab results from Nurse Johnston. "Thanks for getting these back to me so quickly," she said. "And do you have the results for the patient we talked about this morning?"

Nurse Johnston blinked at her. They both waited for a moment while Dani didn't respond. Then Nurse Johnston said, "You're holding them right now, Dr. Martin. I just handed them to you."

"Oh! Of course. I'm so sorry. My mind must have been elsewhere." Dani blushed furiously as Nurse Johnston walked away, shaking her head.

It wasn't like her to lose her focus like that at work. But ever since her beachside date with Cade, she'd had a hard time concentrating.

She knew that Cade's suggestion that they slow things down was completely reasonable. Still, she hated it. The past few weeks had been like a dream. She'd finally been able to connect with someone without any pressure or complications. She wasn't ready to give that up yet, even if continuing on together was a bad idea.

He didn't break things off, though. He just said to slow things down. Those were two different things.

So why did they feel the same?

They'd been unusually distant with each other over the past

few days. There were no more clandestine kisses in their offices, no more meaningful glances after surgeries. Perhaps that was because work had become so busy. They'd barely had a chance to speak to one another at all.

Her phone buzzed in her pocket. It was the first text she'd received from Cade in several days.

Can you come over to my place as soon as you get off from work?

Finally. Maybe after a few days of caution, Cade was ready to relax a little.

Fifteen minutes later, her shift had ended. She headed away from the main atrium of the medical center to the staff dormitories. The halls were nearly empty, as usual. Most of the staff preferred to have their own homes on the island. Dani had an appointment with a realtor to find a place of her own later that week. She couldn't wait; she was looking forward to finally having her own space.

She showered, then began picking out clothes for the evening. As she dressed, she noticed that her phone had received repeated notifications while she was in the shower. Had Cade been trying to get in touch with her?

She picked up the phone and realized there wasn't one message waiting for her. There were hundreds.

She scrolled through them, and her heart sank. It was clear enough what this was all about.

Kim had sent her the worst of it. She'd forwarded Dani the pictures. They were blurry, but they clearly depicted her and Cade in the town square on Horseshoe Cay. The way they were dancing together made it clear that they were more than just friends—as did the kiss that had been caught on camera.

That photographer who'd wanted to take her picture had clearly gone ahead and done so, even without her permission. Dani wondered if he'd recognized her immediately or taken her picture and done his research later. Either way, the damage was done.

The headlines screamed with speculation. Who was this mystery lover of the princess of Lorovia? How involved were they? Was the trip meant to be romantic? Perhaps a proposal was on the horizon and, with the proposal, a wedding and a family. One headline even speculated that she was already pregnant. Dani knew this was typical tabloid nonsense, but it still infuriated her. She might have gained a few pounds since her arrival, but that was merely the stress of adjusting to a new environment. But of course, no tabloid could resist a chance at body-shaming.

She kept getting more texts and alerts, even as she tried to decipher the messages that were already there. It seemed as though she had voice mails waiting from everyone she'd ever met, including her entire family, all of her friends and the Lorovian State Department. She'd have to take the weekend off from work just to return calls.

If there was one silver lining, it was that the tabloids barely showed interest in the fact that she was working as a doctor at Coral Bay. Her family's fear that her career would create a scandal was sorely misplaced. The articles briefly mentioned her profession, then went on to obsess over her love life and the utter fantasy that she was moments away from a proposal.

Had Cade seen the headlines?

What must he be thinking right now?

She scrolled back to Cade's message on her phone. There was nothing more after the message he'd sent earlier.

Can you come over to my place as soon as you get off from work?

And nothing else following her response.

Had he seen the photos before he sent the message?

If he had, the message took on a whole different context.

She'd been looking forward to a fun night of reconnecting, especially after they'd spent the last few days without much contact. But now her excitement evaporated into worry, tinged with panic.

What would he make of the headline insinuation that she was pregnant? She knew how much Cade didn't want children. If he thought she was pregnant, he must be frantic.

Calm down, she told herself. Cade was a practical man. Surely, he'd know that the headlines were nothing more than a grab for attention.

But it immediately became of the utmost importance that she talk to Cade. What if he didn't understand that the story was rumormongering, plain and simple? What if he thought the headlines were true?

She was used to the press interfering with her life. Her family had taught her from a young age that all of her choices would eventually become a matter of public discussion. But rumors that she was pregnant weren't merely hurtful to her. They also touched on a very private grief of Cade's. She knew how afraid he was of passing his brother's heart defect on to a child of his own. She hated to think that these headlines would cause him even a moment's pain.

This was exactly the reason she avoided relationships. It wasn't just about her own difficulty trusting again after Peter's betrayal. It was the fact that anyone she dated was also subjected to the same kind of scrutiny that she'd had to put up with for her entire life. It wasn't fair to someone else to have to go through that.

And now that Cade was getting a taste of exactly what she'd been trying to protect him from, she was certain he'd want to end things. The thought tore at her heart, even though she knew that ending things now was the wisest course of action. If they stopped, she could tell her family that the paparazzi was making something out of nothing, and the tabloids would eventually lose interest and move on to something else.

She left her dormitory and raced down the beach toward Cade's cottage. There was no choice for either of them. If they had to end it, they had to end it. But she hoped he would forgive her first.

Dani had tried to rehearse what she could possibly say to Cade as she raced down the beach. But any words she might have prepared abandoned her the moment he opened his door.

"I take it you've seen the photos," he said, the moment he saw her red, sweating face. She'd nearly run the whole way.

"Yes. Just now. My phone's blowing up with messages, but I wanted to talk to you before anyone else."

He waited while she caught her breath. When she could speak again, she said, "None of it's true, of course. It's all pure speculation. The more outlandish it is, the more papers they sell and the more clicks they get online. But it's just rumors, Cade. I swear. I never wanted you to get hurt like this."

He gave her a long look. "So you're not pregnant."

"Of course not! If I were, I'd have told you immediately. These are baseless rumors, and I feel horrible that you've been affected by them."

He let out a long, slow breath. "Affected by them? That's one way of putting it. When I couldn't get ahold of you, I didn't know what to think."

"I'm so sorry you were upset by this."

"Upset? I'm furious, Dani! You know how I feel about having children. And then, for the past half hour, I've had my face plastered all over the internet, with speculation that I'm about to become a father! People I haven't spoken to in years have been texting me congratulations!"

His eyes burned with rage but, more than that, with hurt. Dani felt miserable. She hated that Cade had been forced to deal with some of his worst memories, simply because he'd been photographed in a public place with her.

"This is all my fault," she said.

He let out a long, slow breath, and she could see that he was trying to control his anger. "It's not *all* your fault. You're not the one who took those photos. If I ever see that photographer again, I'll wring his neck."

"You can't do that, Cade. This is just a small taste of what life in the public eye is like. You can't use brute force against every single member of the paparazzi."

"I can try."

A dark laugh escaped her. "Not if you want to keep your medical license."

His mouth formed a thin, firm line. "If I had known that you were a princess, I could have been more prepared. I would have kept my guard up on Horseshoe Cay, instead of thinking that we didn't have to worry about our secret getting found out since we were away from everyone we knew here on St. Camille."

So he did blame her, then. And he was right. That part was her fault.

"I should have told you sooner," she said.

"Yes! You really should have. Everything could have been different if you'd been honest with me."

"Cade, it was supposed to be a secret. I'm only allowed to tell people I trust completely."

"But why is it all about your trust? What about the fact that

I'm affected by it? I could have made different choices—we *both* could have made different choices about how we conducted ourselves—if you'd shared your secret much sooner. Instead, you didn't tell me, and now this is happening. This is my life, Dani.

"When you told me you were a princess, at first I didn't believe you. Then I took some time to adjust to the idea. And I thought maybe we can make it work. Maybe there's a way to go on as we have been, not meaning too much to each other, but still having fun together."

It was bittersweet to hear he'd been spending the last few days wondering if they might have a chance. So much had changed since her confession on the beach.

"And now?"

"Now... I'm just trying to figure out how to deal with what's happening, minute by minute. My mother reads these kinds of tabloids. I'm going to have to explain to her that no, she's not expecting a grandchild. On top of the fact that she's also not about to gain a royal daughter-in-law."

Dani winced. Some of those headlines really had made it seem as though she and Cade were on the verge of getting married.

"I don't even know what everyone at work is going to think. For years, I've been able to keep my personal life personal. But now I've been getting calls, texts—about us dating, about fatherhood... Dani, it seemed like everyone else knew more about my life than I do. I felt completely exposed. I've spent most of my adult life trying not to feel that way."

"I know the feeling," she said. She remembered how she felt when the photos that Peter had sold were published. She'd felt as though someone had pulled back a protective curtain of privacy that she hadn't even known was there. "I never wanted to subject you to this."

"Dani, I…" He paused, and then seemed to push himself to go on. "Every relationship I've had has been about avoiding getting close, avoiding loss. And then these photos came out. And they reminded me of all the reasons I've made those choices. All this speculation about me becoming a father to a child, about the two of us being on the verge of marriage… I can't do those things."

"I know that," she said. "We've always said from the beginning that that's not where things were going."

He hesitated, then added, "I can't do this anymore, either, Dani."

"I know," she whispered. Still, it hurt to hear him say it. Knowing that something was about to happen didn't change the way she felt about it.

She looked at Cade's blue eyes, looking back at her with concern. That was Cade. Even amid the hurt and anger he was feeling, he still found a way to have concern for her.

"I knew that everything would change once the press found out. I just thought we'd have more time."

"I'm sorry, Dani. I wish there were some way things could be different for us."

Wasn't there a way, though? She knew, even as she said it, that there was no hope, but she couldn't help herself from pointing out that there was one way forward for the two of them.

"I mean, we could always make things official," she said, trying to make her voice sound casual. "You sign on as my consort, fill out all the various palace legal agreements…"

"You can't be serious."

"Of course not," she said quickly. And she hadn't meant it.

Not really. She and Cade had been very clear about their agreement from the beginning. She knew perfectly well that Cade wasn't interested in the kind of commitment that becoming a royal consort required. Who would be?

She couldn't possibly have expected Cade to say that none of it mattered—that he'd put up with anything, go through any amount of inconvenience and suffer any kind of public scrutiny—just to be with her. It was an unrealistic fantasy, and she knew it. Everything that had just happened was proof of just how unfair it would be for her to have those expectations of Cade, and why they'd agreed to no commitment in the first place.

But like most fantasies, it was hard to let go.

"Cade, I'm just curious. If I weren't a princess…and I really did want some of the things these headlines are suggesting, what would you want?"

He paused, and she knew that his hesitation told her everything she needed to know. "Never mind," she said, quickly. "I shouldn't have asked. It was just a hypothetical question."

"I'm sorry," he said.

"You shouldn't be the one apologizing to me right now. I've just gotten your life turned upside down."

"I wasn't apologizing. I just meant that I'm sorry things have to be this way."

And that was the story of her life. No matter what she wanted, things had to be a certain way. She should be used to it by now. She shouldn't be feeling hurt or angry. She was the one who'd brought all the hurt into Cade's life. She was the one who'd kept a secret that had ended up causing all of this turmoil in the first place.

And so it wasn't fair for her to be angry or hurt…and yet, a small part of her was. Cade had every right to be upset. But he also clung to his belief that the way to deal with his feelings was to distance himself from everyone and everything that could cause him pain. She'd never really thought about how it would feel if one of those things he distanced himself from turned out to be her. After all, she'd never intended to get attached to him.

But in spite of all her best efforts, her feelings had changed. Cade's hadn't, and she had no right to expect them to.

"I should go," she said. She'd done what she came to do and assured him she wasn't pregnant. He'd done what he felt he had to do and told her what she'd known all along: that they had no hope for a future together. How strange, she thought, that the things she already knew could still hurt her so much.

The silence stretched between them. Any wild hope she'd had that he might tell her not to go dissolved completely in that silence. She turned and left the cottage, and as she walked down the beach, she didn't allow herself to look back.

It had been a long time since Cade had been struck speechless. As Dani left, he longed to call out to her. He didn't know what he could possibly say, and it didn't matter anyway, because his words were stuck in his throat.

Living on St. Camille, he'd gotten used to one day being very much like the next. There were always different medical emergencies to deal with at work, but for the most part, his personal life was one of stability and routine. He liked it that way. There were no secrets, and thus no unexpected surprises.

But then Dani had come along. No one else had known they were together, and the agreement they had in place to keep their emotions out of their relationship had given him a sense of security. He'd never once felt out of control.

Until this afternoon, when he'd seen the pictures. The initial shock had been severe. If Dani had trusted him with the truth, he could have been prepared. Instead, he'd been blindsided. The headline speculating that she was pregnant had hit him particularly hard. The rumors had brought back all the reasons he was determined never to be involved with anyone again, especially anyone who wanted children.

In his heart of hearts, he did want children of his own. It was a wish he'd never shared with anyone, because he knew it would be impossible. The worry of passing on Henry's heart defect to a child of his own was always present. Atrial valve defects weren't always detectable via ultrasound, which was why procedures like the pulse oximetry screenings he and Dani had performed in the NICU at Coral Bay were so important. He didn't know how he could make it through nine months of a pregnancy, completely helpless to have any control over his child's well-being, with no way to know if his child was healthy until it was born.

By not having children—by avoiding relationships, and thereby avoiding marriage and any possibility of a family— he also avoided loss. But that meant there would be no small fingers to curl around his, like the newborns in the NICU. There would be no baby to cuddle, no child to teach and guide through their own small adventures each day. These were the sacrifices he had to make. The potential for grief was too great otherwise.

He should be relieved that none of the headlines were actually true. But his relief was overshadowed by his frustration with Dani. He couldn't stop thinking that so much could have been different if she'd told him the truth in the first place.

He might not have much experience with royalty, but he felt it was completely unfair that once they'd become involved with each other, she'd continued to keep her identity a secret from him. Before their involvement, he could understand the argument that she could only reveal her secret to the people she trusted most. But once they'd begun their fling, she should have told him, so that he'd known what he was signing on for. At least he could have been prepared. At least she would have acknowledged that it mattered to her exactly how much his life could be affected if their affair were to be discovered.

In some ways, this would be easier if he could regret that he'd ever gotten involved with Dani. But that would be another lie—this time to himself. Thinking about the heat and passion of their nights together, he knew he would have made the same decision, even if he'd known about her royal status. He just would have taken more precautions and been ready for the fallout when it came. And it wasn't only about their physical connection. He'd had fun with her and felt more like himself with her. Their connection had been real in a way it was never supposed to be. And that made him angry with himself, for letting his guard down, and with her, for not being the person he'd thought she was.

And that was the worst part. Because the person he'd *thought* Dani was, was absolutely wonderful. So wonderful that it terrified him.

He'd been so reluctant to admit it to himself, but the person he'd *thought* Dani was, was someone he could be close to. He'd been so concerned about his colleagues finding out about their affair and worrying—in part—about their judgement of him having an affair with a subordinate, even though workplace relationships weren't terribly uncommon on St. Camille. It was a small island, after all. But he knew now that if anyone had discovered their affair, he wouldn't have wanted to end it. It would have been worth any amount of scrutiny from his colleagues to be with the person he'd thought Dani was.

Now that it was over between them, he knew he'd have done anything to be with the person he'd thought Dani was. And that left him feeling off-balance, because he didn't do commitments or relationships. He'd done without relationships for a long time, and this should be proof that he didn't need them.

It was frustrating, then, that he still yearned for her. He missed her conversation, her humor and the feeling of her body next to his. He ached for her in spite of himself, in spite of knowing that the person he longed for had fundamentally hurt him. He wanted her back, and he also never wanted to see her again, because the degree to which he wanted her back alarmed him. He'd been a fool to ever think they could just have a fling. It was for the best that they'd ended things when they did, because if they'd stayed together much longer, his heart would have been in serious danger of becoming entangled.

He didn't think her suggestion that he become her official consort was as casual as she'd tried to make it sound. But he couldn't give it serious consideration. The obligations sounded extensive, and he had a career on St. Camille. If his relationship with Dani became official, would her family understand how important his career was? Or would they expect him to play some over-puffed role in the public relations wing of the royal family? They'd been reluctant to allow Dani to have a career as a doctor; would they understand how important his profession was to him? He couldn't imagine giving up his life in the Caribbean to spend his days attending state functions for a country he'd never even visited. Maybe Dani had been joking, after all. In fact, he recalled, she had been the one to first suggest they keep their fling a secret. From the start, she'd never envisioned a public relationship with him.

A serious relationship between the two of them would never

have been possible. He knew that now. But his heart was having a much harder time accepting that reality than he could have ever predicted.

Even if Dani wasn't royal, he could never give her everything she wanted. He knew she wanted children, but the thought of loving and potentially losing a family again was simply too much to bear.

There were a thousand reasons why ending their relationship was the right thing to do. He knew it, and he knew she knew it, too. He just wished it didn't have to hurt so much.

Dani stormed along the beach, furious with herself.

She couldn't believe she was in this situation once again. Cade was different from Peter, but the end result was still the same. She'd gotten close to someone, and the press had made an appearance just in time to ruin everything.

Maybe it was for the best. Cade was never going to want a deeper relationship with her. And it wasn't fair of her to hope for that, when he'd been clear about his intentions from the beginning. It wasn't as though he'd led her on. She'd agreed with Kim that Cade wasn't right for her. The whole *point* was that Cade wasn't right for her. He didn't want a relationship or a family, and that wouldn't change.

She looked at the tabloid photos on her phone again. She knew she shouldn't, but it was so hard to tear herself away. At least she could get a small laugh at the headline speculating that she was pregnant. Imagine. So she was a little heavier than usual. The press didn't need to leap to ridiculous conclusions about it. Why, she'd just had a period three weeks ago.

The thought stopped her midstep. It had been three weeks ago, hadn't it? Or perhaps four. She'd been so busy that she'd lost track of a few things.

It had to be three weeks ago. It had been the strangest period, though. Just three days of light spotting, and then nothing.

This was ridiculous, she thought. There was no way she was pregnant. There would have been other signs. And she was a doctor, for heaven's sake. She knew her own body.

She hadn't had any nausea, except for a few times in the morning after she'd had some bad soup for dinner from the medical center's commissary. Once she'd realized the connection, she'd stopped eating the soup. But she'd still been queasy for a few days afterward.

She began walking down the beach again, but more slowly. She was going over details in her head. Her late cycle could be attributed to fatigue. She'd been very busy, after all. Her body was a little more swollen than usual, but again, she'd been very busy, with no time to exercise. And she couldn't prepare her own meals while she was living in the dormitory. Which also could explain the nausea she was experiencing, as she couldn't always choose the healthiest meal options when she was busy. There were perfectly plausible explanations for everything she was experiencing. In fact, pregnancy was probably the *least* likely explanation for her symptoms, because she'd been on contraception ever since she and Cade had started their fling.

That stopped her thoughts for a moment. She'd started taking the pill *after* that first night with Cade. And while they'd used protection every night since, on their first night together, they'd used a condom from her purse. Her "wishful thinking" condom—the one Kim had put there years ago.

Most condoms began to break down after a few years. Dani couldn't remember exactly how long that particular condom had been sitting at the bottom of her purse. Had it been two years? Three? Or perhaps even longer than that? She hadn't had any reason to give it much thought. The condom was never supposed to be anything more than a bad joke, but now, nothing could be more serious.

Her worry grew stronger by the moment. They'd used an unreliable condom. And she'd made the biggest mistake a doctor could make: she was trying so hard to explain away her symptoms that she hadn't considered all the possibilities. Especially the possibility that she might actually be pregnant.

She needed to take a pregnancy test. Immediately. Once she had confirmation that she wasn't pregnant, she could put the questions that swirled in her mind to rest. And if she was pregnant… Well, she'd cross that bridge if she came to it.

She changed direction and walked toward town as quickly as she could.

CHAPTER NINE

BEFORE SHE'D EVER arrived on St. Camille, Dani had wondered if it might be difficult to adjust to life on such a small island. Now, for what felt like the thousandth time, she felt awash with gratitude for how close together everything was on the island.

The closest drugstore was only a ten minute walk from the beach. She'd briefly considered going to a different drugstore that was farther away from Coral Bay. That way, she'd be more sure of avoiding running into anyone from work. But the thought of spending an additional minute with the uncertainty that swirled through her mind was unbearable. She couldn't wait. She needed to put her fears to rest as soon as possible, and that meant buying a pregnancy test right away.

She grabbed a test off the shelf, then hastened to the checkout aisle—only to run right into Nurse Johnston, who had apparently gotten off her shift recently as well.

Nurse Johnston gave her a warm smile. "*Bonswa*, Dr. Martin," Her eyes drifted to the package in Dani's hands.

"*Bonswa*, Nurse Johnston. Just picking up a few things." Dani hastily tossed a few random items from a nearby shelf into her arms, but the damage was done. She knew Nurse Johnston had seen exactly what she was holding and had probably seen the tabloid headlines, too.

Her worries were confirmed a second later. "The papers are

saying you're a princess, Dr. Martin. But I hope you know that all of us at Coral Bay consider you a friend, first and foremost."

Dani blushed, feeling grateful. "That's very kind of you, Nurse Johnston. I feel the same way."

"I just wanted to mention it in case you could use a friend to talk to about now." She gave a meaningful look at the items in Dani's arms.

Dani adjusted the items to give more cover to the pregnancy test, for all the good it would do now. Both of them knew perfectly well that Nurse Johnston had seen what she was holding. But any explanation she tried to give would only make things worse. All she could do was stammer, "Thanks. I... I'll keep that in mind."

She paid for her items, double-bagging them in the hope that her purchase would be hidden from any other prying eyes she encountered on the way home. She couldn't imagine what Nurse Johnston would do with the news that she'd spotted Dani buying a pregnancy test. Everyone on St. Camille was kind, but gossip spread quickly. Cade had been right when he'd told her that there were few secrets on an island this small.

Back in the privacy of her dormitory, she took the test and awaited the results.

It was shocking how quickly the tests worked nowadays, she thought. One moment, she'd been taking the test and telling herself she was only doing it as a formality to calm her ridiculous fears. And then, two minutes later, her life had completely changed. The test was positive. She was pregnant.

She sat on her bed with her hands on her knees, letting her mind and body absorb this new knowledge. She'd been denying the possibility of pregnancy so fiercely. And yet, shouldn't all that denial have been enough to clue her in to the fact that something had changed? At the very least, she shouldn't be feeling so surprised.

If she was surprised, she couldn't imagine how Cade was going to feel. Especially after she'd spent the afternoon reassuring him that she wasn't pregnant. Insisting that the whole thing was an exaggerated tabloid rumor, designed to create a scandal. She knew he would be alarmed, and not just because she'd have to go back and tell him that she'd made a mistake, and that everything she'd said earlier wasn't true. She knew that he was afraid for the health of their child, and that he would rather close himself off from relationships than go through grief again.

The strange thing was that she wasn't filled with dread. Less than five minutes ago—before she'd taken the test—she would have been horrified to think of what she would have to tell Cade.

But now, she felt a clarity that she'd never had before in her life.

Her royal duties and responsibilities had often impacted, or even prevented, her pursuit of certain dreams. She'd tried to cope with that by accepting certain limitations. For example, she could be a doctor, but only within the time limit her family allowed. She could be with Cade, but only under the condition that they not become emotionally attached. These weren't just limits that others placed on her. They were limits she agreed to out of a sense of responsibility.

But now that she was pregnant, she realized she'd never wanted anything more than a family.

She knew that learning about the baby would be difficult for Cade and difficult for her family. It wasn't typical for members of the royal family to be single mothers, but it wasn't unheard of, either. This had happened before. But no matter how

Cade—or her family—reacted, her path was clear: she was going to make certain that her child received all the love and support it deserved, no matter how anyone else felt about it.

If Cade didn't want to be involved, she'd make things work on her own. As far as her family was concerned, she'd have to see how they responded. She was sure that once they got over their initial surprise, they would rally around her with support. Her family might place heavy emphasis on tradition, and she had a feeling that some of her uncles would probably be more preoccupied with how to manage the narrative of her pregnancy in the press than with her actual child, but she trusted that they would also be there for her when she needed them.

And she would need them. Princess or not, she didn't think single motherhood would be easy. Despite the clarity she'd felt a moment ago, questions swirled through her mind. How would raising a child affect her career? Her family might want her to raise her child in Lorovia, but what if she wanted to keep working at Coral Bay? How would Cade feel about that? If he didn't want children, then how involved would he want to be? He would probably do the noble thing and help raise his child—but would he do that because it was what he wanted, or because he felt obligated to do so? How would she feel about having Cade in her life just because he felt obligated to be? How would a child feel about that?

There were more immediate problems to worry about as well. The press was sure to explode once her pregnancy was confirmed. She felt a twinge in her heart, knowing that this would affect Cade. There would be no way to hide that he was the father. Whatever reaction he had to the news, it would be public. She could try to ask for some favors from the palace public relations department, but there was probably very little she could do to protect his privacy.

She took a deep breath and told herself to worry about one problem at a time. First, she needed to tell Cade. There'd been enough secrets between them, and she wanted to share this one as quickly as she could. The other questions, such as where she would live and what would happen with her career—those could all be addressed later on. None of it would be easy, but she would make it work. With or without anyone's help.

The next morning, Cade walked into Coral Bay early. He'd had a sleepless night, wondering what it would be like to see Dani at work. They were both professionals, and he knew they would be able to find a way to work effectively together, but he still wasn't looking forward to the awkwardness of trying to be nothing more than colleagues again.

It didn't help that everyone else on staff seemed to be giving him sidelong looks of disapproval. He might have imagined it, but he could have sworn that Nurse Chapel had frowned at him when she'd handed him a file. Dr. Davidson had the look of a man with a suspicion confirmed. Everyone, apparently, had seen the photos and drawn their own conclusions about him and Dani from them. The disapproval he felt in his direction only made him feel worse, as it only served to highlight that he and Dani were no longer together.

He'd never been in this situation before. Should he call a staff meeting? Send a hospital-wide e-mail? Both of those ideas were probably terrible and likely to make things worse. Besides, the rumors weren't just about him. They were about Dani, too, and he didn't want to take any action to address them without consulting her.

Gossip thrives on gossip, he told himself. If he ignored the gossip for long enough, it would die down on its own.

He was waiting in line for coffee at the commissary, when

he overheard a group of nurses having a hushed conversation just ahead of him.

"Are you sure it was a pregnancy test, Marie?"

"Of course. I saw her buy it last night with my own eyes."

"Maybe it was for a patient."

"Then why wouldn't she requisition it from the medical center? I'm telling you, Dr. Martin was buying that pregnancy test for herself, because of all those rumors about her and Dr. Logan in the tabloids."

"Those two have been carrying on for a while. It's the worst-kept secret on the island. I didn't know she was royalty, though."

Cade's blood froze. The line moved ahead without him. He ducked out of the commissary and headed back to his office, his mind racing.

Dani had assured him she wasn't pregnant. She'd insisted that the tabloid headlines were just malicious gossip.

But if that were true, then why had Nurse Johnston been whispering that she'd seen Dani buying a pregnancy test last night?

He didn't want to believe it. She'd looked him right in the eye and told him the tabloids were simply stirring up baseless rumors to get attention. Surely, she hadn't made all that up just because she thought it would make him feel better. Had she?

Another implication hit him like a punch to the gut. If Dani was lying, that meant she was pregnant.

For a moment, wild fantasies came rushing in. That dream of small fingers wrapped around his. A child with Dani's hair and his eyes.

But the images in his mind dissolved as all the old fear came rushing back. He couldn't have a child. More importantly, he couldn't stand the thought of losing a child. He couldn't lose another loved one. Not again.

Perhaps, he thought, Dani hadn't outright lied. Maybe she'd only bought the pregnancy test because she wasn't as certain about her situation as she claimed to be.

But if that were the case, why wouldn't she have told him?

Then again, Dani hadn't exactly been forthcoming with him for most of the time he'd known her. If she could keep a secret about being a princess, then why not keep this secret as well?

But she wouldn't keep a secret this big from him. At least, he didn't want to think she would.

He turned a corner into the next hallway and, suddenly, there she was. They stopped just short of running into one another.

"Cade, we really need to talk," she said.

His unease skyrocketed. "About what?"

"Can we go somewhere private?"

He was about to respond when his pager went off. "I'm needed in the cath lab."

Dani's pager buzzed as well. "Apparently, so am I."

They walked quickly down the hall in uncharacteristic silence. There was so much Cade wanted to ask her, but he had a feeling that not a single one of his questions could be answered in just a few minutes before a cath lab procedure.

As he and Dani stood side by side, scrubbing in before entering the cath lab, he couldn't hold it in anymore. It was a simple yes or no question.

Dani, are you pregnant?"

Her stricken face gave him the answer. "How did you know?"

There was no time to respond. They'd just finished scrubbing in and couldn't delay entering the lab. And it was lucky they didn't, because they walked in to a patient in active cardiac arrest, with one nurse giving CPR and another connecting defibrillation pads.

"Why weren't those preconnected?" Cade barked.

"Never mind that. Give us the history," Dani said.

"Forty-year-old woman who came into the ER last week with chest pain. She was scheduled this morning for a stress test, echocardiogram and MRI," one of the nurses responded. "We were doing a cath insertion when she went into arrest."

Cade raised his eyebrows, and noted Dani was surprised as well. Forty was young to need so much cardiac testing, let alone for a heart attack.

Dani took over the defibrillator paddles. After a few tense moments, the patient's heart was beating, though she still showed signs of tachycardia. Cade pushed calcium channel blockers to regulate the heart rate.

Within a few moments, the patient's eyes were open, and she was breathing on her own. "Don't try to sit up," Dani told her. "You've had a heart attack. You're going to be feeling very weak for a while, but Dr. Logan is going to get to the bottom of things and find out why your heart is acting this way."

As absorbed as he was with the patient, something about what Dani said caught at Cade's mind. Usually Dani told patients "*We'd* get to the bottom of things," referring to the entire care team. But just now, she'd referred specifically to him. Why was she leaving herself out?

He couldn't think about that now. He needed to focus on his patient, who had come in for a transradial cardiac catheterization.

"Do I still have to have the procedure today?" the patient asked.

"I'm afraid it's more important than ever, now that you've

had a heart attack," he replied. "We'll insert a catheter through your wrist and then through a blood vessel into your heart, which will make the arteries show up very clearly on X-rays. Then we'll be able to see what's going on." He tried to infuse as much calm into his voice as he could, but inside, his nerves were frayed.

Once the patient was under local anesthetic, he began with a small incision into her wrist. Dani came and stood beside him.

"Are you planning on going somewhere?" he muttered.

"We'll discuss it later."

What was that supposed to mean? If she was pregnant with his child, then he needed to know where she was going and for how long.

Somehow, he made it through the hour-long procedure. The patient turned out to have a 99 percent blockage in the main descending artery, which meant that without proper diagnosis and treatment, a fatal heart attack could happen at any time. Cade was able to schedule the patient to have a stent placed at the site of the blockage, which would restore blood flow—and not a moment too soon.

"It's funny," he said, as he and Dani wrapped up the procedure and removed their surgical gloves. "The chest pain that woman had last week probably saved her life. She seemed to be in good physical health. If she'd ignored her chest pain, she might have had her heart attack anywhere other than a cardiac cath lab. And we wouldn't have discovered her blockage."

"She was so young to have heart problems," Dani replied. "I suppose it just goes to show that none of us can predict what's around the corner."

He'd been able to get absorbed in the successful treatment of his patient, but the relevance of her words brought him crashing down. "Like, for example, an unexpected pregnancy?"

She blushed. "Just like that. Yes."

"Were you going to tell me?"

"Of course! I was on my way to tell you. But then we had a patient. How could you think I wouldn't tell you? And did you know in the first place?"

"There's a rumor among the nurses that you bought a pregnancy test."

"Nurse Johnston," she muttered. "I was hoping she wouldn't spread that around so quickly."

"I thought we were done with secrets."

"Cade, I was going to tell you. I just didn't have time. Apparently, I had a secret from myself. When I first talked to you yesterday, I didn't think I needed a pregnancy test. I was so sure I wasn't pregnant. We'd been so careful. But then I realized, that first time, we used an older condom from my purse. I didn't think about how old it was at the time. I was just sort of…caught up in the moment. I'm sorry. At the time, I didn't think this could happen."

As angry as he was, seeing Dani so sad cut him to the core. He could be angry with her for keeping secrets, for lying to him about her royal status and possibly lying to him about her pregnancy, but it took two to make a baby, and even in the midst of his anger, he knew that the fact that she was pregnant was not her fault. "Neither of us were thinking about what could happen," he said, remembering the heat of that first night, the way they'd pursued each other with such reckless abandon. Recklessness. That had been the most exciting part of it. And now they were dealing with the fallout. "We had… other things on our minds."

It would be nice to believe Dani hadn't lied to him intentionally. Because now that he no longer had a patient to focus on and the confirmation of Dani's pregnancy was sinking in, a hundred conflicting emotions were hitting him in the gut all at once.

"What do you need from me?" he said. He felt completely overwhelmed by the news, but now that it was confirmed to be true, the only thing he knew for sure was that he had to support Dani and the baby. He'd decided to never have children, but if one was going to arrive, he had every intention of being the father his child needed.

She gave him a confused look. "Need from you?"

"Yes. I know you're royalty, but if there's any way I can support you or support the baby—any way at all—just let me know." He thought he was being remarkably chivalrous.

"Hmm," she said. "Here's something I need from you, Cade. I need to know how you feel about having this baby."

His head spun. He tried to buy himself time. "I haven't had much opportunity to absorb the news yet."

"Neither have I."

Fair enough.

But his brain was still fighting to catch up to the situation. Any relief he felt at the idea that she hadn't lied to him intentionally was overshadowed by the fact that she was pregnant with his child. He'd spent years avoiding the very possibility of that happening with anyone.

The thought of being betrayed again by someone he loved was bad enough to keep him from seeking out a relationship. But the thought of losing another family member, especially a child of his own, was unbearable.

But he couldn't tell Dani that. She was pregnant; she should be focusing on their child, not on his grief. If a child was coming, he'd simply have to find a way to bear it. He wasn't one to shirk his responsibilities.

"I need to know, Cade. How do you feel about this baby?"

He took a deep breath and mustered all his strength. "My feelings are that…if you're pregnant, then I'm here for you. I want to be here for you. For whatever you need. Whatever our child needs. Even if there's nothing between the two of us, I want to be in the baby's life. It's my responsibility, and it's the right thing to do."

"I thought you'd say something like that. I know doing the right thing is important to you, Cade. I know perfectly well what a noble person you are. But what about what you *want*? How do you feel? Are you excited about the baby? Afraid?"

He tried to respond, but couldn't get the words out. A week ago, it would have been the most natural thing in the world to tell Dani exactly how he felt, even about something as shocking as this. But that had been back when he thought she was someone else.

"You can't tell me, can you?" she said, her voice tinged with sadness. "You don't trust me anymore."

"I don't," he said. "But that doesn't mean I wouldn't take responsibility for my own child."

"There's that word again. I grew up in a family where everyone cared about things like duty and responsibility. And those were important things. But I've learned, Cade—I've learned in part thanks to you—that those things aren't everything. Love isn't a responsibility or a chore. It isn't about doing what other people expect you to do. I know what it feels like to live a life based on meeting obligations. And I don't want our child feeling that the only reason its father is in its life is out of a sense of duty, rather than out of joy. Can you honestly tell me that you actually want to be in this child's life? Even though you've always said you don't want children?"

He hesitated. "What I want doesn't matter. The baby's coming, and I'm not going to abandon either of you."

She gave him a smile filled with tears. "Cade, I think I want something from you that you're not able to give. You and I, we decided from the start not to get emotionally involved. We wanted to have fun and to help each other break a long dry spell. And I know now that I wanted the fantasy of a normal life—a relationship without complications. I wanted that with you. But you know as well as I do that that kind of fantasy breaks down the moment a child comes into the picture."

"Don't you trust me? Don't you think I would do anything to protect a child of my own?"

She thought for a moment. "I believe you'd do anything you were capable of. So I'm going to ask you now—are you capable of telling me, in all honesty, that you want a child?"

He didn't know how to make her understand. The truth was, he *did* want a child. He wanted the tiny fingers wrapped around his, and the little body he could lift up to his shoulders to see the world.

But he didn't want the frightening part of it. He dreaded the nine months of pregnancy, during which he wouldn't know if his child had inherited Henry's heart defect. And even if Dani gave birth to a healthy infant, free from Henry's defect, there were plenty of other things that could go wrong. The patients he saw coming into the pediatric unit every day were proof of that. Becoming a parent meant shouldering the burden of constant worry that some harm could befall his child. The world held so many dangers that were out of his control.

That was what made him hesitate. And in that moment of hesitation, Dani said, "I didn't think so."

If it weren't for the fear, he would have promised her anything. Every impulse within him was telling him to beg her to stay. The idea of staying with her, and raising their child together, had woken a dream he'd left buried for years.

The more he thought about the reality of having a child with Dani, the more his anger and resentment toward her fell away. The truth was, he wanted all the things she thought he didn't want. He wanted a family, and what was more, he wanted her, complications and all.

But he couldn't face the risk of loss. All of the complications he and Dani faced made loss even more likely. What if she'd never wanted more than a fling with him, but was acting out of her own sense of obligation because they were about to have a child? What if they tried a long-term relationship and her family felt he wasn't good enough for her, or he didn't match up to their standards? And, of course, what if he lost his child, or Dani, to illness or injury? A thousand things could go wrong. His fear won out. He couldn't tell her that he wanted her because he could lose her.

Instead, he tried to explain. "You know why I've never wanted children. You don't know what it's like to lose a family member. You asked me to be honest with you, so I will be. No, I don't want a child. I don't ever want to go through that kind of loss again."

"So you're going to solve that problem by never getting close to anyone in the first place?"

"It's complicated," he said.

"I used to think that," she replied. "Funny how uncomplicated things get the moment you're pregnant."

"Dani…you know what could happen. You know that both of us could be facing significant grief."

"I know that even with a close relative, the odds of a baby having a heart defect are statistically low. And I'm not going to rob myself of any joy now, just because of something that may or may not happen in the future."

He couldn't agree. As a doctor, he knew of far too many negative possibilities to think about the positive ones.

After a moment, she said, "I need to go home to Lorovia for a while."

"For how long?"

"I'm not sure. There are...so many things to figure out. I'll have to explain to my family about the pregnancy. They'll all have their different opinions about how to handle it publicly. And someone from the palace will be appointed to stay in contact with you."

He hated to think about her working through all of those issues alone. He longed to tell her that he would be there for her. But saying that would mean making a commitment that he wasn't ready to give.

Also, what did she mean by "someone from the palace"? Would they honestly need a liaison to communicate? "You're making it sound as though it might be a long time before we see each other again."

She avoided his gaze. "The chief of staff said I could take as long as I needed. He said it might be a good time for me to be off the island for a while, since my secret identity's been revealed. That will give all the rumors a chance to die down a little. Then, if I ever decide to come back, people will have had time to get used to the whole princess idea."

"*If* you ever come back?" Of all the shocks he'd had over the past few days, this one was the worst.

"Don't worry, Cade. No matter what happens, I'd never prevent you from seeing our child whenever you wish."

While that was reassuring, the thought of Dani not being in his life filled him with despair.

This, he realized, was everything he'd tried to avoid for the past several years. He'd done everything he could to avoid loss, but now he was losing Dani, and it felt as though his heart was being torn out. Even if she did plan to come back, things would never be the same between them. He might see her, she might stay in his life as the mother of his child, but he wouldn't have her. Not the way he used to.

Losing someone he cared about felt even worse than he remembered. He hadn't realized how much life she'd breathed into his days. Being around her had made him feel fresh and alive in a way he hadn't felt before, possibly ever, in his life. And losing her was everything he'd feared.

But he couldn't bring himself to tell her to stay or to take him with her to Lorovia. If losing her hurt now, it would only hurt more if they tried a long-term relationship and it didn't work out. Especially with a child involved. And there were so many reasons it might not work out.

"I don't know what I'm going to do next. But whatever it is, I'm going to do it as me. I need to do something that lets me be my whole self. I think my time with you actually taught me that, Cade, and I'll always be grateful. But I haven't been able to be my whole self with you. We tried to just give one part of ourselves to each other. I don't know about you, but for me, it didn't work."

Dani had said she was coming back, but this felt an awful lot like good-bye. His heart was slowly disintegrating, and he didn't know how to make it stop.

She stood up and turned toward the courtyard entrance. "You know what you said earlier, about how what you wanted didn't matter? That's something I used to think, too. That as long as I was meeting my responsibilities, everything was working out just fine. But then I met you. And I learned that even if someone's going through all the right motions, what they really want matters a whole damn lot." She wiped a tear from her cheek. "I hope you find what you want, Cade."

She left Cade alone, with even more questions than he'd had that morning.

CHAPTER TEN

CADE ARRIVED HOME and slumped into his chair by the fire pit before he even went inside. It had been all he could do to drag himself through his shifts at work over the past few days. The usual things that brought pleasure to his life didn't seem to affect him anymore. Walking along the beach, swimming or watching the sun rise and set no longer gave him joy. Instead, he could barely muster the energy for any of it.

He'd thought about taking some time off work, but ultimately decided against it. If he couldn't be happy, he could at least be useful to his patients.

The only time he'd felt any emotion over the past week was when he'd gotten an e-mail with a "lorovia.gov" address. For half a second, adrenaline had surged through him at the thought that it might be from Dani. But when he opened the e-mail, it was simply a very formal letter from a Lorovian official who'd been designated to be his liaison through "ongoing developments." His child, apparently, was an ongoing development. He supposed he shouldn't be surprised at the formal, careful phrasing. His child wasn't just a child, but also a matter of state for Lorovia. Dani had always implied that that was what royal life was like, but it was strange to experience it firsthand.

It was still difficult for him to even think of having a child without becoming flooded with fear. Dani's words kept coming back to him: Did he think it was best for him to be in his child's life, if he didn't truly want a child? He knew she had a point. As much as he longed to be in his child's life, would his fear of loss prevent him from getting close to a child of his own? Just as it had prevented him from getting close to anyone else in his life?

He missed Dani more than he could have ever imagined. With her gone, it felt as though the sun had left the Caribbean. He hadn't realized how much vitality she brought into his life. For years, he'd done so much alone. He'd eaten lunch alone, spent his days off alone and sat by the fire pit, gazing out at the ocean alone. He missed Dani in the other Adirondack chair next to him. He missed being able to touch her, hold her and feel the heat between the two of them. But most of all, he missed the way they'd been able to work together so smoothly, anticipating each other's needs, and the way she'd always been willing to talk over difficult cases with him. He missed showing her new parts of the island and talking to her after a long day. No matter how warm the weather was, everything felt cold with her gone.

He knew that the gossip surrounding him and Dani was still rampant at work. No one ever spoke about it to him directly, but every time he entered a room, everyone quickly ended their discussions. He wished he could explain, but it wasn't just his secret to talk about. It was Dani's, too, and he hadn't heard from Dani since she left.

The tabloids were getting even worse with their rumors. He'd noticed more photographers on the island lately, eager to get a shot of him. The security at work took care of most of them, but it was irritating to be hounded by press when he was merely trying to go about his business on St. Camille. He'd had several e-mails from tabloids offering him money for exclusive rights to the story of his affair with Dani, which he deleted in disgust.

Dani, for her part, seemed to have completely disappeared from the public eye. He wondered if she was being hounded even worse than he was. He wondered, too, if this kind of attention was something she had to live with anytime she traveled outside of Lorovia. He knew she'd attended medical school under her assumed name, and he was starting to understand, in a way he never had before, why she'd wanted to keep her royal status a secret.

He thought about her facing the scrutiny of the press alone, without him by her side. He wished he could talk to her. But if she wanted to talk, she knew how to reach him. And since she hadn't reached out, he could only assume she preferred to keep him at a distance for now.

He was preparing himself for another lonely evening spent by the fire when his phone buzzed in his pocket. He felt the usual jolt of hope that it might be Dani—but then he saw that it was his mother.

He'd been avoiding the few calls that had come his way lately because he didn't want to respond to any questions, but he knew he couldn't avoid his mother forever.

"Hi, Mom."

"Why, hello there, dear. It's nice of you to answer my call. I hadn't heard from you in so long that I was beginning to worry."

He sighed. "I should have called you sooner."

"You certainly should have. You haven't responded to any of my e-mails, and I've been in a kerfuffle trying to figure out what to do about the wedding."

Wedding? His mother was jumping to some pretty quick

conclusions. "Mom, I don't know what you've seen in the papers, but I have no plans to get married."

His mother laughed. "I certainly have seen the papers, and let me tell you, young man, my friends have a lot of questions! And so do I. But that's not what I called to talk about. I called to tell you that I'm getting married."

"What?" He was stunned. After all the conflict he'd witnessed between his parents growing up, the one thing he'd never, ever imagined was his mother getting married again.

"Yes. Irv and I have finally decided that after five years of living together, we want to make it official. We're going to tie the knot. I know this may sound a little unconventional, but I wanted to ask… Would you walk me down the aisle?"

He shook his head, trying to clear his thoughts.

"Mom, are you sure about this? After everything that happened with Dad? After…" He found that he couldn't quite get the word "Henry" out. "After all our family went through?"

"Those were difficult times for all of us, dear. But they were also a very long time ago."

There was a very long pause as Cade tried to think. He'd always thought that his mother felt the same way he did about relationships: that it was less painful not to get too close. He could understand why she would feel that way, after all she'd been through.

Had he misunderstood her? Had he been wrong?

"Cade? My friends have been asking me if that's you, in those pictures with the Lorovian princess. I don't mean to pry, dear. I know how you like to keep personal things private. But if I'm about to have a grandchild, I'd really prefer to hear about it from you, rather than the headlines."

He sighed. "I don't know how to explain, Mom. It's very complicated. But…yes. There's going to be a child."

"Well, then how complicated can it really be? It sounds very exciting to me."

"How can you say that?" he blurted. His words came in a rush. "How can you call it exciting when you know how it feels to lose a child of your own? Our entire family fell apart once Henry was gone. How could I possibly look forward to this when there's so much to lose?"

"I understand what you're saying," she replied. "You were just a little boy when we lost Henry. It was too much for you to go through and probably too hard to understand what all the adults around you were feeling. But you know what? If I could go through it all over again, I wouldn't change a thing."

"How can you say that? Even knowing what you know now?"

"Because, dear. What I know now is that you don't pass up a chance for love in the present, just because of what happened in the past."

"I don't understand you, Mom. You more than anyone should be worried about what happens if it all goes wrong again."

"Oh, my dear boy. You've got it all wrong. You know, your father and I were having problems in our marriage long before Henry passed, and losing him was not the reason our marriage didn't last. I know those were painful times for all of us. But I'm not afraid of repeating those times. What I'm afraid of is missing out on a wonderful relationship, just because of one bad one that's been over for a long time. I've got a chance to have real love in my life, and dearest, I could lose that chance if I only think about what could go wrong."

He'd never thought about relationships that way. He'd thought his experiences with Susan, and everything he'd seen between his parents, had been a lesson in how relationships inevitably ended.

But Dani had shown him something new. In spite of all his efforts not to get attached to her, she'd brought a freshness, an excitement, into his life. Being with her had felt different from anyone he'd ever been with. Maybe a relationship with her would have been different, too.

"So you really wouldn't change anything?" he said. "Even knowing what you know now?"

"I'd choose it all again in a heartbeat. Maybe some of my choices were mistakes, but those choices led me to you and Henry. Loss hurts, dear, but it hurts because the good stuff is so good. And I wouldn't give the good stuff up for anything."

He hadn't known his mother felt this way. He'd always thought that, like him, she wanted to protect herself from the pain of loss.

"I'm not as afraid of loss as I am of missing out on my chance at love," she continued. "And I'm afraid of that for you, too."

He thought for a long moment.

From a purely logical perspective, nothing his mother was saying made sense. It certainly wasn't what he'd expected to hear from her.

But from an emotional perspective, he understood every word.

His mother was voicing thoughts that had been nagging at his mind since Dani left. He'd tried to ignore them because they didn't make sense. If he knew exactly how painful heartbreak was, then wasn't he making the logical choice by doing everything he could to avoid it?

He hadn't expected his "logical" choice to hurt this much. And deep down, he understood why. He hadn't wanted to let himself understand because he was afraid. Of pain, of loss, of making the same mistakes all over again.

He'd known he was afraid, but he hadn't wanted to admit it to himself. But what was the alternative? Losing everything because he was afraid to take a chance? Losing his child, and Dani and a real chance at love?

More than a chance. He loved her. Of that he was certain. And if his mother, who had been through so much, could take the risk of opening her heart to love, then so could he.

"Mom," he said, "I think I've made a really big mistake."

"Well, mistakes are part of life. Is there anything you can do to fix it?"

"I don't know. What if I try, and it turns out it's too late?"

"Then at least you'll know you've tried."

Dani could tell the palace photographer wasn't happy. She'd been sitting in the palace photo salon for hours, and the photographer had the defeated air of trying to make the best of a bad situation.

"If you could just try to smile," the photographer said, for what felt like the hundredth time.

Dani forced her lips into an upward curve, but the photographer shook her head in defeat. "Something's not right. Maybe it's the light in here."

"Maybe it's time for a break," her grandmother said. "Give us the room." The photographer bowed and left.

Dani knew the problem wasn't the light. The problem was *her*. She'd been home for a week, and nothing had felt right since she'd arrived. She missed her work and the serene peace of the Caribbean. Worst of all, she'd thought about Cade every day, and her heart ached for him.

She was wearing a full gown and was bedecked with crown

jewels. She twisted one of the emerald rings on her finger. No matter how fine her princess regalia was, she couldn't hide the fact that she was heartbroken. She could smile with her mouth, but not her eyes.

She and her grandmother were spending the day together, doing a photo shoot for pictures that would accompany a palace press release announcing Dani's pregnancy. As she was at about twelve weeks, the palace had to make some sort of announcement about her situation. The royal publicist had determined that the best way to deal with Dani's pregnancy would be to portray Dani as an independent, free-spirited woman who had her life completely under control and was deciding to raise a child on her own. Apparently, the best way to depict that her life was under control was for Dani to be photographed in a gown and tiara, indicating her family's support, acceptance and total control of the narrative. "If she looks beautiful enough, everyone will be so caught up discussing the dress she's wearing that they won't be interested in spreading gossip around her decisions," the publicist had explained, and members of her family had all agreed.

But Dani was having a difficult time mustering the enthusiasm needed to play her part. Her heart was still in the Caribbean, with her work, her friends…and with Cade.

The pins holding her tiara in place made her head ache, and she rubbed her forehead to ease the tension.

"Let me help you with that," said her grandmother, sitting down beside her. She pulled out the pins and removed the tiara. Dani sighed in relief as the tightness eased from her scalp. "Danielle-Genevieve. I've known you since you were born. And I can tell when you're not happy."

"I'm sorry, Grandmother. I'm trying my best."

Her grandmother sighed and reached out to tuck a loosened strand of hair behind Dani's ear. "I know, dear. You've always tried to do what was right by the family. But your decisions recently have made me see things in a new light. This passion for medicine…this child that's on the way…"

"I know it's not what you expected."

To Dani's utter surprise, her grandmother laughed. And as her laughter continued, Dani grew more baffled. Surely her grandmother, the head of a family that had emphasized tradition and protocol her entire life, couldn't be laughing at such a moment.

Seeing Dani's confusion, her grandmother stopped laughing and grew more serious. "I only laugh, my dear, because you are so right. You've never been what any of us expected, despite your attempts to uphold your duty—and tradition. But having a baby changes everything, doesn't it? It can certainly change the way one sees duty and responsibility." She placed a warm hand on Dani's shoulder. "And even though you've always taken your responsibility toward this family seriously, sometimes I think the pressure we've placed on you has made you forget that you have a responsibility to take care of yourself, too."

"What do you mean?"

"I mean that I've been very impressed by you, Danielle-Genevieve. By your passion for medicine and your determination to care for your child, no matter what anyone else thinks. Our family may be based on tradition, but if traditions are to survive, they have to be adaptable."

Dani's eyes widened in surprise.

"That diamond necklace you're wearing, for example. It belonged to my great-grandmother. But I have a feeling a stethoscope would make more sense around your neck, my dear."

"Do you mean it?"

"Yes. Let's assume that your decision to be a doctor is a permanent one. And there's no need to have you practice in secret anymore. We all thought the tabloids would get carried away with the story of one of our family holding a profession—in the medical field, no less—but clearly that's been eclipsed by a much more sensational story. It's a silver lining, I suppose. Her grandmother chuckled. "Do you think you'll finish that cardiology fellowship?"

Dani couldn't meet her grandmother's eyes. "I want to, but I don't know if I can ever go back there."

"This is about more than cardiology, isn't it? This is a true matter of the heart."

"I'm afraid so."

As much as her grandmother's understanding meant to her, it didn't ease her heartbreak. She'd missed Cade every day since she got back to Lorovia. She missed his sun-bleached hair, his cinnamon scent and the way he winked when he smiled.

She knew why he was afraid to be in his child's life. He was afraid of loss. But fear of loss was only one side of a coin.

And even if he did try to fight through his fears and be there for their child, it didn't mean he felt anything for *her*.

Tears began to prick her eyes, as they often did when she thought of Cade. Dammit. Now she was going to have to have all her makeup redone if she wasn't careful.

"I'll give you a few moments to collect your thoughts before the photographer comes back in," her grandmother said, leaving Dani to herself.

Dani was grateful to be alone.

As she dabbed at her eyes with the corner of a handkerchief, she heard the door swing open again. Assuming that the photographer had come back, she said, "I'm going to need just a few more minutes to get my game face on."

"That's a shame. I always thought your regular face was perfect."

"Cade!" She was stunned. "How did you get here?"

"I finally responded to the palace liaison who e-mailed me. After I filled out a metric ton of paperwork, flew here and had my picture taken a half dozen times, they let me up here to see you."

A security guard had accompanied him. "Is it all right for him to be here, Princess?"

"Yes, of course. Give us some privacy, please."

The guard nodded and left.

"I can't believe you're here."

"I hope it was all right for me to come."

"Well...why did you come?"

"Isn't it obvious?"

She raised her eyebrows. "Not to me."

"You're right. I have a lot to explain." His mouth worked, and she could see he was trying to find the right words. Finally, he said, "I can't think of the right way to say this, so I'll just spit it out. I'm an idiot, Dani. An absolute fool. I've done the stupidest thing I could possibly do, and I don't know if it's too late to fix my mistake, but I had to come here to try."

"What mistake?"

"There are so many, actually. It's hard to pick just one. But here's the biggest one of all. I pretended to you, and to myself, that I wasn't in love with you."

Dani was glad she was sitting down, because all of a sudden, she was trembling all over. She didn't think she'd be able to stand if she tried.

He loved her?

He walked over to her and knelt next to her chair, so that they were at eye level with one another.

"I know we said no emotions. I know we promised each other we wouldn't get attached. But it happened. I fell in love with you. It was impossible for me to know you and not love you. And I'll understand if you don't feel the same way. But I couldn't stand the thought of never telling you. It was a risk I was willing to take, even if I got crushed. Because the fear of risking my heart is worse than the fear of missing out on love."

"Then you mean—"

"I mean that no matter what you feel for me, I'm going to be a father to this baby. I want this child more than anything I've ever wanted in my life, but I was afraid to admit that because I was afraid of loss. But even more than that, I'm more afraid of not giving this child my whole heart. And I'll give it to you, too, if you'll have it. If you want it."

Tears almost made it impossible for her to speak, but she managed to choke out, "More than I've ever wanted anything."

He kissed her, then, and the feeling of his lips against hers felt like a promise. His arms wrapped around her, and for the first time since she'd returned to Lorovia, she felt as though she was home, really home. The familiar scent of cinnamon that wafted from his neck reminded her of all that could be waiting for her, back in a certain cottage by the sea. Where she'd learned that what she wanted did matter, and was incredibly important, after all.

Finally, they broke apart. Her makeup really was ruined now, and she didn't care the tiniest bit.

"I hope I wasn't too late," said Cade.

"No, Cade. I love you, too…and you were just in time for me to tell you. But are you sure you want all this?" She motioned to the ornate room around her. "You've already gotten a taste of what it's like to have the press involved in your life and some experience with royal protocol. Is it going to be too much?"

He held her face in his hands and looked into her eyes. "Princess Danielle-Genevieve Matthieu DuMaria. I've crossed an ocean for you. I've laid my soul bare for you. I would do so much more. Do you really think filling out a little paperwork could keep me away from the woman I love?"

Love. Her heart thrilled at the word. "But it's not just a little paperwork. It's quite a few contracts."

He ticked off the items he'd spent the morning completing with the palace liaison. "An NDA, a form that bore a striking resemblance to a *job application*, fingerprints, a background check and an extremely detailed contract in which the palace acknowledges that I will continue my career as a physician— and in which I agree to attend no less than three holiday functions and two state dinners each year—"

"You filled out the consort paperwork!" Her face flamed with embarrassment. "Cade, I'm so sorry. I know all of it's *completely* ridiculous, and I wish royal protocol didn't require it."

He gave her that smile again. The one she knew was real, because it made his eye close in a wink.

He put his arms around her waist and held her close. "All of it is completely inconsequential as long as I have the one thing I really want."

"What's that?" she asked, leaning in to kiss him again.

"Your heart."

"I'm afraid that's impossible," she said, smiling. "I can't give you what's already yours."

EPILOGUE

One Year Later

CADE HAD WORRIED that the warm breeze off the St. Camille coast would threaten the wedding decorations, but everything seemed to be holding up well so far.

As the mother of the prince consort, his mother had been offered palace funds so that she could have a lavish wedding. But she'd eschewed that option for something more personal. Dani and Cade had both been thrilled when his mother chose to have her wedding on St. Camille. It meant that everyone important to them could attend. An eclectic mix of people had come to celebrate the day. In addition to their colleagues from the hospital, Dani's parents and a few other members of the Lorovian royal family were in attendance.

After Dani's grandmother had made it clear that she fully supported Dani's career, the rest of the family accepted Dani's decision. If some of her uncles let slip a few mutterings about "breaking tradition," and "unconventional choices," her grandmother silenced them with a glare and a reminder that traditions without flexibility had outlived their usefulness. Dani and Cade returned to work at the Coral Bay Medical Center, with occasional trips to Lorovia to attend required state functions.

Cade found that life in the public eye wasn't as onerous as

he'd anticipated. It helped, of course, that the initial flurry of press coverage and speculation about Dani's pregnancy and mystery consort died down after they married. They'd opted for a quiet ceremony at the palace before returning to St. Camille. The island felt more like home to them than anywhere else, and they both agreed it was the perfect place to raise their child.

At barely three months old, Princess Mathilde-Grace Jeanne Adrienne DuMaria—called Tilly, for short—was the guest of honor at Cade's mother's wedding. And why shouldn't she be? She was perfect.

Cade and Dani sat in the front row, awaiting his mother's walk down the aisle. Tilly fussed a little in Dani's arms. He leaned over and held a finger out to her. Her little fingers curled around his, just as they'd done every day since the day she was born.

All tests indicated that Tilly was in perfect health. Cade, of course, continued to experience the fears of every parent. He was a doctor, after all. He knew that life offered no certainties. But at least he didn't have to worry about his daughter's heart. By all indications, Tilly's was fine.

Her lungs were also in excellent condition. He was relieved that Tilly had finally stopped crying just before the priest leaned over to him and said, "It's time."

He kissed Dani on the cheek and went to the back of the aisle, where his mother was waiting. She'd asked him to walk her down the aisle.

His mother had forgone a traditional white dress for colorful Caribbean garb. She wore a dress with a loose skirt, and a crown of flowers in her hair. She took Cade's arm with a smile.

"Are you ready?" he asked her.

"As I'll ever be."

He walked her down the aisle, his eyes on Dani. She'd looked so beautiful on their own wedding day. But not nearly as beautiful as she did now, with Tilly in her arms.

As they reached the end of the aisle, Tilly grew increasingly fussy. "Go on, dear, if you need to," his mother muttered. "It's all right."

He squeezed her hand in appreciation and sat next to Dani, trying to calm Tilly down. Dani handed the baby to him and she calmed immediately, as she nearly always did.

"Such a daddy's girl," Dani whispered, smiling.

Unfortunately, Tilly's calm was short-lived. Her cries were so loud that Dani and Cade decided to slip away from the ceremony and walk down the beach.

"Oh, dear," said Dani, embarrassed. "I hope your mother won't be too upset."

"Mom will understand," said Cade. Thinking of the way his mother had only had eyes for her groom, he added, "She might not have even noticed."

"Oh, I think everyone noticed," Dani replied, bouncing Tilly up and down. "This girl has got a set of lungs on her. Hasn't anyone ever told her that princesses are supposed to be quiet and demure?"

"I have a feeling she doesn't much care for what princesses are supposed to do. She takes after her mother in that way."

He took Tilly, finally quietened, and held her close, turning her toward the ocean. "You see that, sweetheart? That's the world. And I'm going to show it all to you. There's so much you won't want to miss out on."

"She's got time," Dani said. "But what about the two of us? How are we going to make the most of the time we have?"

He wrapped his free arm around her waist and pulled her

close. "I have a few ideas." They shared a slow, deep kiss, and Cade felt the rest of the world begin to melt away, as it always did whenever she was close to him.

"You know one great thing about being a princess?" she murmured. "With so many of my family members on the island right now, there's a lot of Lorovian security detail here. Which means we can ask one of them to babysit for us."

"Are we going to need a babysitter tonight?"

She traced the lapel of his tuxedo with one finger. "I can almost guarantee that we are." The sun began to make its way down the horizon, turning the sand on the beach into a deep, burnished gold.

They sat down together on the sand, Cade tucking Tilly into the crook of his arm. Dani smiled.

"A minute ago you were saying you wanted Tilly to see the world. But you're holding her awfully tight right now."

"Well, she needs to understand the most important thing first."

"And what's that?"

"How to recognize love when she sees it. And how to grab on as tight as she can when it's right in front of her."

"Even if she's afraid of losing everything?"

"Especially then. Because that's when you know what's most important." His brow furrowed. "I hope she grows up to understand."

Dani dropped her head against his shoulder, and he put his arm around her.

She tilted her face up toward his. "Every child has their own journey," she said. "She'll make her own mistakes, eventually. But until then, it's up to us to show her what love looks like."

"Well, at least we can handle that," he said. "Because I

won't be passing up a single opportunity to show that I love you. Every day, every hour, every moment."

He leaned forward and met her lips with a kiss. Behind them, not far down the beach, they could hear the last few words of the ceremony concluding and the applause from the attendees.

Loss might come, Cade knew. There was no avoiding it. But he was going to teach his daughter how to make the most of her life. When she found love, she wouldn't run from it. She'd run toward it with both arms outstretched.

Just like him.

* * * * *

COMING SOON!

We really hope you enjoyed reading this book. If you're looking for more romance be sure to head to the shops when new books are available on

Thursday 8th June

MILLS & BOON®

Coming next month

TWIN BABIES TO REUNITE THEM
Ann McIntosh

A tidal wave of arousal crashed over Saana as her gaze dropped to that full, wide mouth—unsmiling now, but no less sinfully sexy for that fact.

Against her will, her head suddenly filled with scenes, scents, sensations of being held in Kenzie's arms. There, her every sensual need had been met, ecstasy lifting her higher and higher, until it became irresistible and she was flung into the stratosphere.

Taken to the stars.

Suddenly weak-kneed once more, Saana knew it was time to bring this surreal encounter to an end. The sustaining anger had waned, leaving her floundering and sad.

But she wouldn't allow that to show.

The one person she'd ever completely trusted had betrayed her and deserved nothing but cool dismissal.

Getting a grip on both her emotions and her traitorous body, and although her legs still felt weak, she walked around the car to the semicircular staircase leading to her front door.

"Well," she said, aware of Kenzie's gaze following her

and refusing to meet it again. "This has been delightful, but I'm afraid it's time for you to leave."

She was two steps up when Kenzie replied.

"Saana, I need your help."

Pausing, Saana felt the words echo, shockingly, between them. In fact, it was almost impossible to believe she'd heard them correctly.

Unable to resist, she looked over her shoulder, saying "As surprising as it is to hear you, Miss Independence, say that, I'm sorry. I'm not interested in offering assistance."

Then, as she turned to climb to the next step—wanting to hurry now, to get away—she heard Kenzie say, "I'm pregnant with twins. And I really need your help."

She froze where she stood, trying to process the words, her first impulse to spin around and look at Kenzie to judge whether she was telling the truth or not. To let loose all the questions firing around her brain.

Pregnant? By whom? Had she started a new relationship without telling Saana? Decided she wanted a family with someone other than the wife she'd promised to love and cherish always but had then left behind?

Continue reading
TWIN BABIES TO REUNITE THEM
Ann McIntosh

Available next month
www.millsandboon.co.uk

LET'S TALK

Romance

For exclusive extracts, competitions and special offers, find us online:

- **f** MillsandBoon
- **𝕏** @MillsandBoon
- **◎** @MillsandBoonUK
- **♪** @MillsandBoonUK

Get in touch on 01413 063 232

MILLS & BOON

Desire

Indulge in secrets and scandal, intense drama and plenty of sizzling hot action with powerful and passionate heroes who have it all: wealth, status, good looks…everything but the right woman.